"This is our sister . . ."

Evvy looked at the Trader priest in bewilderment.

The young priest continued: "We are all going on a journey tomorrow, to the holy place."

"Do you mean I will be left here alone?" Evvy asked.

"No, you will go too. In a special wagon, with the Bishops. The shrine is to be dedicated with a purification ceremony."

"Yes?" Apprehension began to stir in her belly. "What do I have to do with it?"

"Ah, Sister Evvy," the priest said, almost with regret, "the shrine is to be dedicated on the first day of spring, the holy anniversary of the messiah's birth. On that day . . . in three weeks . . . you are to be sacrificed!"

*   *   *

"A more than welcome forerunner of a fresh new look at fantasy fiction."

—*Romantic Times* on *Pandora's Genes*

Also by Kathryn Lance

Pandora's Genes

Published by
POPULAR LIBRARY

PANDORA'S CHILDREN

KATHRYN LANCE

POPULAR LIBRARY

An Imprint of Warner Books, Inc.

A Warner Communications Company

POPULAR LIBRARY EDITION

Cover art by Dave Mattingly
Cover design by Don Puckey

Popular Library books are published by
Warner Books, Inc.
666 Fifth Avenue
New York, N.Y. 10103

A Warner Communications Company

Printed in the United States of America

First Printing: May, 1986

10 9 8 7 6 5 4 3 2 1

To Duggo, with love and thanks

Prologue

For a long time after Evvy left, Zach remained standing by the window, looking out at the lightening sky. His mouth was dry, and he felt light-headed. He was almost dizzy with fatigue, but he knew better than to lie down now; if he slept, he would feel worse, more exhausted, when it came time to go.

At last he turned from the window and picked up his feathered lyre. Wrapping it in a soft cloth, he placed the instrument inside his large pouch, then sat in the chair by the bed and waited.

The next thing he knew, there was a discreet rapping and he opened his eyes to full light. The rain of the night had gone and with it the clouds. Bright early sun streamed in the window, and he saw, as if through a gauzy curtain, Robin standing just inside the door, his strong, scrawny old arms holding a tray heavy with food.

The old man seemed embarrassed. "Good morning, Zach," he said, his voice uncertain. He placed the tray on the desk, then spoke quickly. "The Principal ordered me to bring you a good breakfast and food for your journey—" He shrugged off a cloth bag bulging with parcels. "I'll be back in a few minutes to take you to your mount."

Zach yawned. "Thank you, Robin," he said. He stood on shaky legs and, though he had no taste for food, approached the desk. On a large platter were half a roasted fowl, four eggs cooked in their shells, a pot of steaming, fragrant herb tea, and a bowl of fruit.

Robin stood there a moment not moving, then he spoke again. "I don't know what's happened," he said. "The Principal won't say anything except to shout or grumble. But since you returned, Zach, until yesterday he has never seemed so happy. He was his old self—like when he was a boy. I don't know what this trouble is between you, but I hope it will be ended soon. And that soon you will be back with us again." Awkwardly he reached out to clasp Zach's hand, then backed away, as he had when he had first greeted the newly returned Zach only four days—or a lifetime—ago.

"Thank you, Robin," said Zach again. He did not trust himself to say more. Robin turned abruptly and left, closing the door behind him.

He sat and forced himself to eat, knowing he would need the strength the food would give him. He squinted at the clear sky outside the window, trying to estimate how long it would take him to get across the border, back to the Trader empire. He would take the same route he had traveled when the Principal had sent him to fetch Evvy over five years ago, north through the Capital, then following the Principal's own roads along the river, crossing at the Northern Ford, and then proceeding west past the old Garden, now one of the Principal's garrisons, and into the wild lands beyond. He had no more wanted to take that road then than he did now, but at least then, five years ago, he had had a choice, or the illusion of choice; today there was none. If he had refused to go on the journey then, perhaps everything would have been different; certainly the details would have, but he knew on a deeper level that the ultimate result would have been the same: betrayal and dishonor.

He had always been a solitary man, had nurtured his solitude, knowing that the less he asked of others, the less he would want, but now he felt that solitude completely. He was alone. Alone to live, or more likely to die, but either way with no one to know or care. He himself cared perhaps the least.

It did not occur to him to refuse the sentence of exile: his fate in the Capital if he were seen after today might not be death, but in any case he was easily recognizable, and there was nothing he could do here now to help Will or to thwart him. He was known to the people of the District as well as he was known to the Traders, and neither side would trust him or see him as anything other than an enemy.

He was startled by a sound from the corner of his room. He turned and was shocked to see Will standing at the entrance to the hidden door that connected Zach's quarters with his office. Will's curly hair was rumpled, and he wore an expression Zach had never seen before.

"May I come in, brother?"

"Please," said Zach. He indicated the tray. "Share my breakfast. It's too much."

"You need it all," said Will, his voice oddly unsteady, "if you're ever to regain any weight."

"I've thought of one thing more that might help you," said Zach after a moment. "I can give you physical descriptions of the leaders of the Traders. Those I know personally, those I have seen."

"It might be better for you to identify them in person," Will said.

Zach didn't answer. He did not understand what Will wanted. Will's face suddenly twisted, and he turned away. "I've changed my mind," he said. He paused for a beat, then faced Zach again. "No, more than that. I've realized the truth. I don't want to send you away. I never did. I'm . . . asking you to stay and help me. I need you, Zach. I can't do it myself."

"But what about—" Zach left the sentence unfinished.

"It's all in the past. I can't pretend I'm not still angry and hurt. But other things are more important. What matters is for us to work together, to build our civilization, to fight the Traders. I could not have come this far without you, and I need you to continue the work."

Zach set down his cup of tea, untouched. He bowed his head. "Of course I will do anything you ask. My service is yours. My life is yours. I swear I will never disappoint you again."

For a moment Will looked angry again. "For the deena's

sake don't be so formal," he said. Then, abruptly, he sat in the chair Zach had recently vacated and put his head in his hands. "This is not easy for me," he muttered.

Zach did not know how to answer. He was befuddled by lack of sleep, and at the same time he saw clearly what must have happened. "Evvy has been talking to you," he said.

"Yes," said Will distractedly. "She is wiser than both of us." He seemed suddenly to shake off his mood, then he looked directly at Zach. "She and I are going to be married," he said. "She says she loves me and I believe her." He rose, then approached Zach, looking almost himself. "Zach, I need you here."

Zach looked at his brother, not knowing what he felt. He pushed himself to his feet, and the brothers embraced, as they had four days ago.

"Meet me in the stables in half an hour," said Will. He picked up the scarcely touched fowl and broke off a leg and thigh, eating hungrily as he continued to talk. "You must come with me today. Learn the routine again. Can you do that?"

Slowly Zach nodded. Will frowned briefly. "But perhaps you're not strong enough yet?"

"I'm quite well," said Zach. "I'll see you in the stables."

Will left by the same door he had entered. Again Zach looked at the pile of provisions he had planned to take into exile, the bags of clothing and bedding, the weapons, the store of food. Always in his life, those he was closest to—Will, the old woman, Leya, even Evvy, but especially Will, whose moods were like waves passing over water—all could put aside or change their feelings as easily as donning a new cloak. For Zach this had never been true. His head ached, and his fatigue was as great as any he had ever experienced. It clouded his mind, preventing him from knowing how he felt. He was to stay. And Will and Evvy would be married.

PART ONE

THE WEDDING

One

Zach was awakened early by an unearthly, high-pitched howling. For a panicked moment he thought he was still in his Trader prison cell, then he recognized the familiar walls of his own room. He leapt out of bed and quickly pulled on his trousers. The hall was dark, but he could hear running footsteps and then curses coming from the direction of the Principal's quarters. His heart thudding, he ran toward the sounds and collided with Lindy, the young serving boy, knocking the breath from both of them. At that moment the Principal emerged from his rooms, and Zach saw that the bizarre noise was coming from a blurred shape at the end of the hall, behind the Principal.

"Will!" cried Zach. "Are you—"

"No, sir!" shouted Lindy at the same moment. "Don't go near it!" He darted down the hall and past the Principal, who had turned toward the sound.

The next instant there was a sharp, surprised cry of pain from the boy, followed by the Principal's voice, commanding and calm: "Stay there, Zach! Lindy, back away slowly."

A half dozen guards had now appeared, one with a torch, and for the first time Zach could see clearly the cause of the commotion: at the far end of the hall was crouched Napoleon, the Principal's pet fox-cat, its dark-striped fur standing straight out from the top of the large, wedge-shaped ears to the tip of its bushy tail. The howling continued unabated, and now Zach saw that the animal had apparently attacked Lindy. "Lindy, have Wolff attend to that," the Principal said, still sounding calm. He pushed the boy in Zach's direction. Even in the dim light Zach could see the three deep scratches that looked like knife cuts in the boy's forearm. Blood welled from the wounds, and Lindy's eyes glistened with unshed tears.

"Sir," he said. "Please let me—"

"Go!" snapped the Principal. He turned to his guards, who were standing uncertainly, their eyes fixed nervously on the animal.

"It's nothing, men," he said. "The fox-cat has apparently had a nightmare. Back to your stations."

Perry, the Principal's personal guard, started to object, but the Principal cut him off. "Now!" he said. "I'll handle this. Your presence is upsetting him more."

The guards left with Lindy. The fox-cat continued to howl and hiss. Slowly, murmuring soothingly, the Principal began to walk toward the end of the hall. "Will—" said Zach.

"Be quiet! I know what I'm doing!" Again his voice dropped to a soft murmur. "There, there, Napoleon," he said. "It's all right, little one, it's all right."

While Zach watched anxiously, Will slowly knelt and held out his hands to the small animal, which continued to howl and spit in seeming terror.

Zach held his breath as Will withdrew his hand, still speaking soothingly. The creature was more than half grown, and though it had been born in captivity and had been Will's pet most of its life, Zach wondered if it were reverting to the wild state. Or worse, perhaps the animal had rabies, which had not been destroyed by the Change as had some other diseases. "Leave it alone, Will," he said.

"Shh," said the Principal. He reached out again and this time touched the fox-cat, then began to stroke it. At last Napoleon quit making the eerie sounds, and the Principal lifted his pet onto his shoulder. Napoleon nuzzled his master's hair, then relaxed, draping himself across the Principal's shoulder like a cloak. "He's all right now," said the Principal.

"Are you sure? Will, the animal attacked your serving boy."

"Only because Lindy moved too quickly. Fox-cats can sense moods, Zach. I believe all the excitement has him upset."

"He could be sick. At least have Wolff look at him."

"If you insist," said the Principal in a tone that told Zach that he would do no such thing. "But for today I'll keep him shut up in my room." He smiled and yawned. "Besides, both of us have more than enough to attend to today. Are you ready, brother?"

For a moment Zach couldn't think what the Principal was talking about.

"For the wedding," said the Principal, laughing. When Zach still did not answer, he peered closely at him. "Zach? Is something wrong?"

Zach forced himself to relax. "No, brother," he said. "I was just thinking. I suppose I never thought I would see this day."

The Principal smiled sheepishly, suddenly looking like an adolescent boy facing his first challenge. "To tell you the truth, neither did I. And I owe it to you."

Again Zach didn't know what to say. He could not shake a nagging feeling that something was wrong. Perhaps he had caught the fox-cat's nervousness.

"Zach?"

"Ah, Will, it's a happy day," he said. "And I'm happy for you. For both of you." He forced himself to smile, then clasped Will's hand. The Principal returned his grip, then, still holding the fox-cat, turned and went into his rooms.

Zach took a deep breath, then stepped out into the warm afternoon sun. His hair and beard had been freshly trimmed, and he was wearing a new cloak and tunic with the Principal's emblem embroidered on the chest. As always when dressed formally he felt faintly ridiculous; he had to fight an urge to lower his head as he approached the wrought-iron gate that led to State House, where Evvy and the women from the Garden were staying.

This was the second and most important of his errands today. Several hours earlier, dressed less conspicuously, he had guided his mount along the broad avenue, bordered on one side by the teeming mall, on the other by the massive pre-Change marble buildings. He had been struck by the almost palpable mood of excitement and optimism: for days now craftsmen, farmers, and all manner of tradespeople had been flocking to the Capital for the biggest and most lucrative fair held since the District had been consolidated under the Principal's leadership.

Even the frequent public trials of Trader preachers had not seemed to detract from the sense that the District was moving and building toward a new future, a renaissance of civilization and the rebirth of humankind. Everywhere he looked was the evidence of the Principal's vision and influence: from postal notices and schedules for literacy classes to the growing numbers of female children.

When Zach saw all this, especially the girl-children, who were almost all under two years of age, he smiled to himself and could even join for a moment in the feeling of celebration. But he saw other signs too: small groups of sullen, defiantly unwashed citizens, some wearing openly the forbidden double spiral; others with faces reflecting the despair created by a life of hopeless poverty, crouching listlessly in doorways or walking aimlessly in the crowd, swept along but untouched by the celebration. Most of all Zach felt a sense of kinship with these, the hopeless, the frightened, those who seemed to see clearly the coming end of the world. His mood had grown stronger throughout the day; he could no more shake it than he understood it.

Zach was well liked in the Capital, and as he had moved through the unusually crowded streets, he responded almost automatically to the many greetings: "Welcome home, General Zach!" "Congratulations!" "Best of luck to the Principal and his bride!" "May the deenas protect you."

He tethered his mount outside the Hall of Justice, then proceeded to the office of General Marcus, who headed the arm of the military that maintained order in the Capital. With him was General Ralf, one of the oldest and most trusted of the Principal's aides.

Both men rose and held out their hands.

"Zach, welcome," said Ralf. "It's good of you to come on this of all days."

"The work of the District must go on," said Zach, "no matter what else is happening."

"Well, yes, of course," said Marcus. He was a short, round, clean-shaven man, with shiny, well-kempt hair, as meticulous in his dress and manner as Ralf was rough in his. He gestured Zach to a chair. "But drop your serious face for a minute. Your brother is to be a bridegroom at last. I never thought I would live to see it. And such a lovely young bride."

"Yes," Zach agreed. "She's a . . . fine match for Will." The story of Zach's connection with Evvy had never been made known, not even among the Principal's most trusted advisers, nor would it: only Zach, Evvy, and the Principal himself knew the truth.

"And he has changed, or so I understand," Marcus went on. "That is, his dealings with women are apparently not what they were."

Ralf cleared his throat and frowned. "Zach is a busy man," he said. "Perhaps we should get to business."

Marcus looked embarrassed, then spoke again. "Of course I don't mean to criticize him," he said. "I simply meant that I'm glad for him. He never wanted a woman permanent before."

Zach sighed. "I'll convey your good wishes to the Principal," he said. "But there's not much time, and I have some things to discuss with both of you." As quickly as possible, he described the increased security measures that General Red had instituted at the House and the Principal's plans for the deployment of troops throughout the Capital.

The session had lasted nearly an hour; once he had seen that Zach was not to be jollied into a festive mood, Marcus at once concentrated on business while Ralf methodically inspected the plan, asking questions whenever a point was unclear to him. Though Zach had been over the plans in detail with the Principal, he had found it hard to bring his own mind to the task, even as he heard himself repeating the instructions.

Now, approaching State House, Zach forced his misgivings to the back of his mind. He presented himself at the doorway, his heart beating as fiercely as if he were going into battle. A dour woman guard led him to a small parlor where he stood, awkwardly, feeling out of place. After a moment he went to the window and looked through the lace curtains at the crowd that was gathering outside the gates of the Principal's House. At a sound he turned to see Evvy enter, radiant in her soft white gown. A crown of flowers secured a lace veil over her dark, glossy hair, and her plum-colored eyes were enormous.

He could not find his voice; suddenly he felt as awkward as if she were a stranger, rather than the girl he had traveled with for weeks, sharing food, companionship, and danger.

Evvy seemed not to notice his discomfort. She came toward him and took both his hands in hers. "Zach," she said, smiling up at him.

Her smile was so open that he felt himself relaxing and, after a moment, could not help smiling back. "I've come to take you to your groom," he said, his voice unexpectedly gruff.

"I am ready."

"You are a lovely bride," he said then. There was another moment of silence, and he started to turn, then remembered. "I have something for you." He removed a small parcel from his pouch. "A wedding present."

Evvy took the parcel and unwrapped it. Inside the wrapping was a necklace made of hundreds of intricately intertwined, luminous, colored fronds. "Oh, Zach," she said. "It's more beautiful even than the bracelet."

"I used freshly gathered feathers," he told her. He had made the necklace the night before, after the drunken revelry of the Principal's bachelor party had ended. Unable to sleep, he had sat in his room remembering all that had happened in five years. His eyes had fallen on his feathered lyre, hanging on the wall, and he recalled Evvy's pleasure when he had woven a bracelet for her out of one of the instrument's broken strings, a tail feather from a large, flightless new-bird. He made the necklace the same way, twisting and braiding the fronds of several feathers until the many shiny colors blended in an almost fluid way.

She held the necklace in front of her a moment more, then handed it to him. "Please fasten it for me," she said.

She turned her back to him, then lifted her hair and the

veil. Zach carefully placed the necklace around her neck, then, his hand shaking, tied it just below her hairline.

She shook her head and patted her hair, then smiled again. "How does it look?"

"Beautiful," he said truthfully. "Now it is time." Formally he offered her his arm, and flanked by guards, they crossed to the Principal's House.

He left her at the entrance to the Great Hall where the ceremony was to be held, then, feeling more self-conscious than ever, walked to the front of the room where Will and the Minister of Ceremonies were waiting.

The hall was lined with new draperies in the blue and gold colors of the Principal; blue and gold flowers echoed the theme in large vases on each side of the dais. Will, like Zach, was dressed in a new blue tunic, loose trousers, and soft boots; over his shoulders hung a dark cloak edged in yellow. He looked so frightened that Zach almost laughed, forgetting his own nervousness.

Together they stood in front of the nearly two hundred waiting guests. On one side sat a number of women from the Garden, including a tall, handsome blonde who once fixed Will with such a look of hatred that Zach, watching, felt his throat close. She was dressed in the sacred white robe of the Garden, so she could not conceivably be a Trader spy, but Zach kept glancing at her uneasily just the same.

A serving boy handed Zach his feathered lyre, and at a signal, he began to stroke it. He did not play nearly so well as he had before his years of imprisonment, but both Will and Evvy had insisted that nothing else would do for their wedding. The haunting sounds filled the room, and it became hushed until he had finished. He put the instrument down and turned, as did everyone, while Evvy seemed to float among the guests, toward her waiting groom. She looked, Zach thought, like pictures of brides in the ancient paintings. She had pulled the veil over her face, but even so, in her bearing and from the glossy, dark hair that spilled behind the veil, all present could see that she was perhaps the most beautiful woman in a world where all women possessed beauty by virtue of their scarcity.

She handed the bunch of flowers she was carrying to a young girl from the Garden, then held out her hands to Will.

They turned to listen as the Minister of Ceremonies began to read the civil and sacred words. Zach could sense Evvy trembling next to him and realized that his own knees were shaking.

He scarcely heard a word, remembering a similar ceremony nearly twenty years ago, when he had been thus joined to Leya, with Will there beside him as an invisible presence.

The Minister lifted Evvy's veil to reveal her face, flushed and smiling, her plum-colored eyes sparkling. Will looked across at her like a young boy who has just discovered love. It remained only to say the final words, binding them forever, when the room erupted in flame.

Two

It had happened so quickly, there was no warning. One moment the Great Hall was filled with happy celebrants and the next the draperies were burning fiercely, thick black smoke and the pungent scent of fish oil filling the air. There were shouts and screams, the sounds of overturned furniture scraping along the floor, of swords drawn and clashing.

"Will!" Zach heard Evvy's scream, and still reaching clumsily for his sword, he saw the Principal fall against the dais, an arrow in his arm.

The tall woman from the Garden had drawn her sword, and from the corner of his eye Zach saw her run it through a long-haired figure in green. Several of the Principal's men were now battling with shadowy figures by the burning curtains. The guests pushed and shouted in their scramble to leave.

The fire was spreading, its thick smoke choking out the air, and Zach remembered an earlier time when he had been in a burning room—the room he had lived in for a year with Leya and which had become her pyre.

Evvy looked up from where she was bent over Will. "Zach, he's unconscious!"

Zach glanced quickly at the Principal. A thin trickle of

blood showed on his forehead. "Evvy, go!" he said. "I will bring him." She looked up at him, her eyes dazed, not seeming to understand.

"Zach, it was—" she started to say, but he pulled her from Will. "Go! The fire is spreading!" At that moment the blond woman from the Garden appeared. "I'll take her," she said. "Evvy, come with me!"

"But, Zach, I saw—"

"Go now!" Hastily he pushed her toward the woman. He saw that she was strong and competent and knew how to use her sword, and he bent to Will.

Will's face was pale and as still as death. Zach sheathed his sword and bent over him as if he were a sick child. The room was now so smoky he couldn't see beyond his hand. He knelt and lifted Will over his shoulder, onto his back, then began to crawl in the direction of the shouts, choking as the heat singed his face and neck.

There were moans and cries from people lying on the floor, and hissing sounds of water turning into steam. Zach ignored the cries for help and grasping hands and concentrated on moving ahead, stopping only to shift Will's body into a more secure hold. At last he made his way outside, where the Principal's guards had surrounded a handful of struggling prisoners. Most of the guests and soldiers were now passing buckets of water from one person to another in a line reaching from the main doors to the large covered well in the kitchen garden where someone was frantically pumping water into the trough.

Zach laid Will on the soft grass beyond the confusion, then gave way to a prolonged fit of coughing. When he had finished, he looked up through streaming eyes to see Robin, Will's secretary, his face red and bleeding from a cut above one eye.

"Is he—" Robin started to ask, then: "Great Deena! I'll get the physician!"

Zach knelt and felt for Will's pulse. It was fast and faint, but after a moment he opened his eyes.

"Evvy," he whispered.

"She's safe," said Zach.

"My House—"

"They're fighting the blaze. Rest, Will. I promise you we will find and punish whoever is responsible."

As he spoke, he parted Will's hair with his fingers and saw with relief that the head wound was superficial, probably caused when Will fell against the dais. Next he pulled Will's cloak away and, with his knife, began to cut the sleeve from his tunic. The arrow had lodged in the meaty part of his right upper arm. With horror Zach saw angry purple swelling around the wound and realized that the arrowhead must have been poisoned.

Quickly Zach pulled off his belt and fastened it high on Will's bicep above the wound, to prevent the poison from spreading further. Around them he was aware of people shouting and running, with most attention now on the burning House.

By now the physician had arrived, and after a quick look at Will, he exchanged a frightened glance with Zach. "It's chappa!" he said. "We'll have to—"

"Do it," said Will. "Do what's necessary."

Zach felt cold. Chappa was a fast-acting poison made from the crushed bodies of tiny brown spiders. Although not in itself fatal, chappa had killed many men because of its ability to weaken the constitution and cause rapid, often overwhelming, putrefaction of the wound.

Several of the Principal's men had gathered around, looking frightened. "It was the Traders, sir," said Michael, the young captain second in command of security to Red. "With a lot of inside help, must have been. We've caught three of them, but one's pretty badly burned. He—"

"Be quiet!" said Zach. "Can't you see the Principal is wounded?"

"No, Zach," said Will. "Report, Michael. Wolff, continue what you were doing."

Michael continued to report, speaking of fish-oil-soaked torches made of straw, stammering in his fright and shame, while Will kept his calm eyes locked onto the younger man's face. Zach could not understand a word that Michael was saying and realized that the Principal was bringing all of his concentration to Michael, to remove it from his own wounds.

The physician sent a serving boy for water and some healing herbs, then asked Zach to hold the Principal still. "The poison spreads fast," he said. "I'll have to remove the arrow now if we're to have a chance of saving his arm."

Quickly he cut through the shaft of the arrow and pulled the tunic away. During all this, which took only a few seconds, Will never took his eyes from Michael, who continued to talk rapidly but was now looking very pale.

Will's breathing had become quick and shallow as the poison continued to work. When Michael finished speaking, Will dismissed him, then turned to the physician. "Am I dying?" he asked.

Wolff shook his head. "No. But you'll be very sick. I'll do everything I can to save your arm."

Will shut his eyes a moment, then opened them and spoke again. "Evvy—"

"She's safe," Zach repeated, suddenly wondering if it were true. He turned to Robin, who was squatting beside him. "Bring Evvy," he said. Robin nodded and hopped up at once, joining the crowd milling about the Great House.

Now the physician took a thick rawhide thong and set it between Will's teeth, then, using a slender surgical knife, quickly cut into the wound while Zach held Will's shoulder steady. He tugged and the arrow came free, along with gouts of blood.

While the physician cleaned the wound, repeatedly bathing it with fireberry disinfectant and cutting away a good deal of the tissue, several men brought a litter, and at last, bandaged, Will was set on it, covered with his own cloak and Zach's, and taken across the street to State House.

Robin had not yet returned, so Zach instructed Red to have Evvy brought to the mansion, then, on shaky legs, followed the physician behind Will's litter.

Word of Will's injury had spread rapidly, and his men began to gather outside the mansion. Zach stood before them, issuing commands and answering questions.

At last the housekeeper reported that the fire had been put out but not without extensive damage, most of it from smoke. The splendor of the Great Hall was ruined, but the fire had been confined to that one area, and the structure of the House had been saved.

Red reported that the three captured men had readily admitted to being Traders. "They say that God himself told them to prevent this unholy marriage from taking place," he said. "They won't give us the name of a more worldly leader. And unfortunately the one who had been burned died under questioning. We're still working on the others."

Zach thanked Red and dismissed him. He felt suddenly ill. Obviously the attack could not have been accomplished without the help of several of the Principal's own men. But whose? He must discover the truth of it quickly and protect Will at the same time. But who could he trust now to guard Will? Wolff the physician, certainly, and Robin, both of whom had been with Will since the days before he became Principal. The young serving boy, Lindy, worshiped his master. But the others—Odell, even Red and the other generals—some one or more among them must have had a hand in this. All of the higher aides had been with Will since he'd become Principal, but Zach had been away a long time and had no way of knowing what jealousies or rivalries might have arisen in the time he was gone; or who, even, might have become converted to Trader beliefs.

Reluctantly he realized that he did not dare to trust anyone for the time being. He gave orders that the mansion be ringed with double guards and that no one should see Will for the present but those three men and himself. He posted Lindy at the top of the stairs to bar all entry to the room where Will lay. Then he ordered that the generals meet with him as soon as possible.

As Zach watched behind a curtained, glass-paned door, the generals took their seats. They looked incongruous in the dainty parlor, which was arranged with pre-Change furniture and objects, an elegant meeting room for important visitors and guests. Though Zach had seen each of the generals separately since his return, he had not seen all of them together, and not filthy, frightened, weary, as if they had come from battle. For a moment it seemed that time had turned back, and Zach half expected the Principal to appear among them, looking fresh and energetic always, even when he was the most exhausted of all.

The strain of the day was obvious on each of them: old Ralf, whose courage and loyalty had been proven beyond question many times, was looking at his feet, worrying the frayed edge of his tunic with gnarled and grimy hands. Next to him on the yellow-upholstered sofa sat Red, his russet hair matted and greasy, his eyes ringed with soot from the fire.

Quentin and Marcus sat tensely, their big bodies scarcely contained by the ornate upholstered chairs. Of all, only Marcus had taken the time to bathe and change before the meeting, while Quentin, who spent most of the year commanding the Principal's outposts in the south and west, looked almost like a Trader with his unruly hair and beard.

Only Eric, the youngest of the generals present, seemed at ease, his green eyes darting around the room, his face wearing a look of anticipation that was almost a smile.

"Where is General Daniel?" Zach asked Robin, before entering the parlor.

Briefly Robin explained that Daniel was no longer a general. "The Principal doesn't want to see him since what happened at the clinic last year," the old man finished lamely.

Zach nodded. He remembered now that the Principal had told him of some trouble with Daniel. "Send for him later, then," he said reluctantly. He sighed. It appeared now that Daniel perhaps had a motive for the attack, one he could not imagine in the others.

"Yes, sir," said Robin. "Is there anything else?"

"You're certain that Evvy has returned to the Garden?"

"All the women left together right after the attack," the old man said. "For safety's sake."

"Yes, well," said Zach. "After the meeting, prepare a heavily armed party to fetch her back. I'll ask General Ralf to lead it." Robin nodded. "And, Robin, thank you. I'll need to rely on you more even than Will has always done. Please join us and make notes of what is said."

"Yes, sir." Robin seemed pleased; this had been his job for the Principal for years. Of course the Principal's memory was nearly perfect—he seldom forgot anything—but he would often pore over Robin's notes, searching for half-formed thoughts or attitudes that had not come immediately clear in a meeting.

Zach watched as Robin walked into the room, then hesitated a moment more. He closed his eyes and took a deep breath, held it, let it out, and breathed deeply two times more.

This was how Will had always calmed himself whenever he was upset or challenged.

"The Principal is seriously wounded, but the physician promises me he will recover," Zach said without preamble. "He is still very sick," he went on quickly. "He may not be able to resume his duties for several weeks."

"When can we see him?" asked Red, his voice sounding at once relieved and gruff.

"I can't tell you that," said Zach. He had been standing stiffly at the door, wishing that he had the Principal's gift for appearing at ease in any situation. He took three paces into the room, started to speak, stopped, then sank into a chair that had been kept empty for him.

"Great Deena," he said. "I don't know how to say this." He stopped and cleared his throat, then, not looking directly at anyone, went on. "You all must know that this attack was organized by the Traders," he said. "This could not have been accomplished without help from someone within the House." He paused again to let his words sink in, and then he heard the first mutterings as the implications became clear. At last Eric spoke.

"You're not saying that we are suspect?"

"I'm not saying anything," said Zach. "But the Trader spies must have received a great deal of information. They had to know about the security arrangements for the wedding, the plans of the House, everything. This must have required the cooperation of someone, or several men, whose loyalty and service is above question."

For a moment the room was quiet. The generals looked at one another, and Zach saw the beginnings of suspicion appear in narrowing eyes.

"You can't believe that any of us was responsible!" cried Quentin, who had once been Zach's hunting partner.

"We've all been with the Principal since before he became the Principal!" added Marcus.

"I suspect no one," Zach said. "I've told you that. I can't believe it was any of you, but I can't be certain that it wasn't."

"Let us see the Principal, then," said Red. "Let him question us."

"The Principal is gravely ill," said Zach. "The orders are

that no one is to see him now except for Robin, the physician, his serving boy, and myself."

This announcement was met with more angry grumblings and curses. Eric rose from his seat but sat again when Red tugged at his arm. "Take it easy, boy," he said.

"Whose orders are these?" Quentin said then. "Did the Principal himself command it?"

"I ordered it," said Zach. As he spoke, he felt suddenly unsure of himself. At the time of the decision it had seemed the only safe course. But facing these men now, all of whom had battled beside him, all of whom had risked their lives for the Principal and his ideals, he couldn't believe that any of them could have had traitorous motives; none of them had ever done one thing to harm the Principal, not even so much as had Zach himself.

As the generals continued to protest, Zach forced himself to look at each in turn. Eric's face was tight with anger, reminding Zach of the Principal in a rage. Quentin and Red wore almost identical expressions of outrage while Marcus's complexion had purpled, becoming darker as he muttered curses. Ralf, of all, looked more sorrowful than angry, and only he caught Zach's gaze and held it. Zach waited. At last Red, who had always striven to be calm in discussion, spoke. "You are not the Principal, Zach. Let me hear that order from his own lips and I will obey it."

"The Principal is scarcely conscious," said Zach. "I am doing what I think is right in his place. He will support my decisions. And you know it."

For a moment the men were quiet, and then Eric spoke again, half rising in his anger. "No disrespect meant," he said, "but you were away over five years, Zach. You were with the Traders the whole time. I saw you when they brought you in—you looked like a Trader yourself!"

Again the room fell silent. Zach felt as if he had been physically assaulted; a rush of anger filled his chest and he rose, took one step toward Eric, not sure what he would say or do, then Red swiftly stood between the two men. He pushed Eric back into his seat and spoke: "Nobody believes that, Zach."

"Only let us see him," said Ralf, speaking for the first time. "To see for ourselves that he's all right."

Zach took a moment to push his anger away, then nodded. "Not all," he said. "He isn't strong enough for that. Just you, Ralf. You go up now. Robin, go with him and tell Lindy I so ordered it. Then come back and we'll talk about what to do next."

When Ralf returned from his visit upstairs, he appeared shaken. In answer to the half dozen questions he nodded. "It's as Zach says. We m-must do everything we can now to protect him and to c-catch whoever did this."

Zach was exhausted when the last of the generals left. He waited while Ralf and Robin organized the party to the Garden, then climbed the stairs to Will's room. Lindy was standing rigidly at attention outside the door, his eyes red from weeping. Zach clasped the boy on the shoulder and ordered him to get some sleep, then opened the door. The physician was bending over the bed where Will lay, breathing with audible effort.

At the sound of Zach's entry Wolff looked up. Zach gestured. "How is he?"

The other man shrugged. "The poison causes high fever. It's weakened him terribly. But he is fighting it."

"And the arm?"

Wolff shook his head.

Zach quietly pulled a chair up to the bed. At first he thought Will was unconscious, but then he opened his eyes. He was very pale but seemed to be more exhausted than in pain.

"Ah, Zach," Will murmured. "It's all fallen to you now."

"Only the ground floor was damaged," Zach said. "Repairs have begun already. Three men have been arrested and are being questioned. There's no doubt it was the Traders."

"Your old compatriots."

Zach sat back on the chair as if he had been slapped. Did Will, then, suspect him too? He felt his anger at Eric, which had never really dissipated, rising again. He clasped his hands together tightly, feeling all the muscles in his body knotting while he tried to think what to say.

"Zach?" Will was speaking again, his voice drugged and slow-sounding. "Evvy—"

Zach realized he had been holding his breath. He sighed.

"She has returned to the Garden for safety. I've sent Ralf after her."

"Some wedding night I've given my bride." Will closed his eyes, then opened them to slits. "She will be here tomorrow?"

"Yes," said Zach. "Now rest. I'll see to everything until you're stronger."

But Will hadn't heard him. He was asleep. Zach settled himself in the oversized chair and closed his eyes, thinking to rest, but he could not relax. Over and over his mind turned in circles: Who could have been responsible for the attack? One of the generals? He remembered again Eric's words and the look of open suspicion, even hatred, on his face. Was this a cover for his own treachery? Or Red, always the most loyal of men? He alone was responsible for security arrangements in the House. Whom should he trust? Could he trust even himself?

The next day Ralf returned with the news that Evvy had not gone to the Garden. The women who had attended the wedding reported that she had refused to leave the Capital. She had last been seen in the company of one of the Principal's soldiers, but no one knew his name. Zach immediately ordered dozens of men to search the area around the House and on the mall, but it was no use: Evvy had disappeared.

Three

Zach sat at the desk in the front parlor of State House, staring at but not seeing the notes Robin had made of yesterday's meeting with the generals. Across the street stood Will's damaged House, streaks of oily black soot climbing the walls above the first floor like some strange new form of ivy.

His head ached badly and his eyes burned—aftereffects of the smoke. He tried to think what to do, how to handle the disasters that had suddenly turned everything upside down. Upstairs Will lay desperately ill and helpless, relying utterly on him: the betrayer. Zach pressed his hands into his face, bringing bright stars to his eyes. He was not a natural leader, as was Will, nor had he ever wanted to be. What was he to do? And how could he tell Will about Evvy?

He opened the window and took three deep breaths, holding each before exhaling, imagining that he was Will, facing down his own fears. And then he thought: But Will has never been afraid, not, perhaps, until now. In almost the same moment Zach realized that he, himself, was more afraid than he had ever been: afraid of what might have happened to Evvy; afraid of what would become of the District if Will were to die or be permanently impaired; afraid of what might finally happen when Will recovered and Evvy returned, among the three of them.

A loud knocking at the front door brought him out of his thoughts.

Grant and Perry, who had long been the Principal's most trusted personal guards, were standing duty there. "I beg your pardon, General Zach," said Perry hesitantly. "There's someone here who insists on seeing you. It's Daniel son of Martha, sir. He has left his arms outside."

Zach remembered what little the Principal had told him of the circumstances of Daniel's losing his commission and wondered briefly if this could somehow be a trick, but it seemed unlikely that a lone man, unarmed, could do much harm. "Thank you, Perry," he said. "Please show him in."

Daniel entered hesitantly, almost apologetically. Zach was shocked at how much he had changed in five years. Always the handsomest of Will's advisers, Daniel had possessed a youthful and exuberant charm, his natural ease and ready smile only occasionally slipping into impatience and self-importance. Now the youthfulness was gone and with it all traces of arrogance; in their place was stolidity, caution. Daniel had become gaunt, and his clean-shaven face showed deep lines at the cheeks and brow; a large purple bruise above his eye emphasized the look of a man who had suffered. He looked as if he had not laughed in years.

"I'm sorry to disturb you, General Zach," he said. "But Robin said you wished to see me." He paused. "I've wanted to welcome you back all these weeks. I'd hoped for a better moment."

"Have a seat," said Zach. "Would you like refreshment?"

Daniel shook his head. "Thank you, no. I've heard what happened to the Principal and to Evvy. How is he?"

"No worse," said Zach. "His arm is badly infected. The arrow was poisoned."

"So I heard," said Daniel. He paused. "Have you discovered who was responsible?"

Zach shrugged. "We've arrested half a dozen men, two of them temporary guards hired for the wedding. But someone in a position of authority must have been involved. We don't know who."

"It is easier for the Traders to mix with us than you can

imagine," Daniel said then. "I don't know how much the Principal has told you about what happened at the Clinic last year."

"That there was a surprise Trader attack and one of the scientists from the Garden was killed. That the Traders had help from some of the guards."

"Guards under my command," said Daniel. He looked at the floor. "I had no suspicion. I was . . . perhaps too distracted by personal affairs to bring my full attention to the job, and, of course, there is no sure way to tell a Trader from an ordinary citizen. But that's no excuse."

The expression on Daniel's face told Zach that he would never forgive himself. Now he remembered the rest that Robin and the Principal had told him: that Daniel had become infatuated with the young woman scientist who died in the attack. Will had stripped Daniel of his command, fined him, and had him publicly whipped, though he told Zach that he had never suspected Daniel himself. From the earliest days all Will's men knew that those closest to the Principal were expected to obey his laws more strictly than common citizens, to consider themselves at all times extensions of himself and thus fully responsible for their actions.

Eventually the Principal had placed Daniel in charge of the Clinic, which was now run by the Principal's men rather than the women of the Garden. This was the single most important project anywhere in the District: not only did its tests indicate which women were susceptible to the woman sickness, the data gathered were beginning to provide clues to ways of determining which men carried the disease. In conjunction with the testing were classes on methods of birth control and abortion, essential to save the lives of those women who proved susceptible to the disease and had already borne one female child. Because the work of the testing project was so technical, Daniel was more qualified to lead it than anyone else not a woman of the Garden: he was literate; he had grown up in the Garden and was familiar with its scientific philosophy; and he was an able leader and administrator. But Will had never again allowed Daniel into his presence, communicating with him only through intermediaries. Now, looking at the former general, Zach could see on Daniel's face how much this banishment had hurt him.

"Has there been any word of Evvy?" Daniel asked after a moment.

Zach shook his head. "All we know is that she refused to return to the Garden with the other women. They left her in the care of a soldier, but we don't know who."

"Does Will . . . does the Principal know?"

Zach shook his head.

"I pray that you find her soon." A look of sorrow passed over the young man's face, and Zach imagined that he was thinking of his own lost love, the girl who had been killed in the Trader attack on the Clinic. "If there's anything I can do to help you find her . . . anything at all . . ."

"Thank you, Daniel," Zach said. "I believe the most important thing you can do for both Will and Evvy is to continue with the testing project. When things are quieter, I'd like to visit your Clinic and see it for myself."

"Of course," said Daniel. "It would be an honor." For just a moment he smiled, and Zach saw again the young boy who had followed Will from the Garden, serving him bravely and loyally through the long struggle for control of the District. It had been Daniel, in fact, who had helped the Principal rescue Zach from certain death at the hands of the President's men on the night that Zach had rejoined the Principal.

Zach returned Daniel's smile. "Share some brew with me," he said. "I insist." He rang, and in a few minutes Lindy appeared with a pitcher of brew. He and Daniel sat drinking in silence a moment. Zach had always liked Daniel, and he knew that until the trouble last year the Principal had always looked to him as his closest confidant after Zach himself.

Daniel shook his head when Zach offered to refill his cup. "Thank you, Zach, but I must return to the Clinic. Please tell Will—" He stopped, then his face set again into impassive lines. "Never mind. Just one thing. I know that it can't be easy for you now. If there's any way I can help, please call on me."

"I shall," said Zach, getting to his feet. He grasped Daniel's hand. "Thank you for coming."

After Daniel had left, Zach realized he had asked none of the questions he had intended to put to him, but the purpose of the visit had been served to his satisfaction: Zach felt certain that Daniel could not have been in any way connected with the Trader attack.

He was on the point of turning back to Robin's notes when he heard footsteps hurrying down the stairs.

As soon as he saw Wolff's face Zach knew that it was bad news.

"Before the Change we could have cured him," the physician was saying. "There were drugs to fight and subdue the infection, to neutralize the poison. But it is spreading, and it will kill him if I don't take the arm off."

Zach's heart turned over in his chest. Will was right-handed. He wrote with that hand, fought with it. Will was a vain man, too: how would he see himself with one arm only? And the trauma of taking it off—Zach had assisted in a few such operations, always ghastly, but never with a man so sick as Will was now. If only Evvy were here, he thought.

"I'll give him flower-brew before and after," said Wolff. "But it will still be very hard on him."

Before the Change, Zach knew, Will could have been made unconscious without injury, and afterward there would have been drugs to make him sleep and dull the pain. He thought of Jonna and her herbs and wondered if she had found something that would help in such a situation.

"He knows," Wolff went on. "He said he only needs some time to be ready. Lindy and Ralf will assist."

Zach nodded. He forced himself to ascend the stairs, to step into the room.

From the doorway he was hit with the sickening-sweet stench of decay, and he could hear Will take long, slow breaths. He knew that he was preparing himself through deep breathing, relaxing all his muscles preparatory to the ordeal.

Aware that opening the door had already intruded, he spoke quietly. "I'm here, Will."

The Principal lay as before, covered with mounds of blankets. For a moment he didn't move, then his head turned to the door.

"Ah, Zach," he said.

Afterward Will rested in the beautiful pre-Change bedroom with its massive furniture of dark wood, polished over the years to a shiny, living brown. He had cried out only once during the operation, at the end, when Wolff had cauterized the raw stump with a glowing metal wand to seal the blood vessels. Lindy had helped carry Will to the room, his face as pale as Will's and wet with tears.

It had been Lindy's duty to stand next to Wolff and hold the tray on which lay ancient, preserved physician's tools: knives; a saw; metal probes. When the cutting had started, the boy's hands had begun to shake so badly that Zach could hear the metal objects dancing against one another. He looked at Lindy's anguished face and with a pang of sympathy realized that Lindy was in love with the Principal, loved him as truly and deeply as Zach himself had ever loved a woman and that the boy knew, because of who the Principal was and how he was, that his love would never be reciprocated in this life.

When Will was settled in his bed, Zach put his arm over the boy's shoulder a moment in comfort, then told him to get some rest.

"But he may need me," Lindy protested.

"I'll be here," said Zach. "I promise I'll call you if he wants anything."

With a last look at Will the boy turned to leave, and Zach settled himself in the familiar green upholstered chair by the bed while Will slept fitfully under the influence of flower-brew. Wolff had gone to another room to rest, making Zach promise to send for him at once if Will awoke or began to bleed.

After what seemed several hours, Zach gave up thought of sleep. He rose softly, not to disturb Will, and went to the window. All was dark at Will's great House, but he could see the dim shadows of scaffolding where workmen were beginning to repair the damage caused by the fire.

At a noise behind him he returned to the bed. Will had shifted again, as he had been doing all night, unable even in drugged sleep to achieve a moment's comfort. Zach stood looking at his brother, the white-wrapped stump showing against the darker bedclothes. He felt a knot of pity in his throat and again the fear that he would be left alone to rule.

"Zach." Zach started, then looked down at Will. His face was slick with sweat, and his lips were dry and cracked.

"I'm sorry. I didn't mean to disturb you."

"I've been awake. I can't rest."

"I'll get Wolff."

"No. Wait. Talk to me a moment, brother." Zach sat again by Will's bedside. He took a towel and wet it in the small basin, wrung it, then wiped Will's face and neck.

"Thank you." Then: "Zach, tell me. Where is Evvy?"

Again Zach felt a sick fear well up in his stomach. He didn't answer.

"Something has happened to her."

"It was after the attack. We thought she had returned to the Garden with the other women. But she never left. No one has seen her."

Will said nothing, but turned his head to the wall. Zach saw his chest move as he took slow, deep breaths. He held the last breath, let it out, and turned again to Zach.

His face was angry now, and his voice, though still weak, held the familiar tones of command. "Report," he said.

"In truth I don't know what happened," said Zach. Before Will could protest, he quickly told him all he knew from the time he had given Evvy into the care of the woman warrior until Ralf had returned from the Garden with the news that Evvy was missing.

"Of course you have searched . . ." Will's voice was weaker, and Zach could see the effort this was costing him.

"Everywhere," said Zach. "There are parties of men out looking even now. Will, we're doing all we can—"

"You should never have let her out of your sight!"

Although he had been expecting this, Zach had to struggle to contain his anger. His feelings were not lessened by the fact that he had been reproaching himself in the same way. "You were unconscious," he said. "The fire was spreading. I had no choice."

He realized that his own anger must have shown in his voice, because when Will next spoke, his tone was almost conciliatory. "The Traders took her then," he said.

"That's what I've come to believe."

"Who was the woman you gave Evvy to?"

"A tall, strong blond woman. I've since learned that she is Mayor of the Garden. Her name is Katha."

"That one," Will muttered.

"The women told General Ralf that Evvy refused to go with them. She insisted that she needed to speak to someone and refused their help. At last they left her with a soldier."

"Who?"

"It could have been anyone. A man of medium height, light-colored hair, short beard—"

"The deenas take it!" Will pounded his fist on the bedside table, then fell against the pillow with a groan. "I must speak to General Ralf," he said when the wave of pain had passed.

"Of course," said Zach. "But you need more flower-brew. Let me—"

"I need nothing! Send for Ralf!"

"It's the middle of the night. He'll be sleeping. He's not a young man, Will."

For a moment the Principal looked as if he wanted to hit Zach, then his face relaxed and his weariness and pain won the battle with his anger. "In the morning, then," he said. "Tomorrow I must have a full report—"

"Tomorrow you will rest." It was Wolff, just entering. He looked nearly as exhausted as Will as he approached the bed and knelt. "How is it, sir?" he said.

"I can bear it."

"Take this. It will help."

For a moment Zach thought Will would refuse the potion, but the Principal nodded weakly and sighed after the physician held the cup while he drank it down.

"Zach, first thing in the morning you must summon Robin," Will said, not waiting for the potion to take effect. "Tell him to gather the generals, those of them in the Capital. I must have council with them."

"I forbid it," said Wolff.

"You cannot," said Will. "It is urgent—more than you know."

"Zach can see to your army," said the physician. "And to everything else. For a few more days at least."

"He will not be here!" He was half sitting now, propped on his left elbow, his dark eyes seeming to glow in his pale face. Wolff caught Zach's eye, silently asking if Zach knew what Will was talking about. Almost imperceptibly Zach shook his head. He wondered if Will were thinking to punish him for having allowed Evvy to be taken.

"You mustn't excite yourself," said Wolff. "Lie down, sir."

"Will, I will do whatever you wish," said Zach quickly. "Only rest now. We can talk about all this in the morning."

The Principal let his head fall back on the pillow. "I know I'm not well," he said. "But already, now that the poisoned arm is off, I can feel myself growing stronger. I haven't lost my mind from pain, as I can see both of you thinking. If I were stronger, I'd do it myself. But there is no time to waste, so Zach must go."

"Go where?" said Wolff.

"Zach, you must go in search of Evvy. Tomorrow. Go first to the Garden and question the women. Take her fox-cat. It knows her and may be able to help. You must find her, no matter how long it takes, no matter how far you must travel. Do you understand?"

Zach nodded. "But the Traders—"

"I'll be safe. Ralf will take your place until you return. He can rule until I'm stronger." He stopped and licked his dry lips, then went on. "I know that none of this has been easy for you either, brother. But I trust you."

Zach stood. "I'll give the orders now," he said. He started to leave, then turned back. "Good-bye, Will. I'll leave as soon as it's light."

Four

The day dawned gray and rainy, subduing the brilliant colors of autumn. Zach's mount, heavily laden with food and other supplies, picked her way cautiously along the old highway to the Garden. Though not so ill-tempered as his old mount, who had died five years ago, this beast was skittish and had a tendency to turn and try to nip his fingers whenever he urged her to greater speed.

After he had left the Principal and given his orders to Robin and Ralf, Zach had spent what remained of the night preparing for his journey, much as he had done several weeks ago when he thought he would go into exile. Strangely, despite the lack of sleep, he felt less exhausted today than at any time since the crisis had begun—since, in fact, he had returned to the Capital. His mind was clear and all his senses alive, taking in the muted colors of the trees, the muffled crunch of his mount's hooves on wet leaves, the sharp scents of wood smoke and damp earth.

This was, he realized, except for the weeks of his escape from the Traders, the first time in over five years that he had been alone in the woods, responsible only to himself and to his mission.

The misgivings and fears of the previous days seemed to

have dissipated like a fog: despite his concerns for her well-being, Zach was suddenly certain that he would indeed find Evvy and deliver her from her captors. His worries about Will's health and safety persisted, but Will was strong, and those men immediately around him—Wolff, Robin, Lindy, and Ralf—would protect him with their own lives.

By late morning he had reached the Principal's training base, which guarded the neck of the small peninsula where the Garden was located. He stopped and dined with the Commandant, noting with interest the dozen or so women living here, most of them dressed in the Southern-fashion skirts of the Garden.

Then, thanking the Commandant for his hospitality, Zach rode the short distance to the gates of the new Garden, wondering what he would find there.

"I am Zach, delegate of the Principal."

"Our mayor is expecting you," said the young guard, a very thin, strong-looking redhead. "You will want to refresh yourself. After, she will meet with you." She led Zach across the grassy yard to a small outhouse, evidently used as a place for visitors, while two young girls led his mount away, casting frankly curious glances at him.

This was the first look he had had at the new Garden since it had been transformed from the deserted, half-ruined estate Zach and the Principal had found twenty years ago when they had fled the President's men, before the final battle when Will won leadership of the District. Its location provided maximum protection of the women and the secret scientific work they did here.

As always, there were no boys older than puberty here, and Zach let his mind wander again to his own boyhood in the Garden, the rigorous schooling and work schedule, the knowledge that he himself would have to leave when he reached adolescence; although, in his own case, he had stayed nearby, guarding the surrounding area, supplying wood for the Garden, and occasionally helping with particularly heavy work while Leya carried on her experiments within the walls of the Garden, returning to him every few days. If Leya had lived, he might have stayed there his whole life, content in his work and in his family. But he had lost both and had left the area soon after. He had seen no one from the Garden from that time until today.

He shut his eyes tightly against the familiar sense of loss and bitterness, then splashed his face with cool water from the basin standing in the small, tidy room. An old, carefully polished chair on rockers stood in the corner, and he recognized it as his mother's. He combed the tangles from his short wiry beard and the thinning, blond-gray hair, then stepped back out into the soft drizzle.

The guard was waiting for him, looking self-important. She started to lead him back across the yard, to the large pre-Change stone house, but his eye was caught by something.

"Is that your graveyard?" he asked.

"Would you like to see it?"

"Just for a moment." He crossed to the small shaded plot, noting that there were far fewer tiny headstones marking the graves of babies than in the old Garden, and then he saw it, heaped with fresh-cut flowers, the largest stone of all:

ILONA, DAUGHTER OF THE CHANGE
MOTHER OF ZACH AND WILL
BELOVED MISTRESS OF THE GARDEN

There were no dates inscribed; she had been born before the Change and had never known exactly how old she was. According to Will's calendar, this was the Year of the Change 76, so the old woman might well have been over eighty. She had borne her sons late in life, and Zach had never known her as the striking, vigorous young woman she undoubtedly had once been. He stood looking at the grave for a few minutes more, then turned and followed the guard to the main house.

The large living room seemed far cozier and warmer than the long, low wooden log house the old Garden had used for most functions. The pre-Change stone walls and wooden panels had been restored, giving a softness and elegance to the room that was not possible with modern building techniques. The windows were all of glass, and cheerful yellow curtains hung at their sides. Most of the furniture was of recent make; still, it had been finished more carefully than most such utilitarian objects: the chairs and the several long benches along the walls were covered with soft-looking, inviting cushions.

Zach recognized few of the women: Hilda and Gunda were middle-aged now. They had been girls when he had lived in the Garden. Of the older women only Mira, the teacher, whose hair had been white even as a young woman, looked familiar.

They greeted him cordially, and then the front door opened once again and the Mayor strode in. Zach recognized her as the competent-looking warrior who had taken charge of Evvy after the fire had begun. She was surprisingly young: though her square-shaped face was tanned and lined by the weather, and though a livid scar ran the length of her right cheekbone from temple to jaw, she could not have been much older than twenty—scarcely older than Evvy.

"I am Katha," she said. She had no smile of welcome, only a cold, wary look. "Please make yourself comfortable and help yourself to some refreshment."

"Thank you," said Zach. He sat, feeling more ill at ease than before, and accepted a cup of flower wine from a serving girl. "The Principal regrets that he could not come here himself," he said after a moment. "As you no doubt know, he is still recovering from his injuries."

"So we understand," said Katha. "What is his business with us?"

Zach was put off by her manner. He was beginning to realize that Will's dislike of her did not come solely from his long-standing antipathy toward the Garden and its women.

"The Principal has instructed me to try to find Evvy, his intended wife. Since it was women of the Garden who saw her last, we thought this would be the best place to start."

Katha flushed at his words and seemed to take a moment to compose herself. When she spoke, her voice was strained. "The Principal blames us, then, for what happened."

"It is not for me to say what the Principal thinks," said Zach.

"Nothing would have happened to her if the Principal had not insisted on such a pompous public display," said Katha. "Nevertheless, I accept Evvy's disappearance as my responsibility. I have already given a full report to General Ralf."

"Yes," said Zach. "But I thought it might be best to question you myself."

"The Principal does not believe the report?"

"As I told you, the Principal is still recovering from his wounds." Zach sighed. "No one doubts the truth of your statement. But I was hoping that perhaps you might remember some additional detail, something that can help me."

Katha's scowl deepened, and for a moment Zach thought she would refuse to talk to him, but then she, too, sighed. "Very well," she said.

As in her written report, Katha described the first moments of terror and confusion when the flames had suddenly appeared and the Principal had fallen. It had been immediately obvious to her, as it had to Zach, that the fire must have been set by Traders, and it thus seemed to Katha essential for all of the women to return to the Garden at once, for safety.

"But Evvy refused to leave?"

"She was a fool! She didn't seem to realize the danger we were all in!"

"I'm sure she understood the danger very well," said Zach. "But you must have realized that she wouldn't leave the Principal when he had been injured."

"There was nothing she could have done for him."

"Perhaps not. But he was her intended husband."

Katha muttered something, then shrugged. "In any event, I ordered her to come with us. As a Daughter of the Garden it was her duty to obey my orders."

"What happened once you realized that Evvy would not go with you?"

"I felt it would be dangerous to waste more time. One of the Principal's soldiers approached and said he would take Evvy to the Principal."

"Who was this man? Describe him."

"It's all in my report. He was a youngish man of medium height with a light-colored beard. I didn't realize at the time that it would be necessary to memorize every detail."

"What exactly did he say? What did Evvy say to him?"

Katha frowned for a moment. "I honestly don't remember. They talked for a moment or two. Evvy asked him . . . asked him a question. I wasn't listening. I was anxious to be on my way."

"Did you see where he took her? In what direction?"

"No. We left right after that. When I turned to look again, they had disappeared."

"What about the other women who were with you? May I speak to them?"

Katha turned to the small circle of women around her. "Lucille? Gunda?"

Gunda spoke first. "I didn't notice anything. I, too, thought that it would be safest for Evvy to return with us, but I understood her desire to remain with the Principal." She paused, then leaned forward earnestly. "Zach, I can't tell you how sorry we all are about this. I've been searching my memories ever since it happened, and I can't remember anything else."

The dark-haired woman named Lucille spoke next. "It happened as Katha reported," she said. "In the heat of the moment some angry words were said, but Evvy was a true Daughter of the Garden, and I'm sure she did what she thought was best."

"A true Daughter obeys the leaders of the Garden," muttered Katha.

"We're heartbroken about what's happened," said Lucille after a moment. "I love Evvy like my own child."

"We've talked it over a hundred times," Gunda added. "We all believe that the man must have been a Trader agent. That the Traders have taken her for their own purposes."

"That's what I believe too," said Zach.

"What will they do with her?"

"I don't know," said Zach. In truth, he had little idea of what the Traders might have in mind for Evvy. He was certain only that she had not been taken by chance; that the Traders must have known exactly who she was and how important she was to the Principal and his plans.

"Is there anything else we can do to help?" asked Gunda.

"One thing more," said Zach. "The Principal believes that her fox-cat may help me in my search. I would like to take the animal with me."

"The fox-cat is an important part of an ongoing breeding experiment," said Katha. "It's out of the question."

"Katha, you can't mean that!" said Gunda. "We still have Baby's two sons. And Baby might well help. You know how attached she is to Evvy."

"She's lost weight since Evvy left," added Lucille.

"Very well," said Katha. "Let him take it, then. If you will excuse me, I've some work to do." Her face flushed, she stood and strode from the room, slamming the door. For a moment Zach just looked after her, puzzled. Her hostility was nearly palpable, and he could not understand it. The old woman had had negative ideas about men but had never allowed her feelings to interfere with her judgment, as Katha seemed to be doing. If she could not control this aspect of herself, he mused, she would not remain leader of the Garden for long. And then he was struck by how similar Katha's extreme feelings were to the equally negative feelings toward women that Will had harbored most of his life. Yet his antipathies had never caused him problems as long as he had dealt only with his own sex, and perhaps that was true for Katha as well.

"Of course, Baby has a mind of her own," said Mira. "She may refuse to go with you or escape after you set off."

"Perhaps if we explain it to her," said Lucille.

"Do you believe the animal understands human speech?" Zach asked. Although the Principal's pet, Napoleon, seemed remarkably quick, he was certain that it possessed no such thing as real intelligence.

"Oh, not really, not as words," said Lucille. "But she can sense feelings, and often she does show evidence of some reasoning ability. More than one time she saved Evvy from coming to harm."

Zach followed the women to a narrow wooden building behind the main house. Inside were long tables, and racks of animal cages along the walls. "This is where Baby stays when Evvy is not here," said Lucille. She began to call the animal's name. After a moment she was answered by a sleepy "Mowr?"

Zach heard a rustling noise in the back of the room, and then a large orange fox-cat appeared. It had long silky tufts at the ends of its ears and was about the same size as Napoleon, who seemed still to be growing.

Gunda bent and stroked the little animal's back. "Baby," she said, as if she were talking to a child, "this is Zach. He is a good friend of Evvy's." She was speaking very slowly, and Zach thought he saw the fox-cat's ears prick at the mention of its mistress's name.

"Something has happened to Evvy," Gunda continued. She screwed up her face and assumed a look of sorrow. "Evvy is in trouble." The fox-cat flattened its ears and began to growl softly. "Zach is going to help Evvy. But first he must find her. He wants you to go with him. He wants you to help find her."

The fox-cat looked up at Gunda, then at Zach. She sat gazing at him for a moment or two longer, then approached and rubbed her flank against his boots.

"She is very responsive to human emotions," Mira said in a detached way.

"I think she understands," said Gunda. "As much as she can, anyway."

"Thank you," said Zach. He did not know what to make of the animal's response. He knelt and held out his hand. Baby sniffed it quizzically and licked his fingertips. Then she sat back on her haunches expectantly.

"You are welcome to stay the night," said Gunda after a moment. "It is getting late."

"Thank you," said Zach. "I have already made arrangements to rest and supply myself at the Principal's training compound." This was not strictly true, but despite the genuine warmth and good feeling these three women had shown, he did not want to strain Katha's temper more than he had.

Gunda brought him a woven straw pouch with a loose-hanging lid, which he attached to his saddle for Baby to ride in. When the fox-cat and the mount first caught sight of each other, both bristled, the mount whistling in alarm, the fox-cat puffing her fur out all over her body.

"Take it easy, girl," Zach murmured to the mount. He let the beast sniff his fingers where he had touched Baby, then lifted the fox-cat into the saddlebag. The mount danced and reared but calmed after a moment.

"How will you find Evvy?" asked Lucille.

"I will return to the Trader empire," said Zach. "They are essentially nomadic, but they have at least one base, where I was held prisoner. I will disguise myself as a Trader and wander, asking questions, until I can find her."

"Good luck," said Gunda. "All our hopes are with you."

"Yes," added Lucille. "We pray that you find her unharmed."

"Thank you," said Zach. He climbed onto his mount. Beside him Baby's head peeked out of the basket, her ears pricked and her nose twitching softly as she sniffed the wind. "Mowr?" she said quizzically. Zach laughed. He had to admit that whatever intelligence she possessed, the little animal seemed to share his sense of excitement about the mission. With a last wave at Gunda and Lucille he guided the mount through the gate and into the forest.

PART TWO

THE SACRIFICE

One

For several days Zach and the fox-cat traveled to the northwest. He found the little animal a good traveling companion. He had feared at first that she might try to run off or return to the Garden, but she seemed to understand that she was to remain with him. Sometimes she rode quietly in the saddle basket Gunda had provided, but more often she preferred to trot along beside the mount. Occasionally she would disappear for an hour at a time, but whenever he called her name, she would presently return, sometimes bearing the body of a small animal or bird in her mouth. She seemed more than willing to share her kills, and Zach found that letting her hunt saved him time.

At night Baby scampered near the fire, chasing insects drawn by the light, while Zach relaxed with a pipe of newsmoke. He thought often of Evvy and the journey they had shared. His whole life he had been accustomed to long periods of solitude, but his years in the Trader prison had given him perhaps a lifetime's worth, and he realized now that he missed companionship. It began to seem natural to talk to the fox-cat: "Tomorrow we'll try to reach the river," he would say. Or, "That's a fine fowl you've brought us, Baby." Baby, sitting on her haunches, would look up at him alertly, giving every evidence of paying attention, occasionally adding a quizzical "Mowr?" to the conversation.

By late afternoon on the fourth day they had passed the Northern Ford where he and Evvy had crossed the river to the old Garden. His mount was already showing the sluggish signs of her coming nighttime immobilization when he saw the small settlement he was seeking.

At the edge of the tiny farming town stood the Crosskey Inn. It seemed little changed from twenty years ago, when Zach had come here seeking lodging and word of Will. The town was situated on one of the few established routes to the west, and he suspected that the Inn would still be a thriving source of information for a price.

The first time he had come here, the settlement had been dangerous and anarchic, its residents prey to whatever outlaw band had best paid the President's men. Zach noted with satisfaction that it had since grown into a respectable-looking small town, as clean and quiet as any of its counterparts in the District. A smith's shop and a small goods store stood across the main road from the Inn. Next to them a small, well-tended hut displayed a placard proclaiming it the office of the Principal's peacekeeping force.

Zach stopped short of the Inn and stroked Baby's head, speaking to her soothingly. "Stay out of sight and be quiet, Baby," he said. "I'll let you know if I need you." He couldn't be certain that the small animal understood him, but she promptly yawned and withdrew her head into the basket and didn't protest when he closed the flap.

He turned the mount into the stable area and gave her over to a slim adolescent boy with bunched muscles and a wary look. He removed his traveling pouch and Baby's basket, then, buckling on his scabbard, he entered the Inn.

The large rectangular dining hall was exactly as he remembered it, with its low-beamed ceiling, rows of wooden tables and chairs, and dirty straw covering the floor. At one end a fireplace big enough to stand in sent smoke into the air where it mingled with the stink of unwashed bodies and greasy food and the sweetish scent of newsmoke. A dozen or more men sat or moved around in the gloom, and the buzz of voices and clanking of pottery and metal cups created a din much noisier than Zach remembered. Evidently, as the

District had become safer, the number of men traveling on business had increased.

He saw no one he recognized. No doubt the Innkeepers—the stout woman and her three obnoxious husbands—had long since died or moved on. He walked between a long row of tables and approached the bar where a squint-eyed old man was dispensing brew and wine. "Are you the Innkeeper?" he asked.

"Naw, she's most like in the kitchen." The old man jerked a thumb toward a double door on his left. "I'm her second husband, Oscar. You seek lodging here?"

"For the night," said Zach.

"Private's a piece of metal, common's half that," said Oscar. He paused and coughed, then spat onto the rough wooden floor. "In advance," he added.

Quickly Zach considered. One piece of metal was a great deal to pay for a room, but he would need privacy to conceal the fox-cat. He handed the metal to the bartender, who bit it, then placed it in the pocket of his dirty apron.

"Room three, off the loft," the old man said. "Bathing trough and latrine are out behind the kitchen."

Zach mounted the rickety ladder with difficulty, burdened by his parcels, then stooped slightly to stand in the low loft used for common sleeping. It was empty, save for heaps of bedding and a row of flimsily locked cupboards where lodgers might store any belongings that were not too valuable.

The four private rooms were side by side at one end of the loft. He stepped into number three. It was a crudely built cubbyhole with scarcely enough room for the bare mount-hair mattress on the floor. With its tiny chink of a window it reminded him unpleasantly of his Trader prison cell.

Shaking off his claustrophobic mood, Zach set down his parcels. He knelt and unfastened the fox-cat's basket. Immediately Baby thrust her head through the opening. She licked Zach's fingers, then clambered out of the basket and onto the mattress. She shook herself energetically, then looked around and began to explore every inch of the tiny room.

From his personal pouch Zach withdrew an envelope of powdered aromatic herbs and sprinkled them over the mattress and in the corners, in the slight hope of repelling insects. Baby, certain that this must be some new game, jumped at the patches of powder, scattering the grains with her paws. Quite suddenly she sat back and sneezed violently. A moment later she began vigorously to scratch her ear with a hind paw. Zach couldn't help laughing. "Are you telling me the powder doesn't work, little one?"

When Baby had explored the room to her satisfaction, she curled up at one end of the mattress and began to buzz. Again Zach spoke to her soothingly, hoping that she would understand the gist of his words. "I'm going to leave you here for a time," he said. "Don't make any noise and don't do anything unless someone comes into the room. I'll return after dark and take you outside."

Baby watched alertly as he spoke, then yawned and rested her head on her forepaws. He slipped his sword under the mattress; then, taking only his personal pouch and sheathed knife, he left, shutting the door securely. He was certain that his possessions would be safe; any common thief would undoubtedly be terrified at the sight of a fox-cat.

He descended the ladder and went out behind the kitchen to wash and relieve himself, then returned to the Inn. It was deep dusk now, and most lodgers would be returning soon. Feeling refreshed, he returned to the bar. After a moment the bartender noticed him. The man had seemed not unfriendly, and Zach had decided that a direct approach was as likely to work as any other.

"Is the room to your satisfaction?" asked Oscar.

"Quite satisfactory," said Zach. "Now all I require is a bit of refreshment. A cup of brew, please."

"One token," said the old man. Zach gave him a half piece of metal and waited while he counted out change and returned with a pottery mug of brew. He sipped it, feeling the bitter warmth flow down his throat and into his stomach.

"This is very good," he said with surprise.

"The lady makes it," said Oscar. "I sell it. Drink it, too, myself sometimes," he added.

Zach pushed a token across the bar. "Have a cup with me now," he said.

The bartender looked around the room, squinting first one way and then the other. "Thank you," he said. He drew a cup for himself, then lifted it. "To safe traveling," he said. Zach drank with him.

"Are you going afar?" asked the old man, evidently feeling, as Zach had hoped, that the drink entitled Zach to some conversaton.

"To the west," said Zach. "I'm looking for my daughter. She ran off with some Traders."

The old man spat again. "That filthy lot!"

"You've had dealings with them?"

Oscar shrugged. "Their preachers come into town sometimes, when the Principal's men aren't around. Now mind you, some of their ideas make sense. More than the Principal's. I just don't hold with their pushy ways. They won't let a man say his own words."

"Have any Traders come by here recently?"

"They don't stay in civilized places like this," said the bartender. "But I think some was camped outside the settlement a few days ago." He wrinkled his eyebrows, accentuating the squint. "Person to talk to would be Bird," he said. "He sold them some meat. He's been out hunting. Should be back soon."

Zach tried not to let his excitement show. He finished his cup of brew and bought another. He tipped the bartender an extra token. "I'll be having my meal over there. Please tell Bird I want to see him when he comes in."

"Yes, sir," said the old man. "Thank you, sir."

Zach took his fresh cup of brew and sat at an unoccupied table in a corner where he had a clear view of the entire room. The Inn was just beginning to fill with lodgers, and the smell of roasting meat from the kitchen promised that dinner would be served soon. He watched with amusement as the few men near him cast guarded glances in his direction. He was used to it—his large size always drew notice. He sipped at his drink, then reached into his pouch and pulled out his pipe and newsmoke. Slowly he filled and tamped the pipe, then rose to light it with a coal from the fire. He ordered a pitcher of cold draught, then leaned back in his chair, relaxing and letting his mind drift.

He fell into a reverie of newsmoke and remembered the last time he had been there, twenty years ago. The Crosskey was the first inn he had come to after leaving the Garden, and he had earned his lodging here by doing heavy labor during the day—cutting and hauling wood, helping to store supplies, mucking out the animal stalls and human cesspit. He had not minded the work—had in a sense enjoyed it—because it kept him too busy and exhausted to think about Leya and all that had happened at the Garden. In the evenings he had dulled his mind with drink and newsmoke. His purpose had been to find Will, who was at that time a notorious outlaw opposed to the President, but he had not thought out what he would do when he found him.

Zach was startled from his reverie by the clanking of a metal tankard on the table. He looked up to see a tremendously fat, red-faced, hearty man standing above him. "I am Bird," he said. "Old Oscar says you have business with me."

The Innkeeper had begun to serve bowls of stew, and Zach invited Bird to join him. While the woman set their places with large pottery bowls and wooden utensils, Zach explained that he was a woodcutter, a widower, and that his only daughter had recently run off with a band of Traders.

"Oscar tells me you had some dealings with Traders a few days past," he concluded.

For a moment he thought Bird hadn't been listening. Then the fat man grunted. "Sold them some meat," he said. He broke off a large hunk of coarse, dark bread and began to chew noisily.

"Was there a girl with them? Tall, slender, around eighteen years old?"

Bird continued to chew, his face impassive. "They was Traders," he said finally, as if that were answer enough. "They all look alike. Dirty, half starved."

"How many were there?" said Zach. Then, quickly: "Of course, I'll make it worth your while to tell me what you can." He reached into his pouch and withdrew a piece of metal. He set it on the table between them.

Bird took the metal and placed it in his own pouch, then he sighed. "I'd like to help you," he said. "But they was all men. Seven or eight of 'em. One was sick. I didn't see him. They had him in a wagon, all covered up, like. They bought some surplus game birds. Said they were in a hurry—didn't have time to hunt."

"Did any of them mention a girl?" asked Zach.

Bird shook his head. He upended his bowl and drank the greasy remains of gravy, then signaled for another.

Zach felt unreasonably disappointed. Of course, it had been only a chance. He would ask other lodgers—perhaps someone had spotted Evvy in his travels. She was so striking-looking, she would draw notice anywhere.

"I might be able to help you, at that," said Bird after thinking a moment. "Did your daughter wear jewelry?"

"Why do you ask?"

"One of the things they gave me in a payment for the game was a kind of necklace thing. All made of feathers. I can't see I'll have much use for it myself."

Zach's heart began to thump heavily. "I'll pay you for it," he said. "A piece of metal."

"Two," said Bird.

"Get it," said Zach. He knew he should have bargained, but at this moment currency seemed unimportant.

Bird returned to the table just as the mistress brought his second portion of stew. He showed Zach a bundle wrapped in a dirty rag. Zach handed Bird the metal, then unwrapped the parcel. Inside was a jumbled mass of brightly colored feathers. Zach pulled them out and examined them in the light. The feathers were tattered and soiled, but there was no doubt. This was the feather necklace he had made for Evvy as a wedding gift.

He stayed in the dining hall for another hour, talking to various travelers. No one else had seen Evvy or had any dealings with Traders. He ordered a last cup of brew and had begun to drink it when he was startled by a high-pitched yowling and then a scream of anger and fear from upstairs. He dropped his cup and raced up the ladder to the sleeping loft. The door to room three was ajar. A rudely dressed, unwashed man cowered across from it, babbling, "The devil! He's got the devil in there!"

Zach saw Baby standing in the doorway, growling, her fur standing out all over her body. Quickly he shut the door, then grasped the stranger's wrist. The man was quaking violently. There were, Zach saw now, long red scratches on his face and arms.

"What were you doing in my room?" Zach demanded.

"You're breaking my arm!" said the stranger with a sob.

"Did you think to rob me? What were you looking for?"

"'Twas a mistake! I wandered in by accident!"

"What were you doing there?" Zach began to shake the man. By now a crowd had gathered at the top of the ladder.

"*She* ordered me to," the man said then. "She ordered to search your room."

"She? Who?" But Oscar, Bird, and the others were now gathered around. "Let him go," said Oscar firmly. He and Bird pulled Zach away from the thief.

"Get out of here now," said Oscar to the thief. "Sorry, sir," he added, turning to Zach. "Old Pete's a bit crazy. He ain't even allowed in here. I'm sure he didn't mean harm."

Old Pete had begun to babble about the devil again, and Zach decided to let the matter go, rather than risk having Baby discovered. "No real harm done," he said.

Later, after he had smuggled Baby outside and then brought her back, Zach lay awake on the hard mattress, his mind racing. Baby was curled at his head, twitching and making soft whining sounds as she slept.

Zach had learned from Bird that the Trader band had traveled west, which helped confirm his feeling that they were heading toward the town where he had been imprisoned. He also suspected that the sick Trader brother had in fact been Evvy, kept carefully hidden. In any case, this band of Traders certainly had been in contact with her, and they were only a few days ahead of him.

He puzzled again over the attempted break-in of his room. He could not imagine who had ordered it searched. Who was *she*? Most likely the mistress of the Inn, he decided. But why?

In any case, there was nothing he could do about it now. With any luck he would never have to return to this deena-cursed place again. He turned over, causing Baby to growl in her sleep, and willed his mind to be still. He would leave at first light and, if all went well, would find Evvy in a day or two.

Two

Zach had ridden no more than two hours when he began to suspect that he was being followed. It was not that he saw riders behind him—that would not have been possible in the often dense forest, even now that most of the leaves had fallen. Nor did he hear anything specific. But there was a subliminal feel of sound added to the usual noises of the woods—the birds and insects, the whispering dry leaves. Baby, too, seemed to think that something was amiss. More than once she disappeared behind him on the trail, then reappeared, uttering the plaintive cry that he had learned meant: "Stop. I want to ride for a while."

No sooner would he rein in the mount and lift the little animal into her basket than she began to cry to be let down again. At length he became weary of stopping and starting and placed her firmly in the basket. "This is the last time, Baby. If you ask to be let down again, you will stay down until we stop for the evening."

The fox-cat mewled unhappily but remained inside the basket, her ears and nose alertly seeking traces of danger in the air.

He stopped for the night in hilly country, under the protecting overhang of a rock. He considered sleeping without a fire, but it was chilly and looked as if it might rain. Besides, if someone was tracking him by mount, they would be forced to stop for the night as he was.

After dinner, relaxing with a pipe of newsmoke, Zach again tried to puzzle out why the Innkeeper had wanted his room searched. At first he had thought she suspected him of keeping an animal, but if that were the case, why did she not warn Old Pete before sending him in to search?

He laid a last load of wood on the fire and buried himself in his blanket. He was just at the edge of sleep when Baby began to howl.

"What is it?" he muttered sleepily, propping himself on one elbow. In answer the little fox-cat cried all the louder; then suddenly, with no warning, she ran into the trees. Zach thought a moment, then rose and took his sword from his saddle pack, which he had hung in the branches of a tree. He stepped into the shadow of the overhang and squatted, waiting.

After perhaps a quarter of an hour he heard Baby's cries again, in the distance, followed by human shouts of alarm. He tensed, prepared to go to the sounds, when Baby came running into camp, her ears flattened against her head and her fur standing out. She stood by the fire and growled low in her throat. A moment later there was a sound of snapping branches, then three men stepped into the camp.

All were heavily bearded and armed with museum-piece swords. Before Zach could observe further, the largest and oldest approached the overhang. "Drop your sword and come out!" he said.

Zach had no illusions about overcoming three armed men, all younger than he, and he reluctantly complied. He cursed himself for not having trusted his instincts and made camp without the telltale fire. But why had the outlaws not simply waited until he was asleep and slain and killed him? With a start he realized that Baby had probably prevented their doing just that.

His thoughts were confirmed when, after directing one of his companions to take Zach's sword, the grizzled man who seemed to be the leader shouted to another, "Garf, get rid of that devil!"

Baby all this time had continued to stand in front of the fire, her fur bristling, growling a challenge.

"I ain't going near that beast," said Garf, who, Zach could now see, was little more than a boy.

The leader drew his sword and gingerly approached the fox-cat himself. Baby crouched and began twitching her tail and hindquarters as if preparing to spring. The outlaw backed off uncertainly, then approached again, and Zach had an idea.

"Run!" he shouted. "Baby, run! Go as far from here as you can!"

The fox-cat turned her head quickly to look at him. She seemed to consider a moment, then abruptly bolted from the fire and ran directly between the lead robber's legs. As Zach had hoped, he was startled and nearly lost his balance. The other outlaws turned to watch as Baby disappeared into the brush, and Zach took advantage of their momentary confusion to launch himself at the knees of the large man. Holding his knife at the man's throat, Zach roughly pulled him to a sitting position, then held him like a shield. The two younger men stood gaping, their faces astonished and frightened.

Zach forced himself to breathe slowly while he thought what to do next. The eyes of the youngest outlaw suddenly widened, but before Zach could think what this meant, something hit him hard on the back of the head. Now Zach found himself on the ground again, the knife this time pressed hard against his own throat. When the pain in his head subsided, he spoke. "My metal is in my boot," he said. "I will not fight you."

"We don't want your metal," said the outlaw leader. "But may *she* will."

Zach blinked, unable to understand what the bandit was telling him. But he understood only too clearly a moment later when the brush behind him parted and another figure strode into the camp.

"Well, Brother Zach," said the newcomer. "I have found you at last."

Zach was astounded, although he recognized her immediately. "Jonna!"

"Yes. I did not think we would meet again, but God has delivered you into my hands."

The firelight illuminated her startling, misshapen face, revealing the blue eye and its mismatched brown mate. Beneath her hood a stray wisp of coarse white hair escaped.

"Let him up," she instructed the men Zach had thought were robbers. "Tie him."

"You have been following me," said Zach.

"Since this morning. It was chance that we heard about a large stranger at the Inn. I have business to finish with you. I thought it was worth the time to be sure."

Now Zach understood the break-in of his room the previous night. While Jonna's men tied his hands and arms, he tried to think what he might do. Of course she meant to kill him. He had betrayed her trust and, from her point of view, had blasphemed the memory of Yosh, who had been her lover and the leader of the Traders.

He wished now that he had arranged some system for sending word to Will. If he died here, no one would know for certain that Evvy had in fact been abducted by the Traders or where they were probably taking her.

Then he thought of something. "How did you follow me?" he asked. "Traders do not—"

"Traders do not ride mounts," said Jonna. "Or deal with filthy new-beasts. It's true. We came on pack animals. Otherwise we'd have caught up with you sooner. Morgan!" she snapped then. "Bring the animals into camp."

"But, Sister," protested the man Zach had presumed was the leader, "it's dark. And that deena-cursed devil is out there somewhere."

"You're armed, aren't you?"

"Arms don't protect against wild deenas," the man muttered.

"Garf? Eddie? Will you go? Will the three of you go together?"

Garf, the youngest, spoke hesitantly. "It wouldn't be right, Sister, to leave you alone with this scientist."

"The deenas take you all!" Jonna shouted in exasperation. "I'll bring the animals myself!" She turned and strode into the forest. After a moment Morgan followed her, his neck flushing dark red. Zach looked after them with interest. Jonna seemed to have little fear of new-animals or of wild deenas. Despite her position as high priestess of the Trader religion,

Zach had always suspected that Jonna did not really believe Trader tenets, that she had become and remained a Trader entirely because of her devotion to Yosh.

Jonna and Morgan presently returned, leading four protesting pack animals. While her men spread bedding she added wood to the fire, then heated water and prepared an aromatic herbal tea. Zach had begun to shiver with cold and accepted a cup of the liquid gratefully. Jonna had her men move him closer to the fire and cover him, then she ordered them to take turns standing watch.

"You are no doubt curious to know what I want with you, Brother Zach," she said as she covered herself. "I will explain tomorrow. It's been a long day. Sleep now."

Zach's wrists and ankles had begun to ache from the bonds, and he expected to have trouble falling asleep, but he drifted off almost as soon as he had stretched out.

Zach was awakened by the sound of chanting. He groggily opened his eyes and saw Jonna leading the three men in the Traders' morning ritual. In the Trader capital this ritual had always included the burning of a book. He watched as a few wisps of smoke began to rise from some crumpled leaves of paper—apparently they were destroying only a few pages at a time now. He turned his eyes from the sickening sight and tried to wriggle closer to the cooking fire. He was cold and stiff—in the night he had rolled away from his blanket.

Presently the chanting stopped and Jonna saw that he was awake. She ordered one of the men to help Zach sit, then brought another cup of the flowery-tasting herb tea. He drank it quickly, relishing the warmth it brought his chilled body.

After a breakfast of salted meat Jonna ordered Zach to remove his things from the mount and turn it loose. Zach felt a pang at losing the animal, but a mount was well able to defend itself, and if he could somehow manage to escape from the Traders, he might be able to return and recapture her.

For hours they marched through the trees in the same direction Zach had originally been traveling. Jonna said nothing to Zach that the formalities did not require. He wanted to ask her what she intended but kept quiet, realizing that the more time he had, the greater his chance to escape. Besides, he was feeling dizzy and his mind was far from clear—the result, no doubt, of the forced march in the rain.

By late afternoon they came upon a small, empty cabin. From the sign of the double spiral carved above the door, Zach guessed that it was used regularly by Traders in their travels. The cabin had evidently not been constructed by Traders, for it was snug and well built, and soon Jonna's men had created a warm fire. Zach sat next to it bundled in a blanket while his clothes dried on the hearth. He was so grateful to be warm that he scarcely noticed the discomfort of being bound.

Jonna, draped in her cape, sat next to him. She gave him more salted meat and another cup of the flowery tea, then began to talk in an almost friendly, conversational tone.

"You can no longer fight us, Brother Zach. God has seen fit to put you in our path."

"How did you find me?"

"We were traveling to the Capital when one of our men heard that there was a very large, well-dressed stranger staying at the Inn. It is true that this meeting postpones my immediate plans. But it fits quite well into the larger one."

Zach was having trouble following what she was saying. But he felt comfortable with her and found himself making an effort to speak clearly, to maintain his own side of the conversation.

"I understand how you must feel," he said. "I know that you must want revenge."

Jonna did not answer directly. She gazed at Zach for a moment, her mismatched eyes strangely intense, then shrugged. As always when he was with her, Zach sensed the sharp intelligence behind her grotesque face.

"I believe I understand why you acted as you did, Brother Zach," she said. "And I accept my own responsibility in the matter. I never really thought you were a true believer."

Perhaps, Zach thought suddenly, it was because she was not one herself.

"I was . . . unable to think clearly at the time," she continued. "My grief for Yosh was too strong. And the song was truly beautiful." She paused for a moment. "It has been said that an artistic creation becomes something quite apart from the creator."

Zach was startled. For the first time he realized that Jonna must have had some formal education, and he wondered where she had received it. He was also startled by her thought. He had written "The Death of Our Brother" solely in the hope that the Traders might let him out of his cell to sing it at the memorial to Yosh, giving him a last desperate chance to escape. But during its actual composition he had not entertained those thoughts. He had never written a song without believing in it with his soul, and as he wrote, he had put his love for Yosh into the melody, and Yosh's own inspiration and loving kindness into the words. The song had in fact been inspired and had somehow become, as Jonna said, a thing apart from Zach, its creator.

"One thing I have always wondered about," Jonna said then. "From the song—and from what Yosh himself said—I always believed you loved him. I still believe it, even after what you did. Is it true?"

"Yes," said Zach, remembering again his own sorrow when he had heard of the death of the young Trader leader. "Unfortunately his beliefs and mine were opposed in the most important ways. But I always felt, as he himself once said, that in another world we could have been brothers."

"He told me that too," said Jonna. "But I could never understand how beliefs—" She left the thought unfinished. When she spoke again, her voice for the first time held an edge of bitterness. "And what of me, Brother Zach? You must have thought me very stupid to allow you to leave your cell."

"No, Jonna!" Zach said. He was shocked by her words. "I never thought that. I was only glad my plan worked." She did not answer but continued to gaze moodily past him into the fire. After a moment he spoke again. "You were always kind to me," he said. He remembered how she had administered the healing smoke of burning herbs when he had first been wounded, how she had calmly set and bandaged his injured fingers after Galen and his men had tortured him for information about the Principal and the Garden; and, most of all, how she had succored him on the trek to the Trader Empire. His badly damaged hands had been bound to a pack animal, and he had been forced to walk, despite his weakness and injury, without pause except at Galen's whim. More than once he had stumbled, biting his lips to keep from crying out as the bonds pulled on his hands. His exhaustion had been close to total, and only the thought that he must try to survive, to take what he had learned of the Traders to the Principal, had kept him from simply slipping to the ground, falling under the relentless hoofbeats and human feet.

He had begun to think that he could not go on when Jonna had appeared at his side as if from a mist. He realized later than she must have been walking beside him for some time. "Halt!" she commanded in her strange, hoarse voice, and the caravan had slowed, then stopped. In his dazed state Zach had taken a few steps farther than the animal, and as the bonds pulled tighter, he had stumbled, almost falling.

"Yosh left instructions that our brother Zach is not to suffer," said Jonna. With a resentful glance at Zach, one of Galen's men had then come to Zach and untied the bonds. At the relief from the pulling, Zach became dizzy and thought he might faint, but Jonna, though her head reached only to his shoulders, supported him.

"Brother Zach will travel with me," she said in the same commanding tone. "At my pace."

The caravan had started up again, but Jonna drew Zach aside and readministered to his injuries. She made him lie down while she wrapped his hands and wrists in cool cloths soaked in herbs. She bathed his head in the same herbs, massaging his forehead with her strong fingers. After, she had given him a draught of boiled bark and herbs, and as he felt the pain subside, his strength had begun to return. "Thank you, Sister," he had muttered.

Looking at her now he felt again the overwhelming warmth and gratitude. He repeated: "You have always been kind to me."

"I have always hated you," she said ~~after a moment~~, still looking into the fire. "I always knew you meant nothing but trouble for Yosh. Everything I did was because he wished it."

Zach had no answer for her. He was strangely grateful for her honesty. He hesitated, then asked the question he knew she was waiting for. "What do you intend to do with me?"

"I intend to use you, Brother Zach," she said, her voice again bitter. "I intend to get from you the information I need to avenge Yosh. I intend to find out everything there is to know about the Principal—and his scientist allies at the Garden."

Again Zach was silent, again grateful for her honesty. He was not surprised. "You must realize that I will not tell you anything that could harm the Principal," he said.

"I know you told Galen nothing when he questioned you," she said. "But torture is clumsy and unreliable—a man's tool. There are better ways to discover the truth."

With a start Zach now remembered where he had tasted the flowery herb tea before. It was the same potion Yosh had given him long ago in his Trader prison cell, which had caused Zach to lose his will and answer questions almost in a stupor. He now recognized too, the relaxed, trusting mood it had given him.

"I will drink no more of your herbs," he said.

"You'll drink them," she said. "You will drink—or you will die of thirst."

In the end Zach gave in. In part it was because he had already taken a great deal of the drug and was not fully master of the situation. More important, he realized that he must keep his strength if he were to have any chance to escape. He consoled himself with the thought that he would be able to fight the mind-weakening effects of the herbs, since he understood now what was happening to him.

For two days he stayed in the cabin in a dreamlike stupor and talked to Jonna. He felt as if his mind had been divided into two parts. One part was under Jonna's control and could not help answering whatever she asked. The other, a remote observer, watched and listened but made no judgments.

As the questioning continued, Zach discovered that Jonna already knew a great deal about the Principal and his defenses in the Capital. What she wanted was information about the Garden. Zach freely discussed it. After all, the Garden was well protected, and unlike the Principal's House, it could not readily be infiltrated by Trader spies.

"It is a place of ideas and learning," he found himself telling her. "It has been in existence, in various locations, since the Change. The women who work there are devoted to preserving knowledge from the past and creating new ways of living in the world as it has become."

"Filthy scientists, sounds like," said Morgan, who was standing guard.

"Hush, Morgan," said Jonna. She looked at Zach with interest. "Is it true that no men are allowed there?"

"Not to stay. Boys are sent away when they reach adolescence. It is felt that they are too disruptive. And the women maintain strict breeding control."

"What do you mean?"

"The most important purpose of the Garden has always been an attempt to understand and control the woman sickness. For that reason, all mating is directed by the Garden's leaders, using men selected from the population outside the compound. No random mating is allowed. In fact, the Garden's leaders consider unselected sex the most serious possible crime."

Jonna was silent for a moment. "Does the Principal work with the Garden?"

"He has always maintained formal ties with them. Often his soldiers cooperate in the breeding experiments."

As Jonna listened with obvious fascination Zach felt that if she had first met the women of the Garden instead of the Traders, she might have become a valuable member of the Garden, using her intelligence, her knowledge of herbs and plants, and her skills at healing to benefit the entire District.

"It is a pity you did not grow up in the Garden," he said, voicing the thought. "You would have been happy there."

"Am I too old, then, to become a member?" she asked.

Zach was startled. "The Garden is well guarded," he said. "You could never establish spies there. What are you thinking of?"

"I'm asking the questions," said Jonna. "But I don't mind telling you. I am seeking some way to avenge Yosh. Perhaps the best way to do it is through the Principal's own secret scientific organization."

Zach did not allow his relief to show. If Jonna thought she would be able to reach the Principal through the Garden, she was going to be very surprised.

"Your primary target is still the Principal?"

She sighed in exasperation. "We have had spies in his House for two years, and they still couldn't manage to kill him. I will find a better way."

"So it was Traders who organized the attack at the wedding."

"Of course," said Jonna.

"And who took the Principal's bride-to-be?"

"Yes." Jonna smiled now. "That is why, now that we have met with you, we are returning to the central Trader capital. There is a celebration planned in three months' time to be held on the anniversary of Yosh's birth. It is to be a sacrifice. The Principal's chief scientist—his bride—will be burned. And now it will be an even greater occasion, Brother Zach, for you will be sacrificed with her."

Zach felt suddenly chilled. He had never really considered what the Traders might have planned for Evvy. Certainly he had not thought they might do something so monstrous as to burn her alive. He was so shocked that for a moment his mind did not even register the news that he was to be sacrificed too.

He fought to keep his face impassive, but a flicker of his fear for Evvy must have shown, because Jonna said, misinterpreting, "Don't be afraid, Brother Zach. It will be an honor. And when it is over, Brother Yosh will welcome you in the next world."

The next morning Zach and the four Traders set out for the Trader Empire. Now that he was no longer being drugged, Zach focused his mind on the thought of escape. But Jonna was taking no chances and kept him securely tied and closely watched at all times, even when he was performing private functions.

He comforted himself with the thought that at least the Traders were taking him to Evvy. The day of the sacrifice was many weeks in the future; he would have plenty of time to think of a plan. After all, he had escaped from them once before. Somehow he would—he must—find a way to free Evvy.

He remembered his tiny, dank prison cell and wondered if she were being held in one like it. He had known, and Will had known when he sent him, the dangers he would face on this quest: new-animals, human outlaws, the Traders themselves. But of all possible perils, the only one that caused his stomach to knot and sent shivers of fear through him was the possibility of again being imprisoned. Death he had faced many times, and while he did not welcome it, it was an old, familiar enemy. But the thought of confinement in a cell, even for a short while, terrified him.

The closer they came to the Trader Empire, the greater grew his unreasoning fear of prison. Two weeks into the journey, when Jonna said they would arrive in a day or two, the Road Men attacked.

Three

The Principal had been back in his House for nearly two weeks now and, over Wolff's protests, had begun once again, with Ralf's assistance, to see to the day-to-day business of running the District.

The stump where his arm had been ached constantly. Wolff changed the dressing daily, inspecting it closely and removing dead or sloughing tissue. The poison itself had weakened the Principal—only Wolff and Robin were aware of how greatly—and he found that he needed far more sleep than he was accustomed to getting. Still, he was blessed with a naturally healthy body, and each day he forced himself to exercise, walking briskly in his gardens and performing muscle-strengthening and coordination exercises with his left arm. He had never been as strongly right-handed as some men and already was able to eat and sign his name with the left.

One night, less than a week after Zach left, vandals, presumably Traders, had broken into the Clinic and destroyed those written records that had not been removed to the archives for safekeeping, though there had been no more trouble at the House.

The Principal realized that his most urgent priority must be to devise better security against the Traders; he had invited all the generals to dine with him this afternoon and discuss measures that might be taken. Only Quentin, who had returned to his duties in the remote corners of the District, would not attend.

As he lay on the sofa in his office, resting and making mental notes for the meeting, he thought again of Zach's belief that the attack at the wedding could have been accomplished only with the help of one or more of his most trusted men. And yet he could not believe it of any of them. Odell the housekeeper, his private guards, the generals, all had been with him since the earliest days of his leadership or before. Lindy, who had not yet been born when he became Principal, had been raised in this House, the orphaned son of one of his most trusted subordinates. Napoleon, too, seemed to trust all of these men. Although the Principal was not fully convinced that the fox-cat could sense or predict danger, the little animal did seem to be remarkably sensitive to moods, and he was usually at ease with the Principal's aides.

He looked fondly at his pet, who was sleeping in a pool of light on the polished desk. Napoleon opened one eye, then grunted and turned over, exposing his other flank to the warmth of the sun.

The Principal was looking forward to this meeting, but he was anxious, too, not only because of what seemed to be a growing mutual suspicion among the generals themselves, but also because Daniel would be there at the insistence of both Red and Ralf. He had not met with Daniel face-to-face in the year and a half since the disastrous Trader attack on the Clinic that had cost the life of one of the Garden's scientists and had very nearly cost Evvy hers. Now it appeared that the Traders had achieved their aim after all; Evvy had not been taken by accident.

Since he had learned that Evvy was missing, he tried not to allow himself to think of her. When he found images of her crowding his imagination—her startling eyes, her happy laugh, her soft lips—he deliberately dropped a gate in his mind, shutting his fears and longing safely behind it.

But today he could not stop his thoughts. With a sudden sharp pang he remembered again the afternoon after the night that they had lain together and agreed to be married, the night before Zach would have gone into exile if Evvy had not come to him and changed everything. The Principal had arranged for the three of them to lunch together after he and Zach had spent a busy morning on errands in the Capital. Lightheartedly descending the stairs after changing clothes, he had stepped into the long, high-ceilinged hall and seen her gazing intently into the room where they were to dine. She was wearing a creamy yellow blouse and skirt, and her dark hair was pulled into a soft knot on top of her head, secured with a band of the same delicate color.

Watching her, seeing her unseen, he had felt his breath stop. He wanted to stand and gaze at her forever. Then she turned, a pensive, almost sad look on her face; when she saw him, the sadness vanished and her face immediately brightened in a smile of welcome. Unable to speak, he had approached her and put his hand on the smooth, vulnerable nape of her neck. Just touching her calmed him. He kissed her lightly, then walked with her into the room where Zach was waiting, napping in a corner.

He had never felt toward a woman the way he felt about Evvy. He wanted her, yes; more intensely, perhaps, than he had ever wanted anyone, even when in the grip of his uncontrollable compulsion of old. But his desire for her was more than physical; the thought that she was in danger more painful even than the loss of his arm.

She was alive. She must be. The fact that she had been taken, rather than killed on the spot, proved that.

He still had not had word directly from Zach; however, a soldier from one of the western outposts had sent word that Zach had been seen at the Crosskey Inn, where he had stayed many years ago when he had come to join the Principal and his men.

The room was stuffy, and he was groggy from the pain-killing potion Wolff had pressed on him. Confused images filled his mind, from the days when he had been an outlaw, living like the ancient bandit Robin Hood, preying on the President's nobles and soldiers. He saw Zach as a young man, riding into camp, strong and smiling. With him was Evvy, dressed in the royal yellow gown of the President's daughter. He tried to speak to them, to ask them to stay, but his voice had become a feeble croak, and they rode on, laughing and talking, unaware that he was there.

* * *

The Principal came suddenly to himself, aware that his thoughts of the past had drifted into dreams. There was a sharp, impatient-sounding rapping at the door, and then Robin's lined face appeared above him.

"The generals are here, sir," said the old man, looking worried. "I've been knocking for some time."

"I must have fallen asleep," said Will. He felt his mind become slowly clearer, as the dream images and mood dissipated.

"Are you all right? We could put the meeting off to another day."

"I'm fine. I just needed some rest. Tell them I'll be down in five minutes." He smiled reassuringly at his faithful secretary, hiding the wave of pain that came as he sat up. He sat on the edge of the couch a moment to catch his breath, then stood and walked to the mirror. He splashed his face with water from the basin, then dried and brushed his hair. He looked with distaste at his reflection: he was far too pale, and smudged brown circles ringed his eyes, giving them a hollow look. The silver strands in his dark hair seemed to have spread rapidly in the time since he was wounded. He no longer looked a young man but was beginning to seem a middle-aged one.

Awkwardly he fastened his boots with his left hand. The whole time Napoleon stood in front of him, uttering challenging, almost angry-sounding "Mowr"s.

"You know I'm leaving without you, don't you, boy?" said the Principal, amused. "It's a dinner—you'd just be in the way. But I'll bring you a treat, I promise." He scratched the fox-cat's head, then left, shutting the door on Napoleon's pitiful howls.

He could hear the generals before he entered the room. There was a buzz of talk and laughter, and then the short bark of angry words—it sounded as if Eric and Ralf were arguing again. He sighed, then smiled. Some things never changed, and Eric's prickly temperament was one of them.

This was the first important official meeting he had conducted in a very long time. Although he had met briefly with the generals the day Zach had left, he had been too weak and too ill to do more than outline the situation to them. Today he felt far more positive; his memories of the past had strengthened him. Together he and his generals had defeated the President, and together they would devise a plan to restore safety to the Capital. Together they would regain what ground had been lost to the Traders, and then, when Zach and Evvy returned—

He stopped just at the door. The first person he saw was Daniel, sitting alone in a corner, puffing on a pipe of newsmoke. Daniel met his eyes immediately, not with challenge or sullenness but with a sad, almost pleading look. The Principal found himself unexpectedly affected, and he took a deep breath to steady himself, then proceeded into the room.

The other men—Red, Ralf, Marcus, and Eric—immediately got to their feet and came toward him.

"You're looking very well, sir," said Eric. The others echoed his observation, relief obvious on their faces.

"I'm looking very sick," Will said. "But thank you. I feel much stronger than I did a week ago." He was suddenly, acutely conscious of the empty sleeve fastened to the side of his tunic, and he turned slightly to hide his right side as he took his place at the head of the table. Now the generals settled themselves: Ralf at his right where Zach usually sat, Red on his left; then Marcus and Eric, facing Daniel farther down the table, while Robin took his customary position at the foot.

The Principal began to talk, telling what little he had learned of Zach's travels and outlining his ideas for keeping Trader spies away. Then he asked for suggestions from the others.

"As a matter of fact, sir," said Red, "Daniel has been talking to the folk who come into the Clinic, trying to understand Trader ways, and he's come up with a couple of good ideas."

Daniel looked down at his plate, seemingly in embarrassment.

"Well?" said the Principal. "Report, Daniel."

"As you know, sir," said Daniel, still looking down, "the Traders seem to be very superstitious—more so than the general population, I mean. I thought that if we found some well-preserved machine bodies and put them at the entrances to your House and the Clinic, it might make any Trader spies think twice before entering."

"Yes, and what of the people?" said Marcus. "Seems to me that's the surest way to keep them out of your clinic. I don't mind telling you I ain't so relaxed around machines myself."

The Principal frowned, waiting to see if Daniel would continue. After a moment he spoke again.

"I've thought of that, of course. And it could be a problem. But it's a fact that most of the women who come to be tested now come because they have seen the results. They know that by taking the test and following our instructions, they have less chance of dying of the sickness." He paused, then went on, now looking directly at the Principal. "I thought, too, perhaps, that we might raise the amount paid to those who complete the test. I've some metal saved and would be glad to contribute it."

"Buy yourself back into a generalship, you mean?" said Eric.

The Principal was shocked. This was not only an insult to Daniel but to himself, and Eric seemed almost immediately to recognize his mistake. "I beg your pardon, sir, it was just a joke," he mumbled.

"Not a funny one, Eric," said the Principal. He looked at Daniel. Daniel had gone pale and was glaring at Eric, but he said nothing. Will remembered the unspoken rivalry that had always existed between the men, as the two youngest generals. Of all the generals only Eric had not been with him from his outlaw days; he had instead risen quickly through the ranks of soldiers and had nearly single-handedly dispatched the last holdouts loyal to the President in the sparsely populated northern borderland.

Eric seemed about to speak again, but Red put a warning hand on the young man's forearm.

"I think it sounds like an idea worth trying," said Ralf slowly, into the silence. "I'm like Marcus, I'm not fond of machines, but I know the wild deenas are all gone now. If it makes things the least bit safer, I'm for it."

"How will the household servants take it?" the Principal asked Red.

"We might lose some, but that might not be a bad thing.

All I'm worried about is Odell. He's no Trader—he loves luxury too much—but he's near as superstitious as one."

"I'll speak to him myself," said the Principal. "And I agree that the idea is worth a try. Thank you, Daniel. But Red said you had two ideas—"

"This other one you won't like, sir," said Red. "But it's the best of all."

At that moment the double doors opened, and Lindy and two other servants entered, carrying trays of food.

"If I won't like it, let's wait till after we eat. Perhaps you'll find me more receptive on a full stomach." He was beginning to feel almost himself again, and the delicious smells of the food made his mouth water.

Although he hadn't asked for it, Robin had told him that the menu would consist of nothing awkward to eat with one hand. This first course was small pieces of game bird and vegetables marinated in flower wine and vinegar, then arranged alternately on thin wooden sticks and cooked over an open flame.

He helped himself to the skewered meat and began to eat. The other men followed his lead, and soon everyone was relaxed, taking up conversation and bantering. Even Daniel, he saw, began to join in the talk. He noticed with some discomfort that each of the men cast occasional discreet glances at him to see how he was faring.

He had started on his third skewer of meat when the serving boys brought in a rich rabbit stew, steaming fragrantly in large wooden bowls. "Go ahead," he said. "Don't wait for me. Eat your stew while it's still hot."

Red, who had always had a hearty appetite, set down his fifth empty skewer and immediately began to go to work on the stew. He had taken perhaps three spoonfuls when he suddenly uttered a strange cry and pushed back from the table, convulsively kicking his chair over. He fell onto the floor and began clawing at his abdomen, grunting and wheezing, his body jerking spasmodically. For a moment everyone simply stared, then Daniel jumped up, ran around the table, and knocked from the Principal's hand the spoon he had just picked up. "Don't touch this food, sir!" he cried.

FOUR

The Principal understood immediately that Red had been poisoned, and, his heart pounding, he jumped up from the table and shouted for guards. Ralf put out a hand to restrain him, but he shook it off, and, followed by Ralf and Daniel and soon joined by guards, he ran out into the corridor and down the two flights of stairs to the kitchen, where two cooks and a handful of serving boys were bustling about in the hot, steamy room. "Arrest everyone here!" he shouted. A startled, frightened-looking young cook started to make for the herb garden, but Daniel crossed the room quickly and clamped his hand around the boy's wrist so tightly that the youth cried out. Ralf stood in the doorway, looking pale and stunned.

"Get a dozen trustworthy soldiers here right away!" the Principal bellowed. He waited while the frightened kitchen staff was bound, then ordered the guards to place them in isolation, in a seldom used prison area in the basement.

"Ralf, have these men questioned," he said. "Find out who was responsible for this outrage." By now the soldiers had appeared. Their leader, a young sergeant, approached the Principal and saluted. "Sergeant Jeremy," he said, "reporting as ordered."

"I want you and your men to obtain a covered cart—tell

the supply master I order it. Then take every bit of food and drink in this kitchen. All of it, even the seasonings and spices. Take those things and put them in the cart, cover it securely, then take it to the bridge and throw everything in the river at the deepest part. Do you understand?"

"Yes, sir," said Jeremy, looking bewildered.

"No one is to so much as taste anything, and it must be kept covered so that the townspeople do not see it. Until the cart arrives, I want a double guard kept on this room. Nobody is to be allowed in."

"Yes, sir," said Jeremy.

The Principal saw the soldiers looking hungrily at the array of food—the stew still boiling on top of the stone oven; the skewered meat laid out on the long wooden table; roots, vegetables, and fruits hanging in baskets from the ceiling beams. The aromas were tempting, as were the sights, including a half-butchered haunch being prepared for the evening meal. A terrible waste, to be sure, but he would take no chances. Until he discovered what had happened, no one would eat except from freshly purchased or gathered sources.

He had a sudden thought. "My subordinate Daniel will oversee the disposal," he said.

Daniel gave him a quick look of gratitude, then immediately began to issue orders. "You there, start removing those baskets. Sergeant, see that the wagon is brought around to the back gate. . . ."

Satisfied that matters in the kitchen would be well attended to, the Principal returned to the dining room upstairs. Odell was already supervising the removal of food from within. "Destroy all of that food immediately," the Principal told him shortly.

"It has already been ordered," said Odell. "By Captain Robin."

The table had been pushed to one side of the room, and Wolff was bent over Red, who was now lying still. In a nearby chair Robin sat, his face twisted in grief, while Lindy stood in a corner, sobbing loudly. Before the Principal could speak, Wolff looked up. "He's dead."

The Principal nodded.

"It's a fast-acting poison known from before the Change," Wolff went on, standing. He had covered Red's body with the tablecloth. "It has a characteristic odor, which was masked by the herbs in the stew."

"Did anyone else—"

"Even a small amount would have been fatal," said Wolff. "It's our good luck and Red's bad that he was first to eat."

"He was always one for putting it away," said Marcus gloomily.

The Principal knelt by the body of his old friend and pulled the edge of the cloth back. Wolff had closed Red's eyes, but his muscles were still knotted in a grimace, and his skin had taken on a bluish hue.

The Principal looked at him for a moment more, then replaced the cloth. "He will have a full hero's funeral," he said. "The day after tomorrow. Marcus, see to the preparations."

"Yes, sir," said Marcus.

There was no family to notify; Red had once told the Principal that his army was the only family he had ever wanted.

"Will, sit down," said Wolff. He took the Principal's arm and pulled him to an upholstered chair. "You're not well yet yourself. You need to rest and to eat."

"I couldn't eat."

"You must. I've already sent for my wife. She will shop and prepare all meals until the kitchen staff is again secure."

Will remembered Wolff's wife, a plump, very pleasant woman, who was Wolff's unshared, her first husband having died many years ago, shortly after Wolff had married her.

Presently Wolff left with the soldiers bearing Red's body. Robin and Lindy accompanied the Principal back to his office. They walked very close to him, but he would not accept assistance, though he was beginning to feel exhausted. Once he stumbled on a worn place in the carpet and Lindy put out a hand to steady him; irritably he pushed it away.

Robin helped Will settle himself on the couch. "Now, you rest here, sir," he said. "I'll let you know as soon as there's anything to report."

"Thank you, Robin," he said.

He did not lie down but sat against the cushions and thought of Red. He could not believe he was gone. He tried to still his racing thoughts, to concentrate on business, but could not. Red's good-humored face, his ready laughter, and his brave intelligence seemed to be haunting the room.

At last he stood shakily and went to his desk where someone had set a pitcher of fruit juice. Not stopping to consider that it might be poisoned, he drank thirstily, then returned to the couch where he finally fell into a troubled sleep.

Late in the afternoon Ralf returned to report that the food had all been destroyed as ordered and that the questioning of the kitchen staff had produced no results.

"The chief c-cook killed himself before we could question him," Ralf went on. "Some of the men think he did it from guilt, but if you ask me, it was sh-shame."

The Principal sighed. The cook, a quiet and reliable man, had been with him for many years; he tended to agree with Ralf's judgment in the matter.

Marcus had returned to his command of the peacekeeping forces in the District, while Eric had taken temporary command of the House's own guards, tonight reinforced with three dozen regular soldiers.

While they spoke, Lindy brought in some simple food prepared by Wolff's wife and a jug of flower-wine. "I tasted it myself, sir," said the boy, pouring out a cup. "It's safe for you to drink."

The Principal stared at Lindy in horror. "Don't ever do that again!" he shouted. "Am I an ignorant barbarian king who must have a taster?" He hurled his cup against the marble fireplace, then turned to the window, instantly ashamed. He took slow, deep breaths to calm himself. After a moment he turned back to the room. "I'm sorry, boy," he said. "You meant well."

He accepted another cup of the wine and sipped, feeling it begin to warm and relax his body. He was exhausted, emotionally and physically, and what remained of his arm had begun to hurt badly.

Ralf seemed to sense how he felt, because when he next spoke, he sounded apologetic. "It's been a terrible day for everyone, sir," he said. "I'm sorry to t-trouble you, but there's two more pieces of business yet."

"Yes?"

"First of all, Eric reports that there's a crowd gathered outside. There's rumors you were poisoned. Coming on top of the news of your injury, the people th-think... Well, it might be a good idea if you stand at the balcony, let them see you're alive."

The Principal nodded. "And the other thing?"

"It's Daniel's other idea, sir. For stopping the Traders. Like Red said before he... like Red said, you won't like it. But we've all been talking, Robin included, and we think you ought to consider it, especially n-now."

"Well? What is it?"

"We think you ought to start having women from the Garden guard your House, sir."

It was long after dark when the Principal found himself at last alone in his office. Wolff had tried to make him drink flower-brew to sleep, but he had refused. He needed to be alone and to think.

On his desk stood a full pitcher of brew, from a keg purchased that afternoon by Robin, and his favorite pottery mug; Zach had bought it for him one day in fulfillment of a wager over who could drink the most brew in the shortest amount of time. Next to the tray, curled under the fish-oil lamp, Napoleon gazed at him through slitted eyes.

His appearance before the crowd had mysteriously restored his energy. He had worn his heaviest yellow-bordered dark cloak, and, turning to look in the mirror, had been pleased to see that the way it fell obscured the empty place where his arm had been. After checking his appearance he had stepped onto the balcony, then raised his left hand in a salute. He was immediately greeted by a warm cheer that seemed to last for several minutes. The crowd, held back by the guards under Eric's command, was a mixture of his soldiers and of townspeople, men and women both, some of the women holding girl-children in their arms, and, he imagined, with looks of gratitude on their faces. He had spoken a few words, thanking them for their concern and reassuring them that he was well.

"Long live the Principal!" responded the crowd. "May the deenas protect you!"

Heartened, he had continued to speak, talking about his plans for the future of the District, not even aware of what he was saying. He had feared, before he began, that he wouldn't find the energy to speak in full voice, but he was pleased to hear the familiar echo and feel the sense of power, an almost tangible flow of energy that seemed to begin at the soles of his feet and move upward, through his body, then from his mouth and fingertips into the crowd. While he was speaking he felt fully himself again, forgetting the events of the last weeks, his injury, Evvy's capture, even the loss of Red. He had returned to his office restored, his mind racing, ready to begin work.

He wished suddenly that Zach were here so he could discuss with him the idea of having women from the Garden trained to guard his house. He had only briefly discussed the matter with Ralf, who wanted to bring Daniel in to argue the idea.

"He's had women guards at the Clinic," the old man had said earnestly. "He says they're as well trained as your own soldiers, and near as strong. And there's no question of them ever becoming Trader spies, or so he says."

"I said I'll think about it," said the Principal.

"P-pardon me for speaking frankly, sir," Ralf went on. "It's well known you don't like women, except for certain purposes. But just because you don't like them, you shouldn't turn back the suggestion. I don't come from the Garden and I don't know about it. But from what Daniel says, these women are as far from Traders as you can get. I think what Daniel says is right. No matter how you f-feel, you should be thinking about the good of the District."

The old man sat back, flushed. This had been a very long speech for him, and the Principal was touched by his concern. "Thank you, Ralf," he said. "I *will* think about it. Perhaps I'll even adopt it. But as you said before, it's been a long day. Tell Daniel I'll speak to him in the morning."

"Yes, sir," said the old general, leaving the office. "Rest well, sir. I'll be downstairs if there's anything you want me to do."

The Principal poured a cup of brew and shut his eyes. The idea had some merit. But the thought of having his house controlled by women—especially from the Garden—was repellent. Still, as Ralf said, he must think of the good of the District above his own feelings.

He realized that Daniel would have known his objections

even before voicing the suggestion. He had had longer experience with the women and knew their capabilities. The Principal sighed. He had been surprised today to discover that his remaining anger at Daniel had largely disappeared. Both of his ideas had been good ones, and he had acted responsibly and bravely during this afternoon's crisis. Perhaps it was time to restore his commission. Now that Red was gone, he'd need another top aide. And it had been true for many years that he had been able to discuss the subjects nearest his heart better with Daniel than with anyone but Zach.

The thought of Zach brought a new wave of anxiety. Zach would be heartbroken to hear of Red's death. But where was he now? Where was Evvy? Were they together? Were they safe?

He pressed his palm against his face, as if that would stop his thoughts from racing. If only he could find a way to relax . . . He realized with a start that he had not had a woman for a long time. For a moment he thought to ring for Robin, to order him to bring a woman for hire, but he stopped his hand before it touched the bell. What would a woman think when she saw his deformity? How would he himself feel? And what would Evvy— For the first time he thought of how it would be to face her as he was now.

"The deenas take it," he muttered. He drained his cup. Ordinarily he could drink all evening without feeling it, but his injury had made him weak, and he was already beginning to feel light-headed, though it was not an unpleasant feeling. He refilled the cup, set it on the edge of the desk, then gazed thoughtfully into the fire that Robin had laid for him. It had burned down now to glowing coals, and the room was becoming chilled. He rose to place more wood on the fire. Napoleon, thinking perhaps that it was time to retire to the Principal's private rooms for bed, stood up and stretched. The little animal's bushy tail twitched against the cup and toppled it over.

Quickly the Principal reached out to catch the cup before it fell. But only one hand responded, and the cup slipped past it, falling to the floor and shattering.

"The deenas take it!" he bellowed. Napoleon, frightened, hissed and jumped to the floor, then, in one bound, leapt to the top of the mantelpiece where he cowered, making small whining noises.

The Principal stood looking down at the broken cup and the pool of brew now seeping across the floor and into the edge of the carpet, then he abruptly licked the back of his hand, which had been splashed. The bitter flavor changed to a salty warmth, and he pushed the back of his hand into his mouth and clamped down with his teeth to stop the trembling that had begun; but it was not to be stopped. He returned to his desk and sat, burying his face in the crook of his arm, and began to cry, as he had not done since he was a small boy.

After a moment Napoleon uttered a plaintive howl from the top of the mantel, then leapt lightly to the floor and back onto the desk where he began to rub his face and body against Will's shoulder, buzzing in sympathy.

Five

Evvy stood gazing through the tiny window at the broad, grassy park. Although it was not yet winter, the tips of the grass were edged with frost, and she could see her breath in the air before her. She shivered and pulled her cloak tighter around herself, but it did little good; she was so thoroughly chilled and had been for so long that she thought she would never again be warm.

She had been in this cell exactly a week—she'd made a mark on the wall each morning when she awoke—but was not sure how long it had been since her abduction from the Capital. Much of the journey here she had spent tied and blindfolded. It had been many days, perhaps a month or more.

In all that time her captors had not spoken to her directly except to issue commands—"Eat this!" or "Sit down!"—and no one had answered her questions. Of one thing only was she sure—her jailers were Traders.

Once again despair began to well up—and anger at herself for allowing herself be captured so easily. Yet at the time all that had seemed important was to discover more about what she thought she had seen just before the fire broke out.

She remembered again the ceremony, could almost feel her heart hammering as it had then, as the Minister of Ceremonies began speaking the last words before the final vows. From the corner of her eye she could see Will's dark blue cloak; on her other side, so close that she could almost feel the warmth of his body, stood Zach.

As the Minister continued, quite suddenly her eyes had filled with tears. She blinked rapidly, then looked away, holding her breath. At that moment the curtains to the side of the altar moved, and she saw two men, one shockingly familiar, the other a stranger. They seemed to be in a struggle of some sort, but before she had a chance to ask herself what it might mean, there was a sudden roaring noise, a shout, and Will had fallen forward onto the dais.

Shocked to the center of her being, Evvy had knelt swiftly, not realizing at first that the room was burning. Her only thought was that something had happened to Will. She put her fingers to his neck and was relieved to feel a pulse; an instant later Zach pulled her to her feet. Only then did she become aware of the fire. She tried to tell Zach what she had seen, but he wouldn't listen. A moment later Katha, her white coat and sword bloodied, had pulled her away, through the choking smoke, and into the bright sunlight beyond.

She looked behind her in confusion. There was no sign of Zach or Will. She pulled her arm away from Katha, thinking to go back and help them. Someone jostled her, and she nearly lost her balance, then she felt Katha's strong hands gripping her upper arms.

"Evvy, you fool! Come away!"

She looked at Katha without understanding.

"We are returning to the Garden. Now. At once!"

"But the Principal has been hurt," Evvy said. "He's still inside!"

"There's nothing you can do for him. Come away. They may attack again."

"I saw—saw something," she said, beginning to cry in spite of herself.

Katha did not relax her grip. "You are a Daughter of the Garden!" she snapped. "You have vowed to obey the Garden's leaders instantly, without question!"

"But he is my husband!"

"The final vows were never said," said Katha coolly. "And now they never will be."

"You don't know that!" Evvy cried. She took a moment to calm herself. The time she was spending arguing could be better used in helping Will. She tried to pull away, but Katha's hands dug into her shoulders so fiercely that she nearly cried out.

"Evvy, you will come with us!"

Now Gunda, one of the three women who had come from the Garden, put a hand on Katha's arm. "Katha, please. It is Evvy's decision."

Katha cursed and started an angry reply, but then her expression changed subtly, from fury to something that Evvy could not identify. Katha released her grip, and Evvy turned to follow the direction of her gaze. Behind her, staring intently, was the stranger Evvy had seen behind the curtains just before the attack.

"Who is that?" said Evvy.

Before Katha could answer, the man spoke directly to Evvy. "May I assist you, Lady?"

"The Principal—" she said.

"Is safe," said the man. "He sent me to bring you to him."

"We cannot wait any longer," said Katha. "I must think of the safety of the Garden."

"Go, then," said Evvy, feeling at once angry and confused. "My place is here."

"Perhaps we should wait a few minutes more, to see Evvy safe," said Gunda.

"Evvy is no longer one of us," said Katha. "She says so herself." She turned without another word.

Gunda hugged Evvy quickly. "Would you like me to stay with you?" she whispered.

"No, Gunda," Evvy said, wiping her eyes. "Thank you. But I'll be all right."

"The young lady is safe with me," said the stranger quickly. "I am a soldier of the Principal. I will protect her." He indicated the yellow insignia on the chest of his tunic.

"Take care, then," said Gunda.

"May the deenas protect you," added Lucille. They followed Katha to their mounts, and now Evvy found herself alone with the soldier.

"I saw you standing near the curtains just before—" she

blurted. Nervously she looked behind her, but Katha and the two other women had already disappeared into the crowd.

"Yes," the soldier nodded. "And you would like to know what I was doing there. Of course. But first—let me take you to the Principal."

Now Evvy became aware of men running about her, carrying buckets of water to quench the fire. Everywhere on the lawn surrounding the House lay the injured, moaning or lying deathly still. "Where is he?" she asked with the beginnings of panic.

"He has already been moved," said the soldier. "This way." He led her past the kitchen garden, where a line of men were frantically filling buckets from a wooden trough, and into the stable area.

"In here," he said when they came to one of the stables.

Evvy didn't stop to wonder why the Principal was being tended to in a stable. She rushed through the door. It was dark inside, and as she strained to see where the Principal might be, a heavy cloth suddenly fell over her face, and strong arms gripped her tightly. She opened her mouth to scream, and a thick, foul-smelling rag was thrust into it, gagging her. There were at least three men here, and her struggles were useless. She felt her arms being bound tightly and roughly behind her back, and then she was put into a cart. A bundle of straw was placed over her, cutting off all remaining light, and she felt the cart begin to move.

Now, shivering in her little cell, Evvy found her memories of the last weeks becoming as blurred as images from a bad dream. She had been kept bound and blindfolded most of the time, and though her captors had not abused her, they had treated her as if she were an object, a sack of grain to be transported for trade.

For the first few days she had held to a fierce hope that Zach or the Principal would rescue her. Gradually she came to accept the hopelessness of her situation. In the confusion following the attack and fire, it was doubtful if anyone had seen what had happened to her. In any case, the Principal had been wounded, and she did not even know if he and Zach had escaped the burning hall. She remembered again how pale the Principal had looked where he lay fallen, dark blood already soaking his cape where the arrow had pierced it.

If the Principal died, she knew, everything might be lost—all that he had done to build his small civilization, and all the work of the generations of the Garden. None of the Principal's men, except for Zach and Daniel, had grown up in the Garden, with its knowledge of the past, its training in hygiene and medical techniques. None fully understood the importance of the scientific work being done there, from research on the woman sickness to the efforts to restore stable breeding of plants and animals. And none, not even Zach, possessed the Principal's power to lead.

Again and again she remembered the night he had decreed that Zach was to go into exile and that she must return to the Garden permanently. In their anger and stubbornness both men had refused to acknowledge that they had built the District together. It had seemed clear to her then that the only way to insure Will's continued leadership was to persuade him, somehow, to keep Zach with him. She could think of only one way to do it.

She had long known the Principal's reputation for abusing his mistresses, yet she was strangely unafraid of him, even when, understanding what she meant to do, for the first time he had turned the full force of his anger against her. She knew with a calm certainty that the Principal wanted her above all things, and that night she finally understood the power this gave her.

Evvy was brought from her musings by voices in the hall, and then she heard the first of the three metal bars that sealed the door being withdrawn. She shrank against the wall, wondering what was to happen to her.

Two men stepped into the tiny cell from the dimly lit hall. One, an elderly, bearded man, was dressed in long, filthy robes that might once have been light blue; the other wore tattered layers of leather and coarse wool. This man was younger, perhaps Evvy's own age, and his face was deeply pocked with scars.

"I am Brother John, Chief Bishop of the Traders," said the older man. "This is Brother Billy, a probationary minister. We have come to instruct you in Trader beliefs."

* * *

Evvy soon learned that Trader instruction meant listening to tales and lessons and memorizing them by rote. There was none of the emphasis on reasoning or the easy give-and-take of questioning that had been features of her education at the Garden. She had been taught the fundamentals of the old Christian–Jewish religion and had studied the history of the pre-Change past, and soon she recognized that most Trader doctrines came from these sources, though twisted almost beyond recognition by the Traders' peculiar philosophy.

Whereas biblical and historical tales generally presented a picture of humans reacting to supernatural or historical forces, with effect naturally following cause, to the Traders it was the other way around. In their view most effects in the world were seen themselves as being causes. Thus, Noah's "scientific transgression" of building the ark was seen to be the cause of the Flood; likewise, Moses' miraculous receipt of the Ten Commandments, considered by the Traders to be the first among those most evil of artifacts, books, was itself the cause of a subsequent breakdown in morality among humankind. For the Traders, wrongdoing had not existed in the world until words describing it had been written down.

"Throughout history," the bishop intoned, "men have taken the easy way, the evil way. God meant us to live in the world as it is, constructing nothing. But the devil has constantly tempted men to change nature, to transform the natural, holy things of God into the evils of science. Where there are no manufactured goods, no cities, no property, there is no reason to fight. Just as the preacher Jesus was punished for building a cross to reach up into the heavens, so later men were punished for building machines. Our arrogance angered God, and at last He sent the wild deenas into the world to force us to return to His ways."

Evvy could understand the logic behind some of the Trader beliefs: given their limited education, it was natural for them to fear that any tampering with nature might lead inevitably to the sort of disaster that had produced the Change. She was horrified, though, by their simplistic solution, which was to "Trade"—destroy—all remaining links with the scientific past for the "godly" things of nature. She was aware that Zach had been given similar lessons during the years he had been held captive by the Traders, and she wondered how he had responded to the nonsense she was expected to parrot.

One day she became exasperated, exclaiming crossly, "But that makes no sense! If early explorers had not crossed the ocean, none of us would be here now!"

"Oh, no, Sister," droned the bishop, his voice infuriatingly patient. "You see, the world was once united, stretching from one end of the sky to the other. It was only when the columbuses began to follow Noah in building arks that the mighty ocean grew and spread. Finally it isolated different parts of the first perfect world from each other, and men's hearts from other men."

Often the bishop would catechize her, making her repeat the chants and lessons that she had been given. One in particular filled her with horror every time she heard it:

> I believe in the God of Nature,
> Who has given us all green things on earth
> And the holy fire
> And his command that all things of science be burned
> Let the books be burned to ashes
> And the scientists seared unto death.

"I can't say that!" Evvy protested.

"Say it, Sister. Only say it. Even if you don't believe now, by repetition the truth will enter your heart."

"No!" Evvy said. "No, no, no!" She ended by shouting, nearly in tears. "You can't make me say it, I don't believe it, and I won't! I won't!"

After one such outburst the bishop left, seemingly more sorrowful than angry. Evvy expected to be punished, but nothing at all happened except that neither the bishop—nor anyone else—returned to her for more than three weeks by her daily count.

The isolation was terrible, and when Brother John came again, she resolved to do as he asked, just to keep his company, but when he again asked her to bless the burning of books and of scientists, she found she couldn't. "No," she said more calmly now. "I will listen to you, and I will even repeat some of the chants, but I can't say that and I won't."

This time not only was she left alone, but her food became noticeably more meager, and it was served less often.

What would Zach have done in her place? she wondered. Or Will? Whenever she thought of them, she felt an aching longing to see them again or even to receive word of them. She wondered if she would die here of starvation with no one to know. At such times she could not stop the tears of self-pity and would sometimes sob for hours until her throat was aching and she could scarcely breathe.

She felt herself growing weaker each day. One night, when she had begun to think that even death would be preferable to her isolation and despair, Zach and Will came to her in a dream. Zach, dressed in the leather-and-wool clothing he had worn on their journey together, was squatting just in front of her, a look of grave concern on his face. Will stood beside Zach, his yellow-bordered blue cloak covering his shoulders as it had at the wedding, his arms crossed in front of him as he leaned carelessly against the thick wooden door.

"You must tell them what they want to hear," Zach was saying earnestly. "It is not worth your life to hold out for a principle."

"Zach is right," the Principal echoed. "You will betray nothing. And you may make your own life easier. It's important for you to be strong, so you can return to us."

"You may repeat their doctrines a hundred times, but they will not corrupt your soul," said Zach. "I have faith in you, Evvy. I know you will do the right thing."

"Only take care of yourself," said the Principal. "Nothing else is important." He smiled at her and held out his hand. "Only take care of yourself," he repeated. She reached out to touch him and felt again the thrill his touch always created in her. He pulled her into his arms and held her tightly. She looked up into his face and suddenly realized it was not Will at all.

"Zach," she murmured. "Zach."

In answer, Zach stroked her hair. He leaned down to kiss her, but before their lips touched, she awoke. For a moment she lay still, basking in the warmth of the dream images, trying to sort out the confusion at the end. Then she sat up, her mind clear. She knew that Zach and Will—or the deeper promptings of her imagination—were right. She could refuse to say the words—and die here. Or she could repeat them, knowing they were false, and live. Live to return one day to her work and to the two men she loved above all else in the world.

The next morning she asked the guard to send for Brother John, and when he came, he calmly began again, not chastising her but simply repeating himself as if he had not been away more than a day or two.

When he asked her to say the poisonous verse, she took a deep breath, then repeated it over and over, until the bishop asked her to stop.

The amount and quality of her food improved immediately. When she had learned a dozen Trader chants and verses, she was visited again by the young man who had come with the Bishop on the first day.

"I am Brother Billy," he told her. "I am here to teach you the sacred songs."

Without further explanation he began to sing in a high, thin tenor. Although the words of the song contained the usual horrifying images of the death of scientists and the burning of books, Evvy was struck by the melody, which was at once haunting and complex. When Billy had finished singing, she couldn't help asking. "That song is beautiful," she said. "Is it an old product-ballad?"

Looking shy, Billy shook his head. "Some of our songs come from the old tunes. This one was made up by a Trader. At least, we thought he was a Trader. He turned against us, but we have kept his songs, because, no matter what he did, they are godly."

"You have more songs by this same man?"

"Some of them are only for special services," said Billy. "But all of them were written by Brother Zach. In fact, he wrote them here. He stayed in this very same cell for five years."

Six

Zach's back and shoulders ached as he bent into the crossbars, pulling with all his strength. Around him he heard grunts and curses from the other pullers as they strained to move the machine up the steep, muddy hill.

"Faster, you sluggards!" the driver called. "Put your backs into it!" He snapped his short whip in the air but did not strike anyone.

Next to Zach, Garf, the young Trader, suddenly stumbled. His misstep threw the entire line of men out of synchronization, and the giant machine began to roll back down the steep hill, dragging the pullers with it. For one frightening moment it teetered as if to turn over, then righted itself, and at last came to a stop in a rutted depression.

The driver began to curse. After a moment Momus, assistant to the engineer, walked to the front of the line where Zach and the other men were once again gathering for an assault on the hill.

"What is going on here?" Momus demanded.

"It's the new pullers," said the driver. "They're no good on hills."

"You will pull the machine to the top of the hill or all of you will be severely punished," said Momus. "We intend to make camp in the valley beyond, and there is no time to waste."

While the driver and his assistant sorted the team into two straight lines again, Zach heard the young Trader whimper. He looked down and saw that the boy's ankle was discolored and beginning to swell. Garf stumbled again and gasped, his lip between his teeth.

"Don't say anything," the boy whispered.

"You can't walk," said Zach.

"I must," said the boy.

"I'll try to help," Zach said doubtfully. At that moment the puller behind, who had been listening, called out: "Driver!"

The driver, a burly, black-haired man with no front teeth, approached with his whip in his hand. "What's the problem now?" he said.

"This puny one has hurt his ankle."

"No!" said the boy. "It's all right! I can—"

The driver knelt down and examined the ankle. Without warning he grasped it and moved it back and forth. The boy gasped and fell against the crosspiece. "Deenas take it!" muttered the driver. "Herm!" he called to his assistant. "This one's no good. Get a replacement from the drag pool."

"Thought to get out of a little work, did you?" he asked the boy. "Well, you're about to get your wish." He unfastened the boy's hands from the crosspiece, one of six mounted on the long tongue leading from the flat wagon that carried the machine.

"No sir, please, sir—" The boy was speaking rapidly, but the driver struck him across the face.

"Shut up," he said. Then: "The rest of you, take a water break."

Groaning, the five remaining men set down the heavy tongue and sprawled on the frozen ground beside it, waiting for the water boy to come among them. The driver squinted at the top of the hill, looking worried. Zach watched while his assistant pulled the hobbling Trader youth down the long line, past the grotesque metallic jumble of the machine, its rusted brown and pitted green body ridden by an incongruously small metallic sculpture of a woman; past the two other machines, each as fantastical-looking as the first and each with its team of pullers; past the large wagons hitched to pack animals and covered by heavy cloth over wooden frames; and finally to the line of ragged, bound men, shackled together in single file, like the tail of a strange new-animal.

He wondered how the boy would be killed, then put it out of his mind. Perhaps it was just as well that he had been taken from the line. It was obvious that he would not have been able to pull his weight; and from experience Zach was beginning to learn that one more mistake might have meant execution for everyone.

He heard shouts and curses from the end of the caravan as a replacement was chosen for the unlucky Trader boy. Despite the cold, the exertion of pulling the machine had left him covered with sweat, and he began to shiver in the wind. He gratefully took a proffered sip of water and briefly closed his eyes. He was tired, as were all the pullers, but was finding this work easier than some might have. Although it had been many years since he had done hard physical labor, he had been blessed with the kind of body that can easily grow strength; his size, too, helped. That was, he supposed, why the smaller boy had been paired with him: it had been hoped that Zach would be able to carry the weight for both.

He speculated for a moment on what might lie beyond the hill. Although Momus and the others often talked of battles and raids, all Zach had seen in his time among them was endless roads, mostly winding through the hilly, bat-ridden north. He would welcome a battle or any change to break the monotony and in the hope of an opportunity to escape from this strange society and find Evvy before the Trader sacrifice, a very few weeks hence.

His weeks here among the Road Men had shown him that he and Will had been quite mistaken about the kind of world that the Change had created. Of the three societies he was now familiar with—his own, the Traders, and now the Road Men—each had adapted to the Change in strikingly different ways. He was beginning to realize that Will's quest to build civilization among the people of the District was doomed to futility until he spent at least a part of his resources on discovering what lay in the rest of the world.

The Road Men, he was sure, did not represent a direct threat to the District, not in the way the Traders did, but they certainly represented a threat to its expansion or to further exploration or normal trade with the rest of the world.

The fear of deenas was strong in the people of the District and assumed mythic proportions among the Traders; in the Road Men, fear of deenas had been turned around. Rather than shun artifacts of the past, which were superstitiously considered to harbor wild deenas, the Road Men sought them out, almost worshiped them. Thus the custom of constructing assemblages of old parts from dead machine bodies and pulling them along the roads, animating them by human muscle power in imitation of the self-power machines had possessed before the Change.

Likewise, the Traders and the people of the District treated women with respect and deference, valuing them because of their scarcity. The Road Men, while acknowledging that scarcity, treated women as no more than possessions. All women under their control belonged to the chief engineer, although he often shared them with his most trusted aides; they were kept in covered wagons strictly away from sight of other Road Men or their slaves. Zach supposed that Jonna was in one or the other of those wagons but had not seen her or heard her since the night they had been brought here.

When the Road Men had attacked the Trader camp at dawn, Zach—and the Traders—had assumed that they were simply a band of outlaws, perhaps better armed than most. Zach, bound as he was, had been able to offer no resistance to the three fierce men. He was startled by their unusual decorations: although they wore the rough leather-and-homespun garments familiar in the District, they were ornamented with large, circular medallions worn on leather thongs around their necks; other oddly shaped brown-and-green pieces of metal, some resembling small sculptures of women and wild animals, were strung together around their wrists and waists and, in one case, dangled from a piece of wire thrust through a pierced earlobe. At first all of these metallic objects looked unfamiliar, and then with a start Zach realized that he had seen many like them in the past, in the numerous resting places for dead machine bodies.

Although just roused from sleep, Morgan, the oldest of the Trader men, had begun to fight immediately with his museum-piece sword, capably and bravely. The two younger

Traders were inexperienced with their weapons, and one of the attackers easily held them off while his two companions concentrated their fury on Morgan, who soon lay dying on the forest floor. Jonna had tried to escape into the woods when the attack had begun, but as soon as Morgan had been overcome, one of the attackers went after her and quickly returned, pulling her by the hair. While all this was going on, Zach began to cut through his bonds with a sharp rock edge. He had nearly finished when Jonna and the two struggling youths were subdued and the leader of the raid, the man whom Zach now knew as Momus, looked at all of them with satisfaction. "At least one good puller and a woman," he muttered. "A good haul. Tie the young ones up," he added to his followers. "I'll take the woman."

Zach noted with interest that the others obeyed him instantly. He suspected that the short whip the man carried on his belt was at least in part responsible for the excellent discipline.

Only a few strands remained of the bonds tying his hands and feet when Jonna suddenly shrieked in fear and pain. He heard Momus laughing, then saw that he had pushed her to the ground and was roughly fondling her. Without thinking, Zach pulled his hands and feet apart, breaking the remaining strands of rope, and leapt at Momus. He wrestled the man away from Jonna, then struggled with him on the ground for what seemed like several minutes. Momus had set down his sword and knife while he was busy with Jonna, and Zach glanced at the weapons desperately, trying to think how to reach them without losing his grip on Momus.

Before he had a chance to try for the weapons, the two other Road Men pulled Zach away from their leader. One held Zach against the ground while the other began to kick and punch him. Momus stood and dusted himself off, then abruptly pulled Zach's tormenter away from him. "Let him go!" he commanded, glaring. "You'll damage him!" Then, to Zach's surprise, he began to laugh. "You'll make a good puller at that!" he said. "I didn't know it was your woman. It don't matter anyhow, all women belong to the engineer. But I'll let her be for now. Only tell me why she had you tied."

Zach was too astonished to think of an answer, but Jonna

quickly spoke: "He had gone off and left me for another woman," she said. "A pretty one. My brothers and I were just bringing him home."

Momus looked at her, then at Zach, and laughed again. "Looks like there's still a spark there after all," he said. "If he does real good as a puller, there's a chance the engineer will let you be together on occasion."

Jonna and Zach were bound together, behind the other two Trader men, for a march north that took them just under a day and a half. That night they slept under a large blanket next to an all-night fire. They were in bat country now, and although it was winter, they would need the protection of light against the possibility of forays by hunting bats.

"Thank you for helping me this morning, Brother Zach," Jonna whispered hoarsely. It was the first time she had spoken to him since the march had begun. "You could have broken free . . . possibly escaped. Why did you do it?"

"I don't know," Zach said honestly. He had been asking himself the same question all day on the march. When he had first begun cutting himself free, his only thought was to wait for a moment of inattention to escape from both the new foes and the Traders, but when Jonna had screamed and he had seen what Momus was trying to do to her, he had reacted automatically, without thought. Reflecting now, he remembered an earlier time when he would have done anything in his power to prevent the Principal from acting on his own sexual compulsions. Yet his action had been motivated by something more complex: he was beginning to realize that his feelings for Jonna went beyond the relationship of a captive to his jailer.

"What will they do with us?" Jonna asked after a moment.

"I can't even guess. They talk of machines . . ."

"And of an engineer," she said bitterly. She fell silent again, perhaps remembering Momus's attack that morning.

"Whatever our fates," said Zach, "it looks as if you will not get your sacrifice now."

"Perhaps not," she said thoughtfully. Then, more urgently, "Brother Zach, I am grateful for what you did. And I think you are more competent in this sort of situation than the Trader men with me. I want you to take something." She wriggled a moment, then placed a small packet, bound in cloth, in his hand.

"They did not take my herbs when they searched me," she said. "No doubt they did not think them valuable or that they could be used as weapons."

Zach began to understand.

"In this bag there is enough of a certain mixture of herbs to put several men to sleep for an hour or more," she went on. "It does not work quickly, and I don't know if it will help you. But take it."

"But you..."

"I have other things," she said. "And besides, I know how to gather and prepare more."

"Thank you," he said, touched.

"I feel I owe you this much. But do not deceive yourself. If we ever escape this situation and meet again, you and I are deadliest enemies. My purpose in life is to stop the Principal... and to stop you."

Sitting and waiting for the team to be started again, Zach again remembered her words. He had kept the packet of herbs inside his shirt, waiting for the right moment to use it. While he could easily have drugged his team's common water supply at any time, he did not see how this would help him to escape with so many Road Men around him.

"On yer feet!" The driver had returned with a large but sickly-looking man whose skin beneath his tattered jacket showed crusted sores. The newcomer was placed in position, then his hands were strapped tightly to the crossbar. Punctuating his words with sharp cracks of his whip, the driver ordered the pullers to begin work.

Once again the machine began to move up the hill. Every muscle straining, Zach leaned into the crosspiece, digging his heels into the cold, slippery earth. The new puller next to him grunted with effort. Slowly they inched up the hill and at last stood at the crest, looking down into a wooded valley. Patches of snow stood in the shadows of trees despite the recent warmth.

Far across the valley Zach could see faint wisps of smoke, the sign of a small settlement.

The light had taken on the slanted, yellowish cast of late

afternoon in winter, and Zach realized that the day was nearly gone. Now all that remained was to bring the machine down the other side—a job harder in many ways than pulling it up: descent required careful balance and great strength in the thigh muscles. On his first day among the Road Men Zach had watched as a puller slipped while going down a steep path. His loss of balance had caused the other pullers to slip, too, and the heavy machine-wagon had rushed downhill of its own accord, dragging the tethered pullers with it and seriously injuring several of them. He had been drafted into service to replace one of them that very day.

When Zach's team had brought their machine safely to the bottom of the hill, Zach's legs were trembling. After he was released from the crosspiece he had to rest a moment, then he began to help set up the camp for the night.

After eating a skimpy dinner of root stew Zach leaned against a fallen tree and relaxed, trying to make his mind blank. The forest was thick at this altitude, and bare tree branches hung in such profusion that they formed lacy patterns against the purpling sky.

At the periphery of the camp stood the four large shallow wooden wagons, their crude wheels appearing featureless in the dimming light. On each wagon stood the fantastical reconstruction of an ancient road machine. Here and there light glinted on a shard of broken glass, a still shiny shred of silvery metal. As the day faded, the machines increasingly took the forms of monsters from a child's nightmare.

The area was dotted with small camp fires, pottery bowls and metal pots steaming with the aromas of cooking meat and vegetables. Mixed with the smells of cooking food were the earthy scents of the forest; the sweet aroma of new-smoke; the slightly rancid, sour stink of tired and dirty men.

Around the largest fire, which would be tended all night, were grouped the three large, bat-proof tents where the drivers and the engineer gambled and drank until late. The bonfire was tended through the night by sentries wearing leather bat-helmets, thick leather hoods that covered the face and shoulders with slits only for the eyes and nose. The sentries paid little attention to the slaves; any man who managed to slip his bonds and try to escape risked instant death from the talons of a poison-bat, which would not go near a light but would strike at any movement in the dark. Scattered among the smaller fires, which were even now dying down, were the tiny lean-tos under which the pullers and pool-men would sleep through the night or lie awake, wondering what the next day would bring.

As it became darker Zach shivered and pulled his blanket closer around himself. It was nearly time to crawl into his crude shelter. The man next to him passed a glowing pipe of new-smoke, and Zach puffed at it gratefully, then passed it on. Although the circumstances were very different, this camp took him back in memory to Will's camp, to the days when he had first joined Will after being rescued from the Principal's men.

The smoke and his own exhaustion combined to relax him. He was drifting into sleep when Momus appeared, calling for attention. When all pullers were again awake, Momus smiled ironically. "Rest well, men," he said. "Tomorrow we raid the town across the valley. Those who perform valiantly will be rewarded."

Zach stretched out beneath his lean-to and thought about Momus's promise. He did not relish the idea of a raid, but his stomach churned with excitement: This would be his chance to escape.

Seven

The morning dawned cold and cloudy, and Zach shivered while he ate his bowl of tasteless porridge. The Road Men's food was usually adequate, although seldom hearty; just recently it had been skimpier, scarcely enough to support the two dozen Road Men, their women, and the equal numbers of slaves.

Because of the shortage of food, anyone sick or injured was simply killed and his possessions put into the supply wagons. Zach wondered how many casualties they would take in today's raid; he supposed that any lost slaves would be replaced by conscripts from the town.

By late morning the caravan had nearly crossed the valley, and Zach could make out small houses on the other side of the river. Upstream from the town was an ancient, pre-Change bridge made passable by wooden planks fastened to the remains of rotting concrete and metal trestles.

The bridge did not look strong enough to support a machine, and Zach tried to put out of his mind the thought of its breaking through and then plunging into the icy water, pulling him with it.

The other pullers apparently had the same thought, and

the man just ahead of him on the left began to grumble loudly. "This bridge wouldn't support a chicken," he said.

"What's that?" called the driver. "What's that you say?"

"I said the bridge is flimsy! Whyn't you just ask us to march into the water!" He ducked his head but not in time to avoid the driver's lash, which caught him on the side of the face.

"Road Men don't tolerate cowards!" snarled the driver. "Momus! We need a replacement up here!"

"I didn't mean I wouldn't do it—wait!" The hapless puller began to plead as the driver uncoupled him from the crosspiece. "Please, give me a chance—"

"You had your chance," said the driver. He pushed the slave to the ground and began to lash him. Screaming, the man twisted, trying to ward off the blows. Zach turned his head, feeling sick. Momus had already brought up a new replacement, and while he was being manacled to the wagon tongue, two of the drivers bound the first man hand and foot, ignoring his screams of protest, and threw him into the river. His head appeared above the surface once, and then he was gone.

"Anyone else got doubts about crossing the bridge?" asked the driver. "No? Well, get moving. We've wasted enough time."

Trying not to think about the water below, Zach followed the two pullers ahead of him, concentrating all his attention on placing his feet on the strongest-looking boards. The bridge creaked loudly, and the wagon swayed, emitting protesting groans. Halfway across, the man in front of Zach stumbled as his foot went through a rotten plank. The wagon began to tilt, and Zach closed his eyes, using all his strength to hold the tongue steady. After an eternity the wagon settled, and slowly they began to move again. At last the pullers brought their burden safely onto the rocky ground on the other side.

The driver ordered them to rest, and Zach gratefully sat, breathing deeply and willing his heart to slow while the other two machine-wagons crossed.

Now the covered wagons pulled by pack beasts set out. The third, containing the women, had nearly reached the far shore when the lead animal suddenly shied, then broke through the planking. For a moment the wagon teetered, the terrified animals braying and struggling as they tried to regain their footing, then the entire assemblage plunged downward, ripping the wooden supports as it fell. Pack animals, wagon, and large pieces of the bridge fell into the water, disappearing in a spray of foam. The noise of the river swallowed the screams of the women and animals.

From where he was sitting against the wagon tongue, Zach watched as the drivers and other Road Men gathered at the bank, shouting and thrusting branches into the water for the women to hold to, but no one climbed onto shore, and in a surprisingly short period of time there was no sound but the rushing of water.

Zach felt an intense, unexpected pang of grief. Despite their very different aims, he had always felt grateful for all that Jonna had done for him; had admired her quick intelligence and fierce loyalty to Yosh. Though he had hoped never again to have dealings with her, he would, he realized now, miss her.

The engineer began to bellow in his rage, ordering the remaining Road Men and pool-men to cross the damaged bridge at once. Most managed by keeping to the sides where the remaining planks were strongest, then leaping across the ragged gap. Two pool-men misjudged the distance and were lost.

When all had crossed, Momus addressed them. "The engineer has lost his women!" he shouted. "He orders me to tell you that we must replace them from the town! Any man who does not follow orders instantly will be thrown beneath the machines and crushed to death!"

Shakily Zach got to his feet and began to pull with all his strength. Not since his imprisonment had he felt so dependent on the actions and whims of others. If he survived the next hours, he vowed, that would change.

Although far to the north and west, the settlement resembled those scattered throughout the District. Surrounding the town itself was the stubble of grain fields; in the distance, by a stream leading to the river, was a small mill house. The settlement was arranged, as were most in the District, in a rectangle. The dwellings, some built on the ruins of pre-Change buildings, others of wood and straw, all faced inward. Zach was certain that they all bordered on a common square.

Though there was no protective wall, such as had surrounded the old Garden, the small houses were built close together with sturdy fencing closing the spaces between them. In the center of one side of the rectangle was a large barred gate.

Just now a number of men were standing by the gate, wary, holding staffs and farming implements, watching as the party of Road Men assembled.

The engineer, followed closely by Momus, approached Zach's wagon and climbed up onto the front of the machine. Holding tightly to the small metallic sculpture on the front of the machine body, his museum-piece sword in his belt, he ordered the caravan to march forward.

The townsmen standing at the gate spread themselves across the road but otherwise made no move of threat. As the caravan drew nearer one of them, a heavy, dark-bearded man of middle age, stepped out and stood in front of the others, holding a pitchfork, its metal head obviously of pre-Change workmanship, the handle of cruder, more recent manufacture.

Zach, who was pulling in the middle rank, began to fear that the pullers would be expected to keep going until they had forced the men to stand aside—or to march in over their bodies. However, a few hundred feet from the entrance the engineer called, "Halt!"

The pullers stopped, and Zach heard the creak of protesting wooden joints as the order was repeated down the line.

The townsmen held their ground, but Zach could now see looks of uneasiness and fear on their faces. "Machines!" one man whimpered. "The curse of the deenas is among us!"

"Be quiet!" hissed the man Zach assumed was the leader. "I'm Teddy son of Marta," he went on in a louder voice. "I'm mayor of this town. What do you want?"

"We are of the tribe of Road Men," said the engineer. "We demand shelter and food."

"Shelter you can have—for a night or two," said Teddy. "Food is scarce here. We've barely enough to get through the winter."

"Then you'll have to go on even shorter rations!" said the engineer. "Now stand aside and let us in!" His voice sounded brutal, and Zach sensed he was hoping for resistance.

"You and your men can enter," said Teddy. "Those deena-cursed machines—never!" He had, Zach saw, become pale, and sweat beaded his forehead.

"You have no choice," said the engineer. "Momus?"

Momus muttered an order, and the drivers lifted their bows, fitted arrows, and aimed. The townsmen shrunk back, brandishing their weapons. Teddy stood his ground, holding his pitchfork ready to throw.

"Open the gate!" repeated the engineer.

Teddy didn't answer.

The engineer gestured to Momus. "Fire!" Momus said.

The drivers shot together. Three arrows seemed suddenly to sprout from Teddy's broad chest, and he staggered, then fell into the arms of one of his men. The other townsmen hurled their implements to little effect, though the puller in front of Zach was struck by a small ax and slumped forward onto the crosspiece, the force of his fall pulling the wagon tongue downward.

Now the Road Men closed on the remaining townsmen and slaughtered them with knives, swords, and their own farming instruments. When all were dead or dying, Momus grinned, then, with a ceremonial flourish, wiped his bloody hands on his trousers and opened the gate.

The interior of the settlement, now in deep shadow, was as Zach had pictured it. Women and children ran screaming into their cottages as the grotesque machine bodies entered the square. Still bound to the machine, he watched with shame as the shouting Road Men, drivers, and soldiers broke into the houses, taking what they wanted and destroying the rest. He looked away after a moment, unable to bear the gazes of the frightened inhabitants, sensing their hatred for him.

After the first general looting the Road Men quieted down. They slaughtered several new-goats and built a bonfire in the center of the square. There was a large, windowless cabin used for common food storage. This the Road Men emptied and locked into it all the pullers and pool-men.

"You'll be safe and comfortable here," Momus told them, "and it won't take so many to guard you. You did well today, boys. Tonight you'll get your share of the prizes."

Zach sat, leaning against the rough wooden wall, grateful, despite the gloom, for the chance to rest. In the weeks that he had been with the Road Men he had looked constantly for an opportunity to escape. If only his own safety had been involved, he might have taken any of several desperate chances. But for Evvy's sake he had forced himself to be patient and wait.

Jonna had said that Yosh's birthdate was on the first day of spring, and though snow was still standing in the shadows, the lengthening daylight told him that winter had passed its peak and he would have to take a chance soon, even a desperate one. Now, sitting unbound and relatively unguarded, Zach knew that he would never have a better opportunity.

If his prediction was correct, the Road Men would be too busy drinking and carousing this night to pay close attention to the slaves. He would sleep for a while and make no more plans until he saw what happened.

Shortly after the sun went down, with the room lit by a single, smoky fish-oil lamp, the slaves were fed thick slabs of the cooked new-goat. Zach ate hungrily, aware that he might not have a full belly again for some time. To wash the meat down was a barrel of fresh brew raided from the town.

When the men had eaten their fill, Momus returned. With him were three townswomen, tied together and glassy-eyed with shock. Although Zach had been expecting something of the sort, he was nevertheless jolted to see them.

As soon as Momus began to speak, Zach saw that he was quite drunk already, and this gave him hope. "Plenny of food and drink for all!" Momus slurred. "Fer the pullers and poolmen too. You do your job, you're rewarded like the rest. But don't get any ideas about running. Nowhere to go. And the guards have orders to kill anyone who comes out of this room." He cut through the women's bonds, then pushed them into the center of the room. "Have fun!" he called.

The women staggered, then stood, looking at the floor. The oldest, whose tunic had been ripped nearly in half and who was holding the pieces together in a fruitless attempt at modesty, was a stout woman of middle age. The other two, whose clothing was also torn and soiled, were, Zach now saw, very young, perhaps still in their teens. The ordeal they had been through and fear of what faced them that night made them appear older.

As soon as Momus had shut the door some of the men were on the women, pulling at their clothing. But not all.

"This ain't right," grumbled an old man with one eye. "They don't have any more choice about this than we do."

"Well, bad luck for them, but I aim to collect my share of the reward," said a blond youth who already had his hand clasped proprietarily around the wrist of the youngest and prettiest woman. "Besides, looks like they've already been used some. We can't hurt them much worse."

While the men argued, Zach reached inside his tunic and removed the packet of herbs that Jonna had given him. Now was as good a time as any, and if it worked as she promised, he would not only have a chance to escape, he would spare the women a few hours of torment. He walked toward the open barrel of brew, now half empty, and dipped his cup. At the same time he let the herbs fall from his hand into the liquid. Pretending to settle the barrel closer to the wall, he shook it to distribute the drug.

By now the women had been dragged onto the floor. They did not cry out in protest but moaned in despair. Zach looked away, feeling ill, but there was nothing more he could do. Jonna had said that the drug did not work quickly. He kept a mental count and was pleased to see that after a time all the slaves had drunk at least one cup of the drugged brew. The women, too, drank, perhaps to dull their awareness.

Most important, the two men who were guarding the room slipped in twice each to refill their own cups.

After what seemed a very long time all the men were asleep, snoring loudly. As a test, Zach shook the young blond man, and, receiving no response but a loud snore, he crept to the door and pushed. As he had expected, it was barred from the outside. The bar did not fit tightly, however, and by slipping a thin strip of wood between the door and wall, he was able to lift it clear. Just as he did, he heard a rustling noise behind him. He turned slowly, to see the youngest of the women pushing herself to her elbows. Her eyes were wet and pleading, but she did not say anything. He had an impulse to pull her to her feet, to bring her with him, but knew that he could not take the chance. Silently he shook his head. She stared at him a moment longer, then lay down again, her face passive and without hope. He forced himself to turn from her, then pushed the door open.

Peering outside, he saw that it was very late. The bonfire had become glowing coals, though yellow lights shone behind the oiled-skin windows of most of the houses; the laughter and shrieks he heard from within them gave evidence that the Road Men were still enjoying their revelry. As he had expected and hoped, the two guards were dozing too. One was curled up next to the remains of the fire; the other sat slumped with his back to the wall, an empty cup lying on its side next to his hand.

Zach slipped quietly into the square, then disarmed the guards, obtaining two light museum-swords and a sharp knife. He took the bat-helmet and personal pouch from the largest guard, taking the time to check the pouch for flint and metal. Then, slipping the bat-helmet on his own head and keeping close to the walls of the buildings, he crept between two houses and began to run. He did not stop until he had come to the bridge. At the gap in the planking he stopped. Below him he could see the river, its dark, foamy surface phosphorescent in the moonlight. The gulf between where he stood and the undamaged portion of the bridge looked enormous. So much had happened already this day that he wanted to turn back, to rest among the trees until dawn. But he didn't dare. He judged the distance of the gap, took a deep breath, and leaped.

Eight

Evvy could not help liking Billy. The young preacher was so earnest in his beliefs, so eager to teach her the songs, that she found herself working hard to please him. Besides, she enjoyed his company. Unlike the dour bishop who had catechized her in Trader doctrine, Billy was cheerful and solicitous, never failing to ask if she had slept well or received enough food. When one day she confessed that she was nearly always hungry, he had that afternoon brought her a portion of dried meat that he said came from his family's stores.

Despite her liking for Billy, as the weather continued to be cold and wet, Evvy's mood darkened, too; she often found herself cranky and wanting to argue with him. Most of the Trader songs were short and easily memorized; the one they had been working on lately was much longer and so simple-minded that Evvy could not keep it in her mind. It was called "The First Change" and was a catalog of all the "changes" the Traders believed had culminated in the last great Change.

"But it doesn't make any sense!" she said with irritation when Billy had repeated the first stanza three times. "Do you really believe that? That it was evil for the first woman to make clothes to cover her nakedness?"

"Of course," said Billy. "It's in the teachings."

"But humans need clothing. We don't have fur or feathers."

"We need clothes now because she created them in the first place. Her change caused the world to become colder and harsher."

"If you really believe that, then why don't you Traders all go around in your bare skins?"

Billy sighed. "Ah, Sister. I wish you'd try to understand. You don't realize how science has poisoned your mind. You don't see that happiness lies in more than your books and learning. Happiness is being one with nature, living simply under God's law."

"You're right," she said.

"What?"

"I don't see it. I can't. Because it's all nonsense."

Billy sighed again, looking troubled. "Perhaps you should receive more instruction from the Bishop," he said after a moment. "He knows far more than I do and could perhaps explain it better."

At the thought of spending more time with the dour, sour-smelling old man, Evvy decided to stop arguing. She had, after all, learned to say many chants that were against everything she believed; she could just as well learn the songs.

"Sing it to me again," she said quickly. "I promise I'll try to understand."

Patiently Billy began again to sing the first stanzas of the song along with their mind-numbing refrain. By viewing the words as a random collection of nonsense syllables, Evvy found than she was able to memorize, scarcely thinking as she did. The words were set to the tune of an old products-ballad, one Evvy had heard as a child, and while the melody was as primitive as all such tunes, it was lively and even appealing. When Billy left after teaching her the first five of seventeen stanzas, Evvy found herself humming the melody to herself.

After the third of the thick bars that sealed her door settled in its stop, she rose and looked out the tiny window at the clouded sky beyond. Because of the rain, not many Traders were about. She watched as Billy crossed the grassy square, hunched against the wet weather, hurrying toward home. She had been here six months. Looking around the tiny cell, she could scarcely believe that it had been so long; that she had managed to keep her sanity for that amount of time.

She had long since abandoned her faint hope that somehow Zach or the Principal would find her. Too much time had passed. Would she be kept here for five years, as Zach had been? Or longer? Would she spend the rest of her life in this filthy cell? She still did not know what the Traders wanted of her. She had thought at first that they might try to use her in some way against the Principal, demanding something in exchange. But nothing had happened, and now this hope, too, was dead. What, then, was their plan? If they had wanted to kill her, there had been many opportunities both during the abduction and since; besides, they were spending a great deal of time teaching her Trader beliefs. Surely they would not invest so much effort on someone they intended to kill?

She began to pace the few short steps from one side of the cell to the other. She had once begged the bishop to allow her to go outside, to walk in the grass and see the sky, but he had curtly refused, telling her that it would be dangerous for her to be among the Traders.

A sudden gust of wind sent a chilly breeze into the cell, and Evvy sneezed. The inside of her mouth began to itch, and she realized she was getting sick. No wonder; the sanitary arrangements were only rudimentary, and she had been chilled for so long, she could not remember how it felt to be warm.

She wiped her nose on a tattered corner of the filthy cloak her kidnappers had given her, then lay down on the straw pallet to nap: perhaps it would help her to fight the infection.

When Evvy awoke it was dark outside, and she saw that she had slept through her usual mealtime. The small pottery bowl beside the tiny slot in the door was filled with scummy broth, now cold. She began to drink it to keep up her strength, but one sip made her nauseated, and she set it down. She was beginning to feel very ill; her mouth was dry, and she suddenly started to shake with cold. The usual nighttime sounds seemed muffled, as if she had layers of cloth around her head, and a sharp pain behind her eyes throbbed every time she moved. Wondering if she were dying, she lay back and began to cry, without sound, the tears running down her face and into her mouth.

In the morning she felt a little better but still could not

eat. She begged her guard for an extra portion of water, and, grumbling, he brought it. No matter how much she drank, she felt tormented by thirst, and for the rest of the day she lay alternately too hot or shaking with chills. The fever seemed to come and go in a regular pattern, but she lost track of time, and when Billy visited her on the next day, she was surprised. Had he not been here just a few hours ago?

"Sister Evvy!" he said, looking shocked. "You're sick. Why didn't you tell anyone?"

"What good would it have done me?" she said, beginning to cry again, not even lifting her head from where it lay on the filthy straw. "You have no healers, no medicine."

"But that's not true," said Billy. "We have one very great healer, though she is away. But she has taught some of her arts to another woman. I will get her immediately."

"No," said Evvy irritably. "I don't want to see any more Traders. Leave me alone."

"But you need care!"

"I'm so cold and so dirty . . . what use is my life anymore? I'm locked up like an animal . . ."

"That is your illness speaking," said Billy gently. He put his hand to her forehead. "You have a fever," he said. "I will get the healer."

"I don't want her."

"Then I will bring the healing potions myself," he said. She didn't answer. "Will you let me do that?"

"Don't bring anyone else," she said, aware how nasal and rough her voice had become. She began to cough, and Billy looked even more alarmed.

"I will be back in a few minutes," he said.

He returned with a pitcher full of a steaming, pungent-smelling liquid, and a thick, though dirty, blanket. Tenderly he wrapped the blanket around her, then helped her to drink the liquid. It tasted vile, but the fumes seemed to clear her head and chest, and she felt better after she had drunk.

"Why didn't you tell me you were getting sick?" he said.

"I didn't think it mattered," said Evvy. "I thought it was part of my punishment."

"You are not here for punishment," said Billy. He sounded shocked.

"Then why am I here?"

Billy didn't answer right away; perhaps he had not heard her. Her voice was very weak. "I would have brought the blanket before," he said after a moment. "You had only to ask."

"I didn't think the Traders kept stores of manufactured things," said Evvy bitterly.

"We don't," said Billy. "It is my own blanket. But I will find another," he added quickly.

Evvy didn't answer. She was ashamed at taking out her frustration and despair on the only person who had been kind to her.

Billy refilled the cup. "Drink again," he said. "You will feel better."

Too weak to protest, Evvy did as she was told.

Twice each day Billy visited her, bringing the healing broth and once even some freshly cooked winter vegetables. She found herself remembering the time long ago when Zach had been ill and she had nursed him back to health, a man she scarcely knew and had been afraid of but had grown to love.

Gradually the pain in her chest and head subsided, and she began to feel stronger. When her voice was no longer a harsh croak, the singing lessons resumed, although, not wanting to tire her, Billy at first went over only the simple songs she had already learned, to be sure that she remembered them.

The next time Billy visited, it was on a surprisingly warm, blue-skied day. Even confined in her tiny cell, Evvy could sense the promise of spring.

The fine weather had put her in better spirits, and when Billy began to go over the verses of "The First Change" for the first time since she had fallen sick, she repeated them nearly flawlessly. Reciting the words, she felt as she had long ago when she played word games with her younger brother, Daiv. Together they would create a long list, each child adding one item in turn, but only after first repeating all the items that came before.

After an hour or two Evvy had memorized the entire song, and surprised Billy by telling him so.

"All seventeen verses?" he said in astonishment.

"Do you want to hear it?" said Evvy.

"Go ahead," said Billy.

Evvy took a deep breath and began:

"I'd like to tell the world a tale
Of how it did begin
And how the deenas caused the Change
And suffering and sin.
It started when the first of men
Chopped down the knowledge tree
And then his wife constructed clothes
And set the devil free."

Evvy paused a moment, then sang the refrain: "This was the first change . . . the first change." Billy nodded approvingly, and she continued:

"The second Change it happened so
When Noah built an ark
This act of science caused the Flood
And started days of dark. . . .

Each verse advanced the Trader's story through history and myth, the distortions and misunderstandings building and compounding one another. Evvy easily sang all seventeen verses, finally reaching the last:

"The scientists now ruled the world
And hoping to be kings,
They set the deenas loose on earth
And changed all men, all things.
So now the world in darkness dwells
But hope is close at hand.
As we Trade science for the truth,
God soon will rule the land.
We must Trade for God . . . we must Trade for God."

Ordinarily Evvy simply sang as quickly as she could, paying no more attention to the meaning than she did to the strange sounds in her cell at night; the words, however absurd and wrongheaded, were simply syllables to be memorized like the lists she and her brother had used to make.

Today, however, perhaps because of Billy's intense interest, she found herself listening as she sang, and rather than feeling her usual despair and anger when faced with Trader doctrine, she began to realize that the verses were funny. Perhaps it was giddiness caused by relative warmth and the unaccustomed sunlight, or perhaps it was simply a kind of temporary madness induced by months of confinement; whatever the cause, each successive verse struck her as more ludicrous than the last, and she began to have difficulty keeping her face composed and her voice steady. She turned to look out the window as she sang the last verse, to hide her face from Billy, but it was no use; when she reached the final refrain, she could only stutter the ending: "We must T-Trade for G-God . . ." Abruptly she started to laugh, peal after peal, so hard that tears ran from her eyes. She collapsed on her straw pallet and sat doubled up, nearly choking. When she finally had control of herself, she looked at Billy, prepared to apologize. But the young Trader preacher was looking down at her with such a comical mixture of worry and astonishment that she went into a new round of laughter.

At last she finished and wiped her eyes.

"Are you all right, Sister Evvy?" the young man asked solicitously. He looked as if he were ready to run for help.

"I'm f-fine," she said. "Thank you. I'm sorry, Brother Billy. I didn't mean to laugh at your song, it's just that it's—it's so funny!"

Relief spread over Billy's homely features, and he gave a tentative smile. "Well, at least you know all the words," he said. "That's the important thing."

When Billy had left, Evvy leaned against the damp wall, feeling more relaxed and more at peace than she had in months. The laughter had been good for her in an unexpected way. She felt as if she had somehow been healed.

After that day Billy began to spend more time with her. She longed to ask him about Zach but was afraid of the guards' overhearing. Also, though she knew few details of Zach's escape from the Traders, she guessed that he had somehow tricked his captors, including Billy himself; perhaps the topic would be a painful one.

One day they spent the entire singing session on one of the special songs that Zach had written. In spite of the Trader sentiments in the words, Evvy had fallen in love with the melody because of its beauty and because it had been created by Zach. As she and Billy continued to sing together, Evvy began to sing high harmony notes above the melody, as Zach had taught her. The result sounded wonderful, and Billy's eyes widened in surprise and pleasure. They sang the song over and over, practicing until their voices sounded like one multitoned instrument.

"You must teach me how to sing this way, Sister," Billy said with excitement. "So that I may instruct the others."

"I will try," she said doubtfully. "In return will you teach me the rest of Brother Zach's songs?"

"I'll need to get permission," said Billy. "Some of them are very sacred."

"Are they as beautiful as this one?" she asked.

"Oh, yes. All of Brother Zach's songs are beautiful... and godly." Billy fell silent a moment, looking sad, then, hesitantly, "Sister Evvy?"

"Yes?"

"It is my understanding that you were to be wed to the Principal."

"Yes." Evvy dropped her eyes. How long ago the wedding seemed now.

"Did you love him?"

"What?"

Billy flushed. "I'm sorry. I know I have no right to ask such a thing. I only wondered. Because... because the Principal must have the devil truly in him." Billy stopped in confusion. Evvy understood that he was asking only in order to understand; that his experience of Zach and of her contradicted everything he had been taught about the Principal and his allies.

"He is a good man," Evvy said quietly.

"But he serves the devil!"

"I know that you think so," said Evvy. "But just because people do not share the same beliefs does not mean they are not good." She paused, then went on. "I'm sure that Brother Yosh was a good man, yet from the Principal's point of view, Yosh was the most dangerous man in the world." She remembered the brief glimpses she had had of Yosh during the two Trader attacks on the clinic. She wondered what Billy would say if she told him that twice Yosh had tried to kill her.

But Billy's eyes were unfocused, as if he were looking at something far away. "I suppose you're right," he said after a moment. He looked at her and smiled. "Could we sing the song one more time?"

A few days later the Chief Bishop came with Billy and asked to hear this new way of singing; once he had listened he agreed at once to let Billy teach Evvy any of the songs. In return she was to instruct Billy how to sing in harmony.

As they worked together Evvy began to realize that much in this way of singing was intuitive; though he had a good ear and a pleasant voice, Billy seemed to lack the inner ability to improvise harmoniously. Finally she gave up and simply worked the harmonies out herself, then taught them to him as separate melodies.

He began to teach her others of Zach's songs, all of which seemed to her like bright spots of color in the drab surroundings. It was almost as if Zach had written the songs especially for her, as private messages of courage and hope. One day Billy finally sang for her the most sacred song of all, the one that Zach had written to memorialize Yosh, "The Death of Our Brother." The song was so beautiful that Evvy found tears in her eyes at the end of it; when Billy sang it through the second time, she began to harmonize effortlessly, imagining Zach's rich baritone floating beneath her voice as she sang. They sang the song again and again until Evvy's throat ached.

"Zach must have cared a great deal for Yosh," Evvy said at last. "I never knew."

"Do you mean to say you know Brother Zach, Evvy?" said Billy. He seemed startled, as if the idea had never occurred to him.

"Why, of course," said Evvy. "He works for the Principal."

"Then he has returned to the Capital?"

Evvy hesitated before answering. In all the time she had been here, no one had asked her anything about Zach or the Principal. She had simply assumed, because of the attack at the wedding, that they knew everything. Because Zach must now be a special target of their vengeance, she realized she must be very careful about anything she said.

"I knew him long ago," she told Billy then. "Before he

came here, before I knew the Principal. We once traveled together."

"But how could that be?"

Evvy thought again, then began speaking slowly, carefully picking her words. "It all happened a long time ago, when I was a child." Without telling Billy the reasons for her travels with Zach, she told him a little of what it had been like, riding each day, hunting, making camp, then talking and singing together in the evenings.

"He taught me many things," she said. "In fact, it was Zach who taught me how to sing in harmony."

Billy gazed at her a moment, looking sad. "I thought I knew him so well," he said. "But then he tricked us and escaped. I think I understand now why he betrayed us. He did it so he could be with you again."

Evvy did not know what to say. She could see Billy's anger and confusion. "He was like a father to me," she said.

"But perhaps he felt more than fatherly."

"We traveled together, Brother Billy. That is all."

"If I had traveled with you, I would—" Billy stopped, then went on, "I mean to say that in another kind of world . . ." He paused again and sighed. "You are so beautiful, Sister Evvy."

Again unsure of what to say, Evvy laughed, covering her own confusion. "It's kind of you to say so," she said. "But I doubt anyone could be beautiful under so many layers of dirt."

"The dirt does not hide your face," said Billy. "But I was thinking of something else. No matter what you believe, no matter what you have done, you have a beautiful soul. That is the highest compliment a Trader can give."

One morning after a late-winter snow had melted, Evvy went to the window and perceived a new change in the air: it was the unmistakable scent of early spring.

That afternoon Billy brought her a small violet flower.

"This has just come up in the woods," he said. "Since you cannot go out, I thought you would like to have it."

"Thank you," she said, touched. She held the flower to her nose and sniffed. It had scarcely any scent but was so fresh and so delicate that she felt tears start to her eyes.

"It is nearly spring," she said.

"Yes," said Billy. And then he suddenly turned away.

"Billy? Is something wrong?"

"No, it's only that—I wish spring would not come this year."

"You can't mean that!"

The young Trader turned to look at her, his pale eyes brimming with tears. "This is our last meeting, Sister," he said then.

"What? But why? Are you—"

"The Bishop will come and explain everything later. We are all going on a journey tomorrow, to the holy place of Yosh's birth. Most of the townspeople have left already."

Now Evvy realized that in a few days she had seen far fewer Traders outside the cell window than usual; because it had been raining a great deal, she had thought nothing of it.

"Do you mean that I will be left here alone?"

"No, you will go too. In a special wagon, with the Bishops. But there will be no time for songs. I'm going ahead to help create a holy shrine in Yosh's memory."

"Well, we will see each other in the new place, then."

Billy didn't answer. Evvy took a step forward and touched his arm. He started, then turned away again, moving toward the door.

"What is it, Billy?"

"The shrine is to be dedicated with a purification ceremony."

"Yes?" Apprehension began to stir in her belly. "What do I have to do with it?"

"It is for the Bishops to tell you," he said. "I have already said too much."

"But if they are to speak to me, anyway, what's the harm? Why won't we see each other again? Are you in trouble? Is that it?"

"Ah, Sister Evvy," he said, his voice almost a groan. "The shrine is to be dedicated on the first day of spring, the holy anniversary of Yosh's birth. On that day . . . in three weeks . . . you are to be sacrificed."

Nine

When Zach awoke, damp leaves were pressed into his face and his feet were entangled in low-growing branches. Disoriented, he sat, then remembered how he had come here, traveling all through the night till early dawn, when, exhausted, he had pulled off the bat-helmet and crawled into the protecting shelter of some thick brush. With a rush, all that had happened yesterday returned, and he felt a pang of sorrow, thinking of Jonna and all the others who had lost their lives. He realized now that the guards he had drugged had no doubt been killed, too, when his escape had been discovered.

His body ached as if he had been beaten. When he had jumped across the breach in the bridge, he had landed with full force on his hands and knees. The planks just under his legs had begun to splinter, and, trembling, he had held on desperately to the outer supports, then pulled himself farther onto the safe planking, an inch at a time. He had continued to cross the same way, on his hands and knees, every muscle in his body shaking.

Once across he had followed the river south, nearly certain that he would not be pursued but wanting to put as much distance as possible between himself and the Road Men. He squinted at the sky. The sun was already high overhead. He did not know where he was but believed that the Trader capital must lie to the south and east.

He stretched, his joints creaking in protest, then stood and walked to the river's edge to wash. Just as he was bending over the water, he heard a twig snap behind him. His heart thumped heavily as he realized that he had left his weapons where he had slept. He picked up a large, smooth river stone and stood, then turned. The brush where he had concealed himself began to rustle, as if someone were shaking it, and then parted to reveal a small, bushy-haired, orange-colored animal.

"Baby!" At first he could not believe his eyes.

"Mowr?" said the fox-cat. As if it were the most natural thing in the world, she bounded up to him and began to rub her body against his boots.

Although he had heard fox-cats during his stay with the Road Men, he had never imagined that Baby might have followed him, staying out of sight, all this time. Her persistence and loyalty touched him. He knelt and stretched his hand out to her. The little animal began to lick his fingers, buzzing loudly.

Impulsively he scooped her up in both arms and held her to his chest. After the harsh conditions among the Road Men and all that had come before, the warmth was comforting, and when he set her down, he felt stronger and more optimistic than he had in weeks.

"We've a long way to go, Baby," he said then. "It's time to get started." In answer the fox-cat trotted toward the brush, then turned and sat, watching him alertly.

He finished washing, then strapped on his new weapons and slung the bat-helmet from his belt. He began to march south, confident that Baby would follow, but had gone no more than a few paces when he heard the fox-cat's familiar "Mowr?"

He chuckled and turned to see her sitting, licking one paw. "We must be started," he said. "If you want to finish your bath, you can catch up with me."

He started out again but now heard Baby begin to howl, this time her tone clearly commanding. Puzzled, he stopped and looked back. She was sitting in the same spot, an air of obstinacy about her.

"Come along," he commanded.

Now Baby approached him, but instead of falling in step, she took the top of his boot in her mouth and began to pull.

"I don't have time to play games," he said, exasperated. "I'm glad to see you too. But Evvy is in danger."

At that the little animal stood back and let out a drawn-out howl, then began to trot briskly to the east. At the edge of the brush she stopped and looked back, then again made the strange howling noise.

Suddenly wondering if she were ill, Zach took a step toward her in concern. She yowled once again, this time more quietly, and again set out. Finally Zach understood. "You want me to follow you," he said.

In a caricature of human relief, the fox-cat bounded up to him and rubbed against his knees, then set off at a brisk pace, stopping every few feet to be sure that Zach was indeed behind her. After a moment of indecision Zach decided to follow the fox-cat. She was obviously much more intelligent than he had ever given her credit for, and she must have a reason for wanting to go in that direction. In any case, he would have to go east sooner or later; he had thought of following the river only for the certainty of fresh drinking water.

For the rest of the afternoon Baby led Zach east. He began to worry as she veered north but decided to let her continue for the time being. Could she be trying to lead him back to the District? Perhaps she had forgotten Evvy and now felt that she belonged to him; it had been several months, after all, since she had seen her mistress. Yet whenever he mentioned Evvy's name, Baby always responded with a small, plaintive "Mowr," as if she truly understood what was being said.

During the day Baby had caught a large rabbit, and as the sun began to set, Zach skinned and butchered the animal, giving Baby her favorite parts, the liver and heart, then roasted the remains on a long wooden spit. He wished for his pipe and some new-smoke; while grateful for the weapons and for the other necessary items such as flint and metal that he had found in the guard's pouch, he felt vulnerable without his own gear.

He resolved that if Baby did not change direction early tomorrow, he would turn south again whether or not the animal followed. He stretched out under a lean-to of branches and twigs, the folded bat-helmet under his head, and closed his eyes.

But sleep would not come. The sounds of the woods—insects chirping, small animals scuttling about—took him in memory to other days when he had lived in the woods with Evvy and, before that, in Will's outlaw camp. Images of Will filled his mind, and he wondered how he was faring. Had he healed by now? How was he managing with one arm? Suddenly, with an aching longing that surprised him, Zach realized how much he missed his brother.

Except for his five years as a Trader prisoner, and for these past few months, Zach had been near Will for all of his adult life. He knew Will and his moods better almost than his own; even when Will was enraged, even at him, Zach always had understood the cause of the temper and how to calm it. In one matter only had the brothers been opposed, and one time only had their differences remained unresolved.

But Will had changed; Zach believed this truly, and believing it gave him renewed determination to fulfill his mission. He was seeking Evvy for her own sake, of course, but also for Will's. He did not know how he knew, but he sensed that the healing of Will's darker side that had obviously begun with his relationship with Evvy would only be complete when they were reunited.

Something soft brushed his face; he started and half sat, then saw that it was Baby, her body vibrating as she buzzed with affection. He scratched the top of her head, then lay down again. The fox-cat turned around several times and, at last comfortable, nestled her head in his beard at the hollow of his neck. Zach shut his eyes, smiling, and in a few moments he was asleep too.

The next morning Zach awoke feeling full of purpose and almost cheerful. The thoughts of Will had energized him. He looked around for Baby. He was thirsty; he would have to make or get a water skin soon. He finished the remains of the rabbit, then gathered his few belongings and prepared to set out. Just then he heard a great thrashing in the bushes, and repeated sharp "Mowrs," followed by the unmistakable nervous whistling of a mount. His heart pounding, he drew his sword and stood, waiting.

The noises grew louder, and then Zach saw a sight that almost froze him in astonishment: Baby, her fur standing out, seemed to be fighting with a large mount. In the next instant he saw that she was not fighting with it but was herding it before her. And then he realized that this must be his mount that was let go by the Traders all those months ago.

Somehow Baby had managed not only to follow and track Zach but to keep the mount as well. Watching more intently, he saw now how the little animal was able to control the much larger beast: Whenever the mount sought to turn and break away, Baby darted in and nipped lightly at its ankles, her remarkable speed allowing her to avoid the sharp hooves.

The sight was so startling that Zach could not help laughing in relief and gratitude. "Good work, Baby," he told the fox-cat. "This will make our task much easier."

The mount had no saddle or leads, so he would have to ride bareback, a tricky proposition. The mount was as skittish and ill tempered as all such animals but was obviously terrified of Baby. Zach walked slowly toward it, speaking in low, gentle tones. The mount danced away, whistling in alarm, then, with a frightened roll of her eyes, she gradually calmed. He put his hand on the beast's neck and stroked her a moment, then swung himself up. When he was sure that she wouldn't try to throw him, he pressed his knees into her flanks. "Come on, girl," he said. "Let's go."

He traveled south for several days, noting with apprehension the increasing signs of spring. He estimated that he had at best one or two weeks until the day of the sacrifice. This part of the world was more sparsely populated than the District, but as he had hoped, he was lucky enough to come upon a small settlement. Although several of the residents wore the wooden double spiral, they were not Traders and did not know where the Trader capital was. He exchanged his extra sword for a poorly made but serviceable saddle and blanket and a water skin. Once she had been properly saddled and no longer had to bear Zach's weight directly on her spine, the mount settled down and began to travel more quickly.

The landscape began to appear more familiar, more like

the hilly, desolate area where he had been kept prisoner. He had been brought to the Trader town from the opposite direction before. He knew he must be close but didn't know whether it lay to the north or south.

Then, quite suddenly, almost as if it had appeared before him in a dream, he found himself looking from a distance at the village green, surrounded by wretched huts and a few structures, including the prison, built upon the ruins of pre-Change buildings. At one end of the green was the altar where he had sung his famous song.

He was so shocked that for a moment he froze, then he quickly dismounted and led the mount back into the woods to hide it. He had seen no one on the green; he prayed that no one had seen him.

He was not certain what to do next; clearly he must not allow himself to be recognized. Instructing Baby to remain with the mount and be silent, he began to circle around the village, hoping for a sign of Evvy. After only a few minutes he realized that something was wrong. The square was not just temporarily deserted: the entire settlement seemed to have been abandoned. His mouth suddenly dry, he wondered if he had arrived too late.

He cautiously approached one of the huts and looked inside, wrinkling his nose at the stink that still permeated it. There was nothing here. He checked one or two others, but all were empty.

At last he forced himself to approach the prison, then to step inside. Again the fear of imprisonment welled up, almost nauseating him. His heart pounded fiercely and he gritted his teeth, then opened the inner door and stepped into the basement where his cell had been. In the near total darkness he could see nothing. He stood and listened, but all he heard was the distant sound of dripping water. "Hello," he called, but all he received in reply was an echo. The familiar stench of the cells was beginning to choke him, and he backed out without exploring further, to think what to do next.

Just as he turned to push against the rotting outer door, a hand closed on his wrist.

"Halt, stranger!" said a voice in the gloom. "What do you think you're doing?"

Ten

The Principal felt like a prisoner in his own House. Everywhere he went now he heard the alien voices of women, smelled their sweetish, unmasculine odors. He had constantly to fight the irrational, claustrophobic feeling that once again he was a child in the Garden, his every move dictated by women in white, foremost among them the Mistress, his mother.

Yet he had to admit that the two dozen female guards were as capable as any of his own men. And, being from the Garden, there was no danger of any of them falling into the barbarous superstition of Trader beliefs.

Exasperated with the situation and with himself, he sighed. He looked down at the growing pile of papers on his desk, then turned back to the window. Both of Daniel's ideas, as Red had said, had been good ones. Certainly the atmosphere in his House had become more relaxed since the women came; their presence and that of the large rusted machine now resting outside the main entrance gate had eased everyone's fears about Trader infiltrators. A number of servants had resigned immediately when the machine had been installed. Eric had wanted to have them all questioned for Trader beliefs, but several had been with the Principal for many years; he had not the heart for it, nor did he really believe that any of them was capable of treachery. Still, he breathed easier knowing that those who remained were free of the most extreme superstition. Odell continued to oversee the House but uneasily made the sign of the double spiral each time he passed the machine.

The plan to place a machine at the entrance to the Clinic had finally been rejected; too many of the populace were too superstitious.

He felt more than ever that the only proof against falling into Trader beliefs was sound education, such as he and Zach and all the women had received at the Garden. But in a population as poor and superstitious as this, where the primary concern of most citizens was simply filling their bellies, it was difficult to make clear the importance of literacy and rudimentary hygienic knowledge. Just lately the task was beginning to seem beyond him, as were the myriad details of administering his House and his government. Even the most routine of duties, such as hearing the petitioners who visited him twice a month to appeal decisions made by his judges, had recently seemed more arduous than he could bear, and he had twice now postponed that regular meeting. In the past Zach had sometimes heard petitioners in his place, but once again, at a most critical time, he was missing. The Principal had had no word of him for several months now. Nor of Evvy.

He looked again at the unfinished business on his desk, then pushed himself back and stood. "Robin!" he shouted. Almost immediately the old man appeared, looking wary. Although he had long been accustomed to his master's bursts of anger, they had been coming more frequently of late.

"Has the latest message come from General Quentin?" he asked.

"No, sir," said the old secretary patiently. "I have promised to inform you the very minute that a runner arrives."

"Yes, of course," said the Principal, embarrassed at having shown his impatience so openly. "If you have occasion to see General Ralf, tell him I am waiting for his monthly recruitment report."

The old man frowned, then spoke hesitantly. "That report has been on your desk for three days," he said.

"What?" The Principal bent over his desk and pawed through the haphazard scatter of papers. "Why didn't you tell me when it came in?"

Robin opened his mouth in protest, then shut it again. "I'm sorry, sir," he mumbled.

At last the Principal pulled the report from beneath a heap of papers on which Napoleon had been napping. He looked at it a moment and realized that he had reviewed it already yesterday or the day before. How could he have forgotten? To cover his confusion he quickly read through the report again, then initialed it, adding a short note.

"Have this returned to General Ralf at once," he said. "I will be waiting for his reply. In the meantime I will be on the terrace."

Brusquely he strode from the room, nearly colliding with Martha, the thick-bodied woman guard. "Out of my way," he grumbled, and headed for the terrace, Napoleon scampering behind him.

Half the terrace was now taken up with a large wooden cage full of young black-and-white birds. He wrinkled his nose at the sharp odor. Napoleon's ears twitched, and he began to growl deep in his throat.

"Napoleon!" said the Principal sharply.

At the sound of his master's rebuke the fox-cat looked up, then yawned ostentatiously and began to lick his front paws with full attention, as if he had not just then been hungrily eyeing the caged birds. Will chuckled, and then, awkwardly, using the stump of his right arm and his left hand, opened the cage. He was becoming more dexterous every day—his writing was now indistinguishable from his old hand. But he still felt awkward and unbalanced much of the time, and the ghost of his missing right arm often ached unbearably. His thoughts again flashed briefly to Evvy, and he wondered what she would feel when she saw him as he was now. At night, in his dreams, he was still a whole man.

He reached into the cage and caught the largest of the nestlings, a brilliant white bird with bands of fuzzy black just beginning to show on its wing tips. When he had first seen this one, he had named it Patrick.

The birds had been purchased from a farmer who trained

birds to race; they were a new-bird that had replaced the once numerous homing birds that had been used for racing and to carry messages in the past. He had sent Lindy to train for several days with the farmer and had ordered his librarian to search the library for ancient books on homing birds.

He turned to see Lindy stepping onto the terrace with a large pail of water. "Good afternoon, sir," the boy said.

"Good afternoon," grunted the Principal. "We begin training the birds today."

"Yes, sir."

The Principal watched while Lindy swept the droppings from the bottom of the cage and then washed it with soap. The cage was constructed in three parts: a large, wickerwork flying area with perches set into the wall supports at regular intervals; to one side a smaller cage where the birds rested and fed; and, beneath all, under a screen made of woven twigs, an open area that could be easily reached to clean out the droppings. The droppings themselves were saved and given to the gardeners, who used them for fertilizer.

The smaller, inner cage had been constructed with a kind of trapdoor that could be opened from the outside when pushed against but which would not move when pressed from the inside. The first step in training involved placing grain just inside the cage, then putting a young bird on the landing area outside the open trapdoor. After a moment the bird would hop across the threshold for its reward. After all the birds were accustomed to entering the cage, the next step was to train them to push against the trap to open it. This was to be practiced over and over until each bird had learned the procedure.

Training the birds was tedious, but the Principal was finding that he enjoyed it. It was pleasant to be outdoors, away from the pressures of his office and his subordinates. He was pleased to see that Patrick seemed to pick up the trick more rapidly than his nest mates. After a few minutes he let Lindy continue with the training and sat, musing.

Will had learned to like touching the birds, feeling their fierce hearts beating against their soft bodies. He let himself drift in imagination to the day when there would be flocks of trained birds at each of his outposts and at the Garden; he could already see them soaring swiftly from the remote corners of the District, bearing news that would ordinarily take a rider a week or more.

If the birds had already been in place, he might now know what had become of Evvy and Zach. It had been several months now—over half a year—since Zach had set out. He felt sometimes that the intervening time had been lived in a dream and that he was a stranger to himself in that dream. For many years he had lived without close companionship, except for Zach. He had never thought seriously of marrying until his mother had, at her deathbed, urged him to marry and produce progeny to continue his rule. Since the close call at the wedding, he had begun to realize that he had made a mistake by having made no provision for succession. The way his generals increasingly behaved toward each other, especially since Red's death—the bickering, the constant elbowing for position—made him doubt that stable rule would be possible after his death. Alexander had died without heirs or a will; the rumor was that, when asked to whom his empire should pass, in a dying breath he had whispered: "To the strongest."

He must not allow the same sort of chaos to destroy what he had built. From the time he was a young boy he had had a sense of his place in history, of his destiny. It was only with the catastrophes of the recent months that he had begun to doubt: that he could no longer see, as clearly as if they sat before him on his desk, printed books of the future, as finely made as those from before the Change, each of them containing chapters devoted to Will the Principal and his successful efforts to restore civilization, to bring an end to the woman sickness, to establish a great center of civilization where once again the arts could flourish. Never in the years he had ruled the District—never until now—had he been less than certain that he would accomplish these things.

He had accomplished a great deal already, of course; despite the poverty and the bare level of subsistence in which most subjects lived, he had established schools, which were free or nominal to all citizens who could find the time to attend. Though most of the populace still could not read or write, a growing number possessed at least a rudimentary literacy. He had established healing centers, also free, and the Clinic. If he should die now, he thought, these legacies would continue and grow, and his name would live after him—as long as the District remained politically stable.

He could put it off no longer. Consideration of his succession must become one of his first priorities. He must think, and soon, about who should rule in his place in case of his early death, and even, if Zach and Evvy did not return soon, about marriage to another woman who could bear him heirs. Even a week ago such an idea would have been unthinkable—perhaps his brush with death had unearthed a slow process of thought that had until then been deeply buried by his long-standing, almost superstitious, antipathy toward women, and by his belief that he was invulnerable.

He stretched his arm out before him and flexed his fingers, studying his hand. The new musculature was apparent in the forearm. Although he had been forcing himself to walk daily and to exercise the arm, for the first time in weeks he felt an intense need for vigorous activity. Perhaps he would challenge Eric or Marcus to a footrace this evening.

"Sir?" He was brought from his musings by a tugging at his sleeve. "Sir? Are you all right?"

"Yes, of course," he told Lindy. "I was daydreaming."

"I have caught all the birds and put them through the trapdoor once."

"Then it's time to put them through again," said Will.

"Yes, sir." The boy returned to the cage and caught a bird. "Sir?"

"Yes, Lindy?"

"You still miss them, don't you?"

"What?" Will was puzzled, wondering what the boy meant, then he realized that he was referring to Zach and Evvy. Had his thoughts really been so obvious? "Yes," he said. "I do."

"I hope for your sake they return very soon. But until they do . . . well, I'm here to help you any way I can."

"I know," said Will. "And thank you." He felt a sudden rush of affection for all those who had been with him these months: for Lindy, for Robin and Ralf, even for Daniel. They had tolerated without complaint his increasingly short temper; they had attended to work that he had not had the heart or strength to do; they had tried to cheer him with special food and drink, with companionship and jokes. He realized now that all of them must have been worrying about him, unable to end his despondency and too loyal to say anything about it directly.

Although he did not know how he knew, he was certain that the gloomy dream he had been living in had ended. His path ahead was again in sharp focus, as if it were a well-marked trail in the woods: he must devise a clear line of succession, and he must get on with the business of running the District and fighting the Traders. These must, and would be done, even if he were suddenly rendered completely armless; they must and would be accomplished whether or not he ever saw Zach or Evvy again.

He was about to thank Lindy for helping to bring him out of his self-pity when the boy spoke again. "I've just caught Patrick, your favorite," he said. "Would you like to hold him a moment?"

"Thank you, boy." The Principal took the soft little body in his hand and made chirping noises at it. This would be a star pupil, he thought. Patrick would be the father of a long and famous line of homing birds, the strongest links in District's new chain of communications.

He stood and approached the cage, then set Patrick on the landing perch. The bird gazed at him quizzically, its head tilted comically to one side, then turned to look at the grain on the other side of the threshold. Hesitating only a moment, Patrick hopped across the line and into the cage. Will grinned in satisfaction. "Good bird," he said.

"Sir?" said Lindy then.

"Yes?"

"It's good to see you smile again."

In answer Will ruffled the boy's hair and went indoors to attend to business.

Eleven

The next afternoon he and Daniel had a meeting scheduled with the leaders of the Garden. Although he had granted the request from the Garden with misgivings, dreading a confrontation with Katha, today he felt calm and confident, his mood almost buoyant as he approached his office.

He strode to his desk and sat, then asked the others to be seated.

Katha settled herself in the armchair nearest to his desk. She seemed tense, as if poised to flee. Gunda, the fat woman whose red hair was now tinged with gray, sat on the sofa, next to Lucille, the garden's chief scientist, while Daniel, looking ill at ease, chose a bench apart from the women.

Robin brought in a tray of cakes and flower-wine, and the Principal waited with impatience while the women helped themselves to refreshment. He noticed that Katha took nothing and seemed to share his impatience.

After the formalities had been observed, he spoke. "It was good of you to come all the way into the District," he said.

"We've better things to do with our time," said Katha. "But your secretary refused our request for you to visit us."

As always in her presence, the Principal felt assaulted by her tone. Had she really presumed to think that he would travel to the Garden at her whim? "State your business, then," he said brusquely. "I do not wish to waste any more of your time or my own."

Katha opened her mouth, but Gunda, who was now Mistress of the Garden, and therefore senior, spoke quickly. "Katha, please, let me explain. We're very grateful for this time, sir," she said. "We have come to give you a progress report on the testing project . . . and to ask your help."

"Yes, of course," he said, mollified. "What is it?"

"First let us explain what we are finding in our current work," she said. "Lucille?"

Now Lucille began to talk quietly and earnestly. "As you no doubt remember, sir, we believe that the woman sickness is a sort of autoimmune disease, reacting to something in femaleness itself."

"Yes," said the Principal. "That the carrying of the first affected girl-child would set up the sensitivity; the disease would then develop only with the birth of the second."

Lucille nodded and continued. "We further hypothesized that the sperm of men who are carriers are somewhat more mobile or more viable than normal sperm; this is the only way we can explain why the trait does not extinguish itself."

"One of your scientists . . . Evvy . . . told me that you were looking for a way to test the sperm."

"So far we can only determine which men are carriers by inference," she said. "But as a result of all the testing, we have found something new." She paused, then went on, her excitement evident. "Of the hundreds of women we have tested, as many as ten percent who show positive for the trait have produced more than one healthy daughter."

The Principal raised an eyebrow. "That is startling news," he said. "What does it mean?"

"Well, it could mean that there is something wrong with the testing procedure," she said. "It could also—and this is what we find exciting—it could also mean that the illness is becoming less potent or that some women are beginning to develop resistance to it."

Will looked at her, his mind only just beginning to take in the significance of what she was saying. "Then you think . . ."

"It's only a hope. But if it's true, then the woman sickness may no longer be the threat to our survival that we once thought. And if we can identify these women and encourage them to have many children, their resistance should quickly spread through the next generation."

She continued to talk enthusiastically, but the Principal was no longer listening. Although the question of the woman sickness interested him, he did not see it as a scientific problem so much as a political one. Eliminating the disease had always been his highest priority, both because the fact of it contributed to hopelessness and apathy and because it was a very real threat to the survival of the species. But now, if indeed it was no longer as deadly as it had always appeared, he might be able to use the testing project directly to combat the challenge from the Traders. If it could be proven to large enough numbers of the District's population that only science, the antithesis of Traderism, could save them, it would be bound to cut into support for the new religion.

"This is a real achievement," he said when Lucille had finished speaking. "And I'll do everything in my power to help you carry it further. Only tell me what you want."

"Two things," said Gunda, nervously licking her lips. "First of all, and most obviously, we must extend the testing project as soon as possible to as large a group of people as possible."

"We have been discussing expansion, sir," said Daniel, speaking for the first time. "I am prepared to train as many as five new technicians a month, but I know that your budget for the project is already under a strain."

"We will find a way to finance it," said the Principal. "This is too important not to give it every effort. And what is the second thing?" he said, addressing Gunda.

Before Gunda could speak, Katha, who had sat silent during the scientific discussion, leaned forward in her chair. "You speak of resources," she said. "Do you have any idea how you have strained our resources at the Garden by taking so many of our women?"

"I am paying you well for them," he said.

"We have no need for metal!" she said. "As you know very well. We grow or manufacture nearly everything we need. I mean to say—"

"She means to say that our womanpower is stretched thin," said Gunda, smoothly cutting Katha off again.

"Then you want them back?" he asked. Inwardly he felt

relieved; while it was true that the women guards had seemed to improve security, in some respects they had created added problems: a number of his remaining men guards were jealous and angry at being usurped by women while others looked upon them as sexual prey.

"No, sir, it is not that at all," said Gunda. "We are very proud to be helping to protect you. After all, the stability of your society makes our continued security possible. But we need more women with whom we can conduct our breeding experiments, as well as those we can train to carry on the scientific work."

"And soldiers and guards for our own compound," Katha added, her voice still carrying an edge.

The Principal frowned. "The Garden has always survived and grown with those who are born there and those who find their way there."

"That is true," said Gunda. "But fewer come to us now than did in the past, perhaps because we are so isolated. In fact, only those who deliberately seek us out, like the new member we received last week, ever even find us. But those few instances will not be enough now. We must increase our numbers quickly, without waiting for our girl-children to grow up."

The Principal shrugged. "I would be happy to help you if I could," he said. "But as you well know, there are few unattached women anywhere in the world."

"Except for one place," said Gunda. She exchanged a wary look with Daniel. They had evidently discussed this before. "Or, rather, I should say one sort of place."

The Principal suddenly understood. "The state houses of women for hire," he said.

"Yes." She looked unaccountably embarrassed. The houses of women for hire, and other institutions housing young boys for hire, were run by the Principal as a public service. He had nationalized the houses and placed trustworthy men in charge as soon as he had taken control of the District from the President, realizing their importance in an era when many men had little chance of a woman to marry, even shared. There was never a shortage of women in the houses; always there were some who did not wish to marry and preferred to make their own living this way, just as there were always families ready to sell that most precious of commodities—a girl-child. Although he kept the fees at the houses nominal, they were in such demand that the workers made good livings, and the houses themselves brought him a significant tax revenue.

"You want to take women from the houses, then?" he said.

"Any who will come with us willingly," said Gunda. She had colored, her face becoming splotchy, and she did not meet his eyes. Puzzled, he looked to Daniel, but he, too, averted his eyes. Only Katha, whose face was fixed in a glare, continued to look directly at him. Sounding even more uncertain, Gunda continued: "Also, sir, with your permission, we would like to have first chance at any young girls whose families sell them to the brothels. To offer them the choice to come with us; of course we will pay you for anyone we take."

The Principal could not understand her manner or that of the others. Did they think he would fear that the houses would become depleted? They must know how unlikely it was that all women for hire in the Capital would suddenly defect to the Garden; in any case, the shortage of women was so severe that a dozen fewer available would make little difference to the men of the District. And as for the young girls— Suddenly the Principal understood Gunda's embarrassment and her reluctance to open the subject. It had long been known that the Principal was given first pick of all girls just being sold to houses for hire; undoubtedly Gunda and even Daniel did not know that he had stopped this custom long ago, even before he had realized that he loved Evvy. His appetite for very young girls had never totally disappeared, but the uncontrollable compulsion to satisfy it had gone.

He flushed, annoyed and embarrassed that he was evidently still seen by the Garden and even by his own aides as a man who could not master his passions. The annoyance began to grow into anger, and he turned away and took a long, deep breath. Suddenly, without warning, the anger vanished, and the pent-up breath exploded in laughter. The whole thing was absurd. "Of course you may choose women from the houses," he said. "As many as you wish, as often as you wish. And you are welcome to all the young girls whose parents are forced to sell them. In fact, come with me now and we will speak to my head procurer."

Gunda smiled with relief. Daniel looked at him speculatively and seemed about to speak but said nothing.

As they walked from the House, flanked by guards from the Garden, Will felt a sudden prickle of unease. It was all very well to say that his compulsion was gone, but in truth he had not met any young girls in a very long time. Suppose he should see a girl of the type he had always preferred? Would he be able to return to his own House and forget her?

In the large, comfortable living room of the ancient town house that served as the central house of women for hire in the Capital, the Principal explained the situation to the chief procurer. Cyrus, the procurer, a tremendously fat man with a jolly face and hearty laugh, looked out of place among the delicate pre-Change furniture and wall hangings, as did the women from the Garden, particularly Katha in her warrior's garb.

"These women wish to be notified when any young girls come in," the Principal finished. "Send word to Daniel at the Clinic, or to my House, and I will see that they receive the message."

The procurer seemed astonished and looked as if he only half believed him. *Perhaps*, the Principal thought, *he thinks this is a new plan for me to take the girls secretly.*

"As a matter of fact, we got a young one just this morning," Cyrus said. He rang a bell rope at his side, and a serving boy appeared. "Bring the girl who came in this morning," he said. "She's resting now, she ain't even started her training yet," he told the women. "You are welcome to her as long as you pay."

Presently the young boy returned, leading an even younger girl by the hand. She was dark: dusky-skinned and brown-eyed, with long black curls, and her face was frozen in an expression of terror. As soon as she entered the room, the Principal felt a physical jolt, and the ghost of his old compulsion began to rise. He forced himself to continue looking at the girl, to see her as who she was: a frightened child who had been sold by her parents. He breathed deeply and evenly as Gunda rose and went to the girl, gathering her into her arms and speaking soothingly. She whispered in the child's ear at length, and at last the little girl nodded and smiled.

"We will pay you for her—and a bit extra," she said. "And now, may we speak to the other women here?"

"There are perhaps two dozen at the moment," said Cyrus. "I will bring those who are not working."

The Principal stood and took his leave, leaving the women to their task. The girl-child looked at him in curiosity, and he found that he was able to smile at her in return. He had turned and was about to go when a door to his right opened and the women for hire filed into the room. One of them caught his eye, her face strikingly familiar, but he could not think where he had seen her. Of course, he had had many women for hire over the years and could not be expected to remember the name of each, but this girl . . . Suddenly he recognized her: the freckles, the thick yellow hair like straw; she was older now, but there was no doubt that this was Lina, the last girl he had ever bought, purchased during a trip alone in the woods.

He had kept her with him for several months and had even grown fond of her, as fond as he had ever been able to feel in those days. But he had let her go just before leaving to evacuate the old Garden and had never learned what had become of her. All girls that he bought were given metal when discharged, and Robin was instructed to find them suitable husbands if they wished or see them safely in a state-run house for hire.

The girl recognized him, too; her eyes widened and suddenly filled with tears. He saw her glance at his empty sleeve, then look quickly away. Self-consciously he turned again to go, but something kept him from leaving. Perhaps it was the look of recognition, the tears, or simply the desire to find out if she still hated him. As the women continued to file into the room he beckoned her aside.

"Lina?"

"Yes," she said, her eyes lowered. "I am surprised you remember me."

"I could not forget you," he said. "I have often wondered how you were faring." This was a lie; he had not thought of her once since letting her go, but she seemed to draw strength from the remark and looked up at him again, the tears now brimming over.

"I have thought of you every minute of every day," she said. "That is why I am still here, why I have not married. After you there could never be another man."

The Principal was embarrassed; after the way he had mistreated the girl, to be rewarded with such devotion was almost obscene. He remembered again that Lina had been infatuated with him even before he had bought her; perhaps the old romantic tales were right, and it was true that for each person there was only one great love. For Zach it had been Leya; for himself, Evvy; and for Evvy...

"Lina," he said suddenly. "Are you engaged this evening?"

"No, sir," she said. "Not yet."

"Well, then... would you like to have dinner with me? And talk, for old times' sake? Please say yes. Please come home with me now."

Twelve

Evvy awoke before sunrise. She felt as if she had not slept the whole night, though she knew she must have dozed, for her mind was filled with confused images from her past. At one moment it seemed as if she were lying in the sleeping loft above her parents' cabin, listening to the sleepy rustles of her five younger brothers; then the noises changed to forest sounds, and she was riding with Zach, secure and warm in the saddle in front of him; then she was sitting by an evening camp fire, laughing, listening as he sang, the melancholy tones of the feathered lyre reverberating around her. Once again she was a novitiate in the Garden, dreaming of Zach each night, touching with secret longing the feather bracelet he had made for her. And she dreamed of Will. Will, whose dark eyes sometimes sparkled as if he alone held the secret of life, whose animated, mobile face could change from a happy smile to frightening anger as quickly as a ripple could travel the surface of a pond. Will, who from the moment their eyes had first met, had frightened and attracted her at the same time. Will the Principal, who had sent Zach to buy her from her parents, and who, years later, had admitted to her the reputation of his cruelty. Will, nearly her husband, the only man she had ever lain with, whose fingers had seemed to burn her flesh.

Both Will and Zach had saved her life, at risk to their own. But now there was no one to save her. Now, today, soon, she would die. Her flesh would burn literally, as did the books in the Trader services each morning.

Although it was not yet dawn, the nighttime sky had lost its quality of utter darkness, and soon she was able to see the individual thongs that sealed the opening of her tent. She tried to swallow, but her throat was dry, though her eyes were burning with dammed-up tears. She didn't want to die. She was afraid of the pain and of the final farewell to the sky, clouds, trees, and to the two men she loved above all else in the world. If the ancient religion were right, they might again be together, the three of them, in the next world, but she wanted them here now, with a longing that made her throat ache.

When Billy had told her what was to happen to her, she had at first been so shocked that she didn't understand. He made her sit down, then explained that it was an honor, that she would be purified in the flames as her wickedness was burned from her and her life given as an offering in memory of Yosh, who had given his own life to combat the evils of science.

But as he spoke, Billy stumbled over his words, and Evvy sensed that he was repeating them by rote, didn't really believe them.

"How can you say it's an honor?" she asked finally, still trying to calm the beating of her heart, still trying to find a way to believe that this could not be true.

"To die in Yosh's memory is an honor," he repeated. But his voice was shaky. "I was not supposed to tell you, Sister. The Bishops would have explained it later today. I . . . I thought you might feel better hearing it from me. That perhaps I could make you understand."

"I don't understand!" she said then. "I don't understand how you can do such a thing! I thought you were my friend! I thought we cared about each other!"

"We do! I am your friend—" said Billy, but Evvy turned her back on him and began to sob.

"Get out," she said. "Get out. I don't want to talk to you. I don't want to see you again."

"Sister Evvy—" She turned and saw Billy standing at the doorway, his face twisted in anguish, his hands knotted into fists.

"Get out!" she said again. "Leave me alone!"

"I'm sorry," he muttered, and then he was gone and the guards shut the door, stopping it with the three heavy bars.

Later that afternoon Brother John and the other two Bishops came to visit her. "Your instructor Billy has confessed to us his error in telling you of the sacrifice," said the old man without preamble. "He should have left it to us. He will be punished."

For a moment Evvy felt ashamed, sorry that she had caused trouble for Billy, but in the next instant she was angry again. "You have no right! If you planned to kill me, why didn't you do it when you captured me instead of tormenting me for all these months!"

The Bishop continued to talk calmly, as if he had not noticed her anger. "It was necessary for you to receive instruction," he said, "so that you may be purified of your scientific beliefs. The last of them will be destroyed in the clean fire."

"I've never believed any of your instruction!" she said. "It's all filthy lies!"

"I understand you need to say that now," said Brother John. "But you have learned the verses and have repeated them. They have entered into your soul. The process of purification is already under way. It will be completed at the ceremony."

Evvy was so angry that she wanted to strike the Bishop.

"Let us pray together for guidance, Sister," he said after a moment.

"No!" she said. "I won't pray with you! I won't say your poisonous lies again! Leave me alone!"

"As you wish," said the Bishop. "We will return for you tomorrow morning to begin the journey west."

When the Bishops had left, Evvy felt her anger leave with them, as if a clay pot had burst and all the water inside it had poured out. In its place was numbness and disbelief. Surely they could not so coldly kill her? In all the time she had been here she had never seen a human being burned, only books. Although she knew that Traders did not take male prisoners, she had never wondered what they did with the men they captured. Did they burn them? Or was that only reserved for special holy occasions? It simply could not be. Perhaps this was another Trader trick, designed to frighten her into believing in their ideas. Perhaps if she played along, again pretended to believe the nonsense in their chants and songs . . .

She pressed her hands into her face so tightly that stars came to her eyes. Nearly three weeks still remained. Perhaps something would happen before that time.

The next morning the Bishops returned and led her from the cell. She had scarcely a moment to enjoy the fresh spring air, for she was immediately put into a small covered wagon and the journey began. She thought of trying to escape, but someone was with her always, even when she slept. The farther the little caravan moved from the Trader capital, the less hope remained to her. Even if Zach or Will were somehow planning to rescue her, they would have no way of knowing where she had gone.

Once or twice each day Brother John joined her to chant and pray. Numbly she mumbled the chants, simply to avoid talking to him. She missed Billy and one day asked about him.

"As I told you, Brother Billy is being punished for his transgression. He can no longer be trusted to instruct prisoners. He is deeply sorry for what he has done."

"Was he—did you leave him behind?"

"No one was left, for we are moving our capital to the holy birthplace of Brother Yosh. Don't worry about Brother Billy, but rather concentrate on the salvation of your own soul. It is not too late for you to be saved, Sister."

She was kept confined inside the wagon during the entire journey. Although she could see the trees and sky through small openings in the skins covering the wagon, she felt in some ways more confined than she had been in the cell. When the caravan finally stopped, after nearly three weeks, and she was transferred to a comparatively large tent, she was almost relieved.

After her evening meal Brother John and the other two

Bishops came to the tent and squatted, facing her. "We want you to understand what will happen tomorrow," said Brother John. "At first light Traders from all over the region, some even as far as the District, will gather in front of the altar. Then the chanting will begin, and the singing, all in praise of Brother Yosh and the truths he revealed to us. When the voices of praise have filled the heavens, we will bring you from this tent and lead you to the altar. You will be tied to the stake and join us in singing the holy words. Then we will burn the evil artifacts of science, and from that purifying, fire will light the kindling at your feet."

Evvy listened numbly, as if the events he described were going to happen to another person, and not to her. She could picture it all quite clearly, until the moment when the flames began to burn her flesh. When she got to that part, she felt dizzy and was no longer able to imagine anything.

"One thing more," said the Bishop. "Brother Billy has begged to see you one last time. He is outside now, if you wish to see him."

"Yes," Evvy murmured, her mouth so dry that she could scarcely speak. "Please let him come in."

Billy entered and knelt at the entrance to the tent, not meeting her eyes. She saw with shock that both of his eyes were blackened, and fading yellow bruises showed on his cheeks. He looked so miserable that she wanted to hug him and tell him that everything was all right.

At last he looked at her, the yearning and love in his face so evident that she was embarrassed. After clearing his throat once, he spoke. "Good-bye, Sister Evvy," he said. "I will never forget you."

"Good-bye, Brother Billy," she said. She turned away to hide the tears in her eyes.

The sky outside had grown noticeably lighter now, and Evvy moved to the front of the tent and peered out through a narrow space between the thongs. At the edge of her vision, at the end of the clearing, she could see a dark shape where the altar and the pyre would be. Already there were dim forms moving in the semidarkness: Traders crowding near the altar, anxious to get a good view of the day's service.

She turned from the opening in despair. What would Will

do in this situation? she wondered. She could imagine him sitting quietly in the tent, perhaps putting the finishing touches to a weapon he had made, rehearsing in his mind just how he would attack and overpower the guards and make his escape.

And Zach . . . Zach would have created a plan, a means of somehow outwitting his captors, of turning the ceremony to his advantage and then slipping away.

But Evvy, though strong and trained in weapons work, was no match for the large men guarding her, and although she knew she was clever, hers was a practical intelligence, given to solving immediate problems of daily living.

There was nothing she could do. She prayed that she would maintain the strength to be brave, not to beg or to disgrace the Garden in any way.

Thirteen

The sky was rapidly beginning to lighten as Zach found a place among the early worshipers gathering to witness the sacrifice. He still marveled that he had been able to find this site in time. It was only luck that he had been surprised by Father Tree, who had unwittingly told him all he needed to know.

When the hand had closed on his wrist at the entrance to the Trader prison, Zach had instinctively reached out in the darkness and grabbed a handful of rags covering a light, bony frame.

"Take it easy, stranger!" the creaky old voice protested.

Shaking with reaction, Zach pulled the struggling figure into the light. He found himself looking at perhaps the oldest human being he had ever seen, the wizened face deeply encrusted with layers of grime.

"Who are you?" he asked, astonished.

"Better I ask you. This is my home. What are you doing here?"

"Where are the Traders? Where have they gone?"

"To the devil," said the old man, squinting against the sun. "And good riddance to them."

The man's voice was somehow familiar, and now Zach

remembered where he had heard it before. "You were a prisoner here," he said.

"That I was," the man agreed. "Their most important prisoner. Father Tree is my name. I am the spirit of the forest. They locked me up to silence me."

Zach remembered the shrieks and incoherent mumblings he had heard during the long days and nights in his cell. He had once or twice tried to enter into conversation with his unseen fellow prisoner but had given it up when the only response he received was that the man was the son of God and that all who disbelieved in him would be damned.

"What are you doing here now?" he asked.

"They forgot about me. I had loosened the bars in my window years ago. When they were all gone, I crawled out."

Looking at him, Zach realized that the old man was thin enough to have accomplished what he said. "Do you know where they have gone?" he asked.

"I know everything," said the old man.

Zach took a deep breath. "They have taken my daughter," he said. "I want her back."

The old man nodded. "They have no respect for the truth," he said. "They would not let my worshipers come to me."

Zach considered. The old man was confused, but it seemed likely that he knew something about the disappearance of the Traders. It was just a matter of asking the right questions.

"How long ago did they leave?" he asked.

"A year, I think," said Father Tree. "Or maybe it was last week."

From the still-tended appearance of the altar Zach judged that a week was closer to the truth. "Which direction did they travel?"

"You must ask my children."

"Your children?"

"The trees and bushes. If you can read their signs, they will take you to the Traders."

Zach nodded. If an entire town full of people had traveled recently, tracking them should not be difficult. "Thank you, Father Tree," he said. "Is there anything I can do for you?"

"Only tell my worshipers where I am. Tell them they can come to me now."

"How will I know them?" Zach asked.

"They will be looking for me," Father Tree replied. He spoke with certainty and calmness. "I must go back inside now," he said. "I cannot be in the sun for more than a few minutes."

"Good luck to you," said Zach. "I will give your worshipers your message."

Retrieving the mount, he began to explore the woods around the settlement. As Father Tree had suggested, the signs of passage of a large number of Traders were easy to see, even a week or two after the fact. He set off for the west, riding long and hard, and only stopped when the mount began to display the sluggish behavior of her coming nighttime immobilization.

Three days later Zach surprised a party of Trader pilgrims, and after that he traveled parallel to them, in the woods. After a time the woods began increasingly to thin out and were replaced with rolling hills and grassland. At last, breaking the crest of a hill, he came upon a vast plain crowded with the tents of hundreds of Traders. Circling wide, he surveyed the area and discovered a small settlement at the base of a steep hill. He made camp on the far side of the hill, and the next morning left Baby with his mount and weapons, except for the knife, which he concealed beneath his clothing, and walked back to the plain where groups and families of Traders were gathered.

Speaking as little as possible, he learned that the sacrifice was to be held the following morning. That night he explained his plan to Baby, hoping that she understood, then lay down to sleep. He had thought that he might be able to rescue Evvy before the ceremony began but was unable to discover where she was being kept and did not dare to ask too many questions for fear of being recognized.

In the pre-dawn hours he drifted back to the group of Trader pilgrims, and, leaning on a walking stick to minimize his height, his face again hidden under his hood, he walked into the new Trader town, found a place to sit near the altar, and waited.

The altar, he could see as the sky began to brighten, was covered with early spring flowers, as the altar in the original Trader capital had been covered with late summer flowers on the day he had made his escape. In front of it and to one side a thick stake was driven into the ground, all around it a pile of kindling. Behind the altar was the wooded hill, on the far side of which his mount and weapons waited.

The green began to fill with Traders; the larger the crowd grew, the more secure he felt. Only a handful of Traders knew him well enough to recognize him; of these, Jonna was dead. He continued to sit hunched, not removing his hood as did many of the others when the day began to grow warm.

Although no Bishops had yet appeared, the crowd began one of the simple-minded Trader chants. He could not quite remember the words, but Zach moved his lips in the same rhythm as those around him.

Zach was made aware by his growing stiffness that a good bit of time had passed, and finally, when the sun had fully topped the horizon, the three Trader Bishops, the same three who had ruled when he had been here, dressed in their filthy blue ceremonial robes, crossed the green and approached the open altar. Zach was startled as the Bishops began to lead the crowd in one of the songs he himself had written during the time he had been held prisoner. The song had evidently become well known, because most of the Traders around him joined in, and after a moment or so, so did he, with a private sense of irony.

The Chief Bishop now began to address the crowd, speaking of the meaning of this occasion, a celebration of the anniversary of the birth of beloved Brother Yosh. The old man droned on for some time, and then at last, at a signal, the lesser Bishops stepped away from the altar and approached a small tent to one side of the crowd. A few moments later they returned, leading Evvy between them. Zach's heart thumped heavily when he first caught sight of her. Her arms were bound tightly to her sides, and she was dressed in a filthy, tattered gray robe, a travesty of the white gown she had worn at the wedding. She had managed somehow to groom her rich brown hair, and its golden strands shone in the sunlight as they had the first time he had seen her. She was facing away from him, so he couldn't see her expression, but she walked stiffly, awkwardly, once stumbling badly. Perhaps, he thought, she had been drugged.

Now her captors tied her to the stake with ropes at her neck, waist, and ankles. It would be difficult, Zach thought, to free her in the few seconds he would have. If he were unable to loosen her bonds in time, he was prepared to kill her quickly, before the flames could reach her, even if it meant his own capture.

He edged a bit closer along with the rest of the crowd as the Chief Bishop began a harangue about the evils of science. Now he could see Evvy's pale face clearly, her plum-colored eyes enormous. As always when he looked directly at her, his heart seemed to stop; her beauty seemed to have an effect on the crowd, too, which had become hushed, almost reverent.

Zach scanned beyond the crowd, looking for the fox-cat. There was no sign of her, but he had not really expected her to understand his complicated instructions. And then, suddenly, he saw a ripple in the tall grass, as if a small breeze were passing. He could just make out the dark-tipped end of Baby's tail as she stalked, her body nearly flat against the ground, moving in short, liquid spurts toward the altar.

"Our Brother Yosh has commanded us to trade all the evils of science for the goodness and light of God's holy way," the Bishop was saying. "With this consecration of a holy shrine to his memory, we will begin to fully carry out that command. From this day forward, let Trader men and women go forth to the District. Let each Trader teach others of Yosh's holy words, and let no scientists live to spread their evil lies. Let this ceremony today signal the beginning of a new world where science will be no more, and the truth of nature will at last reign on earth."

Listening to the Bishop, Zach realized that the Traders were launching a new, more militant phase in their proselytizing. He wished there were some way he could send word to Will; and he feared more than ever what might happen if he were unsuccessful here this morning.

The Bishop approached a flat rock set on an upright log in front of the altar, on which a pyre, the miniature of Evvy's, was laid. Then, from the back of the altar he took a branch, its bark scraped off to reveal the wood gleaming white like bone, and touched it to a glowing coal in the brazier beside the smaller pyre. Zach could smell the fragrance as the branch began to burn, and then the Bishop touched its flaming end to the small pyre. Zach thought he heard Evvy gasp as the flame touched the tinder, but perhaps it was simply the sound of fire passing from one place to another. He pressed even closer, shuffling on his knees. Although a number of Traders were between him and the altar, he thought he could reach it in one bound.

The dry tinder was already flaming brightly, and now it began to consume the dusty ancient book laid atop it. "Thus we trade the evil work of science, this book, for the clean flame and ash of nature's God," said the Bishop.

There was more responsive chanting and then another song. The tune was hauntingly familiar, and Zach felt a chill as he recognized "The Death of Our Brother," the last song he had written for the Traders, which had apparently become a holy anthem. When the final verse had been sung, the Bishop raised his hands for silence. He took the branch, still burning, and approached the larger pyre where Evvy was bound.

"Just as we Trade the evil things of science for the righteous works of God, so do we purify those things that cannot be Traded. We have before us a woman who has been possessed by the devil. She is a practicing scientist, in service to the Principal, who murdered our beloved leader Yosh."

The crowd murmured angrily. The Bishop raised his hand for silence and continued. "You can see from the fear on her face that she dreads the fire, believing it to be punishment. But it is not so." He approached Evvy and began to talk to her directly. "Be not afraid, Sister. It is our intention only to purify you, to burn out the evils of science that the devil has placed in you. There will be pain, but only that of the dark one, resisting as his hold on the world is loosened. When you have been completely cleansed, and your body is ashes, you will be greeted by Brother Yosh and others who have gone before you to prepare for a world where all traces of science are gone, an innocent, godly world, which the Change only served to announce." He paused a moment. "Do you wish to speak?"

Evvy had looked at the Bishop as he spoke, catching every word, her face composed. Silent tears now brimmed over her eyes and began to trickle down her face, but her expression remained composed, even calm.

"I know that you mean well," she told the Bishop. "I know you are not deliberately cruel people," she continued, addressing the crowd. "But you are all wrong! You don't understand the truth! If you achieve your wish and wipe out all workers in science, you condemn the human race! We are so close to an answer—"

"Enough!" said the Bishop. "Do you wish to recant?"

Evvy looked at him a moment, then at the still-smoldering remains of the book. "No," she said.

The fox-cat had crept to within distance of springing. Zach watched as the tip of her tail flicked just above the top of the grass. The Bishop took another newly scraped branch and held it aloft.

"In the name of the God of nature..." he intoned.

"The God of nature is the true and only God," responded the congregation.

"We prepare now in holiness to sanctify this shrine and to purify this scientist, driving from her the devil of science." He touched the branch to the brazier.

"The devil has been with us always," said the crowd. "The devil is the Change, and his name is science."

"Let the purification begin." The Bishop slowly brought the burning wand down to the pyre. Evvy shut her eyes tightly, tears spilling under her lashes.

It was time to act. Zach reached under his cloak for the knife and, at the same instant, felt his hood being pulled from his head.

Startled, he looked up and found himself staring into a homely pockmarked face, the pale blue eyes wide with surprise. "Brother Zach!" said Billy. "What are you doing here?"

Fourteen

"Billy!" Zach could scarcely believe what he was seeing. Kneeling next to him in the crowd, the pocked scars on his face livid against his pale and bruised skin, was the young Trader who for four years had instructed Zach in Trader beliefs. No longer a tentative, skinny boy, Billy had filled out and grown in the year since Zach had seen him last.

"What are you doing here?" the young man repeated, his face at once astonished and angry. "You betrayed us, you betrayed the memory of Yosh. I gave you love and you repaid it with—lies!" His young face crumpled, and tears began to course down his cheeks.

Zach didn't know what to do. Though moving with theatrical slowness, any instant now the Bishop would set Evvy's pyre ablaze. But he mustn't let Billy sound the alarm before he was ready to move.

"Not all lies, Billy," he said quietly. Billy's gaze had gone to the pyre, and Zach saw his lips move. "What did you say?"

"She is so beautiful," Billy murmured. Then he turned back to Zach, his voice again sharp with anger. "Why did you run away?" he demanded.

"I could not tolerate imprisonment," Zach said. That was the truth, if not all the truth.

The boy looked uncertain. "Then you are still a believer?"

"I am here, am I not?" He looked at the Bishop. The old man had just touched the burning wand to the kindling. A murmuring, liquid sound rose from the crowd like the voice of a stalking animal.

Billy's face darkened. "No," he said. "No, Brother Zach. You never believed." He looked around wildly. All attention, of the congregation, the guards, the Bishops, was on Evvy. "You must be punished," he said distractedly. But he didn't cry out. Again his eyes went to Evvy. With sudden certainty Zach rose to his feet, gripping both of Billy's wrists hard in his own hands. "Billy," he said, looking intently at the boy. "You know why I am here. Don't stop me."

His eyes still full of tears, the boy nodded. All tension left his body. "Save her, Brother Zach," he whispered. "Save her if you can."

Zach let go of the boy's wrists and pushed quickly through the crowd to the pyre. At the same instant the fox-cat let out an unearthly howl, as if all the wild deenas on the planet had been set loose at once, and launched herself at the Chief Bishop, her needle-sharp teeth fastening in his neck. With a terrified scream Brother John fell against the altar. It took a moment for the crowd to notice that anything was wrong, and by then Zach had reached Evvy. The guards had gone to the Bishop's aid while the crowd began to flee in panic. No one noticed as Zach cut quickly through Evvy's bonds, then threw her to the ground where he beat out the flames that had just begun to burn her robe. Her eyes were glazed with shock, and when he pulled her to her feet, she could scarcely stand. "Run!" he shouted, but she didn't move. Baby continued to howl, bite, and claw, occupying the attention of a half dozen Traders. From the corner of his eye Zach saw that the Chief Bishop was bleeding heavily, his throat torn open.

All this had taken only a very few seconds, and now attention began to turn to him. "It's Brother Zach!" cried a voice. "Stop him!" Zach recognized the voice of Galen, who had been an aide to Yosh and had always hated Zach. He slipped his left arm around Evvy's waist and pulled her with him, running into the woods on the hill behind the altar.

"My mount is on the other side of this hill," he told Evvy quickly. "You must run there now!" She looked at him uncertainly, her face still a mask of shock, then she turned and began to run. Zach stood and waited for his pursuers.

A moment later Galen and a man he did not recognize appeared through the brush. Galen's face and arms were badly scratched, and the other man was bleeding from a deep cut on his shoulder. Zach silently thanked Baby, praying that she had managed to escape without serious harm.

"Halt, Brother Zach!" Galen gasped. He brandished a museum-piece sword, but the other man was unarmed. Zach launched himself at the unarmed man, kicking him full in the groin. As the man went down with a cry of pain, Galen swung his sword. Zach stepped inside the swing and clasped Galen's sword arm, then twisted until at last he let go. Zach took the weapon and began to back up the slope. Two more men had appeared, guards, and they started after him, Galen following. He had reached the top of the hill when his foot slipped on a loose rock, and he slid downward, colliding heavily with one of the guards. The man fell against his companion, and the three rolled partway down the hill. Once again Galen appeared above him, brandishing a knife. Zach kicked at the guard nearest him, driving him into Galen's feet, and Galen, too, fell. Zach quickly scrambled to his feet, and then a sharp pain in his left thigh told him he had been cut. Gasping for breath, he backed up a step, then planted his feet and locked his knees. He looked at his foes, struggling to rise, and remembered that Will had once told him that one man against three has an advantage: each of the three will hesitate to strike first. Borrowing another trick from Will, he raised the unfamiliar sword in both hands and brought it down with a full shout. Galen opened his mouth to scream, but nothing emerged but bloody bubbles, and he fell back into the arms of the nearest guard. The other man stood where he was, a shocked expression on his face. Not bothering to retrieve the sword, Zach quickly limped to the crest of the hill. Below him, the two guards began to struggle after him. He picked up a large rock and threw it, catching one on the side of the neck. He saw him go down, then ran to where he had left the mount.

Next to the mount, leaning against a tree, Evvy stood, trembling violently. At the sound of his approach she looked up, and for a moment they just stared at each other.

"Zach," she whispered.

"We haven't much time," he said gruffly. "They are behind us." She didn't move. He took her wrist and drew her to the mount.

"Oh, Zach," she said. She had begun to cry again, and he held her for a brief moment, then helped her onto the mount. He followed with some difficulty.

"You're hurt," she said.

"It's nothing." He pressed his knees into the mount's flank, and she began to gallop down the slope. He could hear shouts in the distance but knew they would soon be safe, since even the slowest mount could easily outrun the pack animals the Traders used for traveling.

Zach turned the mount wide of the Trader encampments, then to the edge of the plain. They traveled west for some distance, till he was certain that any pursuit was far behind. His leg had begun to hurt badly, and now he saw that it was still bleeding.

"We'll stop for a moment," he muttered. Evvy didn't seem to hear him. He dismounted and nearly fell. She sat still, her face streaked where tears had washed away the grime accumulated during her time with the Traders. For a moment he remembered the first day they had been together; then, too, she had been silent, refusing to speak to the strange man who had come to take her from her parents; then, like today, he knew she had been in a kind of shock. He didn't have time to worry about her now.

He sat and examined his wound. His trouser leg was sticky with blood and cut from groin to knee. He hoped that the bleeding had cleaned the wound of dirt; in any case, there was no way or time to treat it more thoroughly here. He pulled off his tunic and folded it several times, then placed it over the wound and tied it with his belt as tightly as he could pull it. With misgiving he saw that the improvised bandage was already showing red. Gritting his teeth, he pressed against the tunic, then pulled the belt even tighter.

Feeling light-headed, he remounted and guided the mount into a wooded area. At last they came to a shallow stream. The deepening shadows of late afternoon and his own fatigue told him it was time to stop. He found a small clearing at the edge of the water, and he dismounted, then helped Evvy down. She looked up at him, no longer crying, then spoke as if they had last talked only yesterday afternoon. "I'm sorry I couldn't help you before, Zach," she said. "I . . . did not seem to have control of myself."

"I understand," he said. "You were nearly—" He broke off. He realized that he was suddenly very dizzy. "We must prepare camp," he said.

Evvy took his arm with concern. "Zach, sit down and rest. You're hurt. I know what needs to be done. Are you still bleeding?"

He looked. The tunic showed only dried brown stains. "No," he said.

"Then sit still." She helped him ease into a sitting position. "Give me your knife." He handed it to her, and she disappeared into the woods. A few minutes later she returned with a bundle of dried stems and roots. She shredded them with the knife, then set the pulpy mass before her on a flat rock. She untied Zach's belt and removed the soiled tunic, then parted the torn trouser leg. She grimaced when she saw the length of the cut.

"It's deep," she said. "It's a good thing you bled—that helped clean it." Taking the pulped roots, she began gently to clean the outside of the wound, wiping away dried blood and dirt. From the sharp sting Zach recognized the material as fireberry root, which contained a mild disinfectant in its sap, and in purified form was one of the most important medicinal herbs used by the Garden.

"I have no way to close it," she said, frowning in concentration. "You're going to have a bad scar."

Zach grunted. At the moment a scar seemed the least of his difficulties. Concentrating on her work, the tip of her tongue touching her lip, Evvy pressed the remainder of the pulp over the wound and, after cutting two long strips from the bottom of her tattered gown, tied it firmly in place.

Zach grunted again. "Thank you," he said. He started to rise and was again hit with a wave of dizziness.

"Sit still," said Evvy peremptorily. "I can make camp." She squinted at the sun. "There's still plenty of time till dark. Rest." While Zach watched, she set about gathering wood and making a fire. She moved efficiently, preoccupied, and did not seem to want to talk.

When the fire was burning, he moved toward it gratefully.

Although the day had been warm with early spring sunlight, his injury and the battle had left him feeling drained and cold.

"I wish we had a pot for boiling water," Evvy said. Then, "May I take the blanket?"

"Of course," he said. He wondered if she were going to sleep now; she had just been through what must have been the most terrible ordeal of her life and must be exhausted. But now she smiled, almost shyly. "While I was searching for fireberry, I came upon the stubble of a soap-root plant," she said. "I want to bathe more than anything in the world. I'll be just around the bend. Please don't look."

He shook his head and returned her smile. She took his bloody tunic and the blanket and disappeared again. When it was nearly dark, she returned, the blanket wrapped and knotted around her, her long wet hair plastered over her shoulders. She spread her gown and his tunic over bushes near the fire to dry. For the first time he noticed that she, too, was limping, and he saw that her lower legs and bare feet were covered with angry red and purple burns.

"Evvy, your legs—"

She grimaced. "Yes," she said. "I didn't really notice until I washed." She smiled weakly. "But it is so good to be clean."

"There's half a rabbit in the mount's pack," he said. "Take some of its fat."

She nodded and retrieved the carcass, then cut beneath the skin and removed a gob of fat, which she smeared over her burns. She pushed the remains of the rabbit onto a sharpened stick and laid it on the fire. At last she sat across the fire from Zach, wrapped in the blanket, her burned legs turned awkwardly to the side, away from the heat. As he watched her comb her still-damp hair with her fingers, Zach felt almost that he had never been apart from her, that she was again the beautiful young girl the Principal had sent him to buy all those years ago.

"It's like old times, eh?" he said, intending a joke, but his voice was rougher than he had expected.

"I never thought I'd see you again," she said. "I feel as if I'm in a dream. I'm afraid to wake up."

He could not think of an answer and simply continued to look at her, unable to stop smiling.

"What happened?" she asked after a moment. "It was all so fast. I thought I heard a fox-cat."

"You did," said Zach. "It was Baby. She helped me find you, and she made it possible to rescue you."

"Baby!" She looked around suddenly. "But did she—"

"I don't know what happened to her," said Zach. "She attacked the Chief Bishop. I think she killed him. When we left, she was still fighting." He was silent a moment, then continued. "If she survived, she will find us." Evvy's eyes filled with tears and he looked away. Privately he suspected that the fox-cat had been killed.

After a moment Evvy spoke again. "Zach, please tell me. How is Will?"

"He was badly injured," Zach said. "At the time I left he was on the road to recovery." He considered telling her about the arm but decided against it. She had suffered enough shock for one day.

Presently the rabbit had finished cooking, and Evvy divided it. When he had finished eating, Zach felt stronger. It was dark now, and stars appeared above the newly budded trees, twinkling over the camp as they had when he and Evvy had been together six years ago. At those times Zach had often imagined that his life had been different, that Leya had lived and that Evvy was their daughter. He had believed then that his decision to take Evvy to the Garden meant that he would never see Will again; just as, more that twenty years ago, he had believed that he and Will would never again be close, as friends or brothers. He remembered again the look on Will's face when he had gazed at Evvy on the day of the wedding and his anguish when he learned that she had disappeared.

At a sound Zach looked across the fire to see Evvy looking at him intently, her eyes dark and luminous in the flickering light. When she caught his gaze, she held it, then smiled.

"How did they treat you, Evvy?" he asked.

"Kindly, in their own way," she said. "No one abused me. But I don't think I could have borne more imprisonment."

Zach shifted position, trying to make his leg comfortable. The night air was rapidly becoming cold, and prickles began to arise on his bare chest.

Evvy added more wood to the fire, then again sat back.

"They're not all bad people," she said. "Just very ignorant. I hadn't realized before how deep their beliefs are . . . or how appealing."

"I've always thought the same way," said Zach. He shivered, then yawned and moved closer to the fire, stretching out beside it.

"Zach, you won't be warm enough."

"My cloak is thick," he said.

"We could share the blanket."

"No, Evvy," he said.

"But—"

"No." He leaned on one elbow and looked directly at her as he spoke. Her eyes widened, then she too lay down, wrapping herself in the blanket like a cocoon.

Zach was drifting off to sleep when she spoke again. "Good night, Zach."

"Good night, Evvy."

Zach closed his eyes again. He could hear Evvy's deep, even breathing from the other side of the fire. He thought of her offer to share the blanket, remembering how she had slept beside him once, long ago, when she had been a child; and he remembered the touch of her fingers when she had tended his wound. It was a long time before he fell asleep.

PART THREE

THE WAR WITH THE TRADERS

One

The Principal stood looking at what remained of the broken body of Patrick, his favorite homing bird. Gray and white feathers lay scattered on the balcony. There was no sign or sound of Napoleon, who, as soon as the Principal had discovered him in the cage, had quickly clambered up a vine-covered column and disappeared among the eaves.

"Robin!" the Principal bellowed. "Robin!"

"Yes, sir?" The old man appeared at the entrance to the balcony, out of breath.

"Who has been caring for the birds while Lindy is gone?"

"I'm not sure, sir," said the old man. "One of Odell's men, I believe."

"Well, find out who it is! And send him to me! The deena-cursed fool left the door to Patrick's cage unfastened!"

Now Robin noticed the still form of the bird. "Yes, sir," he said. "I'm sorry, sir." Rapidly he backed away and disappeared.

The Principal walked to the edge of the balcony and took three slow deep breaths, holding each before breathing out. When he had first found Napoleon with the bird in his mouth, he had felt murderous. Now that the fox-cat had disappeared, however, he felt his anger dissipating. The little animal had, after all, only been following his own instincts. Even the bumbling incompetent who had failed to secure the latch was not wholly to blame. Lindy, who had been dispatched to Crosskey to train birds there, had begged not to leave until he had properly trained a substitute bird handler. "But, sir," he had protested, "no one knows the birds like I do, except yourself, sir. They need an experienced hand to tend them."

He gathered the bird's remains in a cloth, then sighed and sat on a stool next to the cages. Despite Lindy's misgivings, the project to train homing brids was proceeding more rapidly than he had hoped. Patrick, as his prime male breeder, had seemed to him a symbol of its progress. Now Patrick was gone, though his sons and daughters were already breeding and learning to carry messages. Still, what if Napoleon had somehow managed to get into the larger cage and destroyed Patrick's offspring? The simplest oversight could ruin months of work and destroy his new technology before it had really started.

When he had been a boy studying in the Garden, planning the civilization he would build one day, he had been fascinated by all he had read of life in the decades before the Change. Communications then had, thanks to the high degree of technology afforded by oil-burning machines, been virtually instantaneous. Transportation, likewise, had been accomplished by machines, some of which had actually soared through the air, avoiding the delays and dangers of travel by land. Even land travel had been comparatively effortless, proceeding on broad paved roads and rails.

All that had become permanently impossible once the Change had occurred. Most citizens of the District still superstitiously believed that "wild deenas," supernatural and invisible monsters, had caused the Change. The Principal and all who had grown up in the Garden knew that the wild deenas had in fact been tiny viruslike particles of DNA, the blueprint for all life. This DNA had caused havoc first when it was made a part of the hereditary makeup of changed bacteria, created to consume fossil oil accidentally spilled on the oceans. The bacteria had unexpectedly mutated, eating not only all fossil fuel with which they came in contact but also any products derived from that fuel, including clothing, furniture, and, ultimately, special safety seals in the laboratories where harmful bacteria were being manipulated for use in warfare. The result had proved to be the deadliest legacies of the Change: man-created diseases, including the woman sickness, and widespread mutations among plants and animals that had spread rapidly as the changed DNA particles had escaped from their labs and entered the mechanisms of living creatures everywhere.

Although the Principal had always known that he would never be able to achieve the level of civilization that had existed in the late twentieth century—that such marvels, in fact, would never again be possible unless a completely new form of energy were someday discovered—he had nevertheless always had a fantasy of creating a clean, literate world where learning and leisure were a part of every person's birthright. He had come to realize early in his rule that he could probably not hope to achieve even so comfortable a standard of living as had existed in the Middle Ages or classical times. Even the Romans, through their sophisticated systems of aqueducts, had achieved indoor plumbing for the well-to-do.

The problems he had not foreseen were twofold. In the first place, the District required the working power of the largest part of its population just to produce enough food to feed itself. Most of the remaining manpower was absorbed in the army, with its police, protective, and tax-collecting functions. Second, and far more problematic, was the fact that in the decades before the Change, most of the first steps toward achieving a high level of technology had been forgotten. Much that was essential to daily comfort and survival had had to be painstakingly relearned. It was only in very recent years that glazed pottery had been created on any scale.

On the other hand, the success of the testing and birth control clinic was the greatest achievement of the post-Change era. Now that it had been proven in the Capital that the methods did work—maternal deaths were demonstrably down and more girl-children were born every day—he and the leaders of the project had taken the first steps toward setting up satellite clinics in some of the more remote areas of the District.

The first test of the new project had been conducted in a small northern settlement on the outskirts of the Capital. The

Principal had himself ridden out to inspect the facility. A smiling Daniel had greeted him at the door of the clinic, which was in a small restored pre-Change stone building. A handful of women sat on a long wooden bench, their husbands and children gathered behind them. As he entered, the women looked up at him, hiding their mouths with their hands, whispering and blushing.

He smiled at them. "Good luck to you, Mistresses," he said. One, a striking and very young woman with rosy cheeks and dark eyes and hair, reminded him for a moment of Evvy, and he could not stop himself from staring at her. She met his gaze, then lowered her eyes. Her husbands, two tall, gangling blond youths, moved protectively closer to her.

An older woman with the lined face of one who has spent much of her life outdoors rose from the bench and approached him shyly. She ducked her head, then spoke. "Sir," she said, her voice strong and clear, "I want to thank you for this. My daughter took your test in the Clinic last summer. She had her second girl-child this month. It is a great relief to know that it is safe for her to bear children."

"Thank you for telling me this, Mistress," said the Principal.

"My husbands still think it's all nonsense, sir. But I have told all the women I know. I think it's a godly thing you're doing."

He had left the Clinic feeling buoyant and heroic. The Clinic, was, in fact, working. Many women and their husbands by custom entered into voluntary celibacy after the birth of the first girl-child, with the husbands forced to seek sexual relief elsewhere or, if not brothers, with each other. Now this was no longer necessary for all; and the future would be even brighter, for those girls who were born as second and third girl-children would grow up to pass on the trait of immunity to the disease.

After the successful test on the outskirts of the Capital, the satellite clinic was to move to a more remote area, the town where the Crosskey Inn was located; because it was the center of a major trading route, it seemed an ideal site for spreading word about the testing project.

Yes, the Clinic was working, and because of it the people

of the District might now become more susceptible to the Principal's teachings in other matters.

He cast a last look at the remaining birds, then stood and stretched, ready to return to work. On his way to the office he was met by Robin.

"Sir, a message has just come from your chief house for hire. It is marked urgent."

The Principal frowned. It must be another message from Lina. He had received three from her in as many weeks, each requesting to see him. He had put them off, being too preoccupied with the satellite clinic to indulge in pleasure. No doubt she had written "urgent" in order to catch his attention. He smiled, then opened the sealed missive. To his surprise the paper was in the hand of the chief procurer, rather than the shaky, childish scrawl of the girl herself. "Sir," the message began, "Lina is very ill and may be dying. She says she has urgent news for you. Yours respectfully, Cyrus."

Dying! The Principal felt suddenly ashamed. He should have visited her before this, should certainly have sent word that he was busy. Wondering what could be wrong with the girl, he ordered Robin to have the birds' cage repaired, then dressed in a formal tunic and cloak and left for the house for hire.

The Principal sat by Lina's bed feeling uncomfortable and out of place. Her skin was pale and splotchy, and her face had become shrunken and hollow-looking. Every few moments a tremor passed over her body, causing the bedclothes to vibrate. "What is wrong with her?" he asked the procurer.

"We don't know, sir. It came on her sudden, three days ago. She can't hold any food or water. What little she takes she loses almost immediately."

"Send to my House," said the Principal. "I will have my personal physician attend to her."

He whispered her name and her eyes opened. It took her a moment to recognize him, and then she smiled.

"I heard you were sick, so I came," he said. She gave him a weak smile of gratitude.

"It was good of you," she murmured, her voice sounding dry and fragile.

"Do you want anything? Water?"

"Just sit a moment," she said. "Let me look at you."

Will forced himself to keep his gaze steady on her ravaged young face. It had been less than a month since he had seen her last, yet the change was startling. He remembered with unease that he had heard of increased sickness in the Capital and wondered if a new disease had sprung up. Lina's hand fluttered on the bed cover, and he took it, the weight seeming no more substantial than a feather.

He remembered again the afternoon he had taken her home from the house of women for hire. At the time he had not been sure why he had asked her—it was, perhaps, in part curiosity and in part his own loneliness. He had made her comfortable in the two-room suite that he kept for female visitors, where she herself had spent some weeks years ago, then had instructed Lindy to have the new kitchen staff prepare a special meal for two. He had been aware of, and made uncomfortable by, the guarded, disapproving looks of both Lindy and Robin. Lindy in particular seemed upset; though he had not served the Principal during the early years when he had indulged his compulsion frequently, the boy had undoubtedly heard stories. On his way to his rooms Lindy had passed him with a bowl of flowers in his hands. The boy's face was resentful, and he started to speak, then thought better of it and nodded curtly.

Well, the deenas take them all! He had been without a woman for many months now and was entitled to take his relaxation. Besides, he was the Principal, the man on whom all of the responsibilities of the District fell. He was not eased by the knowledge that he had once used just these rationalizations to excuse his brutal behavior toward young girls.

He spent some time smoothing his curly hair, carefully shaving, and checking his appearance in the glass. He was wearing a new tunic of the darkest red, the color of old berry wine, its sleeve made purposely short to fit around the stump of his arm. That and the dark color and rich texture of the cloth helped, he thought, to make his deformity less obvious than would an empty sleeve. At last, satisfied with his appearance and unaccountably nervous, he made his way to the girl's chambers. She rose and smiled in greeting. He saw that Lindy had brought in the fresh flowers and a tray of refreshments.

Almost formally, they sat together and talked of inconsequential matters. The Principal felt ridiculous, as if he were playing a role. He had owned this girl once, had spent weeks with her, weeks during which she meant nothing more to him than an outlet for his pleasure, and now he found himself wondering what she was thinking of him. Lina herself, despite her obvious infatuation for him, seemed apprehensive, wondering, no doubt, if he planned to use her as he had in the past.

He only half listened as she continued to chatter through dinner, telling about her life in the house for hire and about the excursions the procurer sometimes organized to other areas of the District. He began to listen more attentively when she mentioned that some of her clients were Traders.

"Oh, yes, sir, the Traders come to us too. I don't know where they get the money, but ain't they men same as any others?"

"Do they ever speak to you of their plans?" he asked casually.

"Not really, but there's one in particular, a preacher named Jed, tries to get me to go with them. Says Trader women are better off than District women, but I can't see the difference myself."

"If this Jed returns, or any other Traders come to you, will you let me know privately?" He saw from the look of hurt on her face that she now knew that he was not planning to keep her with him. She quickly covered her feelings and nodded. "Of course. You know I will do anything you ask."

She continued to talk and he listened, occasionally commenting or asking questions. He found himself strangely soothed by her presence but with no interest in continuing it beyond this evening. He drank cup after cup of brew, and when it became very late, he found himself telling her stories of his past and his exploits against the President. "Is it true that you fought the President single-handed in the tunnels, sir?" she asked. "Against him and the wild deenas?"

The Principal chuckled. He was aware that many folk legends had grown up around his exploits. "Not quite true, Lina. In the first place, there were no wild deenas, in the tunnels or anywhere else, and in the second—"

"But my first father saw one once, near a dead-machine

graveyard," she said seriously. "It was a little thing, and it had a thousand legs, and it came right for him—"

No doubt a mutant centipede, thought the Principal. "In any case, I did not fight him in the tunnels, though we used them to gain access to the city." She was full of questions, and he talked on and on, surprised at himself. He was aware that he was continuing to talk because of his nervousness, which she seemed to sense. "Now, where was I?" he said. He had just been describing to her the way the tunnel under the river curved sharply upward and how it had taken him and his men nearly a week working in the dark and the damp heat to clear the rubble and debris, afraid every moment that the ancient walls might crumble and the full weight of the river would rush in on them.

"Ah, yes," he remembered. "The river . . . I was just telling you . . ." He paused to pour another cup of brew, spilling more than he got into the container. "The river . . ."

But she was no longer listening. She rose and took the cup from his hand. "Here, sir," she said. "Whyn't you stretch out on the cot here and let me rub your back. It'll relax you."

Dizzy and knowing that he had drunk too much, the Principal let her lead him to the cot and lay on it, closing his eyes. From the sounds of movement and the progressive darkening of the room beyond his eyelids, he knew that she was putting out the fish-oil lamps, and then he felt her strong, knowing fingers on his back.

Later, in the glow of the light from a single candle, they removed their clothes and lay together. She seemed surprised that he wanted her only for lovemaking, that his brutalities of the past were gone, but she quickly adjusted and responded with all the experience of her years in the house for hire and all the ardor of unreturned love. She did not seem in any way repulsed by his arm, only curious; she touched it once gently and asked, "Does it hurt?"

"Sometimes," he murmured. "But not now." He drew her close to him and soon forgot the arm and everything else, abandoning himself to the joy of sensuous pleasure.

They slept and woke, then slept again. Once, in what seemed the middle of the night, he awoke to see her sitting up, looking young and very pretty in the faint, flickering light. She was not Evvy, but she had, he realized now, a charm and intelligence of her own. He took her hand and pulled her down beside him again. "Thank you, Lina," he whispered. "You have made me happy tonight."

"I'm glad, sir," she said. "I think it's different than it was with us in the past. If you don't mind my saying so, you have changed."

"I'm sorry for the things I did to you long ago," he said. "In those days I could not seem to stop myself."

"That's what I always thought," she said. "And I never minded. I loved you too much."

Again he felt ashamed. "I cannot ask you to stay with me," he said. "I have a wife-to-be."

"The whole world knows it, sir," she said. "And how she was taken by the Traders. I hope you get her back. I do. But I also hope that until then . . . you won't forget me."

He had given her a bonus and sent her home the next morning, then sent for her again the following week. Eventually he fell into the routine of seeing her two or three times a month, and occasionally more often. She was unfailingly loving and generous, and he, in turn, tried to be generous with her.

Now she lay before him, as sick as anyone he had ever seen. Her lips moved again, and he could see that she was so weak she could scarcely speak. Where was Wolff?

"I sent you a message, sir," she said.

"I know, Lina. Two messages. I'm sorry I didn't respond right away. I've been terribly busy. We've set up satellites to the testing clinic, and the details—"

"That's what the messages were about," she said.

"What!" He had assumed that the messages were requests to spend the night with him.

"Remember you asked me to tell you whenever Traders came into the house . . ."

"Yes. But what—"

"It was three weeks ago. I sent the first message right after it happened. It was Jed, the Trader preacher I told you about. He told me that it might be the last time he saw me. He kept talking about a new clinic and the evil scientists. I—think the Traders are going to war with you, sir."

The Principal felt suddenly cold. The satellite clinic near

the Crosskey Inn had been scheduled to begin operations yesterday.

"Are you sure about this, Lina?"

"I'm sure about what he said. Men tell me lots of things when we're together. I'm sorry I didn't say more in my message. You said to tell you private."

"Yes, of course," said Will. "You did the right thing, Lina. I can't tell you how sorry I am I didn't respond."

"'Tis all right, sir. I've always known how busy you are." Another tremor passed over her body, and the Principal squeezed her hand. At that moment there was a rapping at the door.

"Pardon, sir," said Cyrus. "The gentleman from your House is here."

The Principal rose as Wolff entered. The other man's face was grim, and became grimmer when he saw Lina's appearance.

"Thank the deenas you are here," said Will. "Lina, you may remember my personal physician, Wolff. He will see to it that you get well."

"Good afternoon, Lina," said Wolff. Then he turned to Will. "I have an urgent message for you from Robin, sir," he said. "He was just about to send a messenger when the call came for me."

"Yes?" said Will, his heart thumping. "What is it?"

"The birds, sir. The ones that you sent with young Lindy? The first one has returned. It was bearing a message in a red band."

"Thank you, Wolff," said the Principal. He leaned over and kissed Lina on the forehead. "Get well, and I will see you soon," he said. Then he crossed the room and without another word went to his mount and started home.

There were four types of bands used to attach messages to the birds' legs. The largest and brightest was red, its color proclaiming, even before the message was unfolded, a serious state of emergency.

Two

By the time Will reached home, another bird had arrived, this one also bearing a red band: all messages were to be sent twice, and in triplicate for emergencies, in case one or more of the birds met with harm or lost its way.

He waited impatiently while Robin opened the intricate clasp, then unfolded the message and handed it to him. In Daniel's neat, small hand, was a chilling message: "Traders attacked Clinic. 2 technicians/3 clients dead. Waiting at Crosskey."

The Principal read the message over twice. "The deenas take it!" he shouted, crumpling the paper. He took three slow, deep breaths, then turned to Robin, who was waiting nervously, his wrinkled face apprehensive.

"The Traders have attacked the satellite clinic," he told the old man. "Instruct Captain Michael to prepare the fastest mount for a relay to Crosskey. Then order Generals Ralf, Marcus, and Eric to report as soon as they can. When you return, I'll have a message prepared." If he had only begun his program of training birds a few weeks earlier, he would be able to send word in a few hours.

When the three generals arrived, he quickly explained the

situation, then told them that he proposed to send a contingent of soldiers to Crosskey immediately.

"Since the very early days we have not tried military action against the Traders," he said. "But I believe it is time to display our power." He paused, waiting for comment, then continued. "Ralf, you will stay in the Capital and rule in my place. Marcus, you, too, will stay—and will be responsible for increased combat training as well as peacekeeping. For the time being we will shut down the Clinic in the Capital. See to it as soon as you leave here. Eric, you and I will go."

"But, sir—" Ralf started to protest, then fell silent.

"Sir, you cannot—" Eric spoke at almost the same moment.

"Cannot what?" said Will. "Cannot lead? Cannot fight?" In one quick move he drew his knife and held it at Eric's throat.

"Sir—I did not mean—" gasped Eric.

"Did you not?" Will replaced the knife in its sheath. "If you prefer not to trust yourself to a crippled old man like myself, you may stay and Marcus will accompany me."

"Of course I know you can lead, sir," said Eric. "You are the greatest leader of men in the world. I was only thinking of your well-being. I'm sorry, sir."

After some further discussion of details the Principal dismissed the generals. Although he was aware that he had acted childlishly, he felt curiously satisfied. He had seen the looks of astonishment and momentary fear when he had drawn the knife. Of course he would never be a first-class fighter again—no man could be with one arm only—but his reflexes and strength were nearly what they had been when he was young, and he was pleased that they had been witnessed.

Later in the afternoon Ralf sought private audience with him, trying to talk him out of the scheme, but Will dismissed him. He wanted to see the situation for himself so that he could decide what further action to take, and perhaps, though he did not like to admit it, he wanted to prove something to himself.

Three days later the Principal, Eric, and their heavily armed, mounted men arrived at Crosskey. The Inn had been temporarily commandeered as barracks for the soldiers and technicians.

As soon as they entered the smoky room Lindy rushed up to him. The boy appeared tense, and there were shadows under his dark eyes. "Sir! How was your journey? I have prepared private quarters for you upstairs."

"Thank you, Lindy," said Will. "How are the birds?"

"Well, sir, General Eric ordered me to stop training after the trouble. I've been sleeping beside them to protect them at night."

"You've done well, boy," said Will.

Lindy wanted to talk further, but Will waved him aside when Daniel appeared from the kitchen area. He led the Principal and Eric to a table in the corner of the Inn.

"This is the situation, sir," said Daniel without preamble. He seemed older and more solemn somehow, as if the horror of what had happened had aged him. "As soon as I received your message, I began to scout the area."

"Not alone?"

Daniel shrugged. "I remembered the old days of fighting the President," he said. "I asked myself what would be the best way of discovering where they were located. Well, sir, I turned myself into a Trader and made my way among the folk of the area. What I found was a small, temporary settlement. With the women and children perhaps there were fifty in all."

The Principal leaned back in his seat and thought. From the corner of his eye he could see the innkeeper and her husbands standing at the entrance to the kitchen, watching closely, warily. His laws provided that in an emergency any citizen was required to quarter and provision soldiers; the measure had seldom been used and had never met with popularity. Of course they would be paid, and of course would complain that the amount was too small to make up for the loss of business.

"Is this settlement an armed camp?" he asked after a moment.

"They are armed, but I saw no evidence of military training or discipline. I tried to discover as much as I could without attracting suspicion. All I found for certain was that they seem to be rather more militant than in the past. That, and there was rather a great deal of disease."

The Principal listened with interest. He had not expected to find such a large concentration of Traders in one place. This would make his task easier. "We must show the Traders that they cannot get away with attacking us," he said. "Sick or not, disciplined or not, we will march on this camp and arrest everyone in it."

"Sir, I'm not sure that is the wisest course—" Daniel looked very serious and was about to go on when Eric interrupted impatiently.

"Don't tell us you're afraid of a few Traders?"

"I don't think it's the best way," said Daniel calmly. "It's true they are not disciplined fighters as our own men are. But they're well armed, as I said, and they are fanatical. They're not likely to surrender without a fight."

"Then we'll give them a fight!" said Eric. "Or do you think they're too strong for us?"

"Don't be stupid!" Daniel's anger showed now. "Of course we're stronger, but that's not the point." He turned to Will. "If we take armed action now, sir, especially with so many women and children in the camp, it may move others to join with them."

Eric grunted contemptuously. "Let me head an expedition, sir," he said. "If they give me any trouble, I will exterminate them. And no other Traders will ever dare to launch an attack on us."

The two young men glared at one another, and the Principal sighed. "Daniel," he said, "your point is well taken. But our power does us no good unless we show it. We will move at once. They undoubtedly know we are here but may not be expecting action so soon. Can you draw up a map?"

"It is done, sir," said Daniel. He seemed on the point of protesting again, then bent over the pile of papers on the table before him. He withdrew a large scroll of leaf-paper with a crude, though neatly drawn, map.

"They are concentrated in a clearing in this heavily wooded area here," he said, pointing at the drawing. "For the most part they live in tents or on the bare ground."

"It should be a simple matter to encircle and trap them," said Eric, studying the drawing.

"Perhaps not so simple," muttered the Principal. "In these dense woods mounts will be all but useless." He closed his eyes and thought a moment. "When Zach returned from captivity, he gave me a full report on the customs of the Traders," he said. "He told me that they always hold religious services at sunrise. Daniel, did you see evidence that this group keeps to that custom?"

"Yes, sir," said Daniel. "They gather—men, women, and children—and say responsive chants, and then a part of a book is burned."

"How long does a service last?"

"I witnessed only one, but I'd say a good half or three-quarters of an hour."

"We'll do it tomorrow morning, then," said the Principal. "Eric, speak to your captains and have the men rest now. We will move on foot, through the night, to encircle them. Then we will attack at dawn."

Waiting in the flickering dark of false dawn, the Principal felt a thrill of excitement he had not experienced since the final battles for control of the District. The largest group of men, under command of Eric, had moved into position in a circle around the Trader encampment and were waiting only for sunrise to launch their attack. Farther back in the woods the smaller group under his command was prepared to provide reinforcements if needed, and to capture any Traders that escaped the main encirclement.

He shifted position on the mossy rock where he was sitting and closed his eyes a moment, remembering again the final days of the struggle for the Capital, when he had been the outlaw, as dedicated to the President's defeat as the Traders now were to his.

He had never doubted that he would prevail; his path to power had seemed to him a clearly marked, shining road. And all of his men had willingly followed him on that road, risking their lives for his dream.

He wondered if the Traders, in their fanaticism, felt the same certainty he had as a young man. With a sudden pang of doubt he wondered if Daniel had been right. If only Zach had been here, he thought then. Zach understood the Traders better than any other man, and his counsel had always been sensible. Zach had been, in many ways, the key to everything he had accomplished.

Will became aware of sudden movement and shook off his mood. Beside him he could see Daniel clearly and realized that the sun was rising. "They're beginning, sir," he said.

Later that day, resting at a table in the Crosskey Inn, the Principal asked himself again what had gone wrong. The question was academic: he of all men knew that a guerrilla army will fight only on its own terms. At first all had seemed to go as planned. The encircling foot soldiers, led by Eric, had stepped into the small clearing just as the nauseating rite of book burning was beginning. "Drop your weapons and surrender, Traders!" he heard the young general call out. "You are surrounded by the forces of the Principal!"

From the shocked and angry shouts that followed, the Principal assumed that the surprise had worked. He raised his arm, prepared to offer Eric assistance in accepting a surrender. In the next instant he heard the sounds of metal on metal and realized that fighting had broken out and, the instant after that, found his own forces under attack by armed men from the surrounding woods.

For a few minutes he was too busy to do more than shout orders and defend himself. After a time he realized that he had underestimated the Traders; suspecting that just such a trap might be set, they had evidently kept the main force of their men away from the camp, in order to encircle and trap the trappers.

The Traders were no match for the Principal's soldiers, and soon the woods were thick with the bodies of dead and dying, most of them Traders. The remaining attackers began to turn and flee, and the Principal shouted orders to capture them alive for interrogation. A large red-haired man, who had seemed to be one of the leaders of the attack, struggled to his feet from where he had been lying and began to run. Quickly the Principal set off after him, glad for all of his practice at foot racing. He had nearly caught up with his prey when someone stumbled into his path and he found himself face-to-face with a wild-eyed young Trader armed only with a pointed stake. He pushed the young man's weapon aside and prepared to resume the chase. But the boy surprised him and attacked, fighting wildly and without technique. Though he had a half dozen opportunities to kill the boy, he fought for surrender instead, satisfied that he had at least one Trader prisoner in hand. He had nearly disarmed his foe when the man he had been chasing returned.

The newcomer stopped in surprise, then suddenly said to the other, "Look it here, 'tis the Principal himself!"

"How do you know?"

"Look at his arm! This is our chance to fulfill the holy plan and avenge Brother Yosh!"

Without warning and with no seeming care for his own safety, the younger man suddenly threw himself at Will. Will thrust and felt his sword go into his attacker, but the momentum carried them both into a tree, and he found himself pinned against it by the weight of the dying boy's body.

Before he could disentangle himself, the red-haired man approached, wielding a long knife. "I thank God for giving me this holy opportunity," he hissed, raising the weapon over his head.

Cursing his own stupidity in allowing himself to become separated from the main force, the Principal twisted and tried to get a grip on his sword handle. Moving as quickly as a fox-cat, his opponent struck at him, knocking him to the ground. The knife had missed and was sticking in the earth. Will struggled to prevent his attacker from retrieving it, but the other man was bigger and stronger and had two arms. A rage began to grow in him, and the beginnings of fear. Was this, then, how he would die, outdone by two ignorant, untrained fanatics?

The Trader raised his arm again, and Will saw the blade gleam in the early-morning sunlight. The knife began to descend, as if in slow motion, and then abruptly his attacker stiffened and fell to the side, the knife rolling harmlessly from his hand.

Stunned, Will looked up to see Daniel holding a bloody sword. The red-haired Trader lay sprawled on the earth, blood spurting from a wound in the side of his throat.

"Thank you," said Will shakily.

"Come on, sir," said Daniel, helping him to his feet. "It's all over. We must get back to the others."

* * *

It had been a massacre. The small contingent of Traders that Eric's men had surprised inside the clearing had refused to surrender and had, instead, fought back with a terrifying fierceness, using swords, knives, sharpened sticks, rocks. Some women and children had even joined the struggle, though more had been captured than killed.

"God orders us to fight the scientists," one of the women prisoners later told her captors. "This is the most holy work there is." Later she, and several other prisoners were found dead by their own hand.

The next day the troops under Eric's command went through the nearby towns and cottages, looking for survivors of the battle. "No one will admit to being a Trader, sir," Eric grumbled. "Or even to seeing any. It's as if they all became invisible." Daniel looked at him sharply as if to say, "What did I tell you?" but said nothing.

As he rode back to the Capital, leaving Eric in temporary command of Crosskey, the Principal reflected that he had handled the matter disastrously. He had "won" the battle, surely enough. A large contingent of heavily armed, trained men will always prevail against an inferior force. But what had he really won? The people who lived in the area of Crosskey must now believe that his true aim was to kill everyone who disagreed with him. Was this what his rule had come to?

Again and again he thought of the piles of bodies, and, as he had when he had first seen them laid out, he felt nauseated. Although he would continue to punish open preaching of Trader doctrine in the Capital, never again would he use massed force. Military action simply would not work against an enemy that conquered by fear and supersition, that took its victims' minds rather than their homes or possessions.

Behind him rode Daniel, just ahead of the wagon containing the medical supplies and the remaining technicians. Lindy was still at Crosskey but would follow as soon as he had trained a bird handler. Thank the deenas that there were still men in the world like these, men he could rely on for their loyalty and, above all, good sense.

But what could he do to prevail against the Traders? Short of wiping them out man, woman, and child, was there a solution? He looked up at the sky, as if hoping to read an answer there. Far above a single bird was soaring, and he thought for a moment of his homing birds.

The next week the first of his soldiers fell ill.

Three

With regret Zach looked again at the twisted body of the mount. It had been his fault—he had not taken sufficient account of the animal's stress under the load of two riders. He had been forcing her to move as quickly as possible, to make up for the hours they had lost that morning, when she had balked at a narrow ditch, then stumbled badly and fallen into it. Quickly Zach had thrown Evvy clear, then jumped, watching helplessly as the huge beast tried to rise and fell heavily, her left foreleg twisted at a grotesque angle.

A sharp pain in his thigh told him he had landed on his injured leg. Evvy was holding her hand to the side of her face but seemed unhurt. If only they had taken a different route this morning, none of this would have happened.

It had been close to midday when they came upon a party of travelers. The strangers had been visible for a good distance across the plain, with their two small covered wagons and a handful of pack animals. The caravan seemed to be halted, and there was no sign of humans about. Automatically Zach had begun to turn the mount farther north; what he knew of the Traders and what he had seen of the Road Men had persuaded him that he wanted as little contact with other groups as possible.

When she had realized what he was doing, Evvy protested. "Zach, they have no fire. And look—" She pointed to where great scavenger birds circled above the encampment.

"They're probably Traders, Evvy," he said. "They have no mounts."

"Then they can't chase us," she said. "Please. They may need help."

At length Zach gave in, motivated in part by his own curiosity. Nevertheless he approached with caution. As they drew closer it became clear that nothing was moving but the pack animals, which stepped about nervously, occasionally braying. Zach dismounted some distance from the encampment, telling Evvy to stay put, then approached, his sword ready.

"Hello!" he called. "Is anyone here?"

At first there was no answer but the braying of the animals, then the curtain at the end of one of the wagons moved. A woman climbed out and stood watching him, shading her eyes with her hand. As he drew nearer he saw from her tattered clothing and the carved wooden spiral around her neck that she was a Trader.

"Good day to you, mistress," he said, still a cautious distance from her. "We saw that your caravan seems to be stopped. Do you require help?"

The woman didn't answer but continued to gaze at him from dark, flat-looking eyes.

"Are your husbands here?" he asked.

"Dead," she said. "All dead."

He moved closer, still suspecting a trick. She shrank back, then started violently as he pulled the curtain all the way open. The wagon was empty, save for some heaped bedding and other household goods.

"In the other," the woman said.

Zach crossed to the second wagon, his sword still ready, but the stench told him there was nothing live here. He glanced at the half dozen bodies and stepped away, breathing deeply to clear his head.

"What happened?" he asked.

"We were on our way to the Capital, to fulfill God's holy plan," she said, her voice as flat and hopeless as her face. "Then a few days ago—a week?—my second-husband fell sick. We kept going, but then the other men—my first-husband and my uncle—got sick too. After that, the children. The littlest one died this morning."

"What sort of disease was it?"

"It was God's will, sir," she said. "He took all the water in their bodies from them. Now perhaps he will take me."

"If you aren't sick by now, you probably won't be," Zach muttered.

"What will I do now?" the woman asked, as if her future lay in Zach's hands.

Zach saw that Evvy had dismounted and was walking slowly toward them. "From what you've said the illness sounds contagious. I'll help you burn the wagon, then I advise you to take the pack animals and the other wagon and return where you came from."

"Burn them?" she said, looking horrified. "Oh, sir, I cannot do that. Burning is for scientists. God requires us to return the holy dead to the earth where they came from."

Zach sighed. The last thing he felt like doing this morning was arguing Trader theology. He met Evvy and explained the situation to her.

"What can we do for her?" asked Evvy.

"You will do nothing," said Zach. "The illness is obviously contagious."

"I think I may already have had it," she said thoughtfully. Quickly she told him how she had fallen ill when she was a prisoner of the Traders. "A number of other Traders were sick at the time. It spreads quickly."

Zach nodded. The filth and malnourishment common among the Traders would be ideal breeding grounds for illness. With a pang he thought of Will and hoped that the disease did not spread as far as the Capital. "I'm not sure what to do," he said, retuning to his present concern. "She doesn't want me to burn the bodies. But I haven't time to dig a large enough grave. And I don't want to touch them."

"Let me speak to her," said Evvy. She approached the woman and began talking earnestly in low tones. Zach could not hear what they were saying but noticed with misgiving that more than once Evvy touched the woman in sympathy. The woman pointed to the mount, and Evvy began to speak very rapidly, gesturing as she did. After a few more minutes he heard something that caused the hair on the back of his neck to prickle: Evvy and the woman were singing a Trader song, one that Yosh had written, a primitive tune about the burning of scientists and books.

When they had finished singing, Evvy turned to Zach. "It's all right," she said. "You can burn the wagon. I convinced her that the illness must have been caused by wild deenas and that the best way to purify the bodies would be to burn them."

"But why would she believe you?"

"Well . . . I told her you are a Trader priest. I'm afraid you'll have to make up some sort of service."

Zach allowed himself a small smile. "How did you explain the mount?"

"That was harder. I finally convinced her that it was part of our disguise. You and I are going to the Capital to kill the scientists and do God's will."

Zach grunted. "Stay with the woman while I prepare the pyre," he said.

The profusion of dried brush on the plain provided plenty of kindling, and after hitching the animals to the remaining wagon and moving it a safe distance away, Zach set the death wagon afire. As it burned he sang an old product-ballad with words improvised to sanctify the holy burning of the wild deenas that had caused the tragedy.

The woman wanted to travel to the Capital with them, but Evvy persuaded her to return to where she had started from, a settlement near the new Trader capital. "We are on a special holy mission," she told the woman gravely. "Just the two of us. Brother John himself ordered it."

They left the woman some of their food, then set out again. Evvy seemed pleased with the way the meeting had turned out, but Zach chafed at the time they had lost. It was this impatience that had led to the accident with the mount.

"Zach? Are you all right?"

"I'm fine, Evvy," he answered. "I was just regretting my stupidity in causing this to happen."

"The mount seems badly hurt."

He nodded and got to his feet. "I'll have to kill her," he said. "Can you help me?"

"Yes." Looking distressed, Evvy followed Zach's directions and held the whimpering beast's head steady, her hands clamped firmly behind its jaws to avoid the sharp teeth. With all his strength Zach plunged his knife through the beast's thick hide and into her neck, severing the carotid artery. The mount cried and bucked, then fell forward, a great fountain of blood soaking the dusty ground around her.

Evvy stepped back, tears in her eyes.

"It was necessary," Zach said, as if to himself. "There is no way to heal the bone. Even before the Change, riding animals with broken limbs were usually killed."

"Such a terrible waste," she murmured.

"It will slow us badly." He sighed. "Well, there's no help for it. I'll butcher her. At least we'll get some use of the body."

When the dying animal had stopped twitching, Zach began the laborious and unpleasant job of butchering it. Though his knife was sharp—he kept it constantly honed—cutting through mount hide was a strenuous business. That thick skin and the nighttime pattern of total immobility were what protected the beasts from poison-bats and certain parasites, but it also made cutting into one a thankless task. It was not for nothing that "tough as mount hide" was a common District expression.

As he worked, Zach heard Evvy behind him, murmuring soothingly to the fox-cat, who had begun whimpering in confusion and fright as soon as he had begun to kill the mount.

Baby had appeared in their camp the morning after the escape, seemingly more dead than alive. She was suffering from a half dozen sword or knife wounds, and her mouth had been cut so badly that the teeth could be seen on one side. Her ear had been taken half off, and her hair was dripping and matted from blood and from fording the stream. Evvy, weeping with joy, had immediately taken the animal in her arms, and despite the injuries, Baby had immediately responded with loud buzzing. While Zach held the little animal, Evvy ministered to her wounds with fireberry root, as she had to Zach's.

Now, a week later, the fox-cat had recovered sufficiently to scamper beside the mount and had even resumed hunting, although she still had some difficulty eating because of her damaged mouth. Perhaps instinctively understanding that her presence would terrify the Trader woman, she had stayed hidden in the grass during the morning's adventure; Zach and Evvy had found her curled and sleeping when they had returned to the mount.

If only nothing else happens, Zach thought. He began to wonder how Evvy would manage to walk the many miles ahead of them on her burned and unshod feet. As for his own leg, though it had been healing with no sign of infection, the feeling of wetness and throbbing he felt each time he moved led him to suspect that he had reopened the wound in his fall. Grimly he continued with the butchering. He would take only a portion of the meat, just what they could carry and eat before it spoiled. A glance upward showed him that scavenger birds were already gathering, waiting patiently for him to complete his task. He wondered briefly if they were the same birds that had hovered over the ill-fated Trader camp.

Presently they set off again, Zach carrying the saddle and mount's pack slung over his shoulder. Although she didn't complain, Zach was conscious that Evvy's feet must be hurting her, and he deliberately kept the pace slow despite his sense of urgency. It had been well over half a year since he had left the Capital. With their way now slowed, it might be many more weeks before they returned.

Until this morning they had covered a good bit of distance each day, camping each night in caves or under overhangs; although he did not know whether or not they were in bat country, each night he had made a large bonfire for protection just in case. Unfortunately, with the new, slower pace, there would be far fewer opportunities to find safe resting places. He would simply have to maintain alertness and, if necessary, stay awake till late tending fire. Again he cursed himself for allowing the mount to come to harm.

"Zach?"

"Yes, Evvy?" He turned to her, grateful for the interruption in his thoughts. Just at present they were hiking around the base of a high hill, following a dry streambed. The way was rough and rocky, and Zach realized with a pang that the pace must be too fast for her.

"I'm sorry," he said, immediately slowing. "What is it?"

She looked at him, her face pulled into a concerned frown.

"I think we ought to slow or rest for a while," she said. "You're limping badly."

His impatience vanished, and he sat on a boulder and smiled. "I hadn't noticed," he said. "I was too angry with myself about the mount. And I was worrying about your feet."

Evvy too sat, spreading the tattered skirt under her. Baby immediately climbed between them and stretched out, buzzing. "The burns are almost healed," Evvy said. "And my feet are getting tougher. In very ancient times no one wore shoes."

"In very ancient times there were no new-nettles," said Zach. Then: "Thank you for being concerned. Just as it used it be, you're always the practical one."

She looked across the river plain, her eyes seeming to focus on something far in the distance. "It's so strange," she said then. "When you talk of how it used to be, sometimes it seems that all that has happened never happened. Do you ever feel that?"

Zach, too, gazed into the distance, wondering with discomfort if Evvy were able somehow to look into his mind. "I do know how you feel. But things are very different now. For both of us."

That night they made camp by the bank of a small pond and ate some of the mount's flesh, wrapped in leaves and baked for a long time. Zach had never cared for mount meat; no matter how long it cooked, it was always tough and stringy and had a slightly rancid flavor. Evvy had been unusually quiet since they had stopped earlier, and Zach wondered what she was thinking. She spread the blanket, and Zach thought she was about to go to sleep, but after a moment she spoke.

"Zach, how long after the wedding did you leave the Capital?"

Zach thought. The days immediately after the attack had seemed to last years, so much had happened. "Three days," he said.

"And Will was recovering?"

He hesitated. He had so far avoided telling her about the Principal's arm. Each time he started to broach the subject something held him back, as if by not telling her he could somehow negate the fact of it. He sighed. "Evvy," he said slowly, "there's something I must tell you."

* * *

Evvy listened quietly, her face reflecting her feelings. "Oh, Zach," she said when he had finished. She blinked and swallowed several times.

"Will is strong," Zach said. "If anyone can adjust to this, it is he."

"Yes," said Evvy after a moment. "I . . . Zach, do you know, in some ways I am relieved. I sensed there was something you were not telling me, and I was afraid that Will was—that Will had—"

"I would not have kept such news from you," Zach said. "Believe me, Evvy. He is all right."

"Or he was when you left."

Zach looked at her. Suddenly he remembered. "Evvy," he said. "Right after Will was attacked, you wanted to tell me something. Do you remember?"

"Yes," she said. "That's what I was thinking of just now. But it may be too late—" She stopped. Before Zach could ask her to say more, there was a sudden howling from the woods.

"Baby!" Evvy's voice was tight with alarm. For a moment there was silence, then another howl, a sound that Zach had never heard the fox-cat make but which was undeniably from her throat.

He was still looking in the direction of the scream when Evvy scrambled to her feet and ran into the woods.

"Evvy! No!" he shouted, but she had disappeared. Cursing his weak leg, he stumbled to his feet and ran after her, his sword in his hand. He heard the howling again, louder and hoarser, and then he saw Evvy standing at the edge of a small clearing, her tattered gown hanging from her like a shroud. Now Zach, too, froze at the sight ahead of them: Perched on a rocky ledge was Baby, her ears flat against her head, her fur standing out, her damaged mouth twisted open in a snarl. Above her, barely visible in the dim moonlight, fluttering like a gust of leaves in a whirlwind, was an inky black form with broad, slowly beating wings. Zach's heart seemed to stop as he heard the unmistakable whirring and recognized a hunting poison-bat.

The bat swooped toward Baby, who struck back, raking the air with her sharp claws. For a moment the bat seemed to falter. Evvy gasped and took a step forward, then suddenly the creature seemed to sense her presence and began to fly directly toward her.

A scratch from a poison-bat's talons was instantaneously lethal. Without thinking, Zach threw himself at Evvy and pushed her to the ground, covering her with his body.

"Zach!"

"Hush!" he said urgently. "Don't say anything! Don't move!" He heard the wings whirring above and braced himself for the attack.

Something brushed the back of his head, and he clenched his teeth. But instead of the sting of knife-sharp talons, he felt a moment of pressure and then a blow on his back. The snarling scream of the fox-cat told him that Baby had used him as a platform to jump at the bat and drive it away.

He did not dare raise his head to look as the fight between the two new-animals continued: the fox-cat's fierce cries and the frustrated squeals of the bat mingled with sounds of brush and leaves being ripped. After a long and anguished squeal there was a sudden silence.

Zach listened but only heard the gentle sounds of leaves brushing against one another. He became aware of Evvy's warmth beneath him. He cautiously raised his head and looked around. Just inches away lay the twisted body of the bat. Next to it, sitting on her haunches and vigorously washing her front paws as if nothing had happened, was Baby. Awkwardly he stood, then helped Evvy to her feet. "Are you all right? I hope I didn't hurt you."

She embraced him, trembling with reaction. He put his arms around her and patted her shoulder in comfort. His own legs were beginning to shake.

After a moment Evvy pulled away, wiping at her eyes. "Baby!"

"I think she's all right," said Zach. He was surprised at how shaky his voice sounded. "Let's get back to the fire."

While Zach added wood to the fire to discourage any other bats that might be in the area, Evvy examined Baby for signs of fresh wounds. The fox-cat, who seemed to think this was a new game, growled gently and batted at Evvy's fingers, her claws sheathed.

"I don't understand," said Evvy. "I thought the poison was deadly."

"It is," said Zach. "A bat can kill a man or a large animal in less than a minute."

"She only has a tiny cut above her eye," Evvy said then. "Do you think she'll get sick?"

Zach considered. "I doubt it," he said. "If the poison was going to affect her, it would have worked by now. Perhaps she is somehow immune." The natural creatures that were the ancestors of fox-cats were said to have been immune to the venom of spiders that were deadly to most other creatures; perhaps Baby possessed a highly developed form of that immunity. If so, this was news that the Garden could use; perhaps someday an antidote or vaccine against bat-poison could be developed.

"We'll have to take turns staying awake to tend fire," Evvy said thoughtfully.

"Yes," said Zach. He did not feel like sleeping now; the aftermath of the attack had left his body feeling as tight as a drawn bowstring.

"Zach, I'm sorry I ran after Baby. I wasn't thinking."

"It's over now." Zach knew that Evvy was remembering, as was he, the night they had been attacked in the bat cave.

Baby, tiring of Evvy's scrutiny, curled up at her feet and closed her eyes.

"Why don't you sleep now," said Zach. "I'll stay up for a while and tend the fire."

Evvy pulled the blanket around her shoulders and lay there, her chin resting on her hands. "I'm wide-awake now," she said.

"So am I," said Zach. Then, after a moment, "What was it you wanted to say before? About the wedding?"

"Oh, Zach. I hope it's not too late. Maybe it doesn't mean anything at all. But right before the attack I saw something moving behind the curtains to the side of the altar. And then two men stepped out, just for a moment. It was hard to see because of the curtains, but they seemed to be struggling. I only had a glimpse of the second man, but Zach, I recognized him. It was Daniel."

Four

"For brave and intelligent service in the Clinic and in the field, I commission you, Daniel son of Lorna, General Daniel."

The Principal placed the heavy medallion around Daniel's neck, then stepped back. Daniel had reddened, though he looked as pleased as Will had ever seen him. "Thank you, sir," he said. "My life is yours. I will obey all your orders instantly, without question and, if necessary, follow you to the death."

The soldiers assembled in the Principal's garden gave a cheer, and Will stepped back to let Daniel bask in the applause. Beside him stood Marcus, Ralf, and Eric, whose sullen face clearly reflected his disapproval. Despite Eric's mood, the Principal couldn't help feeling the old thrill he had experienced whenever one of his men was honored; it was almost as it had been in the old days, except for the jarring sight of women guards flanking the low stage, and except for the crisis.

Marcus dismissed the men, then followed Will and the other generals into the House. "Congratulations, General Daniel!" Will said, clasping the younger man's hand. "I'm sorry I can't hold a banquet for you now—"

"It's not necessary, sir," said Daniel quickly.

"It's always necessary," said Will, "to honor achievement. But with the emergency—well, we'll do it sometime in the future."

"Thank you, sir," said Daniel.

"Come along, men," said Will. "Let's go to my office and have some refreshment while we discuss what to do next."

Just as in the old days, the office seemed comfortably crowded; besides the four generals, Robin sat in his accustomed place at one end of the desk, fresh leaf-papers in front of him for making notes while Lindy bustled in and out, pouring brew and passing a tray of cakes and sweets. Despite the festivity of the occasion, and despite Daniel's obvious elation, Will noticed that all the men looked exhausted and gloomy. They drank and ate for some minutes, congratulating Daniel and making small talk, then presently Wolff came in, his hair disheveled and his eyes sunken from lack of sleep.

"Two more members of the House are ill, sir," he said. "One of the kitchen boys and Martha, the woman guard." Will turned and looked moodily out the window, scarcely believing the misfortune that had come upon the heels of the Trader attack.

It had happened with unbelievable suddenness. Thinking back, the Principal realized that it had begun shortly after the Trader battle at Crosskey. First Perry, the only member of his private guard who had taken part in the battle, had fallen ill, then all of Perry's family, and then one by one, others of the men who had traveled to Crosskey.

At first it had seemed just another of the periodic illnesses that often swept through the District. In a world so primitive, despite the efforts of Wolff and the Principal's healers, serious illness was not uncommon, nor was its frequent sequel of death.

This new disease, however, had spread more rapidly than any other he had heard of, and now it seemed that every third citizen was ill. The deaths were occurring so rapidly that the burial forces were stretched beyond capacity.

Wolff, who was directing the other healers in the Capital, had so far been unable to do more than soothe the symptoms and cover the dead.

"Sit down, man, and rest," said Will. "Have some brew. Then bring us up to date."

The physician sank into one of the armchairs and rested his head against the cushions a moment. He accepted a cup from Lindy and drank deeply. "I know little more than I did the first day, sir," he said. "I cannot find a vector. It may be spreading through vermin or simply through close person-to-person contact, or, for all I know, both. In some ways it resembles an ancient plague of the past that spread primarily through contaminated water. I think it would be a good idea from now on to boil all water used for cooking and drinking."

"It will be done," said Will. "Robin, so order it. And have readers post warnings throughout the Capital and outlying areas."

"Yes, sir," said Robin, rapidly scribbling notes.

"Daniel, you wanted to report on the clinic?"

Daniel looked troubled. "As you know, sir, we have been operating on a reduced schedule since the attack at Crosskey. But . . . there is no longer a reason to stay open on any basis. Quite frankly, our clients have quit coming."

The Principal frowned. "I suppose it's natural, with the plague. Perhaps—"

"It's more than that, sir," said the young general. "At first I wasn't certain . . . then I made some inquiries. It's the Traders, sir."

"The Traders?" Will was aware that Traders had been coming into the Capital in unusually large numbers. But, as Marcus had earlier reported, the plague had hit them as badly as anyone. "Are you saying that they are threatening your clients?"

"Only in a manner of speaking, sir. Their preachers blame the plague on the Clinic. They say it is a temple to science. That we have created new wild deenas, which are causing the plague."

"Confound it!" said the Principal. He leaned back in his chair. He realized at once that what Daniel said must be true. He knew that in times of plague in the past those affected had been quick to blame any supernatural cause for their troubles, accusing witches, planetary bodies, anything but vermin or lack of sanitation.

"Thank you for reporting," he said. "I suppose the best

thing for the time being is simply to close the clinic down. Wolff can use your technicians' help." He turned to Marcus. "Marcus, what is the status of public sanitation?"

"Poor, sir. My men are exhausted and frightened. I've got 'em digging burial pits on the edge of town, but we're short of manpower, sir, and of quicklime."

"Order that all pottery and brick kilns be converted to the baking of limestone," said Will. "Put more men on quarrying from the ruins of pre-Change buildings. Use the lime not just at the burial sites but in all public latrines and cesspits." He glanced at Wolff, who nodded his approval.

"But, sir," said Marcus, "my men are already overworked, and who knows what this disease is? Perhaps it really is caused by the wild deenas, sir—"

"There are no such things as wild deenas!" said Will, slamming his fist on the desk. "Are you as ignorant as a Trader?"

"No matter what the cause, filth spreads disease," said Wolff quickly. "You know that, Marcus. If all bodies and all sewage are burned in lime, it may help."

Marcus grumbled under his breath but said nothing more.

"It seems to me, sir," said Eric, "that the Traders are spreading it with their filthy ways."

Will let out the breath he had been holding. He suspected as much himself, especially since Lina, who was now recovering, had been one of the first victims and had become ill shortly after she met with her Trader client. "Is there any evidence of that, Wolff?" he asked.

"I don't ask a man's religion before I treat him," said Wolff gruffly.

"Beg your pardon, sir," said old Ralf, who had been listening attentively, an occasional grunt as usual his only contribution to the discussion. "Did not General Daniel report that many of the T-Traders near Crosskey were sick?"

Daniel nodded. "And I've been on the burial detail, sir. It does seem as if the ceremonies for death have been largely Trader."

Will thought a moment. With so many people dying, he had suspended his usual injunctions against any form of Traderism and had ordered his men to look the other way when Trader services were held for the dead. This new information could mean then that Traders were becoming sick more rapidly than other citizens. Or, he realized wearily, it could just as easily mean that more of his citizens had become Traders and were taking advantage of the crisis to practice openly. He sighed. Up until this minute—although he saw now that the evidence had been there—he had not considered that his most deadly enemies were likely responsible for this new threat.

"Whatever the cause," he said finally, "we must commit all our resources to fighting it. In addition to the measures we have already discussed, I am considering the following steps. . . ."

When he had finished, he listened as the generals and Wolff outlined their own suggestions. Eric was in favor of having any known Traders run out of the Capital, but the others rejected this as too consuming of resources as well as hopelessly impractical. The Principal was weary and did not feel that they were accomplishing much, beyond venting their frustrations. He was on the point of dismissing the meeting when there was a knock at the door. Robin opened it to a woman guard. "A bird has just come in from the Garden, sir."

The Principal took the message from Robin. Homing birds had only recently been sent to the Garden; this was the first message that had not been a test. He unfolded the small sheet and read it through quickly, then looked up at his men. "It may be good news," he said. "The women think they have found a cure for the plague. Daniel and I will travel there tomorrow."

"The wonder," Lucille was saying, "is that this has not happened before. We have been remarkably free of deadly plagues since just after the Change."

The Principal listened to her with impatience. As always when among women of the Garden, he felt ill at ease. The long meeting room was arranged formally, with chairs and benches gathered in a circle. Most of the women here were dressed in the white scientist's coat of the Garden, with the exception of Katha, clad as always in her warrior garb, and a wild-looking white-haired woman Will had never seen before, who was wearing a long blue dress with a hood that fell across and partially concealed her face.

"It is probable that before the Change, some sort of vaccine or cure could have been found quickly," Lucille went on, "but, of course, that is impossible now."

"The deenas take it, do you have a cure or not?" The Principal regretted his outburst as soon as he had uttered it, but his fatigue and worry had made him incautious. Katha glared at him and half rose, but Lucille quickly began speaking again.

"I beg your pardon, sir, I just wanted to sketch in the background. I want to make it clear that we do not know how the disease is caused or transmitted. We have read Wolff's report, and we agree that it is probably a changed form of an ancient disease. The symptoms are similar—the vomiting and diarrhea, the muscular tremors. They are probably caused by a derangement of the sodium and fluid balance in the body." She paused, then went on. "When the illness first appeared, we began reading ancient medical texts for clues and finally decided, as was done frequently in the past, to begin vigorous treatment of the symptoms."

The Principal frowned impatiently. "Wolff has tried administering fluids, but they are lost almost as soon as the patient takes them in. Well over half his patients have died."

"We lost three women and a child at first," Lucille went on calmly. "I suspect that Wolff's treatment, like ours at first, wasn't vigorous enough. We have been giving fluids literally around the clock. But what is more important is that one of our new members has discovered a herbal mixture that seems to help. Gunda?"

Gunda rose and gestured to the strange woman in blue. "This is Alana, daughter of Alana," she said. "She has been with us for only a few months, but she is already a candidate for Daughter of the Garden. Alana is from the uncharted west, and she possesses a lore of herbs that is remarkable. We have learned many things from her in this time. Alana, please explain what you have discovered."

The woman in blue stood, and as she did, her hood slipped back to reveal the most grotesque face the Principal had ever seen. He heard Daniel's sharp intake of breath beside him. He forced himself to look her directly in the face and was met with a level gaze, frightening in its intensity and impossible to turn from. The woman's eyes were mismatched—one was brown and one blue, and he found himself staring into them. He felt that he was in the presence of an unearthly power and wondered superstitiously if a wild deena was in the woman, if she were the foremother of a race of new-people. With difficulty he kept his face composed and continued to meet the woman's gaze for what seemed like minutes.

Alana's face changed subtly then, and she smiled. The smile was in its own way more grotesque than had been the stare. "Good day to you, sirs," she said in a hoarse, croaking voice. "As Gunda reports, I have some skill in herbal lore. When it was explained to me that the illness forces the body to lose water too rapidly, I remembered a potion my grandmother devised long ago. In large amounts it is a poison, and that is what she used it for. It prevents the body from losing water by sweat or urine, and in a matter of days causes death by the body's own poisons." The Principal listened to her, fascinated and horrified, and wondered who the old woman had used her toxic mixture on.

Alana continued speaking as if she had read his mind. "We lived in the western mountains, you see," she said. "We were a family of women alone and would have been prey to the many wild tribes that live there. My grandmother used this—and some other potions—on anyone who thought to interfere with our family or our land." She sat, replacing her hood, though she kept her eyes locked on the Principal. He shifted uneasily in his seat, wondering if she somehow knew him.

"Alana came to me with the mixture, sir," said Lucille. The Principal forced himself to attend to what she was saying. "She thought that a small amount, a nonpoisonous dose, might reverse the symptoms. We had nothing to lose, so we tried it on three dying women, and two recovered."

"Might they not have recovered anyway?" asked Daniel.

"Of course, we thought of that, but when we saw that it did not cause harm, we tried it on some others, volunteers, who had only just fallen sick. All of them recovered quickly and without experiencing the worst of the symptoms."

"This is a real achievement," Will said, consciously adopting his official voice. "Can you give us a supply of this medicine or teach us how to make it?"

"Unfortunately, sir, it must be made up just before it is administered," said Lucille. "And the ingredients are difficult to find. That is, they are all common, but many of them resemble other plants. One, a fungus, is almost identical to a deadly mushroom. Alana has explained that such lore usually takes years to learn."

"Unfortunately we don't have years!"

"Of course not, sir," said Lucille, ignoring his sarcasm. "But Alana has volunteered to go to the Capital to make the mixture and train others. She has long been interested in the testing Clinic and has wanted to travel to see it."

Will nodded. He felt grateful, yet uneasy at the same time. "We have shut the testing Clinic down during the emergency," he said in conciliatory tone. "But we are planning to reopen it as a treatment center. And of course Alana is welcome to see what she wishes and do as she likes in the Capital if she will help us." He turned back to the grotesque woman. "Can you come today?"

Before Alana could answer, Katha spoke for the first time. "There is one more detail, *sir*," she said. She rose and began to pace, a gesture that brought back all the conflicts they had had in the past. "Alana represents a rare resource for the Garden. We must be assured of her safety. The fact that you have twice been unable to prevent Trader attacks on the Clinic proves that you cannot be trusted to protect her. For that reason I—and six of my best-trained soldiers—will come with her. Besides, I want to see for myself how the women who are serving in your House are being treated."

"Your offer is generous, but it won't be necessary," said the Principal, surprised at how calm he sounded. "You may send soldiers—yes, of course—but there is no need for you yourself to come. I will have my men protect Alana with their lives, and as for the women in my House, they have always been free to come and go as they please."

"Are you afraid to have me so near you, then?"

Will looked up at her belligerent face and forced himself to consider before answering. He took a deep breath and held it, then let it out. He forced his clenched fists to open, took one more deep breath, then spoke. "If you wish to come to the Capital," he said, "you will of course be welcomed. You and anyone else from the Garden. When can we expect you?"

"Within the week," said Katha. She gave him an arrogant half smile and tossed her head, her thick blond braid snapping through the air like a whip.

The two men rode back to the Capital in near silence. The Principal could not shake a sense of foreboding—caused, no doubt, by the always unpleasant contact with the women of the Garden and the thought that he would have to play host to Katha and the unearthly Alana. But the situation held promise, and a feeling of excitement began to dispel his unease. If this cure truly worked, and if he could persuade citizens to come to the Clinic for it, the future success of the Clinic was almost guaranteed.

They had nearly reached the Capital when a messenger on a small, swift mount intercepted them.

"Sir," the young man gasped, "I've been sent to fetch you as soon as possible. There is trouble at the chief house for hire. Physician Wolff requests you there immediately."

When Will entered the bedroom, he was shocked to see that the small form on the bed was completely covered and still. He found himself surprisingly moved. "I thought she was recovering," was all he could think to say. He looked questioningly at Wolff.

"She was," said Wolff. "Until this came." He indicated a stoppered crock of the sort that was usually used to store flower-wine. "It came with this message." He handed Will a folded leaf-paper. Inside was a note: "With compliments of the Principal." Will recognized it; it was a stock card that Robin made up by the dozen to enclose whenever a gift was necessary. On the outside of the crock, he saw now, was a broken seal of gold-colored wax.

"I don't understand," said Will, holding the card in bewilderment.

"You didn't send her anything?"

"No—not since flowers last week, and I wrote a note myself."

"I'm afraid there is still a traitor in the House, then," said the physician.

Still bewildered, Will reached for the crock.

"Let it alone, Will," said Wolff. "It contains flower-wine, apparently from your stock. But it has been mixed with a powerful poison—the same one that was used to kill Red."

Five

The Principal's head ached, and his eyes felt gritty. He was as exhausted as if he hadn't slept in two weeks. Perhaps age was finally catching up with him. In any case, the present crisis was straining him and his abilities more than he wanted to admit.

He tried to focus on the routine paperwork on his desk but found his thoughts returning again and again to Lina's death. That there was still a traitor present in the House seemed obvious, but who? The day after the poisoning all of the serving staff had been questioned, but no one had admitted to knowing anything. The crock of wine that the girl had been sent could have been obtained by almost anyone; likewise the printed note that had come with it.

At Wolff's insistence, no one unknown to him, Eric, or Odell was now allowed in any but the public rooms of the House. Likewise, Wolff's wife had resumed her duties as head cook. Nothing that was fed to the Principal or his aides was prepared by anyone but her. The thought that the traitor might be someone close to him, someone he trusted, gnawed at the back of the Principal's mind. Perhaps, he thought, someone not of the House had simply taken advantage of the recent decrease in guards to slip in and take the wine and the note. Certainly the Traders would feel they had reason to kill the girl, since she had betrayed their plans to attack the Clinic at Crosskey. But how would such a person have known where to find the objects?

The plague itself continued to ravage the Capital. Although Alana and the other women from the Garden had been working tirelessly, gathering herbs and preparing the healing mixture, the reopening of the Clinic had been a failure. Thanks to the Traders, most people seemed to believe that the Clinic had indeed caused the plague. After a full week of operation, the Clinic had served only a handful of patients; only among the Principal's own men had Alana's potion been used, for the most part effectively. But so many men remained ill that his generals had given up all pretense of carrying out any but the most routine of duties.

He pushed his papers into a neat pile and stood; the generals would be here soon. But first he must go downstairs for what had become a painful daily ritual.

The Great Hall where the wedding had been nearly a year ago had long since been repaired and was now in use as a makeshift hospital. Today over two dozen of the House staff and the Principal's soldiers lay on mount-hair pallets, moaning with fever. Despite the efforts of Wolff and those household members who were not ill, the stench of sickness was choking, and the Principal took a deep breath before entering.

He stopped at each bedside, saying an encouraging word to each man who was conscious. At first Wolff had tried to discourage him from so exposing himself to the sick. "We may not know how it spreads, but it's clearly contagious, sir," he said in exasperation the first time Will made a bedside visit.

"I'm healthy as a fox-cat," Will had answered. "Besides, what sort of a leader would I be if I left my men to suffer alone?"

As he moved along the rows of pallets he was heartened to see that many who had received the cure were stronger than they had been the day before; the deaths, though still occurring, came less frequently now. At the far end of the last row of pallets Wolff was bent over a young soldier who lay in a pool of vomit and waste. "I'm sorry, sir," he said, looking up wearily. "This one is gone."

The Principal nodded, feeling numb. "The cure didn't work?"

"It doesn't work equally on everyone," said Wolff. "And he came to us when the disease was already advanced."

"Come to my office when you can," the Principal said, then turned away. Before the healing mixture, well over half of all stricken with the illness had died within a few days. Even with the cure, a goodly number did not recover, simply because they had waited too long. The toll was particularly great among children: the streets outside the House were filled constantly now with the cries of mourning. When he thought of all this, especially of the needless sacrifice of young children, he became so angry that he wanted to kill. But kill whom? Even if he exterminated every Trader in the world, their ignorance would live to cause more misery.

Returning to his office, he reflected again on the ironic circumstance that just when his two most cherished projects—the Clinic and the homing birds—were beginning to succeed, this new threat, one of the deadliest and oldest, had appeared. The Clinic had now been forced to close, and those birds that had been sent to remote outposts now arrived only with more news of the plague and its toll. Just yesterday a bird-borne message from Quentin had announced that nearly a third of his men were dead or dying. All that seemed to prevent the Traders from overrunning him now was the fact that they, too, were falling sick and dying.

He thought again, as he had often lately, of Zach and Evvy, who were presumably in the West, where the plague had started. Was that why they hadn't returned? Had they, too, succumbed to the illness?

One by one the generals—Daniel, Eric, Ralf, Marcus—slipped into the office. All looked exhausted and gloomy, and they accepted refreshment quietly, seemingly not wanting to speak. Presently Robin and Wolff joined them.

The Principal cleared his throat. "It will come as no surprise to you to hear that I have nothing good to report," he said, aware of how weary his voice sounded. "Captain Michael reports that someone has breached the fences surrounding the kitchen garden again."

Eric nodded. "I have already spoken to Captain Michael," he said. "We will post double guards tonight."

"Where will you get the manpower to do that?" asked old Ralf, who looked perhaps gloomiest of all. "I have supplied you with all the troops you have requested, but Marcus and I are strained now in the Capital. There are scarcely enough men to see to the sanitation and burial, let alone to maintain order."

"There was almost a riot this morning by the western bridge," added Marcus. "Two farmers and their wife were bringing in some food for relatives. A mob of people surrounded them and overtipped the cart. The old men and the woman were lucky to get away with their lives."

The Principal listened with his eyes half closed. Once the illness had become an epidemic, the rural farmers that the city relied on to supply a part of its food had begun to stay at home. The produce grown in the city itself was not enough even in good times, and many of its producers had fallen sick themselves. The result had been a growing shortage of food, made worse now by the occasional attacks on the few food growers who did risk traveling to the Capital. And as Wolff pointed out, malnutrition would only make worse the secondary infections that followed for those who survived the plague in the first place.

Deenas take the stupidity of his people! His anger and frustration were all the worse because of his impotence in the situation. Though he hated to admit it to himself, it looked as if the Traders were finally winning: not through military force, or even preaching, but by the simple accident of bringing in this deadly disease.

Was this how his grand plans would end, then? With a starving, decimated Capital, racked with disease and governed by ignorant fanatics? Even now it was clear that his resources were stretched almost to breaking. If things did not improve soon, his government would collapse and with it all hope for the Garden and the future of mankind.

"Sir?"

He shook his head, aware that he had not been listening. "I'm sorry, Daniel. What was it?"

"I was saying, sir, that I think we ought to find some way to let more people know that the cure is working on the soldiers and members of the House."

"We've had readers go about," said Eric scornfully. "No one has paid any attention. What makes you think they will listen now?"

"Because we have had the cure for over a week," said Daniel. "And there is proof that it works."

"Yes," said the Principal listlessly. "Perhaps that is a good idea. Daniel, you find a way to implement it. Perhaps Marcus can give you some men."

"But I have just reported that I have no one to spare," said Marcus. "My troops have been hit hardest of all."

"Oh, well, then, talk to Ralf," said the Principal irritably. His headache had grown far worse, and he had lost all patience with this meeting, which like all those before it was accomplishing nothing.

He reached for a full cup of brew and started to drink deeply but after one swallow spat it out. "What's in this brew?" he demanded.

Ralf took the cup from him and sniffed at it, then sipped cautiously. "There's n-nothing wrong with it," he said. "It's the same as we've all been drinking."

"Then why does it taste so bitter? Robin!"

"I'm here, sir, yes, sir." The old secretary warily stood, awaiting orders.

"Bring a fresh pitcher," said the Principal. "And clean cups."

"Yes, sir. Anything else?"

"A fan. It's so hot—" He loosened the neck of his tunic, suddenly aware that it was soaked with sweat.

"Sir? *Will*?" It was Wolff, his voice sounding urgent. "Are you all right?"

He was on the point of reassuring Wolff when he realized that he was not all right—everything in the room had become blurred, and he suddenly felt violently nauseated. Quickly he stood, muttering that he needed to rest for a moment, and then the room became gray and disappeared.

When he awoke, he was lying on his couch. There was a severe pain behind his eyes and in his belly. He could see, swimming in and out of focus, the alarmed faces of his generals, and, closer, bending over him and wiping his face with a cloth, Wolff.

"Wolff," he muttered.

"Sir? Can you hear me?"

"Have I been poisoned?" he asked, wondering why he was not already dead.

"No, sir," said Wolff. "I believe that at last you have come down with the Trader plague."

"But the brew . . ."

"It often begins so, sir, with a change in appetite or taste."

Will shut his eyes, trying not to let his despair show. He could not afford to become sick himself, not now. He was needed to plan ways to fight the plague and overcome the Traders. Every day might be crucial. He simply couldn't leave his generals to carry on without him. Hard as they worked, there was too much dissension among them, too little vision. He tried to remember what had taken place at the meeting. His last memory was of some scheme of Daniel's. . . .

Suddenly, for a moment, his mind cleared. He struggled to sit, but Wolff gently restrained him.

"Rest, sir," he said. "I have sent for Alana. She will administer the cure."

"No!" said Will. "At least—not now. This may be our only hope."

"Sir?" Wolff looked puzzled and a little frightened. "Our experience indicates that the cure works best when given at the onset of the illness."

"I'll take my chances," Will muttered. "Now bring me something to drink and listen to me."

The Principal lay shivering under several layers of blankets while the final preparations were made. Once he had explained his plan, the generals—and even Wolff, finally—had reluctantly agreed. It was risky, but it was, all could see, perhaps their only hope. It had taken some time to arrange, and during the night and this morning he had felt himself growing weaker. Of course that could be an advantage. If he looked one-tenth as bad as he felt, no one would doubt that he was sick. A tremor took hold of his muscles, and he gritted his teeth, trying to keep the worst of the illness at bay by the force of his mind.

There was a knock at the door, and Daniel and Wolff entered.

"It is ready," said Daniel. "There is a crowd at the park. Some of them are Traders, but not all. When word went out that you had caught the plague, many loyal subjects came. They have been waiting outside, saying prayers for your recovery."

"Perhaps the prayers will do more good than the cure," Will muttered.

"Will"—it was Wolff, speaking very seriously—"you do not have to go through with this. It is not too late."

"I must," said Will. "And we all know it."

With both men supporting him, the Principal made his way to the parlor, where the women from the Garden were waiting. Katha gave him a look of disgust but said nothing. Then Alana stepped forward and handed a pottery crock to Daniel.

"This is a fresh batch, just made up especially for the Principal," she said. Then she looked directly at him with a stare so intense that he felt the skin on the back of his neck prickle. Though she looked like no one he had ever seen, he felt again, as he had when he first met her, that he somehow knew her.

Flanked by guards, the Principal, Wolff, and Daniel slowly made their way to a small platform that had been constructed in the park across from his House, where he frequently addressed his people. With every step he felt weaker and more ill, and he began to fear that he might not have the strength to carry the plan through.

The crowd was not as large as those he was used to commanding, but it was substantial considering the plague, and he felt gratified as he heard his people call to him, "May the deenas protect you, sir" and "We pray you will recover soon."

He heard other voices muttering that he was the cause of the plague, and still others commenting on how ill he looked. It took all of his strength to ascend the three steps to the platform, but as soon as he reached the top and looked around, he felt the familiar surge of power. He leaned against the railing and took a deep breath.

"Sir!" said Wolff urgently. "You are too ill to speak." The original plan had called for Wolff to read an address Will had dictated to Robin. But Will shook him off. "Let me be!" he snapped. "It must be done this way."

"My people!" he said then, his voice shaky but strong enough to carry. The crowd fell into a hush. He could see them leaning forward, straining to catch his words, and knew that he had them. "As you can see, I am sick," he continued. "I have caught the Trader plague."

There was a murmur through the crowd, almost like a long sigh.

"But this is not a death sentence!" he continued. "I will recover! I will recover because the Clinic has discovered a medicine that can cure the plague!"

He paused, and the crowd began to murmur again. He heard a rough voice shout, "Your deena-cursed scientists caused the plague in the first place!"

"Shut up, let him speak!"

The Principal waited until they had quieted, then went on. "Listen to me," he said. "I have seen this medicine work myself. It has cured many of my soldiers. If it is given early enough and often enough, it will cure most cases." He paused again, fighting his growing weakness. "I know that some say that the plague itself was caused by wild deenas from the Clinic. That the Clinic is evil. If you believe that, then I suggest you talk to the women who have borne healthy girl-children. Talk to the women who no longer fear dying of the woman sickness. Talk to them. . . ."

There were nods and murmurs of assent from the crowd. "The cure has been available for a week," he continued, "but none have taken advantage. I am here to show you that there is nothing to fear. I am here because I love you and I do not want you and your children to die. I am here so you will see that there is no harm in this medicine. I am going to take some now before you. In two days I will stand before you again, on the road to recovery." He paused again, then reached for the little strength he had left. "After I have drunk, please, those of you who have sick ones at home, fear no longer. Bring jars and take the cure to your sick ones. These deaths are unnecessary. Let there be no more."

He knew that some would believe it a trick, that he was not really ill, but he hoped that other brave souls would see, and believe, and try the cure themselves. Once it worked, word would spread, and the Trader nonsense would, he hoped, be put to rest at last. If it worked. For a moment he felt a momentary stab of doubt. What if the cure did not work? Had he waited too long? He remembered again Alana's intense, unearthly face. Was she truly the miracle worker she seemed to be? He put the fears out of his mind and took a deep breath.

He was suddenly staggered by muscle spasms and felt his bowels begin to dissolve. Wolff quickly covered him with a blanket and eased him to the chair. Then he dipped a ladle in the mixture and held it out. Will grasped the ladle in his hand, hesitated only a moment, and drank.

Six

As he and Evvy made camp each evening, Zach had an increasing sense that time had somehow been dislocated. Traveling with Evvy, gathering wood and preparing camp with her, sitting by the fire and watching as the summer stars appeared in the sky, had come to seem as natural to him as breathing. Sometimes he almost forgot that he had another life beyond this one, that his mission was to protect and return Evvy to Will, and at such times he was as content as he had ever been.

As she had when she was a child, Evvy often chattered while they traveled. For the first time he heard how she had made her way to the Garden after the two of them had been waylaid by highwaymen, and how she had been taught by the Mistress herself as she was groomed to become a Daughter of the Garden.

"Of course I didn't know what it all meant then," Evvy told him. "All the learning and studying. If I'd known that I was being trained to be a scientist, I don't know what I'd have done."

"You would no doubt have stayed," said Zach. "What choice had you?"

"I would have stayed," she agreed. "The Mistress told me she was certain that was what you wanted me to do."

"I hadn't really thought it out that far," said Zach. "But I felt you would have a better life there than you could have had with your family—or with the Principal as he was then."

"I was happy there from the first," she said. "The Mistress was strict, but she was never as fierce as she pretended to be. I loved the learning. And I loved her. I still miss her."

"So do I," said Zach. "I'm sorry she died believing that I had been killed."

Evvy frowned. "I don't think she ever really believed that," she said. "We talked about you often, and it was always as if you were alive, as if we both expected you to walk through the door the next moment."

Zach felt embarrassed, wondering suddenly what his mother had said about him.

"Zach?" Evvy said after a moment. "Will you tell me about your wife?"

Zach didn't answer. The warmth of nostalgia was suddenly replaced by a familiar, nearly physical pain. "What did the Mistress say about her?" he asked.

"That you loved each other very much. That she died of the woman sickness a year after you were married, and that afterward you took a vow that you would never again be with a woman." Her voice had become faint.

"I felt the evidence indicated that males must be carriers," he said.

"And our research has since proved you right. Zach . . . was she . . . was Leya very beautiful?"

For a moment Zach glanced at Evvy across the fire and tried to remember Leya's face. "She was not as beautiful as you are," he said finally.

Evvy colored, then spoke again. "I'm sorry," she said. "I have no right to ask you about her."

"I don't mind," he said, seeing how uncomfortable she had become. "I haven't spoken of her in many years. But I don't mind." He shut his eyes a moment, fixing Leya's face in his mind, then spoke again. "Her face was sweet and round, not beautiful," he said. "She had light-colored hair, very thick, that fell to her waist. There were freckles across her nose, and her eyes were as light as yours are dark."

"She must have been lovely," said Evvy.

Zach did not answer. He hoped that Evvy's curiosity had been satisfied, but after a moment of silence, she spoke again. "Zach, what happened to your first child?"

"What?"

"I've often wondered. The sickness only comes when a woman has borne her second daughter. So you and Leya must have had a first."

Now the pain was there in full. "She died," Zach said shortly. He rose and picked up a burning branch. "It's late," he said. "I must relieve myself. Go to sleep now. When I return, I'll stand the first watch."

Not waiting for an answer, he stepped into the brush, holding the torch for protection from bats. He leaned against a tree and breathed deeply of the moist night air. Evvy did not know what she was asking, he realized, and did it only because of her interest in him, but he felt the anger and despair churning in his stomach as fiercely as they had twenty years ago.

The next day they set out early, an uncomfortable silence between them at first. Zach's leg throbbed with every step—the constant movement pulled on the wound and prevented it from closing. He had taken to using a stout walking stick, but it helped little, and more than once he saw Evvy looking at him with concern.

That night they were lucky enough to stumble across the ruins of a pre-Change building, and, after making sure that it was unoccupied, built a fire at the entrance to provide safety through the night; since no bat would fly directly over a light, no matter how faint, the glowing embers of a fire would provide protection until dawn.

Both were exhausted from the constant marching; with each day Zach felt more acutely the loss of time that the mount's death meant. Evvy seemed worried too, and asked to see Zach's wound.

"It's all right, Evvy, let it be," he said. He didn't want her to know how concerned he was becoming at its stubborn refusal to heal; he could not help thinking of Will and his poisoned arm.

As dinner, a rabbit caught by Baby, was cooking, Evvy

asked him if he had noticed something unusual in the air. "It smells different," she said. "Do you think it will rain?"

"I don't think that's what the smell means," said Zach, now noticing. "I think we may be near a large body of water, perhaps a river. If so, we are getting closer to home."

"Thank the deenas," said Evvy.

They ate lazily and comfortably, and Zach relaxed, feeling the mood of the last several days returning. Evvy had been unusually silent all day and had not mentioned Leya, nor, he thought, would she again.

"Zach, what are you thinking?" she asked.

"I was remembering the old days when Will and I were outlaws," he said. It was the first thing that came to his mind, and it was close enough to the truth.

"When you fought against the President?"

"Yes."

"My parents told me about the President," she said. "I was a tiny child when he still ruled the northern part of the District. They told me times were terrible then. That he had outlaws working for him instead of soldiers."

"Oh, they were soldiers, all right," said Zach, remembering the fierce, bloodthirsty men he had fought, "but they behaved like outlaws. The President didn't stop them from taking what they wanted—when they wanted it. It saved him paying them."

"That's how my fathers lost their business," said Evvy. "They were fur traders. One day the President's soldiers came into the town. They started taking things. Some of the townsmen put up a fight, so they burned all the houses."

"I'm sorry," said Zach. "That was a common story then."

"We moved to the mountains after that. I can scarcely remember any of it. My parents—especially my second-father—never seemed to feel there was a difference between the President and the Principal. I suppose I felt the same way, until I met Will."

"It's unfortunate but true that there have always been more leaders like the President than the Principal," said Zach.

"I learned that too. From studying history and from talking to Will."

Zach gazed at the fire for a moment. The crumbled walls of the ancient dwelling danced with eerie shadows. "You know, he was always very clear about the sort of leader he would be, from the time we were boys. I think he always knew how difficult it would be."

"Did the men who followed him understand what he meant to do?"

"Some of them. Most of the generals, I think. But at heart they are fighters, not administrators. I believe Will is too. He's never had much fun since he became Principal, even though it's what he always wanted to do."

"How did you overcome the President? He had all the wealth and power."

"But he didn't have the people's loyalty. In the end it wasn't as difficult as you might think. For nearly two years Will waged a kind of guerrilla war, attacking convoys of the President's soldiers, raiding his camps. Eventually we came into the Capital and it was all over in two days."

"How did you get to the Capital?"

Zach mused again, wishing for some new-smoke. He began to tell Evvy about Will's long-held plan to use the ancient tunnels.

"How did you know the tunnels would still be passable?"

"Will's men worked on them from outside the Capital, clearing wherever there were blockages. And I went into the Capital and began exploring from that end."

"You went into the Capital?!"

"It was easy for me. I wasn't known then. I disguised myself as a begger and stayed on the mall for a week. You know the mall, Evvy, it's the best place in the world to hide, with so many people living there, and it was so in the President's day as well. I had memorized a map and quickly located two of the old tunnel stations."

"Were they guarded?"

"No one went near them because of the wild deenas," said Zach. He found he was enjoying telling Evvy these things, reliving them as he did. "The President was the most superstitious of all. I don't think it ever occurred to him that anyone would use the tunnels for traveling. When we finally came up from the underground stations, his men thought we were ghosts from the past. It made the ultimate fight much easier."

"Tell me about it," said Evvy, stifling a yawn.

"Another time," said Zach with a smile. "I think my story-telling is putting you to sleep." Evvy lay on her blanket, and Zach thought a moment, remembering the sights and smells of the President's Capital and his elation when he had discovered that the tunnels converged on a vast series of underground chambers very near the President's great porticoed House. Like all of Will's ideas, this one, too, had worked out nearly as he had planned. Though Will had always thought of himself as a warrior—and he was without a doubt a skilled and brave fighter—it was his planning and vision that had made the District possible.

Zach looked across the fire to see that Evvy had fallen asleep. He put more wood on the fire, then stretched and lay down, trying to put his worries out of his mind.

When he woke, sunlight was filtering through the slatted windows of the ancient room. The remains of the fire gave off an unpleasant charred scent, and he coughed to clear his throat. Evvy was nowhere in sight. He rubbed the sleep from his eyes, then sat up with a groan. The pain in his leg had become more intense. He was afraid to look at it.

"The deenas take it," he muttered. He crawled through the opening into the dazzling sunlight. Evvy was sitting on a rubble of concrete blocks, looking toward the silver ribbon in the distance that must be the river. She did not see him at first, and he gazed at her a moment, wondering how she would fare if he died of his wound. With difficulty he stood, dislodging a stone, and Evvy turned quickly toward him, her face animated and smiling.

"Good morning, Zach," she said. "Isn't it a beautiful day!"

He smiled back, feeling warmed by her happiness.

"We'd best get started," he said. "We'll need to hunt today, and there's still a long way to travel."

"Maybe not," she said. She pointed to the river. "I've seen some smoke. Perhaps there's a settlement over there. They could sell us some food or maybe even a mount."

"And perhaps it's a Trader camp," said Zach.

"It's not. I feel it's not. Besides, we can't go on like this. You try to hide it, but I know your leg is worse. You can scarcely walk."

"I'm quite well," Zach muttered, but even as he spoke, he could see that Evvy knew it wasn't true. She was right. They would have to get some sort of help soon or they might never make it back to the District. "Very well," he said. "We'll go there this morning."

Baby, who had been basking in the sun beside Evvy, stood and arched her back. "Mowr!" she said positively, as if it were all settled.

After eating the last of some summer fruit, they set off across the plain. Baby had become stronger and more energetic each day, and she ran ahead of them and in circles around them, snapping at butterflies among the thick clumps of yellow flowers.

Long before they reached the spot where Evvy had seen smoke, they could see the reddish color of pre-Change building materials, and Zach relaxed, confident now that this could not be a Trader camp.

Shortly after midday they arrived at a small town of red-brick buildings, some nearly perfectly preserved, others obviously restored through crude modern workmanship, and still others a crumbled rubble overgrown with vines and grass. Despite the smoke of the morning, there was no sign that anyone lived here.

"Perhaps it was just campers," Evvy said, her voice disappointed. "But, Zach, I saw smoke."

"I'll take a look," said Zach. "Stay here."

Ignoring the pain in his leg, he stepped around some rubble and sought to enter the largest building. Just as he put his head into the gloom, he heard a snapping noise and then Evvy's cry. "Zach! Look out!"

He whirled to see behind him a very old man dressed in a black robe and cap. He had a weapon trained on Zach. Although he had seen such weapons before, in the Principal's museum collections, Zach had never seen one used, because their manufacture and use had been thought impossible since the Change. But he knew what it was, and he immediately became motionless. The old man was holding an ancient explosive weapon called a gun.

Seven

For a moment Zach and the armed man stared at each other, then Zach spoke. "We mean no harm," he said. "We are travelers."

The old man glanced at Evvy, then back at Zach. "Drop your sword," he said. Zach did as he was told. "And your knife."

Without his weapons Zach felt vulnerable, but the old man seemed more cautious than threatening. He heard Baby begin to growl, and the old man snapped, "Tie your animal!"

"Baby, hush!" said Evvy. She picked up the fox-cat and held it tightly in her arms.

"Now the two of you," he went on in his cracked voice. "Stand over there. No, sit. Might as well be comfortable. Let me take a look at you."

Zach and Evvy sat side by side on a wall made of preserved red bricks, set atop each other with a mixture of lime and sand. Still holding the ancient explosive weapon, the old man approached and peered closely at them. Now that he was so near, Zach could see the opaque film over his watery eyes and realized that he was nearly blind. The gun trembled in his shaking hands as he peered at his visitors. Moving slowly, Zach put out his hands, then seized the gun and twisted it from the man's grasp. Evvy gasped, and the old man started violently, then shrank back.

"We mean you no harm," Zach repeated.

"Nor I you," muttered the stranger. "But a man can't be too careful."

"Does this weapon actually work?"

"In a manner of speaking. That is, it serves to make anyone think twice that it's aimed at." The old man shrugged. "It doesn't fire. But I've seen 'em as do. Out west."

Zach laid the weapon on the wall and stood. "I am Zach, delegate of the Principal. And this is Evvy, the Principal's bride-to-be."

"The Principal? The Principal, you say?"

"You know of him?"

"Most folks do. And Zach?"

"Zach son of Ilona."

The old man suddenly smiled. "Well, Zach. Well, Evvy. Welcome to College. I am Douglas son of Irene. Who'd have thought you would come here?"

"You've heard of us?" Zach had a sudden cold feeling that Douglas might in some way be connected to the Traders.

"More than that. I know you. You were a tad when I left the Garden, but even then you were big for your age. And Zach is not a common name."

"The Garden?"

"You may not remember. Oh, I didn't live in the Garden after I passed thirteen. But I farmed nearby and helped with some of the teaching. I remember you and your brother. He was a wild one, Will. I knew your mother too—" The old man broke off, his wrinkled face still smiling.

Zach thought back. He had a distant memory of an "Uncle" Douglas. Perhaps what the man said was true. "But what are you doing—"

"Here? Son, everyone has to be somewhere. I've been in this town thirteen years now. But come. Let me show you around. You and the young lady. Join me for some food. It's past time for the midday meal."

They ate a filling and delicious stew made of dried beans and summer vegetables seasoned with spicy herbs. Zach noted with interest that the cooking area, adapted from a large, possibly commercial pre-Change kitchen, was nearly as elaborate and well equipped as the Principal's own. Despite his poor eyesight Douglas seemed to know every corner of the place and kept it spotlessly clean.

Although Douglas referred to it as a town, "College" was a simple collection of seven pre-Change buildings. He lived here alone, he said, though varying numbers of other people had stayed here from time to time. "Not too many folk want the contemplative life or the sort of work I do," he mused. "This was once an important center of learning, and I'm working to make it so again."

After the meal the old man insisted on showing them around. Evvy was delighted by a hall filled with the ruins of wooden chairs and tables. At one end of the room hung a large, decaying green board. "Scholars worked here over a century ago," Douglas told her. "That green board was the symbol of a scholarly room, just like my black robe and hat are the symbol of a man dedicated to learning."

There were other halls of learning, none so big, and plaques with scarcely decipherable writing on them. "And now," said the old man with barely suppressed excitement, "I'll show you my real treasure—the reason I am here." He led them into a building that looked at first to be rubble, pulling aside a broken beam and moving what appeared to be a massive concrete block but which was only an empty shell. This revealed a small hole, and, lighting a torch, Douglas led them through it and down some well-preserved steps into a large musty room of the past. Zach squinted, trying to accustom his eyes to the darkness, while Douglas busied himself lighting candles. The room began to take form, and Zach realized that it was a well-preserved and extensive pre-Change library. Someone, undoubtedly Douglas himself, had painstakingly repaired cracks in the walls and had forced timbers in to hold up the sagging ceiling; it was a remarkable job of restoration.

"It's a rare treat to show this place," said Douglas. "Visitors don't come often, and I can't risk showing most of them the library for fear that they hold Trader beliefs."

"Do you know the Traders?" said Evvy.

"Can't avoid 'em these days. When their ideas started to spread, I created false rubble to hide the door in here."

"It's well you did," said Zach. "This library is a treasure."

"All libraries are, and all books treasures within the treasure," said the old man. "Makes me sick when I think of the filthy Traders destroying them. To think of whatever is in them being lost forever."

"The Principal has instituted a program for having ancient books copied," remarked Zach, "though many more are lost every year simply through decay than can ever be saved."

"You might be surprised to know of another way to save the ancient lore." Douglas's face had acquired a crafty look, and Zach looked at him in puzzlement, wondering what the old man was talking about.

"In my travels I learned many things," the old man went on. "It was the brown people of the southern south taught me to make a mixture that can preserve old books."

"What!"

"They use it for ceremonial objects—masks and such. A medicine man gave me a vial of the sacred powder. I experimented and found a way to mix it with certain plant and animal extracts. It stops old paper from crumbling away. You spread it on, let it dry, and when you're through, the book is as good as new. Lasts forever, for all I know."

"This is important news," said Zach. "The Principal would give a good deal to know how to accomplish it."

"The secret is not for sale," said Douglas. "It is free to anyone who cares enough for learning to want it. But I'm too old to travel now. When you return to the Capital, you tell the Principal to send scribes to me. I'll teach them how to do it. This is the only reason I have lived so long, my boy. It is my purpose in life. And every day I live, a few more pages are preserved for humanity's use forever."

He stopped talking at last and led Zach and Evvy to a large table in a corner of the room. On its surface were pots and jars of unidentifiable substances, and next to them, bundles of herbs and pigments. To one side was a small stack of books. "This"—Douglas indicated a small pot half full of a crystalline powder—"is the secret ingredient. Just a pinch is all it takes." He sat. "I've a batch I made up this morning before you came," he said. He poured some viscous liquid into a shallow bowl and stirred it vigorously with a stick, then dipped a feather into the mixture and began to dab it on an open page in front of him. "My only regret," he said as he worked, "is that I can no longer see to read my treasures."

Zach and Evvy crowded closer. Zach could see that the page seemed almost to be healing as the mixture filled in cracks and made the brittle brown edges supple. It also, as it dried, caused the words to fade until they had disappeared from the page.

For the next hour or so Zach and Evvy continued to tour the marvels of College, Baby following them and seeming as interested as they were. Though there was nothing else as spectacular as the library, it was a remarkable place, and Zach found it remarkable that the old man was able to manage it on his own. He grew fruit, vegetables, and herbs, and even a kind of new-grain. He had a small flock of fowl, some pigs, and an old swaybacked mount. He showed Zach a netted trap he had constructed for fishing in the nearby river.

While the old man was checking the trap and cackling over the large bass they would have for supper, Zach and Evvy held a whispered exchange. By silent mutual agreement neither had said anything when Douglas had demonstrated his miraculous book-preserving mixture. Since then, Zach had been wondering whether to mention that what he was preserving was blank pages. He had decided that even though it meant the loss of more books, it would be cruel to let the old man learn what he had done. To his relief he found that Evvy felt the same way.

"Besides," she said, "he will not ruin more books."

"What? You haven't said anything?"

"No." She glanced at Douglas, who was busy rebaiting his fishing trap, and pulled a small bag from her belt. In it was the miraculous powder that the old man had obtained in the southern south.

"It looks like salt, don't you think?" she said. "Well, I noticed he has salt in the kitchen. He sees so poorly, I'm sure he'll never know the difference."

Zach smiled at her in admiration. He should have thought of such a trick himself. Instead he had been worrying for the last hour about the old man and the books. Evvy had managed to find a way to preserve both. He reached out and squeezed her hand. "You're smarter than anyone I've ever known," he said.

When they had returned to the main lodge, Evvy asked Douglas if he had any spare cloth for bandaging.

"What's that? Is someone injured?"

Apologetically Zach told him about the leg wound that wouldn't heal.

"Well, why didn't you say so? Walking won't do that any good. Sit down, my boy."

He rummaged in a homemade cabinet, then brought Zach a stoppered pottery jar. "This may help," he said. "It's a healing ointment made from the leaves of a desert plant. I grow them for the pulp."

Zach opened the jar. Inside was an odorless jelly that felt cool to the touch.

"Now, as for bandages..." Douglas disappeared behind a pile of rubble and returned with a large woven basket. Inside it was a bundle of brightly colored cloths. "There's plenty of cloth here," he said. "I don't recall what all. Most of it is from the southern south. Take whatever you like."

After a moment Evvy had found some worn, clean rags and brought them to Zach.

Zach was dreading this moment. Evvy offered to assist him, but he refused and moved to another room for privacy. With great difficulty he removed his leather breeches, now stiff and grimy from filth and blood, and had a good look at the wound. After cleaning it he relaxed; it was red and oozing but did not seem to be putrid. The ointment eased the pain immediately, and he realized that what it needed was simply rest and time to heal. Perhaps Douglas would give him some ointment to use during the remainder of the journey.

Douglas insisted that his guests stay for a few more days to give the leg a rest. "And don't worry about wasting time," the old man added. "Evvy has told me your problems. Well, you can borrow my mount and ride her to the Capital. It should be less than a week from here."

"I promise I'll repay you for your kindness," said Zach.

"As you can see, I've more than enough for myself," said the old man. "I'm happy to share. There is only one way you can pay me back. Not with money or material things. But by returning and visiting again."

"I promise," said Zach.

"I do too," said Evvy.

For the next few days Zach spent most of his time stretched on a folded blanket, his back propped against a cushion, allowing Evvy and Douglas to bring his meals and fuss over him. At their insistence he confined his walking to the most essential tasks, and found that the leg quickly began to heal. Gone was the pulling and pain that had led him to suspect infection. He watched the old man and the girl with affection as they worked and chatted, Evvy now dressed in a colorful tunic and jacket from the southern south that made her look like an exotic bird.

The last night, the three of them sat in the candlelight in Douglas's lodge drinking a tart fruit-wine that the old man brewed. Evvy watched through dreamy, half-closed eyes as the men talked, the fox-cat curled on her lap.

Douglas had initially decided to leave the Garden, he told Zach, because "the world is a big and strange place. The bit of education I got only made me realize I wanted to see more of it."

"I've sometimes felt that way myself," said Zach.

"Yet you've chosen to stay in one place and serve the Principal."

"The Principal's work is important."

"I suppose it is," said Douglas. "But so is knowledge. I've traveled just about everywhere on this continent, from the southern south where people live as their primitive ancestors did, to the west, beyond the sky-high mountains and all the way to the western ocean."

"I've always believed there was little or nothing in the west," said Zach. He was stretched out on a cot, his leg elevated on a cushion. He took another puff of the pipeful of new-smoke Douglas had offered him, thinking that he felt more at peace here than he had anywhere. Perhaps he would return here, after he had fulfilled his mission, and live for a time with the old man, then journey to the places Douglas told him of. But of course Will would never permit it; he was needed in the Capital. . . . "What?" he said, pulled from the reverie of new-smoke by Douglas's voice.

"I say, there are great stretches of nothing in the west,"

the old man repeated. "Barren desert, blasted rock. But there're great stretches of people too. All kinds of people. Civilizations, just like the Principal is trying to build in his District."

"With leaders like Will?"

"Some like, some different. All are trying to build a new world on the ruins of the old. There are fierce matriarchal tribes out there who castrate all men except their selected breeders. Cuts down on a lot of foolishness in adolescence." The old man chuckled. "There's a rather large civilization that employs its excess men in violent sporting games. Then there are the more traditional feudal societies, some very like the District."

"Why haven't we heard of these societies?"

"Perhaps you have. Perhaps nobody listened." The old man chuckled again and knocked the bowl of his pipe into the hearth, then began to refill it.

"Douglas." Evvy entered the conversation for the first time. "Is the woman sickness as bad everywhere else?"

"I'd say it's the main problem of this part of the world," said the old man. "But it doesn't seem to manifest the same everywhere. I heard tell—but didn't see—that in the northwest it only kills the daughter, not the mother. There's a tribe of women in the southern south that executes any man if his wife gets the sickness—"

"Why, they must have learned that men are carriers," said Evvy, sounding excited.

"They don't have the scientific view like the Garden," said Douglas. "It's more a religious thing. But it works. They don't have the sickness much."

"I never realized that there are so many strange things in the world," said Evvy after a moment.

"Not surprising at all if you take the long view," commented Douglas. "I'm a historian, dear. Like the Principal himself is said to be. Nothing surprises me, for there is a historical precedent for everything. Take these Road Men—"

"You know them?" asked Zach.

"Very well. They made the mistake once of trying to rob me. Anyhow, like I was saying, there's a precedent for them. In the last century, before the Change, there were gangs of men who traveled the roads and worshiped machines."

"Are you saying the Road Men copy these gangs from the past?" asked Evvy.

"Not at all. But it's the same forces at work. Surplus men with no hope of a good living. Fear and superstition, elevating machines to a special, mythical status. Just because the machines no longer work doesn't mean their owners don't get manhood from them."

"What of the Traders?" said Evvy. "Is there a precedent for them too?"

The old man laughed. "The Traders? There've been hundreds—thousands—of sects like them."

Douglas continued to talk, urging more wine and new-smoke on his guests. Zach was surprised to see Evvy accepting wine as often as she did. From the occasional sad glances she cast about the room he suspected that she felt as ambivalent about leaving as he did.

It was growing late when Zach heard music, and realized that the old man was playing a bone flute that looked very much like the one he himself had made for Leya many years ago. As the flute sounded, its tone nearly as haunting as the feathered lyre, Zach gazed at Evvy, aware that he would never again see her in this way. Her eyes were closed and her body swayed in rhythm with the music. Perhaps it was the glow of the fire or the new-smoke, but he thought she had never looked more beautiful.

Presently Douglas put down his instrument and let his head fall back on the cushions. In a moment he was snoring. Evvy glanced at the old man, then stood and approached Zach. She knelt beside him, her eyes sparkling, her smile joyous.

"I'm happy we came here," she said.

"So am I," he said, returning her smile. "And we should be home in less than a week."

"I know," she said, suddenly looking troubled. "Oh, Zach. Wouldn't it be wonderful if we could stay here forever?"

Zach didn't answer. Evvy's lips were swollen and moist, and he could see by the size of her pupils that the wine had affected her. For a sudden, frighteningly intense moment he wanted to reach out and draw her to him, to forget about his mission and his promise to Will, to stay here forever, as she had suggested.

"It's getting late," he said after a moment, hoping that she would not notice the hoarseness in his voice. "We must get an early start tomorrow."

"Yes," she murmured. "Good night, Zach." She hesitated just a moment, then stood and walked slowly to her own cot.

Zach looked after her, aware that an important bridge of some sort had been crossed. Then he shut his eyes and forced himself to think of the coming journey.

PART FOUR

HOMECOMING

One

The Principal stood at the crossroads, his hand shading his eyes, squinting as the birds, now tiny specks in the distance, sped toward his House. On the ground lay an open basket with six compartments; Napoleon sniffed at it, then bounded into the summer undergrowth.

This was the farthest journey yet taken by the new generation of homing birds. He had directed Lindy to mate only those birds that had shown the strongest homing instinct; already, he thought, he could see the results. The young birds seemed to learn more rapidly than had their great-grandparents, and needed very little encouragement to home on their cage.

As soon as more bird handlers had been trained, the Principal planned to send the next crop of hatchlings with Lindy to his farthest outpost to the west, the site of the old Garden. Although he had long been receiving messages, it was time to train birds to home on the outposts so two-way communication would be possible. He had not yet told the boy of his decision; when he had mentioned the possibility a few weeks earlier, Lindy had immediately raised a half dozen objections. The breeding birds needed him; the experience with Patrick showed that no one else could be trusted to care for them; the Principal himself relied on him.

It was, however, clear to the Principal that Lindy needed a wider taste of the world than the confines of the House. He was, in any case, growing too old to be a serving boy. Will had long hoped that he would make a career in the army, but Lindy showed no interest in military service. Perhaps he would ask Odell to take him on as an assistant and future replacement. His service during Will's recent illness had shown his stamina and loyalty, as well as his ability to see to unpleasant but necessary tasks.

He could scarcely remember the hours after he had taken Alana's healing potion; Wolff later told him that he had waited nearly too long for the mixture to help him. He had a nightmarish remembrance of lying in his bed, tossing and moaning, his body expelling everything he tried to take in. But Lindy had gently, repeatedly, cleaned him, and, with Wolff, had patiently stood by to administer the herbal cure every hour. Eventually it had begun to work, and by late the next day he found he was finally able to take liquid and keep it down; the day after, he had appeared before his subjects as he had promised, still weak but undeniably on the mend.

As he had hoped, the word of his cure spread rapidly through the Capital, and soon people began to appear at the Clinic, at first the families of those who had been helped by the woman sickness project, and then others; soon long lines of citizens began to form each day, even before the Clinic opened. There were the sick, those who were strong enough to pull themselves from their beds; friends and relatives of the more severely afflicted; mothers and fathers with feverish children in their arms.

"It is a miracle," Wolff told the Principal. "They come for medicine and instruction and a day or two later are on the road to health. This is how it must have been before the Change, when doctors could truly cure. We must find out what else Alana can teach us."

On his way out of the city Will had stopped by the Clinic and was pleased to see that long lines still snaked down the steps. There were two lines now—one for those who had come to get the cure for the Trader plague, as it was now universally known, and another, shorter line for the resumption of the testing project.

As word of the cure had spread throughout the area, the farmers had begun to return, selling their produce or seeking the cure for themselves. Under Daniel's direction small teams of technicians had gone into outlying areas to bring the cure there. A week ago a team had left for Crosskey, and just today a bird had arrived with the news that the cure was working there as well.

Even the Traders had begun to make use of the Clinic. As Daniel reported during the first week, "A woman came in this afternoon, sir, with two sick children. She was wearing the spiral, didn't bother to hide her beliefs. Both her eyes were blackened. She said her husbands beat her for defying god's will and trying to save the babies. 'If making two innocent boys to die is God's will,' she said, 'then maybe 'tis time for a new god.'"

There was Trader trouble of an unexpected sort when the cure was taken for two days to the satellite clinic outside the Capital. Because of the attack at Crosskey, the Principal had sent a number of heavily armed guards. Not only was there no attack by Traders, but a Trader family who had come for the cure was attacked and driven away by the other patients.

The Principal could not pretend he wasn't elated at this turn of events. The Traders had evidently first brought the plague, and now it was helping to turn the populace against them. The Trader woman's words echoed in his mind: "Maybe 'tis time for a new god." Science was not a god, and Will had no intention of trying to set up an official religion. Still, if the people wanted to believe that the Clinic held more power than the Trader gods, he would do nothing to discourage that belief.

Only one thing marred his triumph: There had been no word of Zach and Evvy. It was now late summer, almost the time when Zach had returned a year ago.

He sat on a rock and scratched his head. Now that the birds had been released, it was time to be getting back to the Capital. He had insisted on bringing the birds himself, simply to escape the stuffiness of his office. The older he grew, the more he missed the fresh air and intense physical activity of his youth, when he and Zach had been confident that they could achieve anything. Those times were gone for good, and the Principal was beginning to suspect that he might never again work with Zach, that Zach might never return from his latest mission.

His mount had been whistling impatiently for some minutes; it was past time to return home. He called for Napoleon and was surprised that the little animal did not come to him immediately. "Napoleon?"

He whistled through his fingers, then, suppressing his annoyance, packed the basket on his mount. Napoleon had still not appeared, and he began to feel uneasy. The fox-cat was trained to come at his first call and usually did so—could something have happened to him? Perhaps he should take a few more minutes and search for his pet.

He stood for a moment in indecision, then he heard a familiar throaty "Mowr." He frowned. Napoleon did not sound distressed, yet there was something strange about his cry. A moment later he saw a small form bounding along the road from the west. "Napoleon!" he called. He started to scold his pet, then stopped. The fox-cat that came into view was not Napoleon but a slightly smaller, orange-colored animal with the tip of one ear missing. Before he had a chance to react, Napoleon himself appeared and ran up to the first animal. For a moment they sniffed at each other, then rolled on the ground in playful combat.

So Napoleon had found a wild friend. Perhaps he should try to trap this new fox-cat and have it taken to the Garden for training. Before he could think how he might accomplish this, he heard the sound of a mount approaching along the same road. At once he straightened, his hand going automatically to his sword as an unfamiliar cream-colored mount approached from the west bearing a very large rider.

As the mount drew nearer, the large rider resolved into two, and his heart seemed to stop as he recognized Zach with Evvy riding in front of him.

He was standing in shadow, and it took them a moment longer to see him. Will watched as Zach cautiously slowed the mount, alertly shifting his body.

Evvy recognized him first. "Will!" she called. "Zach, it's Will!"

He continued to stand and look at them, almost disbelieving his eyes, not daring to speak. Both were dark from weeks outdoors and were dressed in strange, brightly colored woven clothes.

Zach dismounted, then helped Evvy to the ground. He stood looking at Will for a moment, his face expressionless. Now Evvy came running toward him, her brilliantly striped jacket fluttering behind her, and put her arms around him. He hugged her tightly with his left arm and buried his face in the familiar fragrance of her hair. At last she pulled back and looked at him, her smile open, her eyes sparkling.

"Ah, Evvy," he said. He kissed her on her forehead, her cheeks, her mouth. Still holding her tightly, he at last looked up at Zach. "I was beginning to fear you would not return," he said.

Zach smiled. "When you sent me, your instructions were to go wherever I must, no matter how long it took. I'm afraid it took a bit more time than we expected." He approached Will then, and they embraced. Will shut his eyes, savoring the moment and trying to contain his emotions. He thought he was as happy as he had ever been.

Zach stood back and looked at him. "You're looking well," he said.

"So are you. Both of you." His voice shook, and he looked away a moment.

Now Evvy took his hand in both of hers. "Oh, Will, you cannot imagine what's happened to us! And all the things we've learned. How are you?"

"Well and happy," he said. "Now that the two of you are back."

"We have much to tell you," said Zach. He and Evvy exchanged a private look, and for a moment Will wondered what had passed between them on the journey. But then Evvy was speaking again, the words tumbling together in her excitement. "But what are you doing here at the crossroads?" she asked. "Where are your men? It's almost as if you came here purposely to meet us!"

"I'll tell you everything on the way home," he said. "But it's a long way and it's getting late. Let's ride."

The next morning Will woke in the guest room he had ordered prepared for Evvy. He sat up slowly, not to disturb her, and watched for a moment as she slept, her lips slightly parted, her hair a dark tangle on the sheet.

By the time they had arrived at the House and Evvy and Zach had bathed and eaten, it had grown late. Wolff examined Zach's leg and prescribed a good night's sleep. "You can talk tomorrow," he said.

"I have a great deal to report," Zach said. "Some of it important."

Will, standing by the door, shook his head. "We have plenty of time, and you deserve your rest. Good night, brother—and welcome home."

On his way to his own room he had passed Evvy's to make certain that the double guards he had ordered were on duty. A crack of light showed under the door, and he hesitated, then knocked. "Who is it?" she called. He identified himself, and on her invitation stepped into the room. She was sitting on the bed, her head to one side, combing her hair. The tan curve of her neck disappeared beneath a cream-colored dressing gown.

She set down the comb and smiled at him. He could not remember what he had meant to say. He wanted to touch her, but was afraid she would shrink from his deformity. "I stopped to see if you want anything," he said at last.

For a moment she didn't answer, then she rose and came to him. "I want you, Will," she whispered. "I have missed you."

Unable to speak, he had held her, at first gently, then fiercely, the warmth of her nearness intoxicating him, his heart pounding as if it would burst from his chest.

Watching her sleep now, he felt as if she had never been away. He touched her cheek lightly, then dressed and went downstairs to order a special breakfast for the three of them.

For most of the morning they sat and ate and talked. "It must be a relief to return to civilization," Will remarked once.

Evvy responded, "But just a week ago we were in a civilization." Again she and Zach exchanged a private look.

Will, for his part, did not discuss business with them, beyond a mention of the plague and the Trader attack; they had witnessed the plague, too, it seemed, in their travels. So much had happened that they all seemed much older; Evvy had acquired a new gravity and the look of a fully grown young woman, while the lines around Zach's eyes were deeper, his hair noticeably thinner. Will had to stop himself repeatedly from staring at both of them.

Their words tumbling and colliding with one another, Evvy and Zach told Will about their adventures; when he heard how Zach had saved Evvy at the last minute from the Trader pyre, Will had taken her hand and squeezed it, unable to speak for a moment. They told him of College, the civilization Evvy had mentioned.

"We must establish regular communication with Douglas," Zach concluded. "He has learned much about the world that we never suspected, and his library should be examined by your head librarian."

"Also," added Evvy, "he told us about other places where the woman sickness manifests itself differently or they have found other ways to deal with it."

"Here in the District it seems to have become less of a threat," Will said. "The women of the Garden believe that some women may be developing a resistance to it. And indirectly because of the plague, we believe that the testing project will be much more successful in the future."

He went on to tell them about the use of the Clinic as a healing center. "We owe it all to a woman from the Garden," he went on. "A candidate for Daughter. She is from the west and apparently has mastered herbal lore to an extent that we never dreamed of. She has created a mixture that, when administered early enough, prevents the plague from being fatal."

"An herbalist from the west?" asked Zach. "Do you know her name?"

"Alana." When he said the name, Zach frowned in puzzlement. A trace of alarm and something else colored his voice when he spoke next. "Describe her."

Puzzled, Will described the strange woman. "She is a miracle worker," he finished. "Her potion has prevented the worst disaster the Capital has faced in twenty years."

But Zach's face was grim. "I don't doubt that she can seem to work miracles—I've seen some of them myself. But, Will, if this woman is who I think she is, you must have her arrested immediately. I believe she is the high priestess of the Trader empire, a woman I knew as Jonna."

Will could not believe what he was hearing. "But—why would she be with the women of the Garden? Why should she be working with the scientists to cure the plague?"

"I suspect that is a part of her larger plans. She has vowed that her mission in life is to kill you."

"There's no doubt that you are wrong, then," said Will, relaxing. "She administered the cure to me herself. If her goals were as you say—what better chance would she have?"

Again Zach frowned. "I don't know, Will. She is very clever, and her plans may be more complicated than we can imagine. To be safe, have your men take her in. Then let me see her."

"I'm sure there's some mistake," Will said. "But perhaps we can discover more about her without such a drastic step. I will send for Daniel and ask him if he has noticed anything unusual, any chance remarks—"

"Oh, Will!" Now he turned to look at Evvy. Her face was distressed, and for a moment he thought she would cry. "You mustn't trust Daniel, either," she said. "At the wedding, just before the attack, I saw two men behind the curtain. He was one of them."

Two

As the Principal strode across the marble-floored lobby of the Hall of Justice, he could not shake a feeling that disaster was once again about to overtake his plans. There was a fetid, oppressive odor about the building that he had always hated; he imagined it to be the collective stink of centuries of guilt and fear.

If only Red still lived, he would have handled the confrontation at the Clinic differently; would not, as had Eric, summarily arrested the senior women, including the Mayor of the Garden. But the damage had been done, and Evvy, when she heard of it, had been outraged.

"You ordered him to arrest Daniel and this woman Alana," Evvy said. "That is all!"

"I'm well aware of what I ordered," the Principal said wearily. He had just come from a similar argument with Eric.

"None of them could have been guilty of these charges!" she continued. "Even if Alana is who Zach says, the women of the Garden could not have known it! You must let them go at once!"

"Nevertheless," said Will, "they let her escape. Fought for her escape, if Eric's report is accurate."

"What would you expect them to do when your soldiers

suddenly burst in, arresting everyone? Of course they fought! This is not the first time there has been conflict between you and the Garden."

"The deenas take it, we are not in the Garden! This has happened in my Capital! How do I know that they and Daniel were not in collusion?" He had slammed his fist on the desk and stood, glaring at her, then turned and took three deep, slow breaths. Could she not understand? Was she at heart as stubborn, as empty-headed, as all the women he had been forced to deal with?

"Will!" He let out the last breath and turned to Zach, who was speaking as calmly as he always did when Will let his temper get the best of him. "I believe that what Evvy says makes sense. Stop—don't say anything. Let me finish. It seems to me the only fair solution is to have a hearing immediately, with all those who were arrested. At the very least Daniel deserves to hear his accuser."

"I know how you feel about Daniel, Zach," said Will. "But if he were clever enough to stage the attack at the wedding and murder two people, he would surely be clever enough to lie about it!"

In the end he had agreed to meet with the three prisoners immediately, rather than subject them to questioning, which was the usual first step in cases this serious. They had left the office together, Evvy's small face still tight with anger, Zach silent and grim. As they walked along the broad avenue, flanked by guards, Will thought to reach out and take Evvy's hand, but she was hugging her arms to herself, and he was still too angry, even at her, to make the gesture.

He sat behind a desk on a raised platform in the front of the hearing room; he had presided over hundreds of cases here over the years; had heard thousands of excuses, tens of thousands of lies, and occasionally the truth. Never before had he appeared in a preliminary case like this one; never before had he felt so at odds with his own impulses. Before him, Zach and Evvy sat side by side on a wooden bench. After a moment the door opened and Daniel was brought in, his hands bound, heavily armed guards at his side. He had already been badly beaten, the Principal saw with disgust; he would have to speak again to Eric about his brutality. Daniel stood before the bench, looking at the floor, while Will read the charges against him.

"Do you understand the charges?" the Principal asked.

"Yes, sir," said Daniel.

"Let us hear the evidence," said Will. "Evvy, tell the court what you saw at the wedding."

While Evvy repeated what she had seen just before the attack, the Principal studied Daniel's face for some sign of emotion. His features were so badly swollen, it was difficult to discern any expression; once he shifted his weight and seemed to sway. "The prisoner may sit," the Principal said when Evvy had finished. "General Daniel, do you have anything to say to this evidence?"

"No, sir," mumbled Daniel.

Captain Michael of the House appeared next, to testify that Daniel had been present during the fatal luncheon when Red had been poisoned, and producing the more damning evidence that, when Daniel's quarters had been searched, a small jar had been found, which Wolff believed to contain the same poison that had killed Red and Lina. At this last bit of testimony Daniel started noticeably and seemed about to speak. But when Will asked if he had any comment, he again looked at the floor. "No, sir," he said.

Much as he hated to believe it, it seemed clear to Will that Daniel must be guilty. He had never suspected him; had gladly welcomed the young general back; had seen him perform bravely as a soldier and work long, hard hours at the Clinic. How could this have happened? His anger would come, he knew, but for now all he felt was sorrow and disbelief.

"Return the prisoner to his cell," he said at last. "Have him questioned tomorrow, and report all that he says."

After Daniel was led from the room, the Principal braced himself for the next hearing. He stole a look at Evvy, who, from the way she held herself, was obviously still angry. He sighed. "Bring in the women," he said.

The door opened again, and Katha and Gunda entered; like Daniel, their hands were bound, and they were flanked by guards. Evvy started up with a small cry.

"Sit, Evvy," he said. Then, to the guards, "Unbind the prisoners. Then you may wait outside."

Afraid now to meet Evvy's gaze, he looked carefully into the distance while the guards did as they were told. When it was done and the women were seated on benches to his left, he turned to them. Katha's face was set in the familiar lines of hatred, making her appear far older than she was, while Gunda, beside her, wore a guarded expression.

"The charges against you are very serious," he said without preamble. "But I have reason to believe that they may not be as they appear. So I want to hear what you have to say."

"First let us hear the charges," spat Katha.

"This is not a formal hearing," he said, "but very well." He looked down at the sheet of leaf-paper on the desk in front of him. "Harboring and aiding in the escape of a suspected Trader spy; interfering with soldiers of the Principal in performing their duty; resisting arrest; assault; possible murder; and complicity in Trader spying." He ignored an angry murmur from Evvy and turned back to the women. "Well?" he said.

Katha gave a short, harsh, forced laugh. "I suppose you have manufactured evidence to support these so-called charges?"

He took a moment to master his temper, then spoke calmly. "I am here solely to discover the truth of the matter. You may hear the evidence and respond to it." He nodded to the guard. "Bring General Eric."

Presently Eric appeared, looking so pleased with himself that the Principal wanted to strike him. "General Eric," he said, "tell us what happened this morning when you went to the Clinic to arrest General Daniel and the suspected Trader spy called Alana."

"I arrived as you had ordered, sir, with a dozen armed men. The workers in the Clinic were busy with sick children and suchlike, so no one noticed anything until we announced our intention."

"What were your words?"

"'By order of the Principal we arrest General Daniel and the woman from the Garden known as Alana.'"

"And what happened then?"

"General Daniel surrendered at once, sir," said Eric with a mocking look. "But not the woman. At first no one knew which one she was. Then suddenly one of the technicians jumped up from where she'd been sitting at the table, and before anyone could stop her, she ran out of the Clinic and along the portico to the back, by the river. My men and I ran after her, but we were prevented from stopping her."

"Who prevented you?"

"This one, sir." He pointed at Katha. She tensed but did not say anything. "She had her sword out quicker than a fox-cat and blocked the way long enough to let the spy escape. My men overpowered her, but by then it was too late. This Alana had gone into the swampy grass and disappeared."

Katha and Gunda had both sat quietly during this recital. Katha was unmarked, save for a few bruises; Eric had told the Principal that two of his men had been seriously wounded by her and that one was not expected to live.

"What happened next?"

"We placed the warrior under arrest, of course. Then this other one began to protest, saying it was an outrage, we had no right. She tried to prevent us from taking the warrior by holding her. So we took her too. The remaining men closed up the Clinic and sent the patients and workers home."

The Principal nodded. He had heard all this before. "Thank you, General Eric," he said. "That is all." Still looking smug, Eric started to sit. "I said that is all. You may go. Take the guards with you." Not bothering to hide his disappointment, Eric turned and left the courtroom, Katha following him with her gaze. The Principal glanced at Zach and Evvy again. Evvy was biting on a knuckle, looking as if she wanted to cry.

"You have heard my officer's testimony," said the Principal. "What do you have to say for yourselves?"

"We should never have come here," said Katha. "We should have realized that you would try something like this." She spat a harsh word and sat back on the wooden bench.

Quickly Gunda began to speak. "I can appreciate how it must look to you and your men, sir," she said. "But please, try to see how it appeared to us. We were here in the Capital, trying to help your sick citizens, *at your own request*. Alana, who has been with us for several months, has been working night and day to produce the cure that—again—*you* had asked us to provide. In the midst of our work, men who claimed to be your soldiers suddenly appeared and began to arrest the leaders of the Clinic. What could we do but protect ourselves and our own?"

Her words were reasonable, and the Principal wanted to believe them, if only for Evvy's sake. But just as, despite his wishes, he was forced to accept Daniel's guilt, there was something about Katha's manner that had always seemed to him out of character with a leader dedicated to the principles of the Garden.

"My brother, General Zach," he said, indicating Zach, "who spent five years among the Traders, has told me that Alana—whom he knew as Jonna—was not only high priestess of the Trader empire, she was dedicated to the destruction of me and my government. How could such a woman have become a candidate for Daughter of the Garden?"

"Do you accuse everyone in the Garden, then?" demanded Katha, starting to rise. Quickly Gunda put a hand on her arm and silenced her with a look. "Truly, sir, we did not know," said Gunda. "Indeed, I find it hard to believe even now. Do you forget that she prepared the cure for you? That she saved your life?"

"Of course I acknowledge what she did," said the Principal.

He was about to continue when Gunda spoke again, quickly. "General Zach must be mistaken," she said. "When Alana came to us, she was unkempt and ignorant, true, but so are most citizens of the District. She already possessed a rudimentary ability to read and an astounding knowledge of the medicinal uses of herbs, which has already contributed greatly to our scientific knowledge. Never once when she was with us did she evince any Trader beliefs or act in any way like a Trader. She was in every respect a devoted member of the Garden and a worthy candidate for Daughter. Surely, sir, you don't believe that we would knowingly harbor a Trader spy? They are dedicated to our destruction as they are to yours."

"My beliefs are not at question here," said the Principal. "But whether knowingly or not, it appears that you may in fact have harbored not only a spy, but one of the most powerful of the Trader leaders."

"I will never believe Alana is a Trader!" said Gunda, her own anger finally showing. "She once told me she was happier with us than she had ever been in her life. This Jonna that General Zach speaks of must be another woman."

Will turned to Zach with the growing conviction that this was indeed a misunderstanding and that his carefully nurtured relationship with the Garden had been irreparably damaged by a stupid mistake of identity. "Zach? Could what Gunda suggests possibly be true?"

Zach shook his head slightly. "The woman I knew, like Alana, was from the West. She was an herbalist of formidable skill. And her physical appearance was unmistakable. Describe Alana again."

"I only saw her once," said the Principal, "at a meeting at the Garden. But I will never forget her face. She was strangely formed, and her skin was of different colors, like a patchwork. Her eyes, too, were mismatched; one blue and one brown. Her hair was a strange, flat white, and the coarsest I have ever seen on a human. I thought at the time that she might be some species of new-human."

"Did you hear her speak?"

"Her voice was deep and hoarse, almost like a loud whisper." He looked at Zach, who remained quiet a moment, looking grim. Evvy had turned to look at him, too, her face apprehensive, her hands clenched into fists.

"I had thought she was dead," Zach said at last. "But the woman you describe could only be the woman I knew as Jonna, wife of the martyred Trader leader Yosh, high priestess of the Trader empire. There could not be two such women in the world."

"But why would she save my life? That contradicts everything you have said about her."

"I don't know," said Zach. "But I would like to add that Jonna—or Alana—once questioned me closely about the Garden. At the time I did not see any special significance to her words, but I now believe that she must have had a plan to use the Garden. She is a very clever woman and could easily have appeared to be someone she is not."

The Principal sat back in his chair and shut his eyes a moment. He could not dismiss Zach's certainty about Alana's true identity. Neither, he realized now, could he believe that the women of the Garden had been aware of it; obviously, as Zach said, they had been deceived. It was only his own strong feelings against Katha that had led him, even for a moment, to believe otherwise. He took a deep breath and held it; now he must apologize, but how? And how would he persuade the prickly Katha to accept the apology or to trust him again?

At last he opened his eyes. "I'm afraid a great injustice has been done," he said. "There seems no question that the woman, whatever her name, is indeed a Trader spy. But it also seems certain that no one at the Garden knew the truth about her. General Eric acted only as he saw fit at the time, but—"

There was a sudden noise as Katha's bench scraped against the floor and she rose to her feet. The Principal stopped talking and turned in astonishment to see her standing, her hands on her hips, her face pale with fury. Though she was unarmed, she projected an aura of danger and power, and everyone in the room turned to look at her.

"Do you think you can buy us off with a simple apology?" she demanded, her voice shaking.

"Katha—" Gunda plucked at the younger woman's tunic and tried to draw her back to the bench, but Katha angrily pulled away.

"No!" she shouted. "I've kept my silence. But now I will speak. I insisted on accompanying Alana to the Capital because I knew better than to trust you! We have trusted you too many times in the past, and it has always led to trouble for us! First you forced us to move from the old Garden because it suited you to use it as a southwestern outpost. Then, when we sent our women to open the first Clinic, the carelessness and stupidity of your men resulted in the death of one of our scientists. Somehow you poisoned Evvy's mind and took her from us, and now you accuse us of harboring a Trader spy! Don't you see, Gunda? He wants to destroy us! He always has! These charges are just an excuse—"

"Katha, it was a mistake—"

"Katha, please listen—"

Gunda and Evvy were speaking at the same time, but Katha hissed them to silence. "Let him speak for himself!" she said. "Look at him! Ask him what he feels for the Garden and all its women."

She remained standing, her furious eyes locked onto his.

Now the two other women turned their gaze to him, too, and he felt suddenly ashamed.

"I am not on trial here," he said. "But I will answer you. I owe you that much." He paused and took a deep breath, then continued, surprised at his calm. "Some of what you say is true. It's no secret that I have never had any great love for the Garden or for the women in it." He paused and looked at Evvy, wanting to add, "None but one," but did not. She was looking at the floor, twisting a fold of her skirt in her hands. "It is also true that it suited my purpose to move you from the site of the old Garden, but that was not why I did it. I had never before interfered in the affairs of the Garden and never have since. I moved you because I perceived that you were in danger and because I have long recognized how important the success of the Garden is to my own plans."

"That is a pretty tale, but it does not change the fact that you have always wanted to destroy us!"

"Control you, yes!" he snapped, his anger no longer contained. "But destroy you—never. Not even when the old woman was Mistress would I have done that. Why—" He stopped and took a deep breath, then asked because he wanted to know. "Why do you hate me so?"

As soon as he had asked, he wished he could call back the words. Now Katha's face changed subtly, and he realized she had been waiting for him to ask just this question—for how long?

"You should know why," she said with a proud shake of her head. "That you don't—is a measure of your guilt."

"You are free to go," he said, hoping to stop whatever she would say next. "My men were wrong and I was wrong. Go, with my apologies."

"You are afraid to hear the truth," said Katha, her voice now triumphant. "But you will not silence me with a pardon. You will hear the truth—"

"Katha, that's enough!" Gunda was on her feet, frantically trying to quiet her, but Katha shook her off and continued, her eyes fixed on the Principal's face. He had a sudden, strange sense that he had been here before, had heard before what she would say next.

"You will hear the truth," Katha repeated. "And you will know why—if I had known who Alana truly was—I would have helped her in her plan to destroy you. You will hear the truth, *Father*!" She paused, then continued. "Yes," she said. "That is the truth. I am the daughter you had over twenty years ago. The daughter you never knew, the daughter whose mother you murdered."

The room had become absolutely silent after Katha's words, and for a moment the Principal could not get his breath. He gulped at the air, as a man who is dying of thirst will gulp for water, and could not fill his lungs; for a moment he felt as if he were drowning.

He knew with cold certainty that what she said was true. At last he had recovered himself sufficiently to speak, and when he did, could not recognize his own voice. "Your mother then," he said, "was—"

"Was called Leya," said Katha. Her voice was hard-edged, bitter, triumphant. She knew what she was doing, and she rejoiced in it.

He could not doubt her words. They explained everything: her own hatred, perhaps even the old woman's. Her hatred for him, he realized, was a perfect mirror of his own feelings for the Garden and the women there. Suddenly he remembered Zach, who must have known. He forced himself to look at his brother, but Zach was staring at Katha, his face slack with shock. He looked, the Principal thought, like an old man. Zach's lips moved once, he licked them, and finally he spoke.

"They told me the child had died," he said.

"Yes, and so they told my mother," said Katha. "The Mistress did not want her to continue bound to *him*. Another woman gave birth to a dead child on the same day and they switched the infants. There were always babies in the Garden, and you had long since moved out of the compound. After she married you, my mother moved out too."

"I never knew, never suspected," said the Principal, more to Zach than to Katha. "I was a boy when it happened. A child."

"Not too much a child to make a baby. To knowingly commit the greatest crime possible in the Garden!" She was still standing, still glaring at him, her face a crazed mixture of triumph and hatred. He could see Leya now, in the fair hair and skin, and could see himself, too, in the single-mindedness and hatred.

Gunda rose now and placed both her hands on Katha's shoulders and gently pushed her to the bench. "You were never meant to know this, sir," she said. "Or you, Zach. Only a few of the elder women ever knew the truth about Katha's birth."

"But why?"

"The Mistress had her reasons." Gunda sounded weary. "I believe a large part of it was because you had chosen to turn your back on our work. And there was the crime itself, of course. She did not want you to feel you had any further ties or claims on us."

The Principal nodded. Had he been in the old woman's position, he would probably have done the same.

He turned to Zach, the effort making him dizzy. "I didn't know, Zach. I never knew that Leya had . . . I'm sorry."

Zach didn't answer. Evvy looked at him, her face stricken, but she didn't speak.

There was nothing more the Principal could say. Feeling as if he had been physically beaten, he forced himself to his feet. Zach and the women remained motionless. He took a deep breath, then strode to the door and opened it. "Let them go," he instructed the guards, and stepped out without looking back.

Three

It was late afternoon when Zach left the Hall of Justice, but he felt as if days had passed. The things that had been revealed in the hearing room had occurred over half of his lifetime ago; why, then, did the memory of Will's crime and Leya's death seem as vivid and painful to bear as if they had happened yesterday?

After Will had left, the women had remained motionless and silent. Evvy turned to Zach and seemed about to speak; her eyes widened when she saw the expression on his face, and she turned quickly away.

"Evvy." Gunda spoke quietly. "Come with us."

Evvy rose and went to the women. "I will come with you tonight," she said. "We must talk. But I cannot return to the Garden. Katha, I want to—"

Zach heard the bench scrape against the floor.

"Leave us!" said Katha, her voice no longer bold. "Go with *him*. You have abandoned the Garden."

"Katha!"

"No, Gunda, it's all right. Katha, I have not abandoned the Garden and I never will. Nor . . ." She paused. "Nor will the Principal. We are on the same side. We have been all along! Why can't you see that? Why must you hate so much? You need not, Katha, this is the world as it is."

"Do as you please, then," said Katha. Gunda murmured some soothing words, and then rustling footsteps told Zach that they were leaving. For many minutes after he heard the door shut, Zach remained where he was, trying to master his feelings. Once he turned, half expecting to see Evvy at the door, but he was alone in the room.

All these years he had blamed himself for Leya's death, but he had blamed Will, too, because the sickness did not develop until the birth of a second girl-child. Now, for the first time, he saw clearly that the responsibility had been entirely his. Knowing that Leya had already borne one girl-child—stillborn, as he had thought—knowing the danger, he should never have pressed her to marry him afterward, nor have badgered the Mistress until she agreed. The old woman had never denied him anything he wanted. It had been his own selfish young man's lusts that had put Leya in danger. His love for her had killed her. That, and her own love for Will.

He realized now too for the first time what he should have known twenty years ago: She had married him only in the hope that Will would return and become her second husband. He shut his eyes and remembered again the night that he had found them together, his younger brother and Leya, whom he had loved and desired his whole life. The sounds that Leya had been making were not from pain, as he had supposed then, but cries of pleasure; in all likelihood this had not been the first time they had lain together. But he had refused to see the truth then, and a year later had married Leya.

The aftermath of that night—the terrible fight and Will's expulsion from the Garden—had left a legacy of hatred that had forever poisoned relations between the Garden and the District. It had been the cause of Will's and the old woman's mutual antagonism and probably also of his own decision to betray Will and deliver Evvy to the Garden. It was the cause as well of the hatred that obsessed Katha, so much like her father in her ability to lead, and so like him in her inability to forgive.

He had once told Evvy part of the truth but not all of it;

this had been, he now saw, because he had been unable to admit the truth to himself. What had been done could not be changed, but it was not too late to try to undo some of the damage and prevent it from becoming worse. He realized that he had come to a decision without quite being aware of it, and he nodded to himself.

He rose and walked slowly to the door, opened it, and limped into the entrance hall. He stood considering a moment, then, on impulse, crossed the floor and presented himself to the officer in charge, asking to be taken to the dungeon.

Daniel, as an officer of the Principal's army, was in a small cell alone to one side of the large communal cell, nearly empty now because of the recent plague. Zach wrinkled his nose at the stench; though not nearly so bad as that in the Trader prison, it brought back the familiar constriction in his throat and the fear of being confined.

Daniel rose shakily as Zach was let in to the cell. His face was still caked with blood, and Zach quickly told him to sit, then squatted beside him. He dipped his neckerchief into the pitcher of drinking water and dabbed at Daniel's wounds.

"Thank you," said Daniel. He did not look quite so bad now that the worst of the blood was off.

"Eric reported that you surrendered without a struggle," Zach remarked.

Daniel shrugged. "Eric has never liked me," he said, his words slurred through swollen lips. "It doesn't matter." Quickly he went on. "Did the Principal send you?"

"I came of my own accord."

For a moment Daniel let his disappointment show. "It's good of you," he muttered.

"Daniel, I find it hard to believe you are guilty of the charges against you. I know you."

"The evidence is all against me, as you heard," said Daniel. "It does not seem to matter whether I am guilty or not."

"Are you?"

"No."

"I thought not. Well?"

"Ah, Zach. The Principal is convinced he has caught his man. What difference does it make?"

"Perhaps a great deal," said Zach. "If it was not you, then

the traitor is at large, perhaps working in the House. Even if you don't care about your own neck, what about the Principal? He is still in danger."

Daniel looked defiant for a moment, then his shoulders sagged. "All right, Zach. What do you want to know?"

"Tell me everything. How did Evvy come to see you at the wedding?"

Daniel sighed. "First you must understand something. You know that it was through the fault of my men—my fault—that the first attack on the Clinic occurred."

"And you paid for it."

"Yes." Daniel was silent a moment, and Zach sensed that he was thinking again of the girl he had loved, whose life had been lost in the attack. "The punishment was fair," he said. "More than fair. Will could have had me thrown in prison or executed. At times I wished he had."

"He knew that you are a good man. He needed you to continue the testing project."

"I was grateful to be allowed to continue. It is the most important work in the District. But, as you must know, he would not allow me in his presence. We communicated only through intermediaries. I could hardly bear it. I missed being a general, but most of all I missed him. I had served him since I was a boy."

"I know."

"I began to try to think of ways to regain his favor. I knew that my performance at the Clinic was not enough. He expected that. I began looking for something . . . heroic." He paused and took a sip of water, then continued. "As it happened, I had developed an informer. I paid him well, from my own pocket. I needed to be certain the Traders would not infiltrate the Clinic again."

"The informer told you of the attack on the wedding?"

Daniel nodded. "He did not have much information, but knew that someone inside the House was planning something on the day. I had no idea it would be such a large, well-organized attack. I thought if I could uncover the plot and foil it, Will would restore my commission."

Zach leaned against the wall and stretched out his legs. He had suspected something of the sort. Daniel's plan was understandable, but the results had been disastrous. "If only—"

"I know, Zach!" the younger man cried. "I should have sent word to Will, or to you, or Red, about what I had learned. I've cursed myself a hundred times every day since! If I had warned someone, it would not have happened. Will would still have his arm, Evvy would not have been kidnapped—"

"Daniel!" Zach spoke sharply. "It might have happened as it did anyway. Will has never been one to take threats seriously. Now tell me what happened on the day of the wedding."

"I went to the House early in the morning. I got in easily enough—after all, I delivered messages there frequently. Once inside, I secreted myself behind a curtain just off the Great Hall, listening and watching to see what would happen."

"What did you discover?"

"For a long time nothing happened. It was stuffy, and I believe I may have dozed. Then I became aware of whispering. I parted the curtain but could see nothing. I heard two, possibly three, men talking. One said, 'When the music ends, be ready.' Then he said something else I could not hear, and a different voice said, 'Now leave us and don't worry about anything. It will be done as we agreed.' Someone brushed the curtains, and after a moment I looked out. I saw someone dressed in the light blue of the serving staff disappearing around a corner."

"Can you describe him?"

"I had only a glimpse. I do not even know if he was one of the two or three who were talking. But the curtains began to move, and I stepped back into the shadows. A large, heavyset man had found my hiding place but didn't see me. I realized that he was concealing himself too. I thought that this man must be the architect of whatever was to happen. I thought he was alone, Zach! I swear, if I had known how many there were, I would have sounded the alarm at once!"

"Go on."

"There's little more to tell. I heard the sound of your lyre playing. The stranger had still not seen me. I took out my knife and began to creep up on him. I thought I was going to be a hero. The music stopped, and at that moment he turned and saw me. He had a bow and arrows. I think he thought at first that I was in the plot, because he didn't move. I closed on him. Neither of us made a sound. I don't know why. We struggled, the curtain parted once—that must have been when Evvy saw me—and then the stranger's companion appeared from somewhere. He hit me, and the next thing I remember, there was smoke and shouting. Somehow I pulled myself to safety and helped to fight the fire."

Zach looked at Daniel with pity. "Ah, Daniel," he said.

"I considered reporting to the Principal, telling him everything that had happened. If I had had any real evidence, I would have. But I didn't know who on the staff was responsible, and I simply couldn't face his anger again."

"So this is why you have remained silent."

"All these months I've kept my ears open, hoping to get more information on the traitor in the House. But I have heard nothing, and my original informant has never returned." He looked about the cell in despair. "I realize how this story must sound, even as I tell it. But it is the truth. Do you believe me?"

"I believe you," said Zach. He understood Daniel's actions very well and could even sympathize with them to an extent. But it was doubtful if Will would even be willing to listen.

"I knew it was wrong to resume my old commission," Daniel continued. "I've thought many times of telling Will the truth. And I've lived in fear that he would somehow discover the truth on his own."

"He has discovered an untruth, but it's bad enough," said Zach. "What about the other evidence against you?"

Daniel shrugged. "I cannot say. It was coincidence that I was there when Red died. It was the first time I had been inside the House in weeks. I know nothing about the girl. And the poison—they showed me the jar of poison that was said to be found in my rooms. I had never seen it before."

"The real culprit must have hidden it there," said Zach, "to make you look more guilty. But who?"

Daniel shook his head. "I hope, for Will's sake, you find him soon."

"For your sake too," said Zach. "I don't know if you'll ever be a general again, but I will try to get you out of here."

He took Daniel's hand and squeezed it, then called for the guard.

It was early evening when Zach left the prison, and for a while he walked aimlessly, the sounds and smells of summer life scarcely registering. Who could the traitor be? He asked himself this question over and over. It must have been someone with an intimate knowledge of the House and its administration and who was also a secret Trader. Presumably the girl had been killed because—as Will had told him—she gave Will information about the Trader attack at Crosskey. But why would the Traders kill Red? And why, if indeed the man was still at large, had no more attempts been made on Will himself?

A rumbling in his stomach told him it was time for dinner. He purchased two meat pies and a skin of flower-wine from an earnest young boy, then crossed to the mall. He walked slowly through the busiest areas of commerce and at last settled himself in the grass, his back against a tree, on the far side near the river. While summer sounds of music and laughter swirled behind him, he gazed at the water and at the half-submerged, shining marble temple just across from him.

As he ate and drank, the stars began to appear one by one, and he thought of Evvy and their two journeys together. On a level just below his consciousness was the gnawing pain that had been reawakened today; he was aware that he was occupying himself with other matters in part to keep it at bay. Will would be missing him at the House, though perhaps he was as unready for a meeting now as Zach was. He was reluctant to return soon, or perhaps at all this night; it would not be the first time he had slept on the mall.

He finished one of the meat pies and half the second, washing them down with wine, then he let his head fall against the tree. He had a confusing half dream, crowded with images of archers and swordswomen dressed in the white coats of the Garden, then suddenly he felt himself being shaken.

"Brother Zach!"

He opened his eyes and looked up into the misshapen face of Jonna.

* * *

"You do not seem surprised to see me," she remarked. She was sitting cross-legged in front of him, her cloak around her shoulders. Although her face was unmistakable, she had altered her appearance by hacking off the long white hair and applying some sort of dye that made it appear reddish-brown.

Zach smiled without humor. "Nothing would surprise me today, Jonna," he said. "I assume you know that half the Principal's men are out looking for you."

"Are you not one of the Principal's men?" she said in a mocking tone.

"Are you hungry?" He offered her the remaining half pie. She looked at it, then took it and ate hungrily. When she had finished, she accepted the wine skin and drank deeply. "Thank you."

"What are you doing here?" he asked at last.

"I might ask you that same question," she said. "This seems an unlikely bedroom for the Principal's most trusted aide." She took another swallow of wine, then handed the skin back. "I had nowhere else to go. I've spent most of the day in and around the swamps. As soon as I was away from the Clinic, I cut my hair off and changed it with lorna-berry juice. But where can I go?"

"Back to the Trader empire, I would have thought," said Zach.

"With the Principal's men guarding every road out of the Capital? And me looking as I do? It's not likely I'd get far."

"Then what are your plans?"

She shrugged, her expression suddenly bitter. "I don't know. There is no place for me now." She paused and sighed. "It was you who turned me in, wasn't it?"

"I had no choice."

She nodded. "I thought so. No one else would have known. Do you know, I've prayed every day that you would never return, that my identity would never be known."

"I am back in part thanks to your help," he said.

"The sleeping herbs?"

"I don't think I could have escaped the Road Men without them. But how did you get away? All the women were killed in an accident. I thought you were among them."

"To your great relief, no doubt."

"In truth I was sorry. Our purposes have always been opposed, but I've never wished you harm."

She gave him a sly look, then shrugged. "I escaped on the second day," she said. "It was easy. The Engineer sent for me—he does that with all new women—and I used a technique my grandmother taught me, of pinching a certain nerve. He fell asleep immediately, and I took his bat-helmet and slipped out. I can be nearly invisible when I want to be." Zach nodded; he didn't doubt it. "Afterward, I traveled east and made my way to the Garden." She gave him an ironic smile. "Are you going to arrest me now?"

"I don't know," said Zach. "I need to know more." It struck him then that he should have been more surprised to see her; should have sounded the alarm, and yet, despite her vows of vengeance, he felt no threat from her.

"What do you want to know?" she asked. Then: "Give me more wine."

He passed the skin over and thought as she drank. "I need to know first of all what you were doing here in the Capital," he said.

She laughed, again with an edge of bitterness. "I was curing the Principal's subjects of the Trader plague."

"So I hear. Is that all?"

"It is all." She lowered her head, and Zach could not see her expression. "I was a candidate for Daughter of the Garden. Did they tell you that?"

"Yes. I always felt that you would have been happy in the Garden if your life had gone differently."

"I was happy there. It was the only place I ever truly felt I belonged. Even with the Traders, I never felt at home. I don't think they would have accepted me if it had not been for Yosh."

"Have you renounced your Trader beliefs, then?"

She looked up again and smiled. "You must think me a very weak-willed woman. That I believe what I am told to believe. Yet that is, in a way, what has happened. When I made my way to the Garden, it was with the thought of using it as a way to get to the Principal. But once I had been there a few weeks I began to see things differently. I began to see the hope that they offer the world. I learned many things that I had never known. And I taught them things, too, and they honored me for it. I . . . came to love the women of the Garden and what they stand for. I can't expect you to believe me, but that is the truth."

"What about the Principal and your vow to kill him?"

"I came to see also that the Garden can exist only with the help of his government. When I agreed to come to the Capital to treat the sick, I was not certain what I would do. I thought I might still try to avenge Yosh. As you may have heard, I had an opportunity to do so. When I prepared the herbal mixture for the Principal, I could have added a very small amount of a certain ingredient. . . ."

"But you did not."

"No. I realized that to do so would mean betraying the Garden. That if I did such a thing I could never return there. Now I cannot go back in any case."

"I think they would take you in," he said. "They do not believe the charges against you."

"But the Principal does, and he would not allow it. It would only cause more dissension between them."

Zach nodded, knowing she was right. "Perhaps you could return to the Traders and teach them the things you have learned here," he said at last.

"They would burn me as a heretic, you know that. But I think their power is waning. They have never had a truly inspired leader since Brother Yosh. And I have seen—from the work of the Clinic—that results in this life mean more to people than promises about the next."

"I don't know," Zach said after a moment.

"Don't know what?"

"I don't know that I believe you, Jonna."

"Even though I saved the Principal's life?"

"Even so."

She sighed. "I don't blame you, Brother Zach. To tell the truth, sometimes I am no longer so sure myself what I believe or who I am. But you can be sure of one thing. I have forgiven the Principal. And so has Yosh."

"What!"

"He appeared to me in a dream," she said. "It was the third night I spent in the Capital. He said to me, 'Jonna, you have suffered much on my account. But suffer no more. I am at peace and I await you.'"

She spoke simply, and Zach saw again the softness in her face that came when she talked of Yosh, and he believed her.

"What will you do now?" he asked.

"I don't know. I will have to leave the Capital—unless, that is, you have me arrested."

He sighed. "I won't turn you in, Jonna."

"I know it."

"There is one thing you can do for me, if you will," he said then.

"What is it?"

"Tell me the name of the Trader spy in the Principal's House."

Again Jonna laughed. "You believe that the spy is a Trader? No wonder he has never been caught!"

"But if not a Trader—"

"Someone whose aims coincided in part with the Traders' aims. I do not know his name, but I can tell you what he does." She leaned forward and whispered in Zach's ear.

Zach sat back, shocked. It made sense, he realized now. And it also made sense that no one else had guessed the truth. "Who would have thought it?" he said.

"Who would have thought that you and I would end up on the same side of things?" said Jonna. "The world is a strange place."

Zach opened his pouch and took out a small bag full of metal. "Take this," he said. "It may help you to leave the Capital. You must try to get away as soon as possible. If I see you again I will have no choice but to arrest you."

"Thank you," she said. She leaned forward again and kissed him on the cheek.

He squeezed her hand, then got to his feet. "I must take this information to the Principal at once."

"Brother Zach?"

"Yes?"

"Thank you for letting me go."

"I owe it to you."

"And Brother Zach?"

"Yes?"

She held up a small bundle of herbs. "Do you know that I could have killed you just now? With the wine?"

Zach laughed. "I know it, Jonna." He slipped a small,

sharp knife from his sleeve. "Do you know that I could just as easily have killed you?"

Now Jonna laughed too.

"Good-bye, Jonna," he said. "Good luck to you."

"Good-bye, Brother Zach."

Four

The Principal sat alone in his office, drinking and staring at the wall. From the open window behind him he could hear the typical sounds of the mall on a warm summer night; now that the plague was no longer a major threat, the citizens of the Capital had returned to their lives as if nothing had happened. He heard drunken laughter, the angry sounds of a beginning fight, faint strains of music as an itinerant musician played. He realized with a start that he had not heard Zach play the feathered lyre since the morning of the wedding, nearly a year ago. It seemed likely now that he would never hear it again.

The sounds of life should have been cheering—they were an indication that, no matter what else had happened, the society he had established was working. It was its stability that had made possible the widespread cure of the Trader plague. But once again, just when it seemed that the worst threats were behind him, a catastrophe had occurred. This, perhaps the worst of all, meant a serious rift between himself and the Garden and the reawakening of the old bitterness between him and Zach. These were wounds that he feared could never be healed.

As for Evvy, after all that had happened today and all that

had led up to it, he was certain that she would never be able to forgive or even to understand.

He remembered again the hateful look on Katha's face when she had revealed the truth of her birth. Of course she had known the destruction that would be wrought by her revelation; that was why she had made it. It was as if the poisonous feelings pent up in her all these years had finally reached a point where they could no longer be contained; that she had to give them vent no matter the consequences.

That she was his daughter, of his blood, he could not doubt. What to do with this information was beyond his ability to think about for the present. On the one hand, it increased the strength of the ties between him and the Garden; on the other, because of her hatred for him, it left them further apart than ever. Did he even want to acknowledge her as a daughter? He poured himself a cup of brew and drank, his feelings so confused that he did not know what he thought.

If only he had not taken Leya; if only Katha had kept silent; if only, if only . . .

There were three sharp raps at the door, followed by a pause, and then a fourth; it was Lindy's signal. "What is it?"

Lindy looked apprehensive as he entered. No doubt he had heard the gossip, along with every other citizen of the Capital. No matter that there had been no one in the room but himself, Zach, Evvy, and the women from the Garden; even the deepest secrets seemed to spread immediately like a strange new-plant, the truth becoming choked and distorted in its tendrils.

"Pardon, sir," Lindy said. "Captain Robin sent me to see if you want anything."

The deenas take Robin! He had told him that he was to be left strictly alone and would see no one but Zach or Evvy.

"Thank you, boy, but I want nothing," he said.

"More brew? Some food?"

"Nothing!"

"Yes, sir. I'm sorry to disturb you, sir."

Lindy turned to go, and the Principal felt ashamed. Perhaps some company would take his mind off his troubles. "I didn't mean to shout at you, Lindy," he said. "I'm under some pressure just lately. Sit down a moment. Tell me the latest news about the birds."

Looking pleased, the boy settled himself on the upholstered sofa across from the Principal's desk. "The birds that were released yesterday have all returned to the cage," he said. "I didn't bother to tell you last night or this afternoon because you were busy with other matters."

"And what of the training of new bird-keepers?"

"It's a difficulty, sir. No one seems to understand the care that must be taken to keep the cages clean and to handle each bird several times a day."

The Principal remembered the fiasco that resulted in Patrick's death and nodded glumly. "We'll simply have to find more reliable workers."

"Yes, sir."

"Tell me, Lindy," he said after a moment. "Do you know if General Zach has returned this evening?"

"No sir, he has not," said Lindy. "I happened by his room a while ago and found it empty."

"You went into General Zach's room without permission?"

"I'm sorry, sir." The boy looked at his feet. "I . . . I had to return something."

"Something that he loaned you?"

"Something I borrowed." Lindy's face twisted in embarrassment or fear, and then he blurted, "I'm sorry, sir, I should have told you before, should have asked permission, but I did it only to please you."

"Did what?" The Principal didn't bother to conceal his annoyance. Whatever the boy had done, he didn't want to hear about it now. There had been enough unburdening for one day, or perhaps for a whole lifetime.

But Lindy continued to speak, in a rush. "I didn't do any harm, sir, I promise you! Only I just borrowed General Zach's lyre—just the last few weeks, sir. I've been taking lessons."

"How dare you touch Zach's things without permission! And lessons—why on earth have you done that?"

"For you, sir, like I said," the boy continued, bolder. "I'd been noticing how sad you seemed sometimes, with General Zach and your lady gone. I began to think that they might never come back. You said as much yourself once. Anyway, I thought that if I could learn to play the lyre, it might . . . might cheer you up."

"Well, you thought wrong!" shouted the Principal. "No

one is to touch Zach's lyre but Zach himself! I have half a mind to have you whipped!" Napoleon, alarmed at the tone in the Principal's voice, leapt quickly off the desk and onto the windowsill where he watched, growling softly in his throat.

"I'm sorry, sir, sorry, so sorry," Lindy said. His eyes were brimming over. Before the Principal could think what to say or do next, there was a rap at the door, and Grant stuck his head in.

"What is it?" the Principal snapped.

"General Zach is here, sir. He asks to see you."

"Send him in immediately," said Will, his heart suddenly pounding. His dread of the coming meeting drove out all anger at Lindy. "You may go," he told the boy. "We'll discuss this another time."

"I think it's better for the boy to stay," said Zach, stepping into the room. Will looked at him in apprehension, but Zach seemed preoccupied rather than angry or upset. Will saw that he was limping badly, and his face looked unusually gaunt.

"I-I-I'm terrible sorry, sir!" Lindy told Zach. The boy was almost unintelligible in his stammering fear. "I didn't mean any harm! Like I explained to the Principal, I did it only because I thought it would cheer him!"

Zach stopped in confusion. "What are you talking about?"

"Why, your feathered lyre, sir! I only borrowed it for a few weeks. It came to no harm. I even put new strings on."

"My lyre?" Zach seemed to make an effort to remember that he had ever owned such a thing. "You borrowed my lyre?"

"Yes, sir. To learn how to play, sir. To play for the Principal."

Now Zach nodded. "I see," he said. "Of course. It's part of the pattern."

"The pattern, sir?"

"Leave, Lindy! Forget the deena-cursed lyre!" Will could contain himself no longer. "I've already reprimanded Lindy for what he has done. He will be punished. But, Zach, please sit. We must talk. Lindy—"

"Yes, we must talk," Zach said. "But a great deal of what we must talk about involves Lindy. No you don't, boy!" Zach had moved swiftly and grasped the boy by the wrist. Napoleon began to hiss from his perch on the windowsill. "Now sit back down and listen. When I ask you questions, answer."

Looking paler than the Principal had ever seen him, Lindy sat back on the sofa, holding his wrist. Zach stood above him, his face stern.

"Zach, what is going on?" The Principal was baffled. Surely Zach could not be reacting so strongly to the unauthorized borrowing of his feathered lyre?

"*You* know what this is about, don't you, Lindy?" The boy didn't answer, and Zach went on. "It must be a shock. You must have thought yourself completely safe now. All your aims seemed to have been realized. You even managed to see that the only person who might have linked you to the crimes was arrested and charged in your place."

"It's a lie!" the boy blurted. "All lies! I don't know what General Daniel's been telling you, but it's lies!"

Suddenly the Principal thought he understood. Understood but could not believe. "Zach, are you saying—"

"That Lindy is the traitor, the one who was responsible for the Trader attack at the wedding, the murder of Red, and the murder of the girl."

"*Lindy*?" The Principal simply could not accept it. The young serving boy whose only interest in life beyond service to the Principal was caring for birds; the boy who rejected military service as too dangerous; the boy who feared to leave the House for any but the most routine tasks: this boy was supposed to be the mastermind of a plot—and of two murders? For a frightening moment he wondered if the shock of Katha's revelations had unbalanced Zach's mind. "Zach, that's preposterous," he said. "No one would believe it!"

"Agreed," said Zach. "That's why he's gotten away with it for so long."

The boy seemed to have drawn courage from Will's words, and a belligerent look crossed his face. "I've never done anything that wasn't in service to the Principal," he said. "That wasn't for his own good!"

"I know that too," said Zach. "In fact, that's why you conceived the plan in the first place."

The Principal listened in bafflement. "Zach, Lindy—both of you be quiet for a moment. Zach, I can't imagine where you got your information, but what you are saying is ridiculous. Even if the evidence did not point to Daniel, even if I thought that Lindy were somehow capable of the things you accuse him of, what would be his motive? He grew up in the House. You're not going to tell me he's a secret Trader?"

"Not at all," said Zach. "Not a Trader, but someone whose aims coincided in some ways with those of the Traders."

"Are you saying that Lindy wanted me dead?"

"Just the opposite!" He turned to Lindy, who, despite the pose of bravado, had broken out in a sweat. The Principal watched him attentively as Zach continued. "But it didn't happen as you planned, did it, boy? When you made the bargain with the Traders, your only thought was to stop the wedding. The Traders promised you that they would take the Principal's bride but leave the Principal safe. Their real aim all along, though, was to assassinate the Principal. It is only good luck that it did not happen."

The Principal continued to watch and listen, appalled, as Lindy began to shift from side to side, obviously unaware that he was doing so, his eyes riveted on Zach.

"You must have been horrified when you discovered what had happened to Will. But there was nothing you could do about it. To reveal the names of whoever was responsible would be to reveal your own guilt. How did you do it? Did you let them into the House? Did you somehow see to it that Odell hired them as extra servants? You needn't answer. Now that we know the truth, we can find out. Surely someone has seen you in a place you weren't meant to be. Perhaps in Daniel's quarters, concealing the lying evidence of poison? As for the poison itself, you had to have gotten it from somewhere."

The boy had begun to cry now, his face in his hands. He muttered something, and Zach pulled his hands from his mouth. "What did you say?"

"I said . . . said I didn't mean it. I never meant the Principal to come to harm. I didn't want anything to happen to him ever. But once it had been done, what could I do but keep on with it?"

For the second time that day the Principal's heart felt as if it had stopped. His hand shaking, he took a deep swallow of brew. From his post at the window Napoleon continued to emit throaty growls.

"Tell us, then," said Zach. He crossed to the desk and poured two cups of brew, one for himself and another for the boy. Lindy gulped at his, emptying it, then, his eyes fixed on the floor, began to talk. "It's like you say, sir. They told me only that they wanted to stop the wedding. They wanted to take the Principal's lady. They said they'd take her away but wouldn't hurt her. I didn't want anyone to get hurt. I let them in, early in the morning, through the window. It woke up the fox-cat, but then he got shut up and no one found the Traders. I didn't know they meant harm to the Principal until it had already been done."

Will continued to listen, horrified. He felt as if he had not truly awakened this morning but had instead become trapped in an unending nightmare.

"What about General Red?" said Zach. "Why did you kill him? Had he suspected something?"

"No, sir. That was a mistake. I liked General Red. I felt bad for him. The poison was intended for Daniel. Somehow the two bowls got mixed up."

Zach nodded. "And then the girl. Had you come to enjoy killing? There was no reason to hurt her."

"Her I had the best reason for!" the boy exclaimed. His face had changed completely; had become animated and highly colored. At last the Principal realized that Lindy was insane and was confessing his crimes in an effort to justify them.

"She was after the Principal, sir," the boy went on. "She was using her tricks on him, the tricks she learned at the house for hire. After all the trouble I went to to get rid of his first lady, I didn't want another one. She wouldn't have taken care of him as well as I could, don't you see?" He turned now to the Principal, his eyes not quite focused. "Don't you see, sir? I did it for you. I wanted to protect you and take care of you. No one could do it as well as I can. I've been caring for you since I was a little boy. You were going to send me away, make me go into the army. I had no choice, sir, don't you see?"

At last Will did see, and for a moment he thought he would be sick. Lindy was still babbling, tears coursing down his cheeks. "Be quiet, Lindy," he said sharply. Immediately the boy quieted. He turned to Zach. "Thank you," he said.

"If you had not stopped him, who knows what else he might have done. But how did you know?"

"I . . . received some information," Zach said vaguely. "As you know, I couldn't believe Daniel was guilty. After a while I saw how it had to be and why no one had caught the traitor before. What will you do with him?"

"I'll do what's necessary," the Principal said. He glanced at Lindy, but the boy was not listening; he seemed to have retreated into his thoughts. Before the Change, such a person as Lindy would have been locked up and treated and possibly eventually cured. But Will did not have the facilities to care for the criminally insane, nor did he care to. He had no pity for the boy, but strangely no anger or hatred, either; simply a feeling of revulsion and horror.

He stood, feeling that he had aged fifty years in this one day. At the door he instructed Grant to wake Captain Michael and have him report at once. Within ten minutes the young Captain had arrived, swallowing a yawn while he listened to instructions.

"Take this prisoner and put him into a private cell at once," he said. "Bind him and have several guards with you. He is quiet now, but I believe he may become violent. Instruct General Marcus that I want to have him tried and then executed as soon as possible, within the law." He started to turn back, then remembered. "And have General Daniel released," he added. "That is all."

"Yes, sir." Captain Michael looked surprised when he recognized the identity of the prisoner. He pulled the boy to his feet. "Come along, son," he said. Lindy offered no resistance, following the captain from the office like a sleepwalker.

The door shut, and the Principal and Zach were alone. For a moment neither man spoke, then the Principal opened the door again and called for more brew. "I know it's late, Zach," he said, "but please don't leave. I must talk to you."

Five

The next morning Zach awoke with a throbbing head. He slowly opened his eyes and saw by the bright sunshine outside his window that it was quite late, near midday. Feeling disoriented, he sat, his eye falling on the feathered lyre on the wall across from his bed, and all that had happened yesterday and last night came flooding back.

It had been the most emotionally exhausting day of his life, but he knew it had been far worse for the Principal. Zach did not remember ever having seen Will so upset, so drained, not even during the trouble last year, when Zach had returned from the Trader empire. And no wonder. The life that Will thought he knew had suddenly come unraveled around him. First Katha, then Lindy. Zach's exhaustion was perhaps as deep, but the shock was less. Though he had never suspected that Leya's first child had lived or that she might be Katha, he had known of the existence of the child and had known that Will was the father. Likewise, though the questioning of Lindy last night had been difficult and unpleasant, he had not, as had Will, relied on the boy absolutely, treating him almost like a son for more than five years.

After Captain Michael had taken Lindy away and Grant had brought more brew and a platter of bread and cheese, the Principal had begun to drink steadily, heavily, as Zach had not seen him do since their youth. Because of his own tangled feelings, and at Will's urging, Zach matched him cup for cup. The events of the evening and the drink blunted the tension between them, and after a time both men began to feel at ease, almost as they had been before.

As they drank, the Principal questioned Zach about how he had come to suspect Lindy and how he had reasoned out what must have happened. Zach answered automatically, not mentioning Jonna, aware that the Principal was only making conversation to avoid discussing what was between them. Before long Zach began to feel dizzy; Will, as always, showed few effects of too much drink. His eyes only had become slightly unfocused and his movements somewhat awkward. After a time Zach realized that he could hold no more brew. He glanced at the window and saw that faint streaks of light were beginning to appear in the sky. He stretched and yawned, then started to push himself to his feet.

"Zach, wait." Will, still at his desk, was now looking at him directly, his eyes no longer unfocused. "I have planned a meeting for tomorrow, for today. A private meeting of the three of us. You and I—and Evvy. I had Robin send word to her at the house where the women are staying. I've made a decision."

Zach nodded, not knowing what to say. It was obvious that the matters Katha had revealed must be talked about, but he was not certain that it was best to bring Evvy into the discussion. "Very well," he said.

"But before we meet, I need to speak to you. I've been trying to work up the courage to say something all night."

"It's not necessary," said Zach. "It's over with."

"I only want to tell you that I didn't know. I never knew Leya was pregnant. Never suspected. If I had known—"

"If you had known, nothing would have been different," said Zach.

"When you told me she had died of the sickness, I didn't think," the Principal went on. "I suppose I assumed that the two of you had had another child." He paused, drank more brew. "Why didn't you say anything?" he asked.

"You never asked!" said Zach. In spite of himself he felt the old rage and hurt returning.

"At least let me explain," said Will.

"Explain what?"

"Why I pursued Leya. It was because you were who you were. I wanted to do everything you did, have everything you had. I suppose I was jealous of you. I saw that you wanted Leya, so I wanted her too."

"I don't want to hear this," said Zach. "I don't want to hear it, do you understand? If you must ease your conscience by confessing, do it. But not to me."

Will looked ashamed. "You're right, Zach. Only . . . please believe that I'm sorry. We'll leave it at that." He paused, and Zach hoped he had finished, but then he spoke again, his voice not quite steady. "One thing more, I never understood. When Leya died, why did you seek me out? After the way we had parted, I thought I would never see you again."

"In truth, I didn't know," said Zach. His dizziness had grown worse, and it was only by great effort that he was able to keep Will's face in focus. "I think I lost my reason for a time. I remember I had trouble thinking of anything but her. I blamed you for her death. I wanted to see you, to confront you. I think I may even have meant to kill you."

"Perhaps you would have been justified," said Will after a moment.

"Don't talk nonsense," said Zach irritably. "In any case, the worst of the anger went away when I saw you again. I realized that in spite of everything, I had missed you. After a while our friendship and your goals became more important to me than anything that had happened."

The Principal looked at the desk, then again at Zach. "Are you saying that you forgive me, brother?"

"I forgave you long ago, Will," said Zach. "Perhaps it is time for you forgive yourself." He rose then and went to Will, clasped his hand, then crossed to the door leading to his own room.

Despite the fact that he had been up all night, and despite the brew he had drunk, he had trouble falling asleep. He had never seen Will in a mood like this, and it troubled him. He wondered what decision Will would announce tomorrow. And he wondered how his own decision would be received.

* * *

"I have something important to tell you," said Will, sitting again behind his desk, facing Zach and Evvy. Late-afternoon sun slanted in the window, and Zach was reminded of another meeting a year ago, when Will had announced that Zach was to go into exile. "I have thought of myself, my whole life, as a good man," Will continued. "But now I understand that I am not. That through the years I have hurt many people because I never fully considered the consequences of my actions. I thought that because I was a leader of men, because I obeyed my own laws, the other things I did would not make a difference. I know now that I was wrong." He took a deep breath, paused, and then continued. "I hurt you, Evvy, in many ways, first by taking you as a child from your parents. Long ago I hurt Zach terribly by taking the girl he loved for myself and by turning away from the Garden. I hurt the old woman and . . . and Katha in the same way. I want to make up for what I have done and set things right."

Zach listened apprehensively. He could not see the good of going over it again. Evvy evidently felt the same way, because she leaned forward and interrupted. "Will," she said. "Please don't—"

"Let me continue," said Will. "You will both have a chance to speak in a moment." He paused, then went on. "I've been thinking since yesterday afternoon," he said. "I've come to realize what I must do. It will not repair all the damage, but it may help a little to restore things to a balance." He rose and turned to the window.

Zach and Evvy waited, silent. Evvy glanced at Zach to see if he knew what Will was leading up to, but Zach only shrugged. They watched Will's shoulders move as he took three deep breaths, then he turned back.

"What I have decided is this," he said. "I will give up my rule. I can no longer lead other men, no longer set an example for them. I will turn the District over to you, Zach. You will be the new Principal. And Evvy will rule beside you."

For a moment Zach was as shocked as if Will had just announced that he had decided to cut his own throat. He could scarcely believe what he had heard and could not find the voice to speak. After another moment Will sat again. "Well?" he said. "You may speak now."

"You're upset," said Zach at last. "You don't know what you're saying."

"I know very well what I am saying," said the Principal. "I have thought it over carefully. It is what is best for the District and best for the Garden."

"What makes you think," Zach said then, "that I want to be Principal?"

"You will be a good ruler, Zach. Everyone respects you. You are wiser and kinder than most men."

"But I'm not a leader!" said Zach. "I have never wanted to be! After all these years, don't you know that much about me?"

"I understand that you are surprised by my decision," said Will. "But when you think it over, you'll see the wisdom in it." He paused, then turned to Evvy. But before he could speak, she was on her feet, her voice trembling with anger. "I can't believe the things I am hearing!" she said. "Do you really think it is so easy? That you can make things right by turning your back on everything you have worked all your life to build? Do you honestly believe you can simply hand over the keys to Zach and walk away?"

"Of course I can't change what's happened," said Will, his voice weary. "That's why I must take this step. That's why you and Zach—"

"Stop it!" she cried. She was angrier than Zach had ever seen her, and he saw Will take an uncertain step backward as she approached him and continued to shout across the desk. "How dare you presume to give me to Zach as if I were a new mount-hair cloak! Have you lost your reason?"

Will continued to look at her, then he sat again. There was no trace of anger in him, only an unnatural calm. "Ah, Evvy," he said after a moment, "I know that you agreed to marry me because you care about the future of the Garden and of the District. But don't you think I know that you love Zach and he loves you?"

"Please don't, Will," said Evvy. "We had this same conversation a year ago. I told you then that I love Zach and he loves me, but as a father and a daughter! I love you as a wife loves her husband. But it's hard to remember when you are acting so foolishly!"

"Zach, do you love Evvy?"

"It is as Evvy says," said Zach. "Much as I love her, I do not want her for a wife. She loves you, and she wants to marry you, not me."

The Principal sat for a long moment looking at them. "No, Evvy," he said. "Even if what you say was true once, I can't believe you still care for me after yesterday."

Evvy took a deep breath and sat. When she began speaking again, she sounded calmer. "Yesterday, when I heard Katha speak, I was horrified," she said. "I could feel my heart breaking for Zach . . . and for Katha. But also for you, Will. I saw your face when she told you. Thinking it over, I am surprised that no one guessed the truth long ago. It explains so many things. I believe that the greatest harm has been caused not by what you did but because everyone has kept silent about it all these years."

Zach found himself nodding in agreement. He had come to believe the same way. But, glancing at Will, he could see that he had not been listening. "There may be some truth in what you say, Evvy," he said, "but it changes nothing. My relations with the Garden are ruined beyond repair. Only a new leader can set things right."

"What if I refuse?" said Zach.

"Then I will choose someone else," Will said. "Perhaps Ralf . . . if you will not."

"Ralf is an old man. Will you stand idly by if he fails to unite the District, if the Traders decide to take advantage of our weakness?"

"You will not let that happen," the Principal said. "In any case, I will not be here, so it will be no concern of mine." He sat back in his chair, as if the matter were closed.

"I never thought I would see this," said Zach. "You have let Katha do what neither the President's men nor the Traders could. You have allowed her to defeat you."

"That is not what has happened, Zach," said Will quietly. "I leave the District stronger than ever."

"Self-sacrifice does not become you," snapped Zach then, hoping to provoke an angry response, but Will simply shrugged.

Again Evvy and Zach exchanged glances. Will had always had a strong sense of the theatrical, and Zach realized he was capable of going through with his plan simply out of pride and stubbornness.

"Very well," said Evvy. She stood again. "I see you have made your decision and that you mean to stand by it. I know how hard it is for you to change your mind once you have made it up. But before you dismiss us, there is someone else you should explain your decision to."

"Who?" Will looked puzzled.

"Katha," said Evvy. "She asked to come with me today. She wants to talk to you."

"Send her away," said Will. "No good purpose will be served by our meeting."

"What am I to tell her? That you are abandoning her yet again? That you are truly turning your back on the Garden this time? Forever? Is that the message I should carry to your daughter?"

"The deenas take it, Evvy, explain it to her! I'm doing this as much for her as for anyone!"

"Explain it yourself," said Evvy. She crossed swiftly to the door and asked the guard to bring Katha.

"Evvy, you have no right to do this," said the Principal, half rising.

"I have every right," she said. "Zach, I think we had best leave them to—"

"Stay, Evvy," said Katha from the doorway. "You, too, Zach. You may as well hear this too."

For a moment she remained standing in the doorway, her hazel eyes calm, her bearing dignified and proud. But as she stepped in, closing the door, Zach could see that her hands were shaking.

"Sit, Katha," said the Principal.

She turned to him and sat. Their eyes locked, and Zach realized that at this moment he and Evvy no longer existed for them.

"I asked Evvy to bring me here because I have more to say to you," Katha said. "I thought that what passed between us yesterday was an ending, but I believe now that it was a beginning." She paused and licked her lips, then went on. "As you know, I grew up hating you. I believed—the old woman encouraged me to believe—that you hated all of us in the Garden."

"I did," Will said, his eyes still fixed on her face.

"Yes," she said calmly. "I always thought that your purpose was to destroy us. I realized yesterday that I was wrong. My own feelings had prevented me from seeing the truth. I had confused a personal matter with a political one."

"Perhaps I did the same," Will said. "But, Katha, things have changed. I am no longer—"

"Please let me finish," she said. "I want you to understand why I am here." He nodded, and she went on. "I was not meant to know the truth about my birth. I learned by accident when I overheard the Mistress and Gunda talking one night. I was very young, and all I knew about you was that you were the greatest leader in the world. I asked the Mistress to tell me more. She said that you had abandoned us and our work and that you could not be trusted. I began training in weapons work with our Mayor, and I became very good at it. I practiced long and hard. Because of the things I had been told about you, I imagined that I was training to meet you, to defeat you in combat, to seek revenge for what you had done to my mother and to the Garden." She paused and licked her lips again. Will, not taking his eyes from her face, pushed a cup of brew across the desk. She took it and drank, then continued. "By the time I was old enough to be a Daughter of the Garden, I was the most skilled fighter in the compound. I had never been as interested in the scientific work as I was in the physical and organizational side of the Garden. When our Mayor was killed in a hunting accident, I took her place. I was the youngest Mayor the Garden had ever had, younger even than you were when you began your struggle against the President. I felt that my mission was to keep the Garden strong, to protect it from you. My greatest fear was that one day you would return and try to conquer us."

Again she paused. Zach saw the Principal take a deep breath, then he spoke, his voice little more than a whisper. "That is what you thought I intended when I had the Garden evacuated," he said.

She nodded. "I understand now that what you did was at least in part for our well-being. At the time it seemed to me to be the opposite. You must understand: I had been working all my life to prevent such a thing from happening. When the senior women voted to give in without a fight, I felt betrayed. They told me that you were offering us greater safety. Perhaps I didn't want safety."

She took a deep breath and exhaled raggedly. Zach could not take his eyes from them, father and daughter, so unlike in appearance, so like in personality.

"A great deal of damage has been done," Katha went on. "On both sides. This has not been easy for me, and I know it is not easy for you. I think we are alike in this, in our stubbornness. But I believe it is time for both of us to put aside the hatred. Both the Garden and the District will be stronger if we work together."

Will did not answer right away. His face had softened, and Zach sensed that his resolve was weakening.

After a moment Katha spoke again. "If you prefer, you can think of my offer as a—a formal proposal, from one leader to another. You and I needn't work together directly. I am offering you the friendship of the Garden. I want no one else to be hurt by old hatreds."

She stopped speaking then. Will continued to look at her a moment, then abruptly he stood and turned to the window. At last he spoke. "Thank you for telling me this," he said quietly.

"I must tell you something else," she said then, her voice no longer steady. "It is true that I always hated you. But I was always . . . secretly proud of you too. Knowing that I was the daughter of the Principal gave me a secret that made me feel powerful. You were the greatest fighter and leader of men in the world, after all. And I fancied that I had inherited your leadership and fighting skills. The things that I told you yesterday have been inside me a long time. I wanted to hurt you, as you had hurt my mother, as you had hurt me. But I also wanted you to know who I am."

"The deenas take it!" said Will suddenly. Katha moved forward in her seat, her body tense. Zach saw Will's shoulders begin to move in the familiar gesture and knew that he was calming himself. He expected Will to turn back, to tell Katha of his plan to resign. Then suddenly Will's posture changed, and his shoulders began to shake. He continued to stand with his back to them, and his hand went to his face. Zach had never seen Will cry, never when he was injured, not even when he had been a boy. He felt a sense of something breaking, like the ice in a winter-locked river, and knew with sudden certainty that Will at last understood what he had done and what it had meant to everyone in the room. Zach stole a glance at Evvy and saw that she was wiping her own eyes. She half rose, but before she could stand, Katha had crossed behind the desk. Tentatively she put out her hand, withdrew it, then reached out and touched Will in comfort.

"I am sorry," she whispered. Will started, then turned with a choked sob and allowed her to embrace him. Will buried his face in her shoulder, his hand clutching the cloth at the back of her tunic. Zach thought to go, to leave them their privacy. He gestured to Evvy and she nodded. Just as they were at the door, Will spoke, his voice hoarse. "Stay, Zach. Both of you. Please."

Scarcely daring to breathe, Zach returned to his seat. Will wiped at his eyes, then gripped Katha's hand. He took a moment to catch his breath, then turned to her.

"Thank you, Katha," he said then. "Thank you for coming and saying what you have. You have . . . shown me who I am and reminded me of what I must do. Before you spoke, I was on the point of making a terrible mistake, of once again confusing a personal matter with a political one. That will not happen now. Of course I accept your offer. And of course we will work together. I'm sorry it has not happened sooner." He stopped and drew another deep breath, then went on. "I know I can never make up for everything I have done. But I'm grateful that you will give me a chance to try. I would like to speak to you in private, tomorrow, if you needn't return to the Garden right away. Can you come for the noon-time meal?"

Katha smiled wanly. "I will be here," she said. Still gripping her hand, the Principal walked with her to the door. They stood awkwardly facing one another, then the Principal touched her cheek. "I will see you tomorrow, daughter," he said. Katha nodded and stepped into the hall.

Will looked after her a moment. "I owe you an apology, Evvy," he said.

She shook her head. "No, Will," she said.

"I was trying to do what was best for you, for Zach—what I thought was best—"

"The best thing for all of us is for you to continue to lead the District," said Zach quickly. "Thank the deenas you see that again."

Evvy opened her mouth to speak, then rose and took Will's hand. "Zach is right," she said.

"But we cannot be married after all," Will said. "As we now know, I am a carrier of the sickness."

"I am not susceptible," said Evvy. "I have been tested." His face had twisted again, and when he didn't answer, she spoke quietly. "We will have the ceremony at the Garden," she said. "It will serve to unite us formally and truly."

Will held her tightly a moment, then turned away again. He took several long, deep breaths, and when he turned back, he looked sheepish. "Well, Zach," he said unsteadily. "It looks as if you have lost your chance to be Principal."

"I was beginning to think you really meant it," said Zach, weak with relief.

"How do you know I was not just testing you?" said Will, almost himself again. "You'll never know. Now let us have some refreshment."

Reaching for another piece of sweet cake, Zach thought again of how to say what he must. Across from him, on the sofa, Evvy rested her head on Will's shoulder while he talked of his new plans for uniting the District and the Garden.

"I have never known how to deal with women," Will was saying. "You'll have to help me, Zach. Together we'll work out the new relations with the Garden, and then—"

He could put it off no longer. "Wait, Will," said Zach. He stood, then crossed to the window. "There is something I must tell both of you." They looked at him expectantly. He took a deep breath, then turned. "I am going away."

"What?" The Principal half rose. "Zach, no, after everything that has happened, you cannot—"

"Zach, please," said Evvy. "Everything is settled now, you mustn't—"

"I am not going this minute," said Zach, cutting through their protests. "Or tomorrow or even next week." He stopped and smiled. "I will stay until you have found someone to replace me, Will," he said. "And I will stay until the two of you are safely married."

"But where—where will you go?" asked Evvy.

"I do not know. I am going out into the world. The time we spent at College, the things that Douglas told us, persuaded me that I have not seen enough of it. I want to see the west and the ocean beyond the sky-high mountains. I want to see the southern south and perhaps the northern north. I want to visit other societies and learn what there is to learn from them. I will not go away forever. But this is something that I must do."

"But, Zach—how can I get along without you?" Will looked stricken.

"You have managed very well without me in the past, brother," said Zach. "And you have Evvy now. You have never needed me so much as you have always maintained."

"Is this not a bit like what you accused me of, Zach? Of self-sacrifice?"

"Not at all," said Zach. "If anything, it is the opposite. I am no longer a young man. And the things that have happened here have made me realize just how short life is. All my life I have lived for other people. When I was a boy in the Garden, I lived for the old woman. Then I lived my life for Leya, and then for you, and for a time I lived it for Evvy. It is time that I lived for myself."

When he had finished speaking, the others remained silent. After a moment Evvy rose and embraced him. "I will miss you," she said.

"And I will miss you. I'll miss you both. But don't think you can get rid of me so easily. I will be back with stories and marvels you can't imagine." He swallowed hard, then kissed Evvy on the top of her head.

"Ah, Zach." Will suddenly smiled. "Once again you win. You always get your way. I've never known how you do it."

Now he too rose and came toward them, put his arm out. They continued to stand together, their arms about each other, the two brothers and Evvy, listening to the sounds of life on the mall, watching as stars began to appear in the sky beyond the window.